Mark Billingham has twice won the Theakston's Old Peculier Award for Crime Novel of the Year, and has also won a Sherlock Award for the Best Detective created by a British writer. Each of the novels featuring Detective Inspector Tom Thorne has been a *Sunday Times* bestseller. *Sleepyhead* and *Scaredy Cat* were made into a hit TV series on Sky 1 starring David Morrissey as Thorne, and a new series based on the novels *In the Dark* and *Time of Death* will be broadcast on BBC1 in 2017. Mark lives in north London with his wife and two children.

Visit Mark's website at www.markbillingham.com or follow him on Twitter @MarkBillingham.

Also by Mark Billingham

The DI Tom Thorne series
Sleepyhead
Scaredy Cat
Lazybones
The Burning Girl
Lifeless
Buried
Death Message
Bloodline
From the Dead
Good as Dead
The Dying Hours
The Bones Beneath
Time of Death

Other fiction
In the Dark
Rush of Blood
Die of Shame

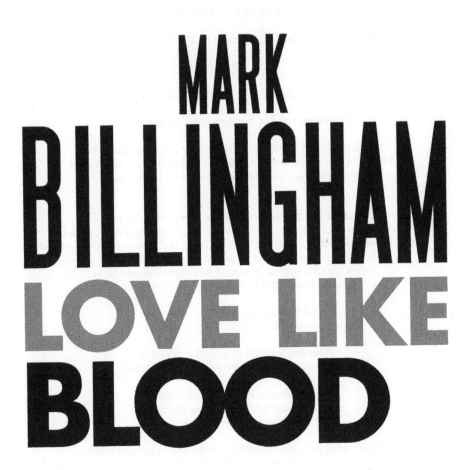

MARK BILLINGHAM

LOVE LIKE BLOOD

Little, Brown

LITTLE, BROWN

First published in Great Britain in 2017 by Little, Brown

3 5 7 9 10 8 6 4 2

A CIP catalogue record for this book
is available from the British Library.

Hardback ISBN 978-0-7515-6688-8
Trade Paperback ISBN 978-0-7515-6689-5

Typeset in Plantin by M Rules
Printed and bound in Great Britain by
Clays Ltd, St Ives plc

Papers used by Little, Brown are from well-managed forests
and other responsible sources.

Little, Brown
An imprint of
Little, Brown Book Group
Carmelite House
50 Victoria Embankment
London EC4Y 0DZ

An Hachette UK Company
www.hachette.co.uk

www.littlebrown.co.uk

For Claire.
And in memory of Banaz Mahmod
and Rahmat Sulemani.

What is honour? A word. What is in
that word 'honour'? What is that
'honour'? Air ...

WILLIAM SHAKESPEARE,
HENRY IV PART I

The conversation stopped as soon as the woman they had come for arrived.

They watched Nicola Tanner's car slow, stop, then reverse expertly into a parking space a few houses down from her own. They watched the woman get out and retrieve something from the boot. They held their breath as she locked the car with a remote and began walking towards her house; saw her lit for a second or two as she passed beneath a streetlamp.

'Good, she's got bags.'

'Why is that good?'

'She's got her hands full. She'll be distracted.'

'OK.'

Their whispered breaths were briefly visible, eyes on the woman as she stepped to avoid a slick of leaves on the pavement and hitched her shoulder bag a little higher.

'What do you think's in the bags?'

'How should I know?'

'They look heavy.'

'Doesn't matter.'

They moved out of the shadows and across the road as the woman turned on to her front path. Quickly, but not too quickly, trying to time it right; heads down and hooded, ready to turn and walk casually away should anyone come along. A dog walker, a nosy neighbour. Emerging from between cars, they were coming through the gate as the woman pushed in her door key and one of them was calling out her name as she bent to pick up her bags from the step.

They had the water pistols out by the time she turned round.

She opened her mouth, but the words, the scream, were quickly silenced by the twin jets of bleach, and a few seconds after she staggered back, blinded, and fell into her house, they were on her.

Inside.

The water pistols were shoved back into pockets and the bags that had been dropped just over the threshold were kicked aside, so that the door could be shut. Folders and files spilled out on to the hall carpet, a bottle of orange juice, a notebook, pens. They stood and watched as the woman spluttered and kicked out at them, inching herself across the floor towards the foot of the stairs.

'Where does she think she's going?'

'She's not going anywhere.'

The woman continued to kick and shuffle until she reached the bottom stair and tried to sit up. One hand was pressed across her face while the other clutched at the carpet. She moaned and thrashed, frantic as her eyes and mouth burned, and the scream that resurfaced was strangled by the bleach that had run down her throat.

'She looks like a crab or something.'

She moved one hand from her face, gasping as she struggled to open one eye. She squinted and sobbed.

'Can she even see us?'

'Doesn't matter, does it?'

'Seriously though, you reckon she can?'

The woman froze when the knife was produced, as one of them moved to kneel down next to her.

'Yeah, just about,' he said.

PART ONE

A PERFECT TEAM

ONE

Who wouldn't welcome an unexpected smile?

At that moment, standing where he was, Tom Thorne was seriously considering the question. There weren't too many smiles flying about in court, as a rule. When the person doing the smiling was the one being escorted from the dock, having just been convicted of murder – in large part thanks to Thorne – it was, to say the least, mildly disconcerting.

Thorne smiled back, raised two fingers for good measure, then left the courtroom as quickly as possible.

The trial had made the front page of the *Standard* and had been deemed worthy of a few minutes on the local TV news, but there wasn't a large crowd outside the Old Bailey. No lawyers reading prepared statements before clusters of microphones, no scrum of cameramen jostling for position. No carefully chosen words about justice, or grief. Just a few members of the prosecution team shaking hands, and the victim's father, talking to a woman Thorne recognised.

He watched the awkward hug, then saw her turn and walk in his direction.

She was somewhere in her mid-thirties and a little below average height. Her round face was framed by brown hair styled into an unfussy bob, the fringe a little straggly. The dark blue skirt and blazer were as practical, as efficient, as Thorne had been led to believe the woman herself was, though of course it might simply have been a case of choosing clothes that were suitable for the occasion. Thorne himself was wearing the dark suit that was only ever dragged out and dry-cleaned for funerals or court appearances. As the woman approached, Thorne adjusted his waistband and told himself that, though he was happy enough to give the funerals a miss, he might need to cut down on the takeaways if he wanted to carry on giving evidence.

He shifted from one foot to another, waited.

'Good result,' the woman said, when she finally reached him.

Thorne had been preparing to shake hands, but the woman clearly preferred to skip the formalities. 'Down to you,' he said.

'Only to begin with.'

'You did all the legwork.'

'Well . . .' She seemed content to accept the acknowledgement and stood looking anywhere but at Thorne, as though putting off the moment when she would have to say what was actually on her mind.

'Course you did,' Thorne said. 'I just came on at the end. Super-sub.'

'That's a football thing, right?'

'Right . . .'

Thorne knew who DI Nicola Tanner was, of course, though they had never met, and he had not been in court the day she had given evidence. Six months earlier, she had led the inquiry into the murder of a young woman named Heather Finlay and become convinced that the killer belonged to a weekly therapy group that Finlay had attended, together with other recovering addicts. With the investigation stalled, Thorne had been brought in undercover to join the group and, after several months of regular sessions, had been able to identify a prime suspect.

The same suspect who, as of fifteen minutes earlier, was now a convicted killer.

'Have you got time for a quick chat?' Tanner asked.

Thorne could not be sure at whose instigation they had begun to move, but as Tanner asked the question they were already walking away from the building, the golden figure of Lady Justice towering high above them, sword raised skywards as if to suggest that she was ready to hand out rather more than an ASBO. 'Yeah, I think so.'

They turned along the main road towards Newgate Street. 'Thank you,' Tanner said.

'No problem.'

Once again, Thorne got the impression that the chat was not one Tanner was looking forward to. It made him a little nervous. Knowing something of her reputation, he wondered if he was about to be pulled up for some lapse in procedure during the latter stages of the Finlay case, or perhaps just told firmly that he needed a new suit.

'Anyway, we should celebrate,' Thorne said, 'and there's a decent pub round the corner.' He nodded towards the Viaduct, a former gin palace that stood on the site of a debtor's prison. There were usually a few too many legal types in there for Thorne's liking, but the place had a nice selection of toasties and the beer was always good.

A few steps further on, Tanner said, 'Can we just go for coffee? Do you mind?'

'Well, a latte isn't my idea of a celebration, but if you'd rather.'

'Sorry.'

'Going back to the office?'

Tanner was looking straight ahead. 'I'm on compassionate leave.'

Thorne took a breath and said, 'Sorry,' because he guessed

there would be good reason to say it, but he worried it was lost beneath the growl of a passing taxi. So he said it again.

Tanner took a few more steps, then stopped. The drizzle, which had been in the air all day, had begun to make good on its threat. She fished in her handbag for an umbrella. 'My partner was killed.' She unfurled her umbrella and looked up from beneath it at Thorne. 'I don't mean my work partner. She was murdered, two weeks ago.'

It took Thorne a second or two to process the two very different pieces of information. 'Jesus . . .'

'Her name was Susan Best.' Tanner smiled, just. 'She was a teacher.'

Thorne nodded. He had been aware of the case; the murder victim whose other half was a copper. It was the kind of news that went around, a Job-related homicide, though the name of the copper involved had never been mentioned. He thought about Helen, his girlfriend, and said, 'Sorry,' again, because he didn't know what else to say.

'Obviously, I'm not allowed to be part of the investigation in any way,' Tanner said. 'I mean those are the rules and they're there for very good reasons.'

Thorne had heard enough about Nicola Tanner to know that rules were something she normally set a lot of store by. It was not a trait they had in common. 'Frustrating though, good reasons or not.'

Tanner's look made it clear just how frustrated she was. 'It's why I wanted to talk to you.'

'Well, I'm not involved in it either.' Thorne had begun to see where this could be heading and was keen to maintain a degree of distance. He might be willing to make the odd phone call as a favour, to pass on such information as he was able to glean, but he had enough going on as it was to do much beyond that. 'Where did it happen?'

'Hammersmith. Susan was killed at our home. I know that's

8

outside your area, but it doesn't really matter because none of this would be on the books anyway.'

'None of what?'

'I need to catch the people who killed her,' Tanner said.

'Of course you do,' Thorne said. 'And I'm sure the team that's on it *will* catch them.'

'I need your help.'

'Hang on—'

'They thought she was *me*.' Tanner stared hard at Thorne, but only for a moment or two before she half turned away, to avoid the rain that was coming at her in gusts from the side, or perhaps because she did not want him to see what became of her expression. 'She was driving my car. They killed Susan, but it was me they were after.'

Now, Thorne looked away too. For a few seconds he watched the traffic crawling past towards St Paul's, the chaotic procession of umbrellas, but he could feel the steady gaze at his back; the scrutiny of the golden figure staring down from the dome behind them. That sword at the ready to mete out punishment.

He stepped across and put a hand on Tanner's shoulder to urge her gently forward.

'Pub,' he said.

TWO

From the bar, Thorne glanced back to see Tanner sitting patiently at the table they had bagged in the corner. He watched her pick up her phone, swipe at the screen a few times, then set it back down. He watched her use the tips of two fingers to straighten the handset in line with the edge of the tabletop before sitting back and folding her hands into her lap.

A few seconds later, she moved the phone again.

Failing to catch the eye of the barman, Thorne looked around at the pub's lavish Victorian interior: ornate marble columns, gilded mirrors and decorated glass. Fine, he supposed, if you liked that kind of thing, though his own taste ran rather more towards spit and sawdust. A wooden sign listed the rules for those entering the old 'gaol', while another inside the door proudly boasted that the pub was among the most haunted in the city and a regular stop on London's ghost tours. Thorne wondered if the spirits were all those of customers who had died while waiting to be served.

'Look at the arse on that last one.'

Thorne turned to see the barman pointing towards a row of

large paintings on the far wall. Three women wearing togas – Thorne supposed they would be called 'maidens' – in various wistful poses. With a statue, what looked like a sheaf of wheat . . .

'Agriculture, business and the arts,' the barman said. 'What they're meant to be. Represent, whatever. The one at the end's got a dirty big hole in her rear end, though . . . see?'

Thorne craned his neck obligingly, but couldn't see anything.

'Some soldier in the First World War . . . shot it or stuck a bayonet in it or something.'

'Everyone's a critic,' Thorne said.

He carried a glass of Glenfiddich and a pint of Guinness back to the table, laid them well away from Tanner's phone. He raised his glass and Tanner did the same and, for a second or two, they stared at one another a little awkwardly. Were they celebrating the result in court or toasting Tanner's murdered girlfriend?

'Right.' Thorne lowered his eyes, then his mouth, to the beer.

After downing half her whisky in two gulps, Tanner began talking. Though they had said nothing else about her dead partner on the short walk to the pub, she spoke as though picking up the thread of a conversation that had only been briefly interrupted. As though Thorne had invited her to carry on where they'd left off.

'After the Finlay case, I did some work with the Honour Crimes Unit,' she said. 'Such as it is.' She waited a few seconds. 'Some of the murder cases that had gone cold. Some of those they suspected were honour killings, but couldn't prove.'

'How many's that?'

'A lot more than the official figures would have you believe, but it really depends which sort you're talking about.' Tanner reached for a coaster and put her glass down. 'Some perpetrators take a lot of trouble to make a straightforward honour killing look like something else. Something sexually motivated, a random attack, a suicide, maybe. Sometimes the victim just mysteriously disappears, goes abroad for a wedding and never comes back, and I've come across at least a couple that look sus- piciously like faked car accidents.'

Thorne nodded. These were scenarios he had come across only rarely, but which were nonetheless familiar. 'What's the other sort?'

Half a smile. 'I knew you'd ask the right questions.'

Thorne took a sip of Guinness. Thinking: Or the *wrong* ones. Up close, he could see that there was rather more grey in Tanner's hair than he had noticed before; that such make-up as there was could not disguise the deep lines around the woman's mouth and the shadowy half-moons beneath her eyes.

A face changed by a fortnight of tears and no sleep.

Tanner smiled and leaned forward. The answer to Thorne's question was clearly the reason they were here. 'Well, the trouble with honour killings ... for the people that carry them out, I mean ... is that any copper with half a brain cell tends to know who they're looking for. It's the father or the brothers or the uncles or some other family combination. Obviously there's a lot of lying and secrecy to deal with, but we tend to get there in the end. Not quite an open and shut case, but pretty close.'

'Not always men though, right?'

'No, not always, but nine times out of ten it's a relative.'

'I'm guessing it's the one time out of ten that you're interested in though.'

Her expression confirmed it. 'Look, there isn't an ounce of anything like nobility in what these people do. None at all. It's murder, pure and simple, pretending to be something else, but some of those responsible do at least accept that they'll be going to prison for it. The punishment is ... part of it, in some twisted way. Some of them are quite happy to strangle their sisters or daughters and then march into the nearest police station and ask for the handcuffs to be slapped on.'

'Men of *honour*,' Thorne said, the beer not tasting quite as good as it did a minute before.

'Others are rather more ... cowardly, if that's even possible. They don't want to get caught, so they pay others to do it.'

Thorne shrugged. 'Makes sense. You know, if you're the kind of scumbag who thinks your own flesh and blood deserves to die for wearing a skirt you don't approve of.'

'Right. Because you can't possibly risk going to prison because you're important. You've got a business to run and a family to keep together. You *matter*.' She took another drink, getting to it. 'Before Susan was killed, I'd become convinced that I'd found several cases where this is exactly what had happened. The methods were different, the locations, but I'm sure those murders were carried out by people who'd been paid by the victim's family.'

'Hitmen.'

'Yes, if you like. Two of them. I think this pair has actually carried out contract-style honour killings all over the world. Pakistan, Turkey, Syria. Like I said, the ones I'm talking about over here were all slightly different, but in every case, somewhere in the files, there was a reference to two men. Two men seen in a car outside a house or watching a college one of the victims attended. Two men spotted hanging around near the scene of the crime. I got a few descriptions, and I've got what I reckon is a pretty decent e-fit.'

'You took all this to your superiors, I presume?'

'Of course.'

'So ...'

'It's not like the brass wasn't interested, but putting all this together did cause a certain amount of friction. There were community leaders getting up in arms, there were complaints. Emails back and forth between various Chief Constables. In the current climate, this kind of thing's a political hot potato, I suppose. I get why they're ... wary.'

'Offending delicate sensibilities.'

'Yes, well fuck that.'

Thorne was taken aback to hear Tanner swear, but there was no doubting her passion; her anger. 'I couldn't agree more,' he said. 'Actually, I rather enjoy offending delicate sensibilities.'

'One of the reasons I wanted to talk to you.'

Thorne smiled, but he was eager to know what the other reasons might be.

'The fact is, having me out of the picture because of what happened to Susan rather suits everybody, I think. But I know I'm right about this, so I'm buggered if I'm letting it go.'

Thorne waited.

'I think these same two men killed Susan.' Her voice had dropped; broken a little. 'I think whoever's been paying them to carry out these honour killings put their hands in their pockets and paid to have me killed as well, because I'm becoming a nuisance. They made a mistake.'

Seeing the look on Tanner's face, Thorne could not help thinking that the men she was talking about had made more than one. 'Why are you coming to me with this?'

'Because you did such a great job on the Finlay thing, and because one of the cases I've been looking at was yours.'

Thorne put his glass down.

'Meena Athwal.'

Thorne remembered the case, because it was one of those that was never solved. They were the ones that stayed with him; those and a few of the killers he had managed to catch. The special ones.

'She was raped and strangled, four years ago.'

'I know.' The words caught in Thorne's throat. Meena Athwal had been a college student. Bright and ambitious, trying to be independent. 'Once we'd done a bit of digging, it made sense to look at the honour killing angle. We brought in a couple of specialists, but we couldn't make it stick.'

14

'Of course not,' Tanner said. 'Because all the likely suspects had cast-iron alibis. The father and the brothers, everyone. Funny, that.'

Thorne was trying to remember: witness statements, house to house. Had there been any mention back then of two individuals who might have been the men Tanner was talking about?

'So, what exactly do you think I can do?' he asked.

'I don't know yet. I just wanted to see what you made of it, that's all. What your . . . inclination might be.'

Thorne's inclination at that moment was to down another pint as quickly as possible.

'How did you know, by the way?' Tanner asked.

'How did I know what?'

'When you were in that therapy group. How did you know which of them it was?'

'A smile,' Thorne said. 'A particular sort of smile. I could see they'd worked out that I was pretending to be something I wasn't and I knew straight away it was because they were pretending too.'

'You got another one today,' Tanner said. 'A smile.' She stood up and grabbed her handbag. 'Same again?'

'Please.' Thorne watched Tanner walk to the bar, raise a hand and succeed in attracting the attention of the barman immediately. She struck Thorne as someone who tended to get what they were after.

What your inclination might be.

As if she didn't know *exactly* what it would be.

Thorne downed what little was left of his first pint, began to tear the corners off his beer mat. He already had the feeling that the smile he had received from a killer might turn out to be the high point of his day.

THREE

As soon as Amaya Shah had pushed through the glass doors of Barnet College and out into the fresh air, she buttoned up her coat and began looking around. People moved quickly past her and away up the concrete steps, most hurrying towards the Mitre or the cheap pizza place on the other side of the road, a few heading left towards the shopping centre. Plenty were loitering in small groups near the doors, talking and smoking; making plans for the rest of the day. Others were already gathered at the bus stop. There were plenty of faces she recognised, of course – other students, members of staff – but none that concerned her. She checked again, to be sure, as she always did.

Then she reached up and removed her hijab.

As she was tucking the blue headscarf carefully into her shoulder bag, Amaya looked up to see Kamal marching towards her across the precinct. A wave and that wonky smile she adored so much.

Another look around. There would be no touching, no embrace, not until they were somewhere they both felt safe, but the caution had become second nature.

He nodded towards her bag. 'I thought you didn't wear that here.'

'I don't,' Amaya said. 'I just make sure I've got it on when I come out, that's all. My brother was waiting for me once.'

'And he wasn't happy about it.'

'What do you think?'

'So, you put it on then take it straight off again?'

'Right. Like you were wearing that shirt when you left home.'

Kamal touched his fingers to the shiny material of the two-tone shirt, red and gold like a sunset, tight across his muscular chest. 'You like it?'

Amaya nodded. 'What's in your bag? Nice sensible sweater, maybe? The stupid one with all the stripes?'

'Arsenal shirt.' That wonky smile again. 'What d'you fancy?'

She thought about it for a few seconds then nodded across the road. 'Pancakes.' She grinned and pulled the hood of her anorak up against the drizzle. 'Chocolate sauce . . .'

Amaya ordered precisely what she'd told Kamal she wanted, while he plumped for a banoffee waffle with ice cream. They drank popcorn tea and vanilla milkshakes. From their small table in the window they each had a good view of the street outside; the parked cars and the passers-by.

Kamal said, 'Did you get my text?'

Amaya nodded, ate.

'So, we doing this, or what?'

She looked at him. His perfect teeth and beautiful skin. He had cleared his plate quickly and now sat staring at her, slender fingers drumming on the tabletop, buzzing with it. It was his strength that had brought them this far, enough for her to feed on and cling to, but his excitement also made her nervous. How could he be quite so confident? Why did he never want to talk about what might happen if things didn't work out the way they wanted?

17

'Not sure about the running away bit,' she said.

'Only if we have to.'

'You know that's not what I want, though.'

'Course, but we might not have any choice.'

Amaya nodded again, but she struggled to believe it would ever come to that, in spite of everything. The shouting and ... worse. Whenever she thought about her mother, she always saw that beaming smile, felt those meaty arms around her, could conjure the smell of the spices that clung to her clothes, to her hair; the garam masala, cardamom and cumin. Her father was different, of course, but she retained her faith in the fact that, above all else, he loved her. That his desire to see her happy would outstrip everything else when it came down to it. She understood the things he had to say in front of his friends, his wife and sons; the appearance that needed to be maintained for all those other important men.

She understood the importance of reputation.

But at the end of the day, he was still her dad.

'We need to tell them at the same time,' Kamal said. 'Our parents. You remember that, right?'

'Yeah, course.' Amaya looked away, pushed what remained of her pancake through a smear of chocolate sauce. Her ma would already be preparing the evening meal; bent over pots and pans or chopping, chopping, chopping ...

'What's the matter?' Kamal leaned forward and touched her hand, just for a second. 'You haven't said anything already?'

'Not to them.'

'To who?' Suddenly, Kamal was not sounding quite so confident. Nerves, fear in his whisper.

'I told a friend in college.' She looked at him. 'It's OK, a white girl. She won't breathe a word to anyone.'

'Nobody else? Tell me.'

Amaya knew that she had to be truthful. If what they were planning was ever going to happen there had to be honesty, and besides, Kamal was the last person in the world she would ever lie to.

'My brother takes my phone sometimes.'

'So? He doesn't know your PIN number, right?'

'He made me tell him.' Amaya closed her eyes. She did not want to remember how. 'Said I shouldn't have secrets from the family, that there was nothing to worry about if I didn't have anything to hide.'

'I *told* you,' Kamal said. 'I told you to always delete my messages.'

'I do,' Amaya hissed at him across the table. 'I'm not stupid. Just . . . he might have seen something before I deleted it. I'm just saying.'

Kamal looked serious, but only for a few seconds before he shrugged and the smile came back. The smile that was never far away. 'Well, all the more reason to tell the 'rents sooner than later, right?'

'I suppose,' Amaya said.

They said nothing for a while, looking at their phones and glancing out at the street every few seconds, the spatter of drizzle crawling down the window as it began to grow dark outside.

'So, what about this party, then?' Kamal held his arms out. 'If you think this shirt is good, wait until you see what I've got lined up for tonight.'

'It's tonight?'

'Come on, Amee.' He growled in mock frustration. 'I sent you a message last week.'

Amaya stared at him, wide-eyed, sarcastic. 'I deleted the text, genius, like you *told* me.'

'You still coming though, yeah?'

'It's so late. I'd have to leave after dinner.'

'It's a *party*. Look, I can use my dad's account to get us an Uber back.'

19

Amaya thought about it. 'Well, someone's got to keep an eye on you, I suppose. Stop you getting into trouble again.'

'Ha bloody ha.'

'I could always tell them I'm going round to Sarah's house to study. She's the girl I was telling you about.'

'There you go.'

'They'll want her number, but that's not a problem. I've lent her notes plenty of times, so I'm sure she'll cover for me if I ask her.'

'Make sure you stash some decent party clothes in your bag. None of your Primark rubbish, OK? I don't want you showing me up.'

Amaya grinned and stuck her tongue out. She was already thinking about what to wear, picturing the silver top she'd bought at River Island and sneaked into the house the week before. It was at the back of her wardrobe in an old suitcase, where her brother would never find it.

Kamal reached across and took her plate. He picked up the fork. 'And if you want to keep that gorgeous figure, you'd better let me finish this.'

FOUR

It was hard to think properly, to clear sufficient headspace for it, with the voices from the next room and the multicoloured chaos of discarded toys and games at his feet. One of those occasions when Thorne wished he was alone. Back at his own place on God's side of the river; the flat which was currently being rented by two young beat officers based at the local station. His girl-friend's flat, just south of Brixton, was certainly no bigger than his own, but there could be little argument that, for the time being, the current living arrangements remained the most sensi-ble option for both of them, despite the twice-daily journey to and from Thorne's office in Colindale. It was close to where Helen worked in Streatham, Helen's son Alfie was happily settled in a local nursery, and they were within easy reach of emergency childcare, in the helpful, if irritating shape of Helen's sister Jenny.

One of those rare occasions.

Most of the time, Thorne would admit – when pushed – that it was oddly comforting to come home at the end of a shift to this. A welcome distraction. Noise and clutter and a lively three-year-old who was always pleased to see him.

Easy to forget about murder for a few hours.

Easier . . .

Helen appeared from the narrow hallway that led to the bedrooms. She did not need to tell Thorne that after a day at work and a few full-on hours with her son – feeding him, bathing him, getting him to bed – she was exhausted.

She sighed, said, 'Fingers crossed.'

'Brown bear again?'

She closed her eyes and shook her head. 'Only three times tonight. I sneak a new bit in every time I read it, just to keep myself interested. I'm really tempted to kill him off next time.'

'Go for it,' Thorne said. 'Chapter twenty-six. "The bear-trap".'

Helen smiled as she walked across, nudging aside a squeaky dinosaur with the tip of her trainer, then dropping on to the sofa next to Thorne. She reached behind her, dug half a plastic jeep from beneath one of the cushions and tossed it on to the carpet.

'Shall I heat up some of that pasta?'

'In a bit,' Helen said. She turned and looked at him, imploring. 'Must. Have. Wine.'

Thorne heaved himself up and went to get the white wine from the fridge. He took out a can of beer for himself while he was there, though he was still feeling the effects of the lunchtime Guinness. He could almost hear Phil Hendricks telling him what a lightweight he was turning into, how the years were finally catching up with him. The truth was that Thorne probably wouldn't bother to argue. A few months before he'd had a good session at lunchtime with a confidential source and every intention of going back to work afterwards. On a muggy afternoon, four pints to the good, he'd fallen asleep on the Tube and woken up in Edgware.

He carried the drinks across, sat down again.

'Good result today,' she said.

Thorne nodded. 'Few and far between.' He'd texted Helen as soon as the verdict had come in, but they hadn't had a chance to talk until now. She had already been preoccupied with Alfie by the time Thorne had got back to the flat.

'You were a bit . . . weird during all that.' Helen took a drink. 'When you were going to those therapy sessions.'

Thorne turned to face her. 'How was I weird?'

'I don't know . . . just getting into your part, probably. Like Robert De Niro or something.'

'Oh, come on.'

'I swear. I mean, it wasn't like I was rummaging around for your secret coke stash, but I did get a good idea what it must be like living with a junkie.' She smiled. 'I kept thinking you were lying to me about things. Well, more than usual, anyway.'

'More than usual?'

'You know, everyday things. We both do, don't we? Everyone does. I was lying just then about Alfie's bedtime story. I only read it twice, but three times sounded better. Listen, I'm not talking about anything important. Just stupid stuff.'

Thorne considered it for a few seconds. He raised his beer can, but didn't drink. 'I don't think I was being weird.'

Helen laughed. 'And addicts don't think they're addicts, do they?' She took another drink. 'I'm just saying . . . you were a bit strange to live with, that's all.' She paused, timing her punchline perfectly. 'A bit *stranger* . . . '

'Bloody hell.'

'What?'

'Like you're so easy to live with.'

Helen was a picture of innocence. 'Never said I was.'

The truth was things *had* been a little strained between them since the events nine months before in Helen's home town of Polesford. The case they had worked on there had been shocking enough, but it had precipitated a personal revelation that they were still struggling to live with. A secret that only seemed to grow darker once it had been shared.

'Worth it though,' Helen said. 'The weirdness.' She was clearly still enjoying the wind-up. 'For today, I mean. Like you say, it doesn't always go the right way, does it?'

Thorne nodded. During a trial a few months before, a medical expert had produced evidence that the accused had still been five milligrams over the legal alcohol limit during an interview and therefore unfit to be questioned. Thorne could only watch as a solid murder case had fallen apart faster than an Arsenal title challenge.

'Good piss-up afterwards, was it?'

She had smelled it on him immediately, of course.

'Not bad,' Thorne said. 'Patting ourselves on the back. The briefs raising a glass to Heather Finlay, then swapping stories about cars and holiday homes. The usual.'

'Bloody hell.'

'What?'

'You are happy that you won, right?'

Thorne looked at her.

'Well, how about letting your face know about it?' Helen finished her wine and stood up. 'You murder squad boys need to learn how to celebrate.'

Thorne smiled and watched Helen go to the fridge to get herself a refill. She asked if he wanted another beer and he told her he'd had quite enough at lunchtime.

He could still taste that Guinness, fizzing on his tongue. Worsening, the more of Tanner's story he'd heard.

Thorne could not see any good reason to mention the meeting with Nicola Tanner. Chances were that nothing was going to come of it anyway, but the fact was he and Helen rarely talked about work if they could avoid it: a murder squad; a child abuse investigation team. The people, maybe, but not the work. Now and again there were occasions when steam needed to be let off, or stories were simply too funny or bizarre to remain untold, but otherwise there was an unspoken agreement to try and leave the Job on the doorstep.

That didn't mean it wasn't in their heads, of course, a shadowy voltage charging the distance between them, but it wasn't the subject of chit-chat.

'Why don't I do the pasta?' Helen said, removing the bowl of leftovers from the fridge.

'No ...' Thorne tried to get up, but Helen was already bending down to the cupboard.

She said, 'You always manage to burn the pan, anyway.'

Thorne sat back, tried once again to focus.

We brought in a couple of specialists, but we couldn't make it stick.

Though his shift had been set aside for the court appearance, Thorne had gone back to the office as soon as he and Tanner had parted company. At Becke House, there had been more congratulations on the outcome of the trial, offers of yet more drink at the end of the day, but Thorne had made his excuses and slipped away at the first opportunity. He had seated himself at a computer in a quiet corner and gone back through the files on the Meena Athwal case. Every statement, every CCTV log, every piece of what might have become evidence four years before, had the investigation ever got out of first gear.

He had found what he was looking for quickly enough.

A friend of Meena's had told a police officer that, more than once, Meena had said she thought she was being followed. She had mentioned two men. It had been logged but later ignored, once it had been decided that Meena had been the victim of a random attack. After all, those who chose to sexually prey upon strangers rarely worked in teams.

Had they got it horribly wrong?

Could these have been the same two men Tanner had mentioned?

Helen was saying something, and when Thorne looked up he caught movement to his left and looked to see Alfie standing in the doorway. One foot balanced on the other, a perfect expression of practised helplessness and misery.

'Hello, mate. You OK?'

Alfie shook his head and lowered it; as good a con-artist as Thorne had ever encountered.

Helen turned and removed the saucepan from the heat. She sighed, rolled her eyes at Thorne. 'Come on, then . . .'

Alfie was smiling by the time Helen had reached him and taken his hand to lead him back to bed.

Half a minute later, Thorne could hear the familiar rise and fall of her voice coming from her son's bedroom. Brown bloody bear . . .

Thorne reached down and picked up a toy; a miniature basketball hoop on a plastic handle, the ball at the end of a stripy cord. He decided he might just as well focus on that for a while.

He flicked up the ball, missed.

He put down his beer and tried again.

Nicola Tanner sat halfway up the stairs, looking down at the unsullied oatmeal blandness of the hall carpet. The nice *new* carpet, the smell of which, two weeks on, had still struck her like a slap when she'd opened the front door half an hour earlier.

She hadn't had any choice.

Blood, mess . . . disorder. The stain had needed to be removed, of course, but it still felt as though she had erased the last of Susan. The last part of her that had been real. There were still . . . things, clothes and books, but she kept putting off that trip to the charity shop. Dropping off the cardboard box and turning to leave, as though its contents were no more than unwanted junk without any real meaning.

She pulled her overcoat tighter and thought about her meeting with Tom Thorne. He had been polite, which was a surprise considering some of the things she had been told about the man, but she wasn't sure there was anything beyond that; any real interest.

Why should there be?

26

But she couldn't do this on her own. They hadn't taken her warrant card away, but compassionate leave was still leave, at the end of the day. That said, wouldn't any officer, working or not, step up if they had to? Surely no copper worth the name would stand by and do nothing if they genuinely believed a crime was being committed.

It was bending the rules, though, no point pretending it wasn't, and that was not something Nicola had ever done, reserving a special kind of scorn for those who did. No, the simple fact was that she needed help. She required some degree of legitimacy if she wanted to carry on with this; if she was going to start turning over stones again.

She stared down, empty; cried out for the day. She was still angry at herself for losing control, though sitting in that pub she had been aware, even as the tears had come, that they might be doing her a favour. Thorne was clearly no pushover, but she'd known plenty like him who couldn't resist a sob story.

There had been so much blood.

Like misshapen wings, or the rust-coloured remains of them, by the time Nicola had opened the door that night and found Susan's body. Soaked into the pile, and that strange scattering of white spots that she was later told was bleach. Was it too much to hope that Susan's eyesight had gone by the time they'd snuffed out the life, so much life, in the rest of her? That she had not been able to see them killing her?

Christ, what was she thinking? What did it matter? Susan was gone, and all because they had thought she was Nicola. Because Susan's own car had been in the garage that day.

Oatmeal.

How sadly, *stupidly* dull was that?

Her arms wrapped around her knees, Nicola felt a smile begin to form, creaking into place; so rare these last two weeks that she could not help but be aware of it. No, she could not imagine living with a brightly coloured hall carpet, or walls that were anything but white. She could not imagine an uncrossed t or an undotted i; an open-ended arrangement or a spur-of-the-moment decision.

She could not imagine life without the woman she had loved. Still loved.

But she could imagine the men who had done this looking up at her and begging for their lives. She could imagine the horror on their faces, the slow realisation, and she could imagine their screams as she let the bleach fall – one nice, fat drop at a time – into their eyes.

She let her head drop and shook it. The few moments of fantasy, of imagined revenge, were natural enough, she knew that. But she also knew that it was *just* fantasy; that with both men hog-tied and helpless, with a bottle of Domestos in her hand, she would never do it.

She raised her head.

She was, and always would be, as inoffensive, as predictable, as that carpet.

She got slowly to her feet, turned round, and climbed the stairs to run herself a bath.

FIVE

Even Kamal had been forced to admit that the party wasn't up to much. A semi-famous DJ getting paid a small fortune to put together a crappy playlist on his iPod. Smirnoff Ice at eight quid a pop and nowhere to sit down. They had stayed less than an hour and, in the end, Kamal had been the one to suggest that they leave; his lips pressed close to Amaya's ear, still needing to shout above the din of some house hit for thirteen-year-olds they could have heard on Capital Radio any afternoon.

'This is rubbish. Waste of a good shirt.'

Amaya was certainly not arguing. She had spent most of the time alone, while Kamal had prowled around. Eking out her drink in a crowded corner and scanning faces as the coloured lights danced across them, just in case.

'Shame.' They had changed position and now Amaya was the one doing the talking; pointing at the idiot behind the decks and shouting her sarcasm. 'I was thinking of asking him to DJ at the wedding.'

Kamal had grinned and grabbed her arm. 'Come on, let's get out of here. At least we can still get the Tube. I won't have to explain an Uber to my old man.'

On the train they ate chocolate bought from the station kiosk; jabbered happily about Amaya's college course, Kamal's job at his father's printing business.

'We might have to chuck both of them in,' Kamal said. 'Do something else.'

Amaya looked at him. 'Hopefully not.'

'Yeah, hopefully. But it might come to that.'

'What do we do for money?' Amaya asked. 'If it does come to that. What do we live on if you don't have your job?'

'I find another job.'

'Yeah, because that's so easy.'

'I go on benefits if I have to.'

They stopped talking as the train pulled into a station and watched as several people got off. They were overground now and the carriage was emptying, stop by stop.

The doors closed and the train moved away again.

'But if you lose your job that's probably because they're not exactly thrilled about us getting married, right?' Amaya looked at Kamal. He nodded. 'So, that means moving away.' She leaned closer to him; the rattling of the carriage made conversation only marginally easier than it had been at the party. 'And getting involved with all that official stuff – benefits or signing up for council housing or whatever – is a really easy way of somebody finding us.'

Kamal nodded, chewed at a fingernail. 'I'll sort it all out, don't worry.'

'Plus, I want to carry on at college.'

'Yeah, obviously.'

'It's a good course, you know? A good qualification.'

Kamal took her hand. 'Look, I'm only saying these are things that *might* happen, but we'd be stupid if we didn't think there's a possibility. I mean, remember why we're doing this in the first place. You know what it's like for me, right? And I know *exactly* what it's like for you, because I've seen it with both my sisters.' He reached for Amaya's hand. 'I'm just talking about the way it could go if they don't like it. If they really don't like it, I mean. I'm talking about the worst-case scenario. Yeah?' He waited. 'Amee . . . ?'

Amaya was looking at a man sitting on the other side of the carriage, a few seats down and to their left. He was leaning against the divider, bleached-blond hair pressed to the Perspex, watching them. He wore a green jacket spattered with what looked like white paint, a dirty brown T-shirt underneath and dusty boots. Kamal caught the stranger's eye and quickly looked away.

It was as though the man took this as his cue.

'Yeah, you'd better look away.' He sat up straight, staring at Amaya. He pursed his lips, made kissing noises.

At the end of the carriage, a middle-aged woman was engrossed in her copy of the *Standard*. Amaya looked at her and watched the woman raise the newspaper a little higher.

Amaya glanced at Kamal. His head was lowered. She squeezed his hand, feeling him tense next to her, before her eyes slid quickly back to the man in the green jacket.

'Look at you,' he said. A low, smoker's voice, the words thick with drink. 'All ballsy, aren't you? But your boyfriend's shitting himself. Look at him, for Christ's sake.'

Amaya was afraid to take her eyes off the man. She said, 'What's your problem?'

The man leaned forward, closing the gap between them. 'Your lot,' he said. 'You're my problem. You're everybody's problem.' The train slowed as it approached the next station, but the man carried on talking. 'You don't need to be hiding inside them stupid black sacks either or have hats and beards.' He waved a hand towards them, looked them up and down. 'Makes sense, I suppose, sitting there dressed like normal people, trying to blend in so you can catch us off guard.' He nodded towards Amaya's feet, to the bags containing the clothes she and Kamal had left home in. 'What's in the bags?'

The doors opened and the woman with the newspaper got off quickly, leaving the train through the doors furthest away from Amaya and the man in the green jacket, her eyes fixed on the platform ahead of her.

'I asked you what was in the bags.'

Amaya looked quickly left into the next section of the carriage and saw that there were only two passengers remaining. A young boy was busy with his phone and a smartly dressed Asian man sat a few seats further along. He was old, at least forty or something, and just for a second, he caught Amaya's eye and shook his head. She was still trying to work out what it meant when the other man spoke again.

'Mind you, I suppose you wouldn't waste a decent bomb on an empty train, would you? No point going to heaven or whatever you lot call it for that.' He got to his feet suddenly, steadied himself on the hanging rail and shouted at the two other passengers, playing to what little audience he had. 'Hardly worth blowing themselves to kingdom come for the three of us, is it?' He pointed at the Asian man, who was watching him. 'Not like *you'd* be much of a loss, mind you.'

Amaya leaned close to Kamal, one hand wrapped around his and the other pressed against her thigh, trying to control the tremor that was causing her foot to bounce off the floor of the carriage. She leaned in to whisper, 'It'll be fine, he's just drunk,' then sat up straight again when the man turned to loom over her.

'So, *he* gets virgin dolly-birds, does he?' He nudged at Kamal's leg with a dusty boot. 'So what, you get blokes who've never got their ends away? That how it works? Like some mental . . . raghead gang-bang—'

32

He stopped, startled for a moment as the Asian man from further along the carriage arrived suddenly, ducking in front of him and dropping into the seat next to Amaya.

'Hello, here's the other one.' He narrowed his eyes as though struggling to focus on the newcomer. 'Who the fuck asked you to get involved?' He stepped away and all but fell back into his seat, spread his arms out behind him.

The Asian man leaned close to Amaya and whispered quickly. 'Next stop.'

Amaya nodded.

'Eh? Who invited you?'

With the man in the green jacket seemingly more interested in his newest victim, Amaya took her chance to lean in and pass the instruction on to Kamal.

'I don't need an invitation.' The Asian man was well spoken and his voice was calm and steady. 'It's a free country.'

'Yeah, and some of us want to keep it that way, don't we? Which means getting shot of the likes of you.'

The train was slowing again.

'I'm every bit as British as you.'

'I seriously doubt that.'

'Is it British to bully strangers?'

'You cheeky fuck.'

'To abuse them?'

'You *want* a slap? Is that it?'

Amaya was counting down the seconds as the train got closer to the next station, the darkened houses and gardens giving way to steep sidings and a sparsely lit car park; signs and posters passing in a blur and slowly becoming readable. The colour had risen to the bully's face and she could see that he had clenched his fists. He turned his dead-eyed stare on her.

'Don't know which of you to start with.'

They were almost at a standstill.

'What about your pussy-arsed boyfriend?'

She held his stare until the train juddered to a stop and then the man next to her said, 'Go,' and the three of them were out of their seats and away through the doors before they had fully opened.

They ran along the platform, and just before they turned towards the stairs, Amaya looked back to see that the man in the green jacket was getting off the train behind them. He spotted them and began walking.

The Asian man took her arm. Said, 'Quickly.'

They ran up the short flight of metal steps, Amaya digging into her bag for her Oyster card until Kamal nodded ahead and she almost shouted in relief when she saw that the barriers were open.

They tore through them, and out.

Looking behind them as they walked quickly down past the car park towards the road, Amaya could see no sign of the man from the train.

'It's OK,' the Asian man said.

Kamal was still turning to look back every few steps. 'Shit . . . shit . . .'

'Don't worry, it'll be OK.' Now it was their rescuer who was digging into his pocket, producing car keys and pressing the fob. Lights flashed fifty yards away and Amaya and Kamal hurried after him to the car.

'I'll run you home,' the man said as they climbed in.

Amaya closed the rear passenger door and slid in next to Kamal. 'Thank you . . .'

'Yeah, thanks.' Kamal grabbed Amaya's hand. They were both breathing heavily.

'No worries.' He started the car. 'So, where am I going?'

'Between Whetstone and Barnet,' Kamal said. 'Not far.' He looked at Amaya, squeezed her hand.

They waited. Amaya shuffled forward, caught the man's eyes in the rear-view mirror, but before she could speak the door had been yanked open and the man in the green jacket was squeezing in, forcing her and Kamal to move across.

He said, 'Hello again.'

He didn't sound drunk any more.

There was a soft *clunk* as the central locking was activated, which was when Amaya began to cry.

SIX

It was just before six o'clock, three days after Thorne had met Nicola Tanner, when she called him. He was playing pool with Phil Hendricks in the Grafton Arms, a pub opposite his flat that had seen a good deal of their custom over the years.

The landlord had made a good job of not looking too thrilled to see them back.

Thorne had driven to Kentish Town straight from work, ostensibly in response to a complaint from his tenants that the boiler was acting up. Thorne knew about as much about faulty boilers as he did about astrophysics. He'd taken no more than a glance at it and said, 'I'll get a plumber over,' then, after a cursory look around – a few more stains on the carpet, some Coldplay CDs which made him feel like raising the rent immediately – he'd walked across the road to meet Phil.

To relax and talk about nothing important for a while, to maybe win a few quid.

'We might have another one,' Tanner said.

Thorne said, 'Right.' Thinking: *Another what?* Then: *We?*

Hendricks chalked his cue and mouthed, 'Who's that?'

Thorne shook his head, listened.

'A missing couple,' Tanner said. 'Bangladeshi. Families reported them missing two days ago.'

'A couple?'

'As far as honour crimes go, it's not uncommon. A wife who runs away with another man. A girl who refuses to marry who-ever her parents have promised her to and runs off with the boy she loves.'

'How old are they?'

'They're both eighteen.'

'Well then, maybe it's just that,' Thorne said. 'Love-struck teenagers getting away from their families.'

'In which case they might be in danger.'

'So, now you're investigating crimes before they happen?'

'They might not be missing at all,' Tanner said. There was a pause, for effect. 'They have to be *reported* missing, to avoid suspicion.'

Thorne said nothing, watched Hendricks lining up his next shot.

'Nobody's taking it very seriously, that's the thing, so I think we've got a good chance to look into this without putting too many backs up.'

Except mine, Thorne thought.

'Look, if you're not interested—'

'I never said that.' Thorne looked across at Hendricks and rolled his eyes. 'I'm just assuming they're not taking it seriously because it's two adults, that's all. There's nothing to indicate anything sinister going on, is there?'

'Not at the moment. Nothing obvious.'

'Or anything to connect this to the Meena Athwal murder?'

There was silence for a few seconds. Thorne could hear Tanner's frustration, anger even, crackling down the line.

'It would be a lot easier if we talked about this in person,' she said.

Thorne had the feeling he sometimes got arguing the toss with a senior officer. Though fighting losing battles was something of a speciality, on this occasion he simply couldn't be arsed.

And Meena Athwal had been missing before she'd been found dead.

He sighed out a 'Fine'.

'Any chance you could come over later?'

'Tomorrow no good?'

'Sooner the better.'

'It'll be late.' Thorne looked at his watch. There was plenty of pool to be played yet. 'What time do you go to bed?'

'I'll be up,' Tanner said.

When he'd taken down the address and hung up, Thorne told Hendricks about the call and his meeting with Nicola Tanner in the Viaduct; her ideas about a team of hitmen carrying out honour killings to order. It took him about as long as it took Hendricks to polish off his remaining balls and casually pocket the black into the corner.

'You've been practising,' Thorne said.

Hendricks walked across and picked up his pint. He shook his head. 'I still can't get over Tanner being gay.'

'She just keeps it a bit quieter than you,' Thorne said. 'Then again, so does Elton John.'

Hendricks had known Tanner a while and had been the pathologist responsible for the post-mortem on Heather Finlay. They had always enjoyed something of a spiky relationship at work, and back then he had actually told Thorne he thought Tanner was homophobic.

Thorne began gathering the balls from the pockets, rolling them down the table. 'Must just be you she doesn't like.'

'It all seems slightly . . . tenuous,' Hendricks said. 'This missing persons business. Sounds like she might be a bit obsessed.'

'She's got every reason to be,' Thorne said.

38

'I suppose.'

'Pain can do that to people.'

Hendricks began racking the balls, arranging the spots and stripes in their correct position within the triangle. 'How's Helen?'

Thorne looked at him, but he understood immediately why his friend had made the connection between one kind of grief and another. Hendricks had been with them in Polesford. He was close to Helen and, Thorne suspected, someone she was more likely to confide in.

'Yeah, she's doing OK, I think.'

'Good.'

'Got her hands full with Alfie, but otherwise ... you know.' Thorne made a mental note to call Helen on his way to Tanner's, to let her know he'd be late.

'She'll be fine,' Hendricks said. 'She's a scrapper.' He smiled at what was coming, seemingly happy to move the conversation on to ground a little less heavy. 'Well, she'd have to be, living with you.'

'Don't you bloody start. The two of you been comparing notes?'

'On the rocks, is it?'

'Are you going to break or not?'

Hendricks picked up the white ball. 'I can't help feeling sorry for her, though. I mean, not exactly a match made in heaven for her, is it?'

'Like you're such a bloody catch,' Thorne said. 'I'm surprised you haven't turned Liam straight.' It was ironic, considering the horrors of Polesford, that it had been where Hendricks had met Dr Liam Southworth, his current partner.

Hendricks just smiled and tossed the cue ball in the air; clearly still fully loved-up. He smacked the ball down on the table. 'And *this* isn't much of a match either, mate. Three-one now, is it?'

'I'm hustling you.'

'Chance would be a fine thing,' Hendricks said. He leaned down and broke, sending the balls scattering. A stripe dropped softly into one of the side pockets.

'Jesus.' Thorne picked up their glasses. 'I'll get them in, shall I?'

'Maybe you *should* help Tanner out with this.'

Thorne waited.

'She might be on to something.'

'Or she might just be obsessed, like you said.'

'Well then, just do it because it's something different. A bit of a break or whatever.'

'Honour killings, right. Like a week in Barbados.'

Hendricks was eyeing up his next shot. 'OK, then, how about doing it because she's asked you for a favour and you're being nice.' He leaned down. '*Nice.*' He sank a second ball in the corner and grinned. 'Look it up.'

SEVEN

It wasn't a big house, two storeys in the middle of a modest Victorian terrace in Hammersmith, but Thorne reckoned that, in line with the madness of London house prices, it was probably worth well over a million. He rang the bell and waited, wondering if Nicola Tanner would be able to stay, now that there weren't two salaries coming in. Did teachers get a pension? Had Susan had life insurance or mortgage protection? Thorne certainly didn't and it suddenly struck him, standing there, that he didn't know a lot about Helen's arrangements either.

Did she have a will?

Had she thought about who would take care of Alfie if anything happened to her?

If anyone was likely to have made provision for all eventualities it would be Nicola Tanner, Thorne decided. Though he guessed there would be plenty of grieving to do yet, before confronting such practicalities.

Tanner opened the door wearing baggy black jeans and a thick sweater and said, 'Right, I've got some coffee on.' Then, as an afterthought, 'Thanks for coming at such short notice.'

'It's fine,' Thorne said. 'I was only half an hour away.'

She stepped aside to let him in, and, as he walked past her, she said, 'You've been drinking.'

'Sorry?'

She waved his barely concealed irritation away as though it were unimportant. 'Just ... Susan drank. I mean, well we all drink ... *I* drink ... but Susan drank a *lot*, is what I'm trying to say. Too much. She'd been getting more of a handle on it lately; well, a bit ... but it wasn't easy. I tried to help, obviously, but it's got to be up to the person with the problem in the end, hasn't it? Sorry, I really didn't mean to sound judgemental just then. I tend to notice it, that's all.'

She turned her head as a cat darted from a doorway, ran halfway up the stairs, then turned to look at them.

'Mrs Slocombe,' Tanner said.

Thorne nodded his understanding; of the joke and of the bizarre, gabbled speech that Tanner had just delivered. She had spoken as if she were nervous or excited; leaning towards him, a hand pressed to her face, her arm, her chest. Thorne smiled and waited, and tried hard to ignore the smell of the new carpet.

She led the way to a small living room and told him to make himself comfortable while she went to fetch the coffee.

Thorne sat down and reminded himself that he was doing this for Meena Athwal. That slim possibility. He thought about what Hendricks had said; it was definitely not because he was being nice.

The room was neatly laid out, and immaculate. Bleached floorboards, a pair of identical grey sofas with blankets folded across the arms, a small TV set on a polished pine trunk. There were shelves lined with books in one alcove next to the fireplace, their spines arranged by colour: orange, then green, then black. Thorne turned to look at the four framed prints in a square on the wall behind him. Simple pencil sketches: fruit and flowers; a matching pair of nudes; an old woman's face with a delicate criss-cross of lines beneath her eyes.

He sat back, and then – though it was clearly too late already – he leaned forward again to check that the soles of his shoes were clean.

Tanner came back in carrying the coffee things on a tray and told Thorne to help himself. 'I've already had too many.' She took a pair of glasses from a handbag by the side of the sofa and put them on. 'I won't sleep.'

He poured, stirred in milk and sugar. 'Look, before anything else, I just wanted to say again how sorry I am about Susan.' He tried to set the spoon down quietly. 'I read about it.'

Tanner had already picked up a sheaf of papers that had been laid out on the coffee table when Thorne came in. She nodded, head down as she turned over a page. Susan's murder had made the newspapers, the story running for a day or two until something even more brutal had happened somewhere else, but Tanner understood that Thorne was talking about the material contained on a police computer; that he had gone to the trouble of looking and now knew every terrible detail.

'Good.' She held up the sheets of paper. 'So you know what kind of people we're dealing with.'

Thorne nodded. He knew enough to think that Tanner should probably be rather more concerned than she appeared to be.

'Amaya Shah and Kamal Azim.' Tanner read her notes. 'Both eighteen. Kamal lives in Whetstone and Amaya's a bit further north, up towards Barnet, which is where she goes to college. The Wood Street campus.' She leaned forward to pick up another sheaf of papers and handed it to Thorne. 'I made a second set for you.'

Thorne glanced down at the top sheet. The names and addresses were underlined, other details laid out in bold where necessary. He would not have been surprised if the sheets had been laminated. 'How did you even find out about this? A missing persons thing. I mean, you're on leave from a murder investigation team.'

'I put a flag on the computer system,' Tanner said, as though the answer were obvious. 'Anything in this . . . area. A colleague of mine is keeping an eye on it and he let me know when this one came in.'

'You're obviously good at getting people to do favours for you.'

'Right now, people are sorry for me.' Tanner shrugged. 'I'm not above taking advantage of that.'

'Obviously.' Thorne wondered if he would be sitting there himself had the woman on the sofa opposite not been so recently bereaved.

Tanner smiled, as though she knew exactly what Thorne was thinking. A tacit admission that she had taken advantage of him, too. 'Dipak Chall's a good DS, but he's not exactly a close friend,' she said. 'No . . . he might not have done this normally.'

Thorne looked up at Tanner's mention of her colleague's name, its implications. 'He knows what this is about, does he? What you're actually up to?'

'Of course. And he's a hundred per cent supportive, I can promise you that.'

Thorne went back to the notes, turning the pages as Tanner continued.

'They went missing three nights ago. Amaya had told her parents she was studying with a girl she knew at college. Kamal said he was going to a friend's. They used their Oyster cards at King's Cross just after eleven thirty, but we can't say for certain which line they were taking.'

'Going home?'

'Probably. So, Northern line towards High Barnet, but they never used their Oysters to touch out, which means we don't know where they ended up. They disappeared from the train.'

'If they *were* running away together, they could have gone

44

anywhere from King's Cross. Piccadilly line to Heathrow. Victoria line to the coach station—'

'I don't believe they were running away,' Tanner said.

'CCTV?'

'Like you say, it's a lot of lines to check. Over a hundred stations and that's just if they were heading north. Hopefully, the missing persons team will get round to looking at the Northern line first. Like I said on the phone, it's not high priority.'

Thorne put the papers down and picked up his coffee. He watched as the cat he'd seen earlier crept around the door, slunk across to the sofa and jumped up. As it settled down on the seat next to Tanner, he said, 'What makes you so sure they aren't running away or that this has got anything at all to do with those other cases?' He sat back. 'Seriously. Why is this an honour crime waiting to happen?'

'Or one that's already happened.'

'So . . . ?'

'I saw the transcripts of the parents' emergency calls,' Tanner said. 'Dipak got hold of them for me. There's something a bit hysterical about them.'

'For God's sake, their kids are missing.'

'OK, wrong word, but like you said yourself, these are eighteen-year-olds. Something a bit . . . predictable, then. Both sets of parents called within half an hour, that first night, and there's nothing to indicate they know one another. As if it was co-ordinated, somehow. Both fathers went marching into their local stations the next morning, demanding to know what was being done, both saying more or less the same thing. Word for word, actually. "My daughter's a good Muslim girl."' She looked down at her notes, turned a page to check. '"He's a good Muslim boy. He would not just disappear without a good reason."' Exactly how you'd expect them to act if they had nothing to do with it.' She stopped, pointed at Thorne. 'I know what you're going to say. "Because they *didn't* have anything to do with it."'

'Well, someone's got to say it.' He nodded across. 'And it doesn't look like the cat's about to chip in. Look, I'm just about willing to accept the basic . . . premise. The contract killings, the link between the cases. I mean, I'm *here*, aren't I? But just because these two teenagers don't come home one night . . . how many other Asian kids are on a missing persons list right now? How many of them are going to turn up safe and sound after sneaking off to some festival or other, or buggering off to Magaluf on the sly with a few mates?'

Thorne felt strange being the naysayer, when he was usually the one on the receiving end of such unwelcome words of advice. Such warnings. In Polesford he had been accused of looking for a crime where there was none; of chasing shadows. It hadn't been the first time.

He looked across at Tanner as she put down the file. She took off her glasses, pinched the bridge of her nose.

She seemed tired, suddenly.

'I'm good at my job,' she said. 'And please don't take that as any kind of suggestion that you aren't.'

'Not in a million years,' Thorne said. He had ignored the warnings in Polesford and eventually he had been proved horribly right. The shadows he had chased, and caught up with, had been far darker than even he had been expecting.

'I know Amaya and Kamal have not gone to any festival. I know there's something iffy about the two of them going missing. Something too textbook. I know it every bit as much as I know that two men came to my house two weeks ago to kill me, and why.'

Thorne had seen the forensic report, and knew she was right about that much, at least. Evidence confirming that there had been two individuals in the hallway with Susan on the night she was killed.

Two men who had thrown bleach into her eyes before stabbing her to death.

46

'I'm good at my job and this is me doing it, simple as that. I'm not doing this because I'm bored and I need something to do. It's not because I want revenge for Susan and I'm certainly not seeing honour crimes around every corner because I'm ... "crazed with grief" or anything like that.' She picked up the file again. 'Don't make the mistake of believing that I'm not thinking clearly.'

Thorne picked up his own set of notes. He sensed that Tanner's words, her assertions, were not aimed solely at him; that rather they were the result of one or more heated conversations with herself.

'You said Muslims.' He turned a page. 'Amaya and Kamal. Good Muslims.'

Tanner put her glasses back on, nodded.

'Meena Athwal was a Sikh.'

Another nod. 'As was the victim in one of the other cases I've been looking into. The third was a Hindu.'

'So they're ... multi-faith hitmen? These two.'

'The majority of honour crimes in this country occur within the Muslim, Sikh and Hindu communities and most of them are south Asian. But honour killings have also been documented in Jewish and Christian communities. Actually, I think the only ones without any blood on their hands are Buddhists and Rastafarians.' A half-smile. 'Maybe Jedis.'

The joke came from nowhere, and while Thorne was relieved to be shown a sense of humour, he nevertheless had a picture of a woman who was as uncomfortable with banter as she was with bullshit. Who would stand there, stone-faced, the only member of a group failing to see the funny side of something. Or else the teller of a joke that was misjudged or simply unfunny; the colour flooding her cheeks while others smiled awkwardly or wandered away.

He said, 'Where do we start, then?'

'The parents seem as good a bet as any,' Tanner said. 'Let's go and see how hysterical they are three days on. You good for tomorrow?'

Thorne held up a hand. 'Hang on. You'll need to give me a day to try and get some shifts swapped around. See if *I* can call in a few favours.'

'Fair enough.' Tanner leaned across to refill his mug, and when she sat back the cat arched its back for a few moments as though irritated by the disturbance. 'She was Susan's cat, really,' Tanner said. 'She would always go to her first, you know?'

'Pheromones or something,' Thorne said.

'Well, she was hers more than mine. Mine now though, obviously.' She reached a hand across tentatively to stroke the cat. 'I certainly couldn't bear to be without her.'

Thorne watched Tanner move a finger gently back and forth beneath the animal's chin.

Not a woman crazed with grief, perhaps, but transformed by it nonetheless. Struggling to see what might lie ahead, needing to, when she was only capable of taking one small step at a time.

'She's getting used to me, I think.'

Thorne smiled and drank coffee that was far too strong and decided that he would have that conversation as soon as he could.

Those awkward practicalities.

He would let Helen know that if the very worst were to happen, whatever her bloody sister or anyone else might have to say about it, he wanted to take care of Alfie.

EIGHT

It was a small printing business; a minute's walk from Finchley Central station, between an estate agent's and what appeared to be a pop-up selling electronic cigarettes and associated items. There were no customers, but two women, who Thorne presumed to be the mother and sister, were at work behind the counter. The younger girl was wearing jeans and a white sweatshirt emblazoned with the logo *Azim Kwikprint*, but both were wearing hijabs. Thorne and Tanner had taken out their warrant cards as soon as they came through the door, and as they approached the counter they saw the older woman move closer to her daughter and reach for her hand.

Tanner made the introductions.

The older woman nodded and turned without a word to walk away into an office at the back. The daughter's gaze had already returned to her computer screen. She typed for a few seconds then pulled some papers towards her. She glanced up and flashed a smile that seemed friendly enough, but before Tanner or Thorne could speak she had turned away from the counter to follow her mother.

'She looked scared,' Tanner said.

'Did she?'

'The mother.'

Thorne picked up a ream of printing paper. 'Your son's been missing for three days and two coppers walk in. How else are you going to look?'

'I suppose.'

The paper was cheap, but Thorne knew it was even cheaper at the megastore on the nearby trading estate. He wondered how a place like this, how any independent, stayed in business. There weren't any small electrical shops on this high street any more, or sports shops like the one he'd bought his Spurs scarf and football boots from when he was a kid. He couldn't remember the last time he'd seen a record shop anywhere.

Record shop. He could imagine Helen laughing. Calling him 'Grandad' and asking him what things were like in the war. On reflection, Thorne wondered if perhaps there might be a few more record shops opening soon, now that vinyl was having such a resurgence.

'Here we go,' Tanner said quietly.

Thorne put the paper back on the display and watched Hamid Azim emerge from the room at the rear of the shop. He said, 'Just a second,' as he walked straight across to the door and turned the sign to CLOSED. He said, 'Right,' as he walked back to take his place behind the counter.

He was small and trim, his hair and beard streaked with grey, his eyes bright behind lightly tinted, rimless spectacles. He wore a maroon sweater over a white shirt; brown slacks, sandals and socks.

He said, 'Have you found Kamal?'

'I'm afraid not,' Tanner said. She introduced herself and Thorne a second time.

Azim leaned across the counter to shake hands with each of

them. 'His mother is in pieces. We all are. But what can we do except sit and wait for news?'

'I'm sorry that we don't really have any,' Thorne said. 'We just have a few more questions.'

Azim looked at them. 'I told the officers everything when I went to the station.'

'Obviously the more information we have the better.' Tanner took out a small notebook and pen. 'You might have remembered something since then that could help.'

'Of course, I understand.'

She smiled and opened the notebook. 'So, would you say that for Kamal to just disappear without saying anything was out of character?'

'Definitely,' Azim said. 'I told them the same thing at the station. He would never do anything like that. This is why we are so worried. No phone calls, no messages, nothing.' He shook his head. 'Not like him at all.'

'You hadn't argued?'

'No.' Instant, definitive.

'No family rows?'

Azim waited a second or two this time, made eye contact with Tanner. 'No.' He shrugged. 'He bickers with his little sister, but that's only normal, isn't it?'

'What about work?' Thorne looked around. 'Any problems, issues with money?'

'Kamal works hard,' Azim said. 'And he's sensible with the wages I pay him. He doesn't drink, he doesn't take drugs, nothing like that. I know he likes to enjoy himself, go to parties and so on, and that's fine, of course. We want him to be independent.' A smile appeared, but not for very long. 'I know every father would say the same thing about their son, but he's a good boy.'

'So, very out of character to be arrested for being drunk outside a nightclub and verbally abusing a police officer?' Tanner smiled, ignoring the look from Thorne.

51

'What?' Azim shook his head. 'No, you must have that wrong.'

'Three months ago,' Tanner said. 'They let him off with a caution and obviously he decided not to tell you about it. I mean, he's eighteen, so no reason he would, is there?'

Azim stared at the floor, muttered something to himself.

Tanner turned a page in her notebook, as though looking for a name she could not instantly recall. 'Did you know the girl who disappeared at the same time ... Amaya Shah?'

Azim shook his head. 'He had never mentioned her. I was surprised when I heard that they had been together that night.'

'Did Kamal have a girlfriend?' Thorne asked.

'Friends who were girls, yes, but not the way you mean.'

'Really? An eighteen-year-old boy?'

'There is a girl he is very fond of back in Bangladesh,' Azim said. 'In Dhaka. They have known each other since they were children.'

'Childhood sweethearts, that kind of thing?'

'Exactly. We have always hoped they would get married one day.'

'*We*, meaning ... ?'

'Everyone.'

'How did Kamal feel about that?'

Azim looked puzzled.

'A girl in Bangladesh. How often did they even see each other?'

'We use the internet. Skype.'

'All the same.'

'As I said, he was very fond of this girl.' Azim turned his attention to Tanner, as though he had decided that she was the one in charge, or perhaps just the more naturally sympathetic. 'So, what is being done to find my son? It's very hard to imagine that anything we're talking about is going to help a great deal.'

'We're doing everything that can be done,' Tanner said. 'You understand that because Kamal is legally an adult, the process is not the same as it would be if a child were to go missing.' She looked at him. 'That's not to say we aren't taking this extremely seriously.'

Azim shook his head slowly, nodded around at his shop. 'We go about our business,' he said. 'We have to. We print our brochures and our fancy letterheads and all that, but we might just as well be robots. While our son is . . . nowhere, life has stopped for all of us. It's stopped.'

Thorne watched Tanner slip the notebook back into her bag. It certainly went with the part she was, to some extent, playing, but he guessed that someone as methodical as she was got through a fair number of them in the course of a year.

He wondered if Azim would give her a discount if she bought in bulk.

Faruk Shah sighed, a crackle in his chest. 'She told us she was going to study at a friend's house,' he said. 'That girl Sarah, from the college. The girl confirmed it when my wife called her, but she told us the truth on the second day.'

Next to him, Shah's wife Nabila nodded.

Amaya's somewhat surly elder brother had shown Thorne and Tanner up to a small flat above a convenience store in East Barnet before returning to work downstairs. The living room was overheated and seemed barely large enough to contain the widescreen TV and two leather sofas on which the four of them sat. The plum-coloured carpet felt deep enough to lose sight of their feet in. The ceiling was low and featureless, and the claustrophobic atmosphere was not helped by air that was thick with cigarette smoke. Shah had hastily stubbed one out when Tanner and Thorne were shown in, but he was already lighting up again.

'Perhaps if that girl had told us the truth straight away.' He tossed his lighter down on to a glass table. 'Apparently, some girls are brought up to think that lying is acceptable.'

'Amaya lied,' Thorne said. 'About where she was going. I'm sure you don't think there's anything wrong with how you brought *her* up.'

Shah grunted and sat back.

'Amaya is a good girl,' his wife said.

If Kamal's father had appeared every inch the no-nonsense businessman, Amaya's looked as if he had just got out of bed. He was dressed, but had clearly made little effort; a belly sagging over tracksuit bottoms, an unbuttoned shirt. Unruly tufts of hair curled from the neck of his vest, and a beard that Thorne guessed was normally neatly trimmed, had evidently gone ungroomed.

'Do you know Kamal Azim?' Tanner asked.

Shah shook his head.

'But you know who he is.'

'We know, yes.'

'Do you know his parents?'

'How could I know them if I don't know him?'

'It's possible,' Tanner said. 'Had Amaya even mentioned his name?'

'Yes, she'd mentioned him. We thought he was just a friend.'

'And that was OK?'

'Of course, why wouldn't it be? We never suspected it could be anything else.'

'Is that what you think now?'

'It looks as though they ran away together,' Shah said. 'This is what the police are telling us, so what else are we supposed to think?'

'How do you feel about that?' Thorne asked.

'How do I *feel*? Our daughter is missing.'

'About Amaya lying to you, I mean. Running away with someone you had never even met.'

'Why does that make a difference?' Shah sat forward again. 'How is what I feel about one thing or another going to help find my daughter and this boy?'

'We'd like to know.'

Amaya's mother was looking down at her hands, folded neatly in her lap.

'We want her to come home,' Shah said. 'That is the most important thing. But yes, of course, she will certainly be in trouble when she does.'

'What kind of trouble?'

Shah shook his head, blew out a thin stream of smoke. 'That is a matter for my family.'

'Not any more it isn't,' Thorne said.

'I would never ask you how you would discipline your child.' The anger was building. 'I would never dare to do that.' Shah waved his hands around as he spoke, ash falling on to the carpet and the smoke from his cigarette drifting across his wife's face. 'That is your business.'

Thorne nodded, as though it were a perfectly reasonable point. 'It's my business to try and find out where your daughter is, and if she *has* run away, I have to ask myself if the way you impose . . . discipline could have had something to do with it.'

Shah glanced at his wife, and when he looked back to Thorne his face had softened considerably. 'I can promise you it is not something you need to worry about, because we never had to discipline Amaya.'

'You're lucky,' Thorne said.

'Very,' Tanner added.

'It was never necessary, was it?' Shah glanced at his wife again.

Nabila Shah shook her head.

'She works hard at home and she works hard at college. She has never been disrespectful and she does everything that is expected of her. We have never had any trouble.'

'Until now,' Thorne said.

'Yes, until now.'

'She *was* a good girl,' his wife said again, raising a hand to arrange the folds of her soft, crimson hijab.

She said it like a line she'd been given.

They sat together in a Starbucks outside the Spires shopping centre. Thorne watched Tanner staring at her receipt. Saw her smiling.

'What?' he asked.

She held up the receipt. 'I'd normally keep these,' she said. 'Make a note of all my expenses on a job.' She screwed up the slip of paper and picked up her coffee. 'Never done anything like this before.' Her eyes widened. 'Off the books.'

Thorne stared past her through the window. Saturday shoppers crowding the pavements. On the High Street a car slowed, searching for a parking space, and the driver behind leaned on his horn. 'Well, I'm none the wiser,' Thorne said. 'Not really.'

She looked at him.

'Shah and Azim.'

Tanner was rather more decisive. 'They're certainly not stupid. They're all upset enough and they're all making out like they accept that Kamal and Amaya have run away together. They're shocked, course they are, but they've forced themselves to accept that it's the only explanation.' She sipped her drink. 'They're not pretending that they're going to win liberal parents of the year, mind you, but that would probably be too much of a stretch. I'm guessing they've been coached. Told how they should behave, what they should say.'

'You've got no doubts?'

'None,' Tanner said. She shook her head. 'Skype. Did you hear him?'

'What?'

'The people that do this stuff use it to get round the law against forced marriage. Young girls being married off on

56

Skype to men in Bangladesh or Turkey or wherever. Then they stick them straight on a plane to ... consummate the marriage.'

Thorne saw the look on Tanner's face, but distaste was not certainty. It did not mean that anyone had committed murder. 'You don't for a minute think that maybe they seemed upset because they were? The Shahs and the Azims? I've seen some very good liars in my time, but I've also come across plenty of people I thought were dodgy as hell, when they hadn't done anything wrong. I know you must have, too. Something like losing a child can do strange things to people. How they act.' He looked at her. 'Talking of which, why didn't you tell me about Kamal being arrested?'

'I didn't think it was very important,' Tanner said. 'Just fancied throwing it at his father, see what the reaction was. It was only a caution. Drunk and shouting his mouth off, a couple of poppers in his pocket.'

'Still. I'm not very happy about you knowing things that I don't.'

'Fair enough.' Tanner did not look thrilled about being reprimanded, however gently. It was clearly not something she was used to. 'It won't happen again.'

'If we're going to do this together ...'

After a few seconds of silence, Tanner sat back and shook her head. 'My only problem is not letting them know I'm on to them. Not letting them see how angry I am. That they can sit there, bleating on about their missing children, asking us what we're doing to find them, when they've handed money over so that two men can ... do whatever.' She looked at him. 'If I wasn't a hundred per cent sure before, I am now.'

Tanner's certainty was pretty persuasive and Thorne could not deny that the conversations with the two sets of parents – well, those that did the talking, anyway – had not given him any reason to walk away from this.

That prickle at the nape of his neck he had learned not to ignore.

'What?' Tanner had clocked the look on Thorne's face.

'Just something Helen said to me once. If everyone loves their kids, some of them have got a strange way of showing it.'

'I like her already,' Tanner said.

There was one thing, though, that continued to nag at him. Something that Tanner had not considered, or more likely was choosing to ignore.

These two men . . .

If they had tried and failed to kill her once, wasn't there every possibility that they would try again?

NINE

Obviously it paid to be nice to your regulars, but Angie made a point of always being extra nice to customers she hadn't seen before, in the hope they might *become* regulars. So she'd turned on the chat and the big smile for the pair that had wandered in just before the lunchtime rush, told them to let her know if there was anything else they needed. Refills, extra toast, whatever. The younger man, Irish by the sound of it, had been keen to tackle one of Angie's all-day full English breakfasts, while his friend – a Pakistani, she reckoned, though he didn't really have any kind of accent – had just asked for orange juice and a muffin.

'Never mind him,' the Irishman had said. 'I'll eat enough for both of us.'

Angie had grinned. 'Well, you're a big lad.'

The big lad had sat back and stretched. 'Right enough.'

Once she'd taken the food over, brought a bottle of ketchup across from another table, she sat with a magazine and watched them from the corner of the counter. Turned that smile on again whenever one of them looked up and caught her eye. It was easy enough to listen in to their conversation too, despite the growl of traffic moving past on the Holloway Road just six feet from the door. It made sense to know who your punters were, that's what she always told herself. It was fun to have a nosy now and again and it was how she got through the times when the place wasn't busy. No harm in it, was there? It was just a question of looking like you weren't actually listening at all, and trying not to mind too much that your customers' lives always sounded so much more interesting than your own.

While the Irishman ate, his mate looked swiftly through the pile of newspapers he'd brought in with him. When he'd finished, he laid the papers to one side and started scrolling through his phone. After a few minutes he put that down, too and picked a small piece from his muffin.

'Still nothing,' he said.

The Irishman shrugged, his mouth full. 'Should be any time now.'

'I hope so.'

'No worries.'

'I always worry until we get the rest of the money. One of us has to.'

Angie turned the page of her magazine. She waved as one of her regulars wandered out.

'It'll be grand.' The big Irishman swallowed and took a slurp of tea. 'There's always some old bloke comes along with a dog.'

Glancing over, Angie could see that the Pakistani was watching the Irishman eat. It was not a spectacle he seemed entirely comfortable with. After a minute or so, the Irishman looked up and grinned. He speared a slice of bacon and held it out, a fat drop of grease plopping on to the red vinyl tablecloth between them.

'Want some?'

The Pakistani shook his head, looking bored as much as anything else, but the reaction certainly seemed to amuse his mate.

'No, course you don't. Sorry.'

The older man let out a long, slow breath. 'Don't you ever get tired of that stupid joke?'

The Irishman was still grinning. Apparently not.

'You know I'm a vegetarian.'

'Why it's still funny,' the Irishman said.

'Really?'

'It's a religious thing as well though, yeah?'

The Pakistani sighed. 'I'm a vegetarian.'

That explained the muffin, Angie thought. Mind you, there was a vegetarian breakfast on the menu, and she could easily have done him an egg sandwich or something. Maybe the bloke just wasn't very hungry.

She turned another page, wondering what dogs had to do with money.

'Anyway, you know I don't give a toss what you are. Never have, mate. Couldn't care less what you or anyone else believes in, because it's all nonsense.' He sliced a piece of fried bread in half. 'But you know, I'm just a pig-thick bogtrotter and religion's always been nothing but trouble where I come from, so . . .'

'So.'

'My choice, right?'

'Well, I don't believe that faith is something you choose.' The Pakistani sat back. 'It's something you have or you don't have. Like the colour of your eyes. A part of you.'

'You can choose to change the colour of your eyes.' The Irishman pushed half a tomato on to his fried bread and bit into it. 'They have these special contact lenses.'

They sat in silence for a few minutes. The Pakistani quietly finished his muffin while the Irishman began to slow down a little, the all-day breakfast beginning to look like something it would take him all day to eat.

'I reckon it's a good thing,' he said. 'That we don't really get on, like.'

'A good thing.'

'Well, yeah ... when you work with someone who's a friend, or someone who becomes a friend *because* you work with them, it can cause problems, can't it? You get touchy about things. Upset.'

The other man nodded, considering it.

'I think it's what makes us a perfect team. You know, the fact that we don't actually have a lot of time for each other. Keeps us sharp, I reckon.'

'I can't deny that we're a good team,' the Pakistani said.

'Better than good, I'd say.'

'We do an excellent job, I wouldn't argue with that.'

'We're *efficient*, right? That's why people pay us to do a job, and I think we're efficient because we're so different. Because, if we weren't doing this, we wouldn't be giving each other the time of day, would we? Come on, be honest, would we?'

'I doubt it.'

When a sausage sandwich was pushed through from the kitchen, Angie picked it up and carried it across to a table by the window. She slowed and smiled as she passed the two men whose conversation she had become so interested in, but neither of them looked up at her.

'Course we bloody wouldn't. We'd be avoiding each other like the plague.' The Irishman was brandishing a fork as he spoke, a gobbet of baked beans stubbornly clinging to the tines. 'The truth is, you don't like me a whole lot because I couldn't care less about religion or any of that.' He muttered something that Angie couldn't quite catch above the noise of plates clattering in the kitchen. Something about hats and beards. 'If a woman's show-ing her ankles when she should be wearing one of those stupid things that makes her look like a sodding postbox. All that carry-on. You dislike me, because I do this for the money, pure and simple.'

'I've always been well aware of why you do it,' the Pakistani said.

'Not like you *don't* take the money. But that's not why you do it, right? It's a whatever ... a higher calling.'

'I do it because it has to be done.'

The big man nodded, as if he were impressed. 'Yeah, I've known a few people in my time who did things that'd give anyone bad dreams ... you know, back at home ... but you're cold as you like, no question about that. Coldest I've ever seen.'

'We are doing these things for very different reasons, that is certainly true.' The Pakistani brushed crumbs from his shirt. 'But we also go about them in very different ways.'

'I can't argue with that.'

'You are more ... emotional.'

'Oh, I can get a bit worked up, definitely.'

'For me, it's not like that. I know what I'm doing is right and virtuous, but in the act itself there is no more feeling than if it were a goat, or a pig.'

Angie looked up from her magazine. What the hell were they on about now? The Irishman was smiling as he laid down his knife and fork and sat back, having finally given up. He raised a hand, and when she looked at him he pointed to his plate and shook his head.

'You beaten?'

'I'm as full as a fat girl's knickers.'

As she came around the counter, laughing, the Pakistani took out his wallet and removed a twenty-pound note. He leaned across the table and said, 'I don't dislike you.'

'Doesn't bother me if you do,' the Irishman said.

Angie walked across and began gathering up their plates. The Irishman helpfully passed over his used cutlery and dirty mug.

'I have no strong feelings about you one way or another.' The Pakistani slid the note beneath his empty glass, seemingly oblivious to Angie's presence. He took out his phone to check it again. 'I admire any man who works for a living, who does his job well.'

The Irishman grabbed a napkin and pretended to dab his eyes. 'Oh, I'm filling up over here.'

Turning from the table, Angie heard the scrape as the Pakistani pushed back his chair.

'What I dislike,' he said, quietly, 'is the fact that you seem to enjoy it so much.'

TEN

When Thorne called from his office in Colindale, Tanner answered almost immediately, and it was apparent that she had already programmed Thorne's number into her phone.

'I was just about to call you,' she said.

'Go on.'

'No, you first.'

Thorne looked around. A few desks away, DI Yvonne Kitson was in the middle of her own phone conversation, while other officers appeared mesmerised by whatever was on their computer screens. Their boss, DCI Russell Brigstocke, was attending a 'strategic diversity' meeting at some country-house hotel and was almost certainly chewing his face off with boredom by now.

Nobody seemed to be paying Thorne any attention.

'These two men,' he said.

'Right.'

'I was thinking about how it works.' Thorne checked again to make sure he was not being overheard. 'So, let's accept for the time being that the parents of Meena Athwal, the families of Amaya and Kamal ... decide their son or daughter needs to be killed. They don't just pick up the phone. It's not like the killers advertise, is it? Someone else arranges it.'

'Obviously. The deal is brokered.'

'So, where do we start looking for our broker?'

'I've already got an idea about that,' Tanner said. 'But there's some other stuff I need to talk to you about first. Things I need to show you. When's a good time?'

'The rest of the day's buggered,' Thorne said. He had a mountain of paperwork that couldn't wait any longer and several other cases demanding his attention.

Murders he knew had happened, victims he had seen with his own eyes.

'What about tonight, then?'

'OK.'

'I can come to you, if that's easier.'

Thorne wasn't too sure that it would be. Driving home via Hammersmith was not ideal, but wouldn't going to Tanner's place again and getting back late be better than bringing all this home with him? He had still not said anything to Helen about what he was doing, and even if he did, he wondered how he and Tanner would be able to talk openly about the case with Alfie tearing about.

He explained the situation.

'Your son?'

'As good as,' Thorne said. 'He doesn't go to bed until seven and only then if we're lucky.'

'I'll come just after seven then,' Tanner said. 'It's my turn anyway. I'll bring a bottle.'

It looked as though the arrangement had been made.

When Thorne got home, he told Helen that a work colleague from a different team was coming over; that cases they had been working on separately might be connected. He told her he would explain later. Helen did not seem overly concerned one way or another, though that might have been due to the fact that she was already preoccupied with getting Alfie ready for bed.

Or perhaps it was because she was not used to seeing Thorne so keen to tidy up.

Tanner arrived at seven fifteen with a clanking carrier bag from which she produced two bottles of wine. 'I wasn't sure what you'd both like,' she said. 'I had plenty knocking around. Found it stashed all over the house, you know, after Susan.'

Thorne carried the wine over to the fridge. He offered to open a bottle for Tanner. She reminded him that she was driving and asked for water.

As Thorne walked back across to the small table in the kitchen, Tanner nodded towards the hallway that led to the bedrooms. They could just make out Helen's voice. 'Bedtime story?'

'He wants the same one every night,' Thorne said, sitting down.

'My brothers' kids were all the same. How bloody hungry can a caterpillar be?' A smile made no more than a fleeting appearance, and Tanner was quickly into work mode and turning away; removing a laptop from her bag and opening it on the table. The moment the system was awake, she began working at the keyboard. A few seconds later, she double-clicked the track pad, then turned it so that he could see.

'Dipak sent me this.' She pointed at the still CCTV image that filled the screen. Blurry, black and white. 'Woodside Park, so we were right. They were going home.'

'Got off two stops early.' Thorne leaned in. Two Asian teenagers he guessed were Amaya Shah and Kamal Azim, moving towards the ticket barriers. Another man, older, his hand on Amaya's arm as though pushing her through.

'I've seen all the footage and it's obvious they're in a hurry,' Tanner said. 'Looking behind them several times, like they're trying to get away from someone.'

'What about him?' Thorne pointed at the older man. He too

was Asian; well dressed, fortyish. Only the side of his face was visible in the still, but Tanner had just said she'd seen much more. 'You think he's one of them? Didn't you say you had a decent e-fit?'

'I've got something better,' Tanner said.

'Right . . .' Thorne waited.

'We'll get to that.' She smiled again and this time not simply because it was the appropriate response. Thorne could sense she had something important up her sleeve, and he was surprised that someone who was anything but a drama queen would milk the suspense.

He was amazed to see her enjoying it.

They looked up together as Helen appeared at the end of the hallway.

'Got him off,' she said.

'Brown bear does the business again,' Thorne said.

Tanner was still smiling. 'I'm Nicola. Sorry for being a nuisance.'

'Don't be daft.' Helen moved across to shake Tanner's hand, then told Thorne she was going for a shower. He said he'd keep an ear open for Alfie and that he'd try to be as quick as he could.

'I brought some wine,' Tanner said, pointing to the fridge.

When Helen had left the room, Thorne asked again about the broker they had talked about on the phone; how those that required the services of the two killers Tanner was after might go about securing them.

'It's the multi-faith thing I'm struggling with,' he said. 'If it was just about Muslims or Sikhs, or just about Hindus, there are all manner of groups and organisations that might be able to front for these people.'

'I struggled with that too,' Tanner said. 'For a while.'

'Where would all three of them come together, though?' Thorne was thinking out loud. 'Some social thing? People who all support the same football team?'

Tanner was already typing again. She said, 'I'll show you where I'd got to.'

She turned the laptop around again and Thorne found himself staring at the home page of a website called *The London Sikh and Hindu Forum*.

'I started with this and a few others like it,' Tanner said. 'Places where the Hindu and Sikh communities would come together.'

'Makes sense,' Thorne said. 'Stuff in common.' The truth was, he knew as much about the two religions as he did about boilers, but he could see that the site made great play of the sort of 'stuff' he had been thinking about. It was open to all Hindus and Sikhs of any age and background, even welcoming non-Indians simply interested in the culture, and promoted care for all members, mutual respect and the honouring of the Indian motherland.

As Tanner scrolled down, Thorne was taken aback to see a swastika prominently featured. He simply pointed at it. Said, 'Eh?'

'It's an important symbol in a lot of Indian religions,' Tanner said. 'The Nazis borrowed it.'

'Who's he?' Thorne was pointing to a man pictured at the bottom of the page, above an elaborately drawn *Namaste*. He wore an open-necked black shirt and a broad smile. His palms were pressed together in greeting and there was a red mark or *tika* in the middle of his forehead.

'Arman Bannerjee,' Tanner said. 'Local businessman.'

Thorne saw her face darken. 'What?'

'We've had a few run-ins.'

'I take it you went to some of these meetings?'

'A couple, yes. This group and a few others. Not quite so open to non-Indians as they claim to be. Or maybe it's just non-Indians who happen to be coppers poking around where they're not wanted.' She was still looking at the man with the wide grin and the gesture of warm welcome. 'Bannerjee complained,' she said. 'Him and several others, eventually.'

'You think he might have sent those men to your house?'

'I'd upset quite a few people by the time I stopped.'

Thorne nodded. It had been the worst thing imaginable that had forced Nicola Tanner to stop, and even then, the compassionate leave had been something she'd had little choice about. He said, 'Upsetting people is good, sometimes. Shakes things loose.'

'No Muslims involved though, right?' Tanner was already looking for another website, typing in the address. 'So I'd started looking for a group where all three religions would come together. Sikhs, Hindus *and* Muslims. I talked to some of the groups within those communities working against honour-based violence and it turns out a few of them had already been doing some digging of their own. Which brings us to this.' She hit the enter button and Thorne watched while the page loaded.

'*London AHCA?*'

'Anti Hate Crime Alliance. It represents all three of the major south Asian religions.'

Three young men stood together in the centre of the page, smiling. One was heavily bearded and wore a Muslim prayer cap, another wore a turban and was sporting a T-shirt with the slogan *Don't Freak, I'm A Sikh,* and the third had the *tika* on his forehead that marked him out as a Hindu.

'Most of these morons in the BNP and the English Defence League don't know one religion from another,' Tanner said. 'They think all Muslims are terrorists, and if that wasn't bad enough, think anyone remotely Asian-looking is a Muslim, so plenty of innocent Sikhs and Hindus are getting the shit kicked out of them by these idiots and getting rightly pissed off about it. They formed this group to start organising some opposition and obviously, it made sense for the Muslim community to be involved.' She pointed to a tab marked *Forthcoming Meetings* in a column on the left. 'They're pretty busy.'

'Gives someone who's looking to send certain kinds of messages to certain kinds of people the perfect opportunity.' Thorne shook his head. 'Last place you'd think of.'

'I don't see why,' Tanner said. 'Just because you don't want to get beaten up for no good reason doesn't mean you aren't also the kind of person who'd have your daughter killed for shaming you.' She quickly opened two new web pages, shrank them and positioned them next to one another. 'Some members of those groups I mentioned . . . Karma Nirvana and the Halo Project . . . had been going to these meetings for a while and heard one or two opinions they didn't like the sound of.'

Thorne couldn't argue. 'We should go along ourselves.'

'I think we should.'

'I mean, preventing violence is one of our jobs, right?'

'Absolutely,' Tanner said. 'There's a meeting tomorrow. Now . . . ' As she began to type, that smile appeared again, the one that was so pleased with itself. ' . . . best till last.'

Thorne leaned forward. 'Porn site next, is it?'

Tanner didn't hear or didn't bother to acknowledge him. She said, 'Look what popped up on YouTube this morning.'

It was obviously mobile phone footage; the kind Thorne had seen plenty of times before. The phone was usually the first thing to come out when anything dramatic happened.

A punch-up, a car crash, a terrorist attack.

'Some kid on the Tube with them,' Tanner said. 'Filmed the whole thing.'

For a few seconds the image was blurry, jumping around until it became clear that they were inside a carriage on an underground train. Thorne could hear the voice of the kid doing the filming; mumbling his commentary, keen to stay anonymous.

Bloody hell, look at them . . .

Amaya and Kamal, frozen in their seats. A big man in a paint-spattered jacket standing above them, shouting and swearing, making threats. An Irish accent. An older, Asian man in a suit, sitting next to Amaya and answering back; standing his ground in the face of the abuse. The same man Thorne had seen in the CCTV still.

He's going to deck him in a minute.

'That's how they did it,' Tanner said. 'How they got Amaya and Kamal off the train. One of them making threats and the other one stepping in, like he was trying to save them.'

'Bastard,' Thorne said.

'Two of them.'

'I mean the kid doing the filming. Jesus ... why didn't he do something instead of sitting there with his phone?'

'It doesn't matter now,' Tanner said. She was right, and besides, it was time for her big reveal. She leaned forward, waited for the right moment and paused the video. 'There.'

Not pin-sharp, but still a very decent close-up of the two men who had tricked Amaya and Kamal into getting off the train.

Who, in all probability, had been paid to murder them.

'That's them,' Tanner said, sitting back. 'Those are the men who killed Susan.'

ELEVEN

After Tanner had gone, Helen opened the wine she had brought and sat with Thorne on the sofa, waiting.

He told her all about it. He told her about Tanner's murdered partner and the honour killings investigation it was connected to; that *he* was now connected to.

Helen took a minute once he'd finished. She said, 'Well, I wouldn't be much of a girlfriend if I didn't remind you that it isn't your investigation. If I didn't tell you how stupid you were being.'

'Meena Athwal was mine,' Thorne said. 'It looks like she was killed because her father, or her brothers, or all of them, paid to have her killed. How could I—?'

Helen held up a hand. 'I'm just saying, that's all. I'm not willing to argue about it. I haven't got the energy. I know what you're like, anyway, so what's the point?'

Thorne nodded, happy to be let off the hook.

'Once you've made your mind up about something.'

'I'll consider myself told,' Thorne said.

Helen sat up and turned to look at him. 'The other day I was out with Alfie in the park and he stopped because he wanted me to carry him. I told him he was a big boy, and that I was tired, and that he was perfectly capable of walking.' She smiled as she remembered. 'He just stood there in the middle of the path and refused to go any further. So, after arguing the toss with him for five minutes, I just carried on walking and it got to the point where I could hardly see him any more when I turned round, but he stayed exactly where he was. Just stood there and wouldn't move an inch . . . stubborn little sod.' She took a sip of wine and shrugged. 'I had to go back and pick him up in the end, but guess who he reminded me of?'

'Well it can't be genetic, can it?' Thorne said.

Helen's smile slipped a little, because suddenly they were on dangerous ground. Officially, Alfie's natural father was a man named Paul Hopwood; a police officer who had been killed on duty only a month or so before Alfie was born. Paul almost certainly *was* Alfie's father, but the affair between Helen and another officer eight months before his death meant that there would always be doubt. Always doubt and always guilt.

'Obviously not,' Helen said.

Thorne wondered if now might be the time to have that conversation about practicalities, but the mood had already changed. The moment, if it had ever been there at all, was gone.

'She doesn't *look* like the sort who's going to get you into trouble,' Helen said. 'Tanner. So you might get away with it.'

'Don't troublemakers always look like that?' Thorne asked. 'Like the trustworthy ones?'

'No, most of the time they look like you.' Helen laughed. 'You've always been a shit-magnet. You can see it a mile away.'

'Was Paul like that?'

Helen blinked. 'No.'

Thorne thought: Didn't stop you shagging someone else though, did it? He said: 'So, why the affair?'

'Because I'm an idiot,' Helen said. She had another drink and another after that, and suddenly she looked pleased with herself. 'Actually, *no*. I had an affair because I met someone I fancied and I wanted to shag him. That's why.'

'OK.'

'And can we talk about something else?'

'Fine.'

They sat in silence for a minute; silence that was always a little heavier without Alfie around. Then Helen said, 'It's like that song. The one about angels . . .' She nudged him. '*You* know. On one of your stupid cowboy compilations.'

Thorne thought about it. '"It Wasn't God Who Made Honky Tonk Angels."'

'Yeah, that one.'

'Kitty Wells.'

Helen shrugged, because she didn't care. 'It's all about how men can cheat or whatever and that's acceptable somehow, but when women do it, men say it's because they're weird or whatever. Like it's something in their naturally wicked nature. A woman can shag someone just because she feels like it, you know? God's got bugger all to do with it.'

She said something else after that, but Thorne was thinking about Meena Athwal. About Kamal and Amaya. The men who had done these things, whatever they believed, were not carrying out divine will, and faith of any sort had nothing to do with any of it. It was murder, plain and simple.

Tanner had been right. They were just men.

And God, of any sort, had bugger all to do with it.

Thorne glanced up and saw that Helen was looking at him. 'It's a good song,' he said.

'Yeah, it's all right.'

They dug the remote from between the sofa cushions, and put the news on, and Helen was asleep on Thorne's shoulder before it had finished.

TWELVE

Walking towards her front gate, Tanner froze, just for a second, when she saw a figure emerge from a car twenty yards ahead of her. She reached quickly to unzip her shoulder bag: pepper spray and telescopic baton inside. She relaxed when a hand was raised, and when the man moved through the bleed from a streetlamp on his way towards her she recognised DS Dipak Chall.

She zipped her bag up again and carried on walking.

For a week or so after Susan's murder, a patrol car had been stationed permanently outside Tanner's house. It was understandable, of course, but in the end she had told her boss that it was no longer necessary, fed up with coming and going with mugs of tea as much as anything. A car still passed along her road as part of the local night shift, which was fine, but she did not feel the need to be protected.

She certainly did not want to be watched.

Had she not seen his face, washed orange beneath the lamp, she would have recognised Dipak Chall quickly enough anyway.

That lazy, loping walk. Gangly and drooping like a bored teenager, even though he was in his early thirties.

She reached the front gate before him and waited, taking out her keys.

'Ma'am.'

'What's happened?'

'Nothing. I just ...'

She looked at him. 'How long have you been sitting there, Dipak?'

'I just got here, really. I was passing, so I thought I'd look in.' He saw the look on Tanner's face that told him she was not buying it. 'OK, about half an hour, but I was on my way home and it's not like it's out of my way.'

She couldn't remember where he lived. 'Do you want to come in?'

Chall looked a little surprised. 'Yeah, I mean, if that's OK.'

'Why wouldn't it be?' Tanner nudged the gate open with her foot. 'It's freezing out here, and I can just as easily tell you off over a cup of tea.'

They leaned back against the polished worktop in Tanner's kitchen. She passed Chall a coaster for his mug, and said, 'I don't need nannying, you know.'

'Course not.'

'I can look after myself.'

'I know.'

'Good. So I won't expect to see you lurking outside my house again, all right?'

Chall smiled as he stared down at his tea. 'Got it, ma'am. No lurking.'

'And you don't really need to call me ma'am, not when you're standing in my kitchen drinking tea.' She shook her head. 'I mean wouldn't you be far better off going home to your ... going home?' Tanner hedged her bets, suddenly aware that she was still unsure as to the details of her sergeant's domestic set-up. She was almost certain he was married, but did he have kids? Months before, when they were both working on the Heather Finlay case, she had chided herself for her ignorance about someone she had worked with for almost a year by then, had resolved to put it right.

She hadn't, because in truth it was more than simple ignorance. It was a symptom of her reluctance to involve herself in her work-mates' lives, to forge what she'd always seen as meaningless social relationships with colleagues outside the Job.

The truth was, she'd only ever allowed one person to get really close.

Standing where she was now, in the spotless kitchen of a house that now felt a lot bigger and quieter than it had a fort-night before, she could see just how peculiar that was. How pig-headed.

A terrible change had been forced upon her, but she could choose to make easier ones.

She said, 'You got kids, Dipak?'

Chall shook his head. 'We're working on it, though.' He reddened slightly. 'I mean, we'd like to.'

'You want one? A couple?'

'I don't know. Three, maybe?'

'Nice.' Tanner sipped her tea. Outside an interview room, chit-chat was not her strong point. 'Listen, thanks again for getting me that CCTV stuff.'

'Not a problem,' Chall said.

'Well, it's not your case, so you might have got yourself into trouble.'

'It's fine.'

'You still might.'

'Was it any use?'

'Oh yeah, that was them. And we know how the men who took them did it, too. How they got Amaya and Kamal off

78

that train.' She held out her mug, touched it to Chall's. 'So, cheers.'

'You think it's your pair of hired honour killers?'

Tanner nodded. 'I'm as sure as I can be.' She hadn't been lying when she'd told Thorne that Chall knew what she was working on, but she hadn't told the sergeant quite all of it. She was wondering whether now was the time when she heard him say 'Hello' and looked up to see that the cat had wandered in.

'Who's this?'

'Mrs Slocombe,' Tanner said. She glanced over and saw Chall nod, clearly with no idea what the joke was. Unlike Tom Thorne, he was a little too young to remember the innuendo-laden sitcom it came from. 'Susan's cat. Well, my cat now.'

They watched the cat rub itself against the leg of the kitchen table, then move across to butt its head against Chall's shin. He leaned down to stroke it and it quickly slinked away again.

'Are you religious, Dipak?'

He looked at her, took a few seconds. 'Well … in theory, I suppose. I don't really do anything about it, though.'

She smiled. 'Probably some official guidelines saying you're not allowed to ask questions like that at work.'

'It's OK, we're not at work.'

'I'm not trying to be nosy.'

'I know.'

'It's none of my business.'

'Look, it's fine, and I get why you're asking.'

'I'd like to know what you think, that's all.'

Chall looked down as the cat made another approach, but this time he ignored it. 'No, I'm not as religious as maybe I should be, but it doesn't make any difference to the way I feel about all this stuff. *Honour*, or whatever they choose to call it. However they try and dress it up.' He looked across at her. 'It's fucking disgusting.' He blinked, as though surprised at what he'd said. 'Sorry.'

79

'It's fine,' Tanner said. 'That's exactly what it is.'

'Didn't mean to swear.'

Tanner laughed. 'You can swear as much as you like in here. Just don't spill anything.'

THIRTEEN

It wasn't clear if AHCA meetings were held in different locations each week, but tonight's was being held in the main hall of an independent Hindu academy in Highbury. Looking for it on the map, Thorne could not help but notice that the location formed the third point on an almost perfect triangle, with both the Sikh temple in Finsbury Park and the mosque in Stoke Newington within a mile or so.

'Home fixture for everyone,' Tanner said, as they walked from Thorne's car.

'Stamford Hill's not far either.' Thorne pointed towards the district of the city just two miles to the north of them, which was home to Europe's largest concentration of Hasidic Jews. 'I wonder why there isn't any Jewish representation? Plenty of them been on the receiving end from right-wing nutters.'

'Racists' wet dream, this,' Tanner said. 'Turning up here mob-handed, they'd have a field day.'

Thorne hadn't really considered it before. He had spotted a couple of patrol cars in adjacent streets and now he wondered if there might be other officers in unmarked vehicles on alert nearby. 'Nice easy night for local burglars,' he said.

The possibility that the meeting itself might be a potential target for the likes of the English Defence League was clearly one that the organisers had considered. A small group of men loitered near the entrance to the school, and though Thorne couldn't say for certain to which religion each one belonged, he was sure he wouldn't want to fall out with any of them.

He and Tanner were deemed worthy of a second glance as they walked in, but no more than that.

'What if we were EDL in disguise?' Thorne muttered.

Tanner looked at him.

'Good job no one can see my flag of St George underpants.' Thorne could not resist the stupid joke, but knew Tanner was right and that the muscle outside the doors was probably necessary. These meetings were being held to debate the shocking increase in hate crimes, after all, and there was no doubt that racists of a particularly vicious stripe believed that the previous year's Brexit vote had been a mandate to carry them out.

Inside, at least a hundred chairs had been arranged at the front of a large stage, set with a table and a microphone on a low stand. What appeared to be enough food to feed a small army had been laid out on three separate trestle tables along one wall; groaning foil platters covered in cling film below colourful posters of India and pictures of assorted Hindu deities.

Empty chairs were being taken quickly, so Tanner and Thorne grabbed seats near the back.

Thorne looked around.

Notionally, the meeting might have been arranged along interfaith lines, but positions in the audience seemed to have been taken strictly according to religion. Thorne might have struggled to tell some Sikhs and Hindus apart, were the two groups not largely separated by the Muslim contingent.

Thorne was aware of Tanner shifting in the seat next to him. She was wearing a long skirt and dark jacket, and though he didn't think she had dressed any differently from the way she might otherwise, he still wondered if she was feeling altogether comfortable. Tanner was not someone to be easily cowed, and nobody seemed very bothered that she was there, but as a white woman she was definitely in a minority of one. Thorne looked across at the only other women he had seen since they'd come in. Several groups of five or six, in hijabs or brightly coloured saris, were gathered by their respective tables of food, which he guessed they had prepared.

He found himself smiling as he remembered what Helen had said to him the night before; her words about a woman's right to shag any man she fancied, whenever she felt like it. He imagined her marching up on to the stage and making the same speech to this audience.

He turned to Tanner. 'OK?'

'Why wouldn't I be?'

Audience chatter dwindled as three men walked slowly up a small set of wooden stairs to the stage and took their seats at the table. The man in the middle – a local imam – introduced himself. He spoke for ten minutes or so then passed the microphone to a Sikh community leader who said much the same things, but seemed a little more passionate about them. Thorne recognised the final speaker to be Arman Bannerjee, the face of the website Tanner had shown him the previous night. He was easily the most charismatic of the three and, watching him speak, it was not hard to see why he had become such a successful businessman.

'What's his business, anyway?' Thorne whispered to Tanner.

'Furniture.'

'I could do with a new sofa for the flat.'

All three speakers had talked about the urgent need for unity in the face of the attacks to which members of their faiths were being subjected. Whether it was Muslims being targeted, or Sikhs and Hindus being mistaken for Muslims, such violence was unacceptable, they said, and had to be opposed. They were all keen to stress that, whatever happened, they must not let the ignorance and hatred of others lead to an increase in tension between themselves.

The applause for each speaker had been polite, but somewhat muted. Once the discussion was thrown open to the floor, things quickly began to get rather more heated.

'Speeches are all very well,' one man said, 'but we need an effective response. We need to *do* something.' The comment received widespread approval, and when someone proposed organising street patrols, someone else quickly suggested arming them. Another man got to his feet and began shouting about a Sikh temple that had been firebombed three weeks before in Harrow. It was time to fight back, he said, and if that meant meeting violence with violence, then so be it. This received the most enthusiastic reaction of the evening, and the man had to shout above the applause and the attempts at placation from the stage. 'We wouldn't have to do this ourselves,' he said, 'if the police cared a bit more.'

An elderly man sitting in front of Thorne turned round and nodded at him, grim-faced. Thorne smiled and the man turned away.

Was it that obvious?

When the meeting itself had finished, chairs were pushed back so that smaller groups could gather to talk about what they'd heard, while many of the others made straight for the food. Walking past the platters of samosas and cutlets, kebabs and salads, Thorne started to feel hungry, but he and Tanner kept on walking until they reached the foot of the stage, where the three speakers were talking in whispers.

They stood and waited. Bannerjee caught Tanner's eye and gave a barely perceptible nod to acknowledge that he had seen

84

her. He did not look overly pleased, or perhaps it was just surprise.

After another minute or so, he waved them across. He introduced Tanner to the other men and Thorne introduced himself. The Sikh, whose name was Jagtar Dhillon, reached over to shake hands with them both. The imam, Shahid Mansoor, shook hands with Thorne and nodded respectfully at Tanner.

Tanner nodded back.

'It is good to see you here,' Dhillon said. 'You heard what our friend in the audience said about the police not caring.'

Bannerjee's smile was as thin as it was brief. 'I don't think the two detectives have come tonight because they're concerned for anyone's safety.' He looked at Tanner. 'Though I'm sure they *are*. It's a rather more ... contentious issue.'

'A serious issue,' Thorne said.

Bannerjee looked at him. 'Absolutely.'

'How can we help you?' Mansoor asked.

By now, two other men had arrived and were listening from a few feet away. They were both in their early twenties, dressed in jeans, shirts and sweaters. They were eyeballing Tanner and making no attempt to disguise it.

Thorne did exactly the same to them.

'I have been working with a unit tackling honour-based violence,' Tanner said. 'And my investigations have led me to believe that a number of killings have been carried out ...' she paused as the imam began shaking his head, 'within the Muslim, Sikh *and* Hindu communities, probably arranged by the same person and carried out by the same two men.'

'What men?' Dhillon asked.

Tanner reached into her bag and produced a printout of the freeze-frame from the YouTube video. She held it up. 'These two men. They are paid to carry out these murders on behalf of the families.'

Mansoor peered at the picture. 'I don't know what you expect me to say.'

Thorne looked at him. 'Yeah, it's a tricky one. How about "that's terrible" or "that's awful"?'

'Why should I need to say something that would be obvious to anybody?'

Tanner nodded as though in agreement. '"To kill one human being is to kill all of humanity." Doesn't it say that in the Quran?'

The imam looked at her. 'The Holy Book says all sorts of things.'

'Can you prove any of this, though?' Dhillon asked. '"Led me to believe", you said. "Probably," you said also.'

'I will prove it,' Tanner said. 'And I would do so a lot quicker if I could count on your help.'

'What can we do?' The imam's words sounded more like a dismissal than an offer.

'Whoever is behind this is spreading the word through organisations like yours.'

'It's the perfect way to reach out to all three religions at once,' Thorne said.

'These men are being hired by someone who has the necessary contacts.'

Thorne wasn't sure if it was done for effect, but he saw Tanner's eyes drift away towards the crowd that was gathered around the food tables; the smaller groups still debating in the hall. He watched the two younger men look at each other and he saw Dhillon's expression darken.

'Are you suggesting it's someone here, in this room?'

Tanner held up the photo again. 'There will be people in this room who don't believe that what these men are doing is "terrible" or "awful". A few who actually believe it is the right thing to do. You must accept that, surely?'

Dhillon looked away. Mansoor sighed and shifted from one foot to the other.

Bannerjee laid a hand on the imam's arm, nodding in sympathy, though for what, it was unclear. He turned to Tanner. 'I had hoped this might have all gone away.'

'Two teenagers have gone missing since the last time we spoke,' Tanner said. 'This is a problem that is getting worse.'

'Well, I'm afraid I can only tell you what I told you last time,' Bannerjee said. 'And the time before that—'

'You can't think this is *right*? You can't have any ... tolerance for this?'

Bannerjee shook his head, impatient. 'Of course I don't, but I am not going to stand here and debate the so-called honour system with you. I am just going to remind you that by spreading this kind of ... scare story ... all you are actually doing is perpetuating the idea that we are all somehow the same. That this is the kind of thing we do. We don't eat this or that, we wear funny clothes, we go around killing our wives and daughters. In some ways you are no different from the people we have come here tonight to organise against.'

'That's ridiculous,' Thorne said.

'Is it?'

'We're talking about murder.'

'I have *said* I will help her.' Bannerjee jabbed a finger in Tanner's direction. 'I have said I will keep an ear to the ground or whatever. But then a week later or two weeks later she's back and it is starting to feel not as though she wants our help at all, but that we're being accused of something.'

Tanner put the photo back in her bag. She said, 'I'm sorry you feel like that, but the fact is, I'm going to keep coming back.' She turned to include Dhillon and Mansoor. 'So you'll all have to get used to it.'

Bannerjee nodded, expressionless. He stepped towards Dhillon, and Mansoor, the imam. 'We'll expect to see you again soon, then,' he said. 'But now we are all very hungry, so please excuse us.'

The three moved away together, talking in whispers, nodding, followed a few seconds later by the two younger men who had been watching and listening.

'Never hurts to rattle a few bars,' Thorne said.

Tanner was still watching Bannerjee and the others. 'We'll see.'

A few people had already left and others were drifting towards the doors at the back of the hall. Thorne and Tanner did the same. Thorne leaned in past Bannerjee and helped himself to a couple of samosas on their way out.

Walking towards the school gates, Tanner said, 'More than a few.' She looked at Thorne. 'More than a few back there who believe in this rubbish.' It felt colder than it had when they'd arrived. Tanner took a scarf from her bag and Thorne fastened his leather jacket to the neck. 'A recent survey claimed that two thirds of young British Asians believe that families should live according to the concept of honour. *Seventy* per cent of Sikhs and Muslims. Three per cent said that they sanctioned honour killings. They were actually happy to say that.'

'How's it working?' Thorne asked. 'This particular set-up.'

'Hard to be sure.'

'Best guess.'

'Well, whoever wants something like this done asks around, maybe talks to someone they think might be sympathetic at their local mosque or temple or gurdwara. That person mentions it to somebody else and it goes down a line until it reaches our broker and he makes the arrangements. Money probably changes hands half a dozen times.'

They were almost at the gates when Thorne turned at the noise of footsteps behind them. One of the young men who had been loitering by the stage was hurrying to catch them up.

'Hello, Ravi,' Tanner said.

Thorne looked at her.

'Mr Bannerjee's son.'

'Dr Bannerjee,' the young man said. 'He has an honorary degree. He has two, actually.'

Thorne nodded, like he was impressed. 'How can we help you?'

'Easy.' Ravi stared at Tanner. 'Stop hassling my father.'

'You think that's what I'm doing?'

'I know it is.'

Thorne looked at him. Jeans and trainers; a black, military-style jacket. He didn't know if Bannerjee's son was a student, whether he had a job, but to Thorne he seemed no different from any other nineteen- or twenty-year-old. 'Does this stuff not bother you? I know you're a Hindu . . . I don't know how ortho-dox you are. Is that the word?'

'Devout.'

'OK, then.'

'Look, maybe I'm not as devout as my father, but I don't see what that's got to do with anything. He's still my father, and you need to leave him alone. I'm not sure what he believes and what he doesn't, but he hasn't done anything.'

Tanner nodded. 'It was you that made the complaints, wasn't it?'

Ravi looked embarrassed. 'Well, I encouraged him to say something, yeah. He's my dad and he deserves a bit more respect than you're giving him. That's all.'

Before she could respond, Tanner's phone rang, and when she looked at the screen she stepped away. 'I need to take this.'

Thorne watched her walk towards the road, then turned back to Bannerjee's son. 'Sometimes, there's only so much respect to go around, you know what I mean? Right now, ours is all being used up on the memory of some dead kids. Respect for them and for the loved ones, the *innocent* loved ones, of two missing kids.' He saw Tanner waving him across and walked over to her as Ravi jogged away in the opposite direction.

'That was Dipak,' Tanner said. 'The murder investigation team called the missing persons unit and they called him.'

Thorne knew what was coming. Suddenly, it felt even colder.

'They found Amaya's body.'

FOURTEEN

Thorne waited until he got to Colindale and had pulled into the car park at Becke House before he called Hendricks. It took a good deal of willpower, but, despite weekly reminders from Helen, he had yet to install a hands-free system and the last thing he needed was to get stopped for using his mobile at the wheel. Nothing a 'lid' liked more than nicking a 'suit', and a gung-ho traffic officer – a black rat – would be drinking free for a week or more if he managed to get penalty points slapped on a DI's licence.

'Favour,' Thorne said.

'As per bloody usual.' Hendricks yawned. 'Up comes your name on my phone, complete with a very fetching headshot I should add, and for a few precious moments I think you might be calling just to see how I am. Just for a natter, you know? I'm a fool to myself.'

'How are you, Phil?'

'I'm ticking along, mate, thanks for caring.'

'Pleased to hear it. Now, there's a body I need you to look at.'

'Well course there is,' Hendricks said. 'I'm not that stupid.'

Amaya Shah's body had been discovered the previous after-noon by a dog walker, in thick woodland between South Herts golf club and the stadium that had once been home to Barnet FC. If there was a glimmer of good news to be found in such a grim discovery, it was the fact that this area of north London was Thorne's territory, even if it had been a different team that had been on call and caught the case.

It made sense, Thorne thought, that the killers had chosen to dispose of the body close to where Amaya had last been seen alive. They would have been well aware that CCTV would pro-vide the final sighting of their victim, so the subsequent discovery of the body close by would lend credence to the theory that she had been attacked and murdered by a stranger shortly afterwards.

All part of the fiction they were being paid to construct.

Over the course of several phone calls the night before, Thorne had managed to ascertain that the body had been found in a shallow grave beneath leaves and branches with the victim's handbag discovered under a bush nearby. Credit cards and a driving licence had provided the Homicide Assessment Team with a provisional ID. Signs on the body indicated that she had been strangled and the fact that she had been discovered naked certainly suggested that she had been sexually assaulted. Whether this was the case and, if so, had taken place before or after she had died would be down to the pathologist.

'Would probably have come in overnight,' Thorne said. He stared up through the windscreen at the building he was unlucky enough to work in. Three storeys of shit-coloured cement and peeling olive woodwork. 'Or last thing yesterday. Amaya Shah . . .'

'Right.' There was a pause while Hendricks checked paper-work, humming to himself. Thorne could hear a radio playing in the background. He recognised the voice of Neil Diamond and an ident told him it was Magic FM, but Thorne decided that now was not the time to take the mickey.

'Got it,' Hendricks said. 'Her father formally identified the body first thing this morning. PM's down for this afternoon.'

Sitting in his car, Thorne pictured the man he had spoken to in that overheated room above a shop in Barnet, his face as the sheet was drawn back. Had the tears still come, staring down at the lifeless body of the daughter he had, in all probability, paid to have killed?

Had it been much of an effort?

'One of yours? The PM?'

'Not as it stands.'

'Can you make it one of yours?'

'Might be nice if you told me why,' Hendricks said.

'Remember you thought it would be a good idea if I helped Nicola Tanner out?'

'The night we played pool, right? Five—one, as I remember.'

'Bit of a break, you said.' Thorne brought Hendricks up to speed as quickly as he could. The meeting at Nicola Tanner's house. The disappearance of two teenagers that had now become a murder; one they believed was down to the pair of contract killers Tanner had been talking about.

'So, where's the boy?'

'God knows,' Thorne said. He doubted that the body of Kamal Azim would ever be found. The kind of random sex-attacker that the killers – and those paying them – wanted Amaya's death pinned on did not routinely go around murdering young couples. 'I'm betting they've taken a lot more care getting rid of him.'

'Yeah, OK, I'll have a look,' Hendricks said. 'Any particular reason you want me to do it? I mean it goes without saying I'm the best.'

'There you go then.'

'So, nothing to do with the fact that it might be better for you in the long term if you've got a mate involved?'

'Not especially.'

'Right. Only I'm looking at the paperwork and this isn't actually your case.' Hendricks waited, enjoying himself. 'This is one of Yvonne Kitson's.'

'I'm about to get that sorted,' Thorne said.

DCI Russell Brigstocke had changed a lot in the fifteen years or so that Thorne had worked with him. What had once seemed a stylish quiff now appeared to have been an attempt to draw attention away from the onset of baldness. Though he still occasionally produced a pack of cards in the pub, the passion for magic tricks appeared to have waned; gone the same way as the brief fixation with Pilates, the hill-walking and the moped. The man's endearing enthusiasms, watered down little by little as he had moved, albeit unwittingly, from the job of detective to one that was closer to that of a politician, or CEO.

His feelings for Tom Thorne had gone largely unchanged, though, even if the mix was never the same from one day to the next. Admiration and anxiety in wildly varying measures.

Both were there in his expression as he sat and listened.

'Have you spoken to Yvonne about it?'

'Not yet,' Thorne said. 'But I'm sure she won't mind. I thought I should check it with you first.'

'Oh, did you?' Brigstocke sat back and folded his arms. A theatrical pose of surprise at Thorne following procedure which any other officer would have considered standard. Compulsory. 'Well, thanks for ... running it by me.'

'Come on, Russell. What difference does it make whether it's me or Kitson? Anyway, I think she's got more on her plate right now than I have, so ...'

'It's her case, because she caught it. I know you're not a fan of systems, but we do need to have one. It's not like we can just put names into hats any time we catch a murder. We can't let people pick and choose.'

94

'I know that.'

'So why should I give it to you?'

'I should have it because I think it's connected to an old case of mine. Four years ago.'

'Which case?'

'Meena Athwal.'

Brigstocke repeated the name. He closed his eyes and took a few seconds' thinking time. 'Raped and strangled, right? Unsolved.'

Thorne nodded. He was pleased to see that it had not taken Brigstocke long to recall the case. A politician's poise when it came to sitting on the fence and a CEO's flair for a budget, but a detective's memory. 'If you let me have the Amaya Shah case, I think I might be able to solve it.'

'So, what? Same killer, you're saying? A serial?'

'Not a serial,' Thorne said. 'Well, not really ... and two killers.'

Brigstocke blinked. If he was trying to hide the genuine curiosity on his face, he was making a poor job of it. He said, 'I'm listening.'

The DCI's expression changed several times as Thorne told him about Nicola Tanner; the theory about honour killing that she – and now Thorne too – had come to believe was the truth. It darkened as Thorne explained Tanner's very personal connection to the men they were after; he shook his head when Thorne talked him through the interviews with the parents of Amaya Shah and Kamal Azim, and his eyes widened in disbelief at the description of the encounter at the AHCA meeting the previous evening.

When Thorne had finished, Brigstocke sat back and took off his black hornrims. He said, 'Jesus.'

Thorne waited. It wasn't clear if his boss's expletive was one of shock or horror. Or if it simply meant that he thought the whole thing was ridiculous. Thorne picked at the torn fabric of his chair. He stared out of the window at the ragged line of

95

cranes above the trading estate on Aerodrome Road; the railway line, and the grey ribbon of the M1 just beyond it. He said, 'Why don't I dig out the Meena Athwal file? A witness talked about Meena seeing two men—'

Brigstocke raised a hand, put his glasses back on. 'Fine,' he said. 'You can take the Shah case, but only if it's OK with Yvonne Kitson.'

Thorne nodded, guessing that would cost him no more than a large glass of wine in the Royal Oak at the end of the shift.

'And keep me informed, obviously.'

'Goes without saying.'

'And I don't even want to *hear* about you working with an officer who's officially on compassionate leave.'

'I haven't been,' Thorne said. 'I won't. I mean, obviously I can't stop her if she decides to show up and make a nuisance of herself, but I'll definitely let you know if that happens.' Trying to suppress a smile, he stood up and walked towards the door. 'You know very well how I feel about coppers who won't do as they're told.'

Thorne fetched himself a coffee from the recently upgraded machine in the corner of the incident room and took it back to the office he shared with DI Yvonne Kitson. She wasn't around, but that suited him.

He sat down at his desk and picked up the phone.

He would certainly need to talk to Kitson about the new arrangements as soon as possible, but before he got round to writing Amaya Shah's name on his whiteboard he wanted Nicola Tanner to be the first to know. It would be the first piece of good news she'd had in a while.

FIFTEEN

The post-mortem suite was more or less the only place where Phil Hendricks took things seriously. The work he was there to do, at least. It was as if the necessary combination of focus, compassion and skill engaged a part of his brain that filtered out the sarcasm and the smartarse remarks. If that was not the case, then he certainly kept them to himself until the job was finished.

Then it was game on, as always.

Thorne watched his friend work, struck, as usual, by the delicacy with which he employed the often gruesome-looking tools of his trade. The graceful movement around the steel slab, so at odds with his physical appearance: the tattoos and shaved head; the multiple studs and rings in ears, lips, nose and quite probably several other places that Thorne tried his best not to think about.

'Nearly there,' Hendricks said, glancing across at him, the Mancunian accent, often so blunt and abrasive, softened as it always was within these sterile, white walls; the voice flat, though not matter-of-fact, as he reached for the hand-held recorder and

dictated the latest set of findings for the report he would be writing later on.

Tissue samples, microscopy, organ retention.

Thorne dry-swallowed and stole a look at his watch. The PM
suite was far from warm, but there was still sweat where the
plastic of the blue apron made contact with the back of his neck.
He had already been given the headlines, told the things he most
needed to know, more than half an hour earlier. But he would
not be going anywhere until the job was finished.

His job was to observe, whatever that felt like, and bailing out
once information ceased being useful would have felt ... disrespectful to Phil, somehow.

To Amaya Shah.

'OK, we're about done.' Hendricks gave final instructions to
his assistant, who was still taking photographs and whose job it
would now be to sew up the corpse's chest cavity. The pathologist walked towards the doors and Thorne followed, the two of
them removing their aprons and letting out a long breath in sync
with one another.

Tanner was waiting for them outside.

'Ay ay, it's your secret helper,' Hendricks said, tossing his
gloves and apron into a biohazard bin.

Thorne looked to Tanner for a reaction. If an experienced
detective inspector was at all offended at being thought of as
anybody's 'helper', she didn't show it. Not that Hendricks had
been right, of course. Though Thorne was now nominally the
lead investigator on the case, while Tanner had no official role at
all, he still wasn't altogether sure who was going to be helping
who.

Thorne's knowledge of the most famous detective double act
of all time was based purely on a few episodes of the TV series,
but there had been enough moments already when he felt rather
more like Watson than Holmes.

'Philip,' Tanner said.

Hendricks laughed as he stepped across to shake Tanner's hand and he was still laughing half a minute later when they walked into the dismal office he shared with three other pathologists in the basement of Westminster Hospital.

'I've told you before,' he said. 'Only my mother calls me Philip, and only then if she's annoyed with me. You don't always have to be quite so ... formal.'

Thorne was pulling chairs across. He knew that Hendricks had come close to using a word that was rather less flattering.

'Fine,' Tanner said.

The three were forced to sit close together; closer than Tanner would have liked, Thorne suspected. He watched her draw her feet back, so that they wouldn't make contact with anyone else's.

'Listen, Nicola.' Hendricks looked embarrassed suddenly, as though regretting his earlier remark. 'I just wanted to say about Susan ...'

'I know. You're sorry for my loss.'

Hendricks glanced at Thorne.

'Sorry,' Tanner said. 'That came out a bit ... snappy.'

'It's OK.'

'People just get on your bloody nerves, sometimes.' She looked at Hendricks. 'Not *you* ... just ... it's that stupid tone of voice, when they're telling you how sorry they are, you know? The endless nods and the bloody murmuring. I know everyone means well and some of them even feel genuinely upset, but it always manages to sound so fake. They have this stupid way of cocking their head.' She demonstrated. 'Like they're talking to a simpleton ... and this simpering look all over their faces, and why do so many of them think it's the done thing to touch your arm or your shoulder? Your arm, usually.' She reached across to lay a hand on Thorne's arm. 'Like that. Like, "I'll just touch the poor thing's arm ... actually, I might even stroke it ... *there there* ... because that's bound to make her feel better."' She let out a long-suffering sigh. 'Look, I *know* that's how everyone does these things, probably exactly how I do them, but honestly, sometimes I just want to shout at people. Or punch them.'

Hendricks nodded slowly, then sat back and held out his arms. He said, 'Go on, have a pop.'

'It's all right.' Tanner was reaching for her bag. 'I'm fine now.'

'Go on, treat yourself.' Hendricks leaned forward and stuck his chin out. 'Do you the world of good.'

'Thanks for volunteering, Phil.' She opened her notebook, smiled as she looked down at it. 'All those piercings, I'd probably just cut myself.'

Hendricks laughed. 'Well, don't say I didn't offer.'

'I'll do it,' Thorne said.

Tanner shifted in her chair and looked at them both. 'Right then.'

The pleasantries were evidently over with and Thorne took his cue to begin the *un*pleasantries.

'Amaya was raped then strangled,' he said. 'The killer used his hands.'

'What he didn't use was a condom.' Hendricks moved his chair to within reach of his computer and began typing. 'So, we've got a good semen sample to work with.'

'How soon can you get that off?' Thorne asked.

'I'm emailing the lab now,' Hendricks said. 'Telling them to expect it.'

'Rush job.'

Hendricks looked at him. 'Brigstocke going to authorise that?'

'We've got one dead teenager and another one still missing,' Thorne said. 'Rush job.'

Hendricks carried on typing. 'The killer's strong too.' He glanced back at Tanner who was scribbling in her notebook. 'Hyoid broken, larynx crushed.'

'Anything under her fingernails?'

Thorne shook his head. It was unusual, as the victims of strangulation often clawed at the hands of their attacker.

'No reason why there would be,' she said. 'There's two of them, so easy enough for one of them to hold her down while the other one strangles her.'

'We'll get DNA from the semen, so—'

'Don't hold your breath,' Tanner said. 'Because you won't get a match.'

Hendricks looked at Thorne. *That's you told.*

'It's the same as Meena Athwal, right?'

Thorne nodded. Even if he had not gone back to the files just a few days earlier, he would remember the girl's body; the state of it. The swollen tongue and the dried froth around her mouth.

Tanner smiled grimly. 'Pretty much identical, all of it. You didn't get a DNA match then, so chances are we won't get one now. This pair's too clever. They won't be in the database.'

'You always this bloody optimistic?'

'We should talk to some of their friends,' Tanner said. 'Amaya's and Kamal's.'

'I can't see much point. Not when we already know who we're looking for. We need to get those images out and about.'

'I'm not arguing with that, but we might get some more on the parents, and remember that Meena Athwal's friend had information about Meena being followed? We might get lucky with someone who knew Amaya, so it's got to be worth doing.'

'Makes sense,' Hendricks said. 'What do I know, though? I just do the slicing and dicing.'

'OK, I'll send someone to talk to them,' Thorne said.

Tanner was already shaking her head. 'We should do it ourselves. We know what we're looking for. Plus, we're good at it.'

Thorne checked his irritation and reminded himself that, off the books or not, Tanner had a very personal stake in catching the men they were after.

He guessed that she probably wasn't invited to a lot of parties.

He thought: Watson. Definitely Watson.

SIXTEEN

Danny Mirza worked at a fast-food restaurant in Holloway, close to where he lived with his parents, and only a mile or so away from where he and Kamal Azim had gone to school together. The cartoon chicken on the sign outside looked rather more cheerful than those coming out of the kitchen and was there, Thorne imagined, to prevent pissed vegetarians stumbling in by mistake and give the more obtuse carnivores a clue as to what they were in for. After letting Danny Mirza know that he had arrived, Thorne looked at the menu, complete with helpful pictorial guide, high above the counter. To be fair, the chicken appeared to come in as many different ways as any diner could imagine. As long as it involved frying.

He ordered a basket of hot wings, took them to a table in the corner and waited for the boy to join him.

'Is this going to take long?' Danny asked, sitting down. 'The boss is going to knock it off my lunch hour.'

'Shouldn't do,' Thorne said. The wings weren't as spicy as he would have liked, but he was hungry. 'Just a few questions about Kamal.'

'You won't find him, you know.'

'No?' Thorne thought the boy was probably right, but he doubted that their reasoning would be quite the same.

'He's too smart, isn't he? If he doesn't want to be found, that's it.'

'Why wouldn't he want to be found?'

Danny looked at him. 'Come on, you've spoken to his dad, right?'

'He's trying to get away from his parents.'

'Yeah, well he didn't want to, did he? It was only a last resort kind of thing, if it all kicked off. I suppose it must have.'

'So why would it have kicked off?'

Danny leaned a little closer in and lowered his voice. Looking around as he ate, Thorne could see that the majority of the other customers and staff were Asian. 'There was this girl back in Bangladesh, lined up for him to marry. Years ago, right?' He smiled, proudly. 'My boy Kamal wasn't having it, simple as that.'

Thorne dropped a chicken bone into the basket. He licked his fingers. 'Not simple though, is it? Not when your parents and everybody else are telling you it's the right thing to do.'

'Not everyone. *I* told him not to do it.' Danny shrugged. 'It's not like this girl was even fit or anything. I mean, you seen a picture?' Thorne shook his head. 'She was like two years younger than he was and she didn't speak English or anything. Ridiculous, I swear.'

'OK, but wasn't it more because Kamal already had a girl-friend?' The news of Amaya Shah's murder had yet to be made public, and though the pictures from the YouTube video were being circulated to newspapers in connection with her disappearance, Thorne was happy to keep it that way.

Danny smiled again, grinned. 'Yeah, and I've seen *her* picture, too.'

'Tell me about her.'

'Well, she's gorgeous, isn't she? God knows how Kamal

103

managed to pull someone like her. Jammy bastard didn't stop talking about her, showing me all these photos on his phone. You seen her?'

Thorne said that he hadn't. Only a white lie, because the Amaya he had seen, the marbled flesh shifting beneath a pathologist's fingers, was not the one that Kamal Azim had fallen in love with.

Not her at all.

'So, he wanted to be with her, like who wouldn't? But he knew his old man wouldn't be over the moon about it, so he told me that if they had to, they were going to disappear. Abroad even, if it came to that. Said he'd let me know where they were, once they were settled.' He looked at Thorne. 'I haven't heard anything yet, if you were wondering.'

Thorne took a serviette and wiped his fingers. He said, 'Did Kamal ever say anything that made you think he was worried, or scared about anything?'

'Like what?'

'Like someone was watching him.'

'Don't think so.'

'Did he ever say anything about anyone following him?'

Danny shook his head. 'He told me his girlfriend's brother was a bit of a nutcase, but I think that was more about her than it was about Kamal, you know?'

Thorne reached for another chicken wing. 'OK.'

'What do you mean, following him? Why would anyone be following Kamal?'

'I'm not saying that anyone was.'

'You think something's happened?'

'We're just checking out all sorts of things, that's all.' Thorne looked at the boy. 'Just questions I've got to ask.' He nodded down at his food. 'These are good. You do them?'

Danny said, 'I'm on the burgers.'

'Maybe I should have had one of those,' Thorne said.

'Anyway, we're about done. Oh, and tell your boss if he tries to dock your wages I'll have the Food Standards Agency up his arse, OK?'

As he was standing up, Danny hesitated. He said, 'He's just getting himself and his girlfriend settled, then he'll call me, yeah?'

'Thanks for your help,' Thorne said.

'He's my best mate, you know?'

Thorne watched Danny Mirza walk back to the kitchen. He decided to stay and finish his last few wings, before driving to Barnet College where he was due to meet up with Tanner. He quickly wiped his fingers again when his phone rang and he saw Brigstocke's name on the screen. He wondered what on earth he could have done to upset his boss when he had only been on the case twenty-four hours, then reminded himself that he had managed it several times before.

'I've had Lambeth on the phone,' Brigstocke said.

'Right.' The Forensic Science Laboratory. The standard call to let them know the DNA sample had yielded no results.

'You're a lucky so-and-so, Tom. You push to get Kitson taken off it so that you can step in and next day, bang, you get a DNA match. Yvonne's going to be spitting feathers.'

'You're kidding.' Thorne stood up and walked towards the door. This was something Tanner would want to hear as soon as possible.

'It's not all good news, though. I mean not as far as your theory's concerned, anyway. Tanner's theory.'

'Go on.'

'The DNA from the semen sample is a match for Kamal Azim.'

Thorne said nothing. He had been about to start telling Brigstocke that there had to have been a mistake, but then he remembered that Kamal had been arrested three months before. The drunk and disorderly outside a nightclub. A DNA sample would have been taken then as a matter of routine. There was nothing he could say. He had argued with his boss any number of times, would have done so again had he felt it was remotely worthwhile. But there was no arguing with DNA.

'So, we really need to up the search for Kamal Azim, right?' Brigstocke said. 'I know he's not the prime suspect you were expecting, Tom, but you can't choose them any more than you can choose your cases.'

Thorne pushed through the door on to the street. 'Right,' he said. It had started to rain and umbrellas were going up around him as he walked towards his car.

Barnet College was only twenty minutes away.

Twenty minutes to process the news and to work out how the hell he was going to break it to Nicola Tanner.

SEVENTEEN

She was waiting for him outside the entrance to the college, grim-faced beneath a black umbrella she did not offer to share. Her expression darkened further when he told her about the call from Brigstocke.

'It doesn't make any sense,' she said.

'Maybe it does.' Thorne turned away slightly so that the rain was at his back. 'We don't really know what kind of kid Kamal Azim is, do we? We're just making assumptions about him based on what we know about his parents. We've just been presuming he's a nice lad because we've been presuming he's a victim. So, maybe he and Amaya haven't had sex yet. Maybe he's desperate to do it and she doesn't want to and maybe he gets aggressive.'

'Do you really believe that?' Tanner looked at him. 'What about the men on the train? The men in that CCTV footage?'

'We know Kamal had sex with her,' Thorne said. 'We have to ask the question.'

'What if he had sex with Amaya before they were snatched?'

'On the train?' Thorne saw the distaste on Tanner's face, the frustration and the anger, before she turned away. 'Look, I'm just running through the conversation I'm going to be having with my boss, OK? When I'm standing there like I don't know what "DNA match" means and I'm trying to persuade him that I shouldn't be trying to find Kamal Azim even though it looks very much like he raped and strangled his girlfriend.'

'You won't find him.'

Dead or on the run, Thorne knew that Tanner was probably right. Neither of them spoke for half a minute, until Tanner said 'There' and Thorne turned to see a young girl coming out through the glass doors at the front of the college. She raised the hood of a bright green sports top and looked around.

Tanner waved and the girl hurried over.

'Sarah?'

The girl nodded. 'You the one I talked to on the phone?'

Tanner produced her warrant card, then gave Thorne a look that prompted him to produce his.

'Can we get out of the rain?' the girl asked.

'Good idea,' Tanner said. 'Any thoughts?'

The girl nodded towards the pancake house on the other side of the road.

Tanner and Thorne ordered coffee, while Sarah Webster asked for pancakes with chocolate sauce. 'These were Amaya's favourite,' she said. 'We used to come in here all the time and she'd always end up eating half of mine. Never put a pound on mind you, flukey cow.'

The girl looked as if she could do with gaining a few pounds herself. She had short blonde hair and a rash of spots around her mouth. One ear was lined with studs and the lip-ring was one Phil Hendricks would have been proud of.

'Did Amaya talk about life at home much?' Tanner's notebook was open on the table in front of her.

'Yeah, a bit.' The girl licked chocolate sauce from her knife. 'I mean, it wasn't hard to see why she preferred being at college, you know?'

'How strict were her parents?'

'Well, they're a damn sight stricter than mine, but it's the religious thing, isn't it? My mum couldn't really care less what I get up to and that's not great either, but I'd rather have that than be told what I can wear and who I can be with and stuff. I think I'd rather be ignored than controlled. She had to sneak out of the house and hide clothes and all that. She had to lie about where she was going. Well, she said she was with me, didn't she? The night she went missing.'

'She asked you to cover for her.'

Sarah nodded, spooned a large piece of her pancake into her mouth. 'Had her dad on the phone the next day, didn't we? Screaming and swearing at my mum, calling her all sorts, like it was her fault.'

'Were they ever violent towards her? Amaya's mother and father?'

'I don't think so, but her brother was the one she was afraid of. He might have got nasty a few times. I can't remember any bruises or anything like that, but she was off ill quite a lot. So ...'

Tanner glanced at Thorne. He drank his coffee, happy enough to let her ask the questions.

These questions.

'Did she ever tell you that she was frightened about anything in particular?'

'She was frightened most of the time,' Sarah said.

'Did she ever mention being followed?'

Sarah shook her head.

'Did she ever mention seeing two men? Maybe outside the college or watching her house.'

'No, I don't think so, but like I said it was her brother she was most scared of. He turned up at the college once or twice.

Keeping an eye on her, you know? We were sitting in here one day and she pointed him out, standing on the other side of the road just staring at us.' She stopped eating and looked at Tanner. 'You think he's hurt her?'

'Right now, we don't know what's happened,' Tanner said.

'She's run away, right?' The girl waited, then began nodding when she didn't receive an answer. 'I mean she told me that her and Kamal had been talking about it. They wanted to get married and she said running away together was something they'd have to do if their parents reacted badly.'

'You think they would have?'

'Well, I don't know much about Kamal's family, but by the sound of it hers certainly would have.'

Thorne put his coffee down and looked at Tanner before leaning towards Sarah Webster. He said, 'Is there any reason why Kamal would have wanted to hurt her?'

The girl stopped eating and stared at him as though he'd suddenly begun speaking in a foreign language. 'Kamal?'

Thorne was aware that, next to him, Tanner was putting her notebook away. He kept his eyes on the girl. 'Is there?'

'Why the hell would there be?'

'Sorry ... I know this is difficult, but is there anything Amaya ever said that would lead you to believe he might hurt her sexually?'

Sarah looked like she'd bitten into something sour.

'We do have a reason for asking,' Thorne said.

'No way.' Sarah shook her head. 'Kamal could never have hurt her. They loved each other to bits.'

Thorne could feel Tanner's eyes on him. 'OK. Again, sorry for asking ... but were Amaya and Kamal having a sexual relationship?'

The girl laughed and looked down at her plate.

'Right.' Thorne nodded. 'They're eighteen. Of course they were.'

'No, you don't understand.' She looked up. 'It wasn't like that. Yeah, they loved each other and everything, but he was her best friend. He wasn't her boyfriend, not like *that*.'

'You're right,' Thorne said. 'I don't understand.'

Sarah Webster grinned and folded her arms, staring at Thorne and Tanner as though they were idiots.

She said, 'Kamal's gay.'

EIGHTEEN

'It's not fair,' Muldoon said. 'Just because you always do the driving, why should you be the one who picks what we listen to on the radio?'

Riaz said nothing, his eyes on the house.

'What's this racket anyway?'

'It's Sabina Yasmin,' Riaz said.

'Oh well, in *that* case.'

'She's one of the great Bengali singers. Maybe the greatest.'

Muldoon shook his head, let it fall back. 'What's she wailing about, anyway?'

'She's singing about the fact that she can't be with the man she loves.'

Muldoon laughed.

'What?'

'Ironic, don't you think?'

'Not particularly.'

Though they were parked, Riaz had left the engine running so that the car would stay warm. He flicked the wiper stalk once to clear the film of drizzle that was beginning to impede their view. He took a drink from a bottle of water then put the bottle back into the cup holder.

'Why can't she be with him?' Muldoon asked.

Riaz grunted.

'Why can't she be with the man she loves? In the song?'

'What does it matter?' Riaz snapped.

'I just think it's weird, that's all. Like, you can have something like that in a song, but not in real life. In a film or whatever, you get to sing about it, with thousands of those stupid dancers or whatever, but in real life you get the likes of us turning up. Funny, that's all.'

Riaz said nothing. He leaned forward as a car drove slowly past, then back again as it accelerated away.

'Bollywood, isn't it?'

'What?'

'Them films with all the singing and dancing.'

Riaz nodded.

'All a bit stupid, don't you reckon? I mean, it would be nice just for once to have the odd one of them that was a bit more . . . realistic, all I'm saying. Like a film about the sort of thing you and me do.' He nodded, smiling. 'Now, that'd be something worth seeing, don't you think?' He waited, but Riaz showed no inclination to tell him what he thought. 'I'd have none of that mental singing and dancing business for a start, and we'd need good actors, obviously. To play us, I mean.' He sucked his teeth while he thought for a few seconds. 'Liam Neeson would be good as me. Yeah, I'd be happy with that . . . when he was a bit younger, like. Or that other bloke, whatever he's called. Mind you, he's a bit short.'

Riaz reached to turn the music up a little.

'Colin Farrell.' Muldoon turned to study his partner. 'What about you?'

'What about me?'

'You ever thought about who they'd get to play you?'

113

'No.'

'I mean there's not so much choice, I wouldn't have thought.'

Riaz sniffed and turned to look out of his window. An emergency light came on in one of the driveways on the other side of the road and a few seconds later a small, thin fox sauntered out on to the pavement. It looked both ways and scratched itself, then trotted daintily away.

'Oh, and I tell you what else,' Muldoon said. 'I was thinking about what you were saying the other day, about me enjoying the job. You know, enjoying it too much?' He looked at Riaz. 'Yeah, well, I don't think you're being very fair.'

'So, we'll have to disagree,' Riaz said.

'What's wrong with enjoying your job? If you enjoy something, surely you're going to better at it.' Muldoon held his arms out. 'Come on, you've got to give me that much, surely?'

'I don't mean you enjoy it the way someone would simply enjoy doing their job well. Painting a house nicely or scoring the winning goal in a football match. Not like that. Not like taking pride in it.'

'I'm not with you.'

'*Enjoying* is not perhaps the right word.'

'OK then.'

'Luxuriating in it.' Riaz nodded his head in time to the music and tapped his fingers against the steering wheel. 'No. *Revelling.* I dislike the fact that you revel in it quite so much.'

Muldoon stared out of the window and thought about it.

'Yeah, well—'

Riaz held up a hand. He leaned forward again and a few seconds later Muldoon did the same. Riaz flicked the wiper stalk again and the picture became clearer.

Muldoon turned off the radio.

They watched Nicola Tanner's car slow, stop, then reverse expertly into a parking space a few houses down from her own.

PART TWO

WORSE THAN WORDS

NINETEEN

Everyone stood up as the procession of teachers entered and climbed the short flight of stairs to the stage, followed a few seconds later by the headmaster. When the teachers sat down the children did the same and, once the coughing and sniffing and the scraping of chairs had stopped, the headmaster began to speak.

'This is a very special assembly,' he said. 'Special, because this morning we are here to pay tribute to a friend and colleague.' He turned to acknowledge the men and women in a line at the back of the stage then looked back out at the hundreds of pupils staring up at him. 'To someone who taught many of you.' He gave a small nod towards the wings and, a moment later, a face appeared on the screen behind him.

A woman with dark curly hair and a crooked smile; a sprinkling of freckles across her nose, a gap between her teeth.

There was more sniffing, a few sobs.

The headmaster nodded, then said, 'A special morning and a very sad one.'

Thorne was struck by how young the man at the lectern was, how pleasant-looking. At least that's how he seemed, relative to the memory Thorne had of the white-haired sadist who had taken such great pleasure in handing out detentions or canings and, on one memorable occasion, knocking Thorne and the boy sitting behind him to the floor with a window-pole. The fact that the teachers looked like sixth-formers was not the only thing that jarred with Thorne's recollections of his own school. The hall they were sitting in seemed nowhere near as cavernous as the one in which he had sat fidgeting through tedious assemblies and terrible plays. In fact, the whole school felt far smaller than the concrete monstrosity he remembered.

They always did.

Thorne had been inside schools many times since his own education had ground unceremoniously to a halt almost forty years before. He'd been part of a team that had broken up a decent-sized MDMA operation run by fifth-formers in Tottenham. He had led the investigation into a fatal stabbing at a junior school, where both perpetrator and victim were barely out of short trousers. Only nine months earlier, he had earned the undying gratitude of a classroom full of eleven-year-olds, when he'd marched away a maths teacher whose internet history revealed an interest in his pupils that went far beyond long division.

The schools might only have felt smaller, but they certainly seemed to have become a lot more dangerous.

That smell was always the same, though, and Thorne had never been able to work out why, or exactly what the smell was. He couldn't believe that, post Jamie Oliver, the kitchens were still turning out boiled cabbage and treacle sponge. Or that schools used exactly the same cleaning products in the corridors as they had back when he was being told off for running in them. He looked round at the rows of children – younger ones at the front, those with bras or bum-fluff gathered at the back – and wondered if it might not simply be them.

Maybe five hundred kids always smelled like this.

'Susan Best was a teacher who loved what she did,' the headmaster said. 'She had a gift for making learning fun, for making all her students keen to learn. Those of you lucky enough to have been in one of Miss Best's classes will always remember her, and not just because of today. Not because of what's happened. You'll remember her because of the effect she had on you and because she was the kind of teacher that *all* pupils remember.'

Thorne glanced to his left. He wasn't sure whether Nicola Tanner was staring at the headmaster or the picture on the screen behind him. Her hands were clasped together in her lap.

'She was the teacher we all wish we'd had.' The headmaster smiled and gathered up his notes. 'One of those that stays with you.'

When he had finished, the head boy came up to talk about a charity they were setting up in Miss Best's name. He urged his fellow students to put some of their pocket money into the buckets that would be going around afterwards. He was followed by the head girl, who told a funny story which made the younger kids laugh, then said, 'She was called Miss Best and she *was* the best,' which started a few of the older girls crying at the back of the hall. When the music teacher began playing the piano they got to their feet and hugged one another, then sobbed their way through a hymn and an old Pete Seeger song.

'How Great Thou Art'.

'Turn, Turn, Turn'.

Thorne mumbled, as self-conscious as singing always made him – unless he was drunk or howling along with Hank Williams in the car – while Tanner sang loudly next to him; her voice high and tuneful, both hands clutching the single sheet of paper that had been laid on every chair. The lyrics to the songs and the same photograph of Susan Best that was being displayed on the screen. Thorne guessed that Tanner had provided it, and he wondered if she had chosen the music, too.

Her favourites, or Susan's.

He wondered why she didn't reach for the tissues that he knew were in her handbag. Or use a sleeve. Why she didn't let go of that piece of paper, not even for a second, to wipe away the tears that were pooling and threatening to spill.

Instead, she faced forward and sang, unaware that next to her, Thorne was almost tempted to lean across and wipe them away himself.

Afterwards, the headmaster led them to Susan's classroom, where some of the kids she'd been teaching at the time of her death were waiting to make a small presentation.

Walking a few paces behind the headmaster, Tanner said, 'Thanks again for doing this.'

'Not a problem,' Thorne said.

'I'm grateful, really.'

She had asked him only three days earlier; the same day they had interviewed Sarah Webster and Danny Mirza. The day that Sarah had dropped the bombshell about Kamal.

'There's this thing,' Tanner had said.

'Thing?'

'Susan's school. A memorial kind of thing. A bit weird I know, considering we haven't even had a funeral yet, but they're keen to do something, so . . . '

Thorne had nodded. The funeral could not take place until the body was released and that was unlikely to happen while the official investigation into Susan Best's murder was still ongoing. He and Tanner both knew that while those investigating remained unaware of the existence of a particular pair of hired killers, it would be ongoing for a good while yet.

120

That was something he and Tanner needed to talk about.

'So, when is it?'

'A couple of days,' Tanner had said. 'I'm not really sure how I feel about it, to tell you the truth.'

'Oh.' Thorne did not yet know Tanner quite well enough to be surprised at how she felt about anything, but he thought what the school was planning sounded nice. Then he began to wonder why Tanner was telling him about it.

'Thing is, it's a long way for Susan's mum and dad to come. So, at the moment, it's just me.'

Thorne looked at her.

'How would you feel about going with me?' She did not give him time to hesitate. 'Susan wasn't ... out, you see. I mean obviously the other members of staff knew, well most of them, but not the kids. No point giving some of those little buggers a stick to beat you with, is there?'

'I suppose not.' Thorne remembered a chemistry teacher he and his classmates had decided was gay. He remembered the nicknames and the stupid rhymes, the stammering and the red face. It wasn't a memory he was proud of, or that he'd ever shared with Phil Hendricks.

'I'd just feel a bit happier going with somebody else,' Tanner had told him. 'That's all. It avoids ... questions, you know? Awkwardness.'

'So, who are they going to think I am? Or you, come to that?'

Tanner had shrugged, seemingly unconcerned about Thorne's worries now that she had his tacit agreement to accompany her. 'Well, we're ... friends, and we're there because we're Susan's friends.'

'Friends?'

'Yes.' She had smiled then, and quickly turned away to do something else, but not before Thorne had seen the mask slip a little.

121

Inside the classroom, the headmaster said a few words to the dozen or so fourteen-year-olds who were waiting in silence, reminding them about the prearranged procedure and the fact that a counsellor was on hand in the nurse's office for a day or two, in case any of them were still upset and wanted to talk about how they were feeling. Then, having been introduced as a 'close friend of Miss Best', Tanner sat down at what had been Susan's desk. She inched her chair carefully forward and her knees underneath. Standing behind her, Thorne watched as she moved her hands slowly across the surface of the desk, careful to cover each scratch or indentation in the wood.

Her hands where her lover's might once have been.

She didn't look up until the headmaster gave a signal and the first child stepped forward.

There were poems and cards and small bunches of flowers. A collage of leaves and seashells signed by everyone in the class. One by one, the children approached, said 'Sorry' and handed something across the desk. Tanner took the gifts and arranged them neatly, nodding her thanks and passing a tissue to any child who needed one.

There were several packs in her handbag.

Towards the end, a tall, blond-haired boy stepped forward and handed over a picture he had painted. A woman with a shock of dark curly hair and a crooked smile. The gap in her teeth a little bigger perhaps than it had been, a few too many freckles against livid pink skin.

Tanner looked up from the picture and saw that the boy was studying her. 'Thank you,' she said. 'That's really nice.'

The boy nodded, as if he knew how nice it was. 'She was your girlfriend, wasn't she? Miss Best.'

Thorne saw Tanner stiffen a little. Clearly, Susan had not been quite as discreet as they had thought. The headmaster must have seen it too, because he leaned across to Thorne and whispered, 'Ryan Smedley. He's a very bright boy.'

Tanner tried to smooth out the wrinkles on the picture where the paint had hardened, then laid it down gently next to all the other offerings. She looked up at the boy who was waiting patiently; several other children restless in the queue behind him.

'Yes,' Tanner said. 'She was.'

TWENTY

They ordered a takeaway from a curry house near to Helen's flat. It had been her idea to invite Nicola Tanner, then Thorne's to ask Phil Hendricks along. Hendricks had tried to tempt them all across the river, so that they could order from his and Tom's favourite restaurant in Kentish Town, but Helen had pointed out that it wasn't worth organising a babysitter on the off-chance they might get a couple of pappadoms on the house.

'It's OK, I suppose,' Hendricks said, when they began to eat. He looked at Thorne. 'Not the Bengal Lancer, though.'

Thorne shook his head sadly, mouth full.

Helen rolled her eyes. 'Let it go.'

'Nicola doesn't know what she's missing, that's all.'

'Tastes great to me,' Tanner said. 'I've been more or less living on cheese on toast for weeks.' She looked at Helen. 'I wasn't really the one that did the cooking.'

Helen took the reference to Susan as an opportunity to ask how things had gone at the school. She had watched Thorne get ready that morning, pulling out the suit he had last worn at the Heather Finlay murder trial. She had laughed as he had flopped on to the bed, complaining about being Nicola Tanner's 'beard'. She had told him that, if anything, he should be flattered to be asked.

'Hasn't she got any friends she could ask?' Thorne had pulled a face at the unbearable agony of fastening the top button of his shirt. 'I know she's got brothers.'

Helen had handed him his tie on the way out of the bedroom. 'Maybe they were all busy.'

'It was fine,' Tanner said now, helping herself to rice. 'The kids were nice.'

'Great that they wanted to do that.' Helen said.

'Yes, it was.'

'To remember her, you know?'

Tanner took another spoonful and it seemed clear that, for the time being at least, she had said as much as she wanted about the memorial for her late partner. Instead she asked Helen about work and soon the four of them were swapping tales of colleagues they had in common or had once crossed paths with.

A custody sergeant who had smoked some 'evidence' and driven his car through the front window of Vision Express.

A DC who was into rubber.

A DCI who had hanged himself in his garage.

When the leftovers had been put into the fridge and the four of them were at the table with beer or coffee, Tanner said, 'Makes sense, him being gay.'

'I think it makes sense that everyone's gay,' Hendricks said.

Thorne laughed, but Tanner didn't look at either of them. 'Kamal.'

'Oh, right.' Hendricks grinned and winked at Thorne.

'They were saving each other,' Tanner said. 'Amaya and Kamal. I wouldn't lay money against Amaya's parents' having someone lined up for her and we know Kamal was promised to this family in Bangladesh. God knows how much trouble he'd have been in if they'd found out the real reason he didn't want to

125

marry the girl back home. I've seen honour killings where the victim was murdered simply because they were gay.' Now, she looked at Hendricks.

He stared down at his beer can, every trace of mischief gone from his expression.

'So, they marry each other,' Thorne said. 'Once it's done and they're settled, they're free to lead the lives they want.'

'Right, but the families get wind of it. So the word goes out.'

'Isn't it possible though that Kamal's family *didn't* know about him being gay?' Thorne looked to the others, then back to Tanner. 'Everything you've told me about this stuff, it's likely that Kamal would be targeted by the Shahs anyway, just because he's run away with their daughter.'

Tanner shook her head. 'I think there's every chance that both families are in it together.'

'Really?'

'Why not? The relationship is unacceptable to the Shahs and the Azims, so they join forces. Come up with the money together.'

'Bloody hell,' Helen said. 'This is horrible.'

They all turned to look at her. Helen's own job on a Child Protection Unit meant that she came across crimes that were deeply disturbing on an almost daily basis, so the fact that even she was appalled at what she was hearing was enough to give everyone pause.

'We need to go at them,' Tanner said. 'Be a bit more proactive. I think Amaya's brother is a good place to start.'

Thorne put down his drink. 'Hang on—'

'You heard what Sarah Webster said.'

'I know.'

'He was the one Amaya was really scared of.'

'I'm not arguing with you.' Thorne took a moment once he had everyone's attention. 'I just think everything's getting a bit messed up here. We've got a team in Hammersmith looking into

126

Susan's murder, right? They're busy checking out people you might have put away, anyone who might have a grudge against you, whatever, and we know they're looking in the wrong places—'

'That can't be helped—'

'They're wasting their time, which apart from anything else is pissing away time and money for no good reason.'

'Like I said—'

'Then we've got my investigation into Amaya Shah's murder, which nobody knows is connected and which my boss thinks is all about tracking down Kamal Azim, who is still technically our prime suspect.'

'Technically.'

'Yeah, but whichever way you look at it, we're withholding crucial information which could help catch the men we know are responsible for killing Susan.'

'So, tell your boss.' Tanner's voice dropped. She sounded sulky. 'If you really think you need to.'

'Isn't that what you want?' Thorne leaned towards her. 'To catch them?'

'Obviously.'

'I mean, I don't want to sound stupid, but I thought that was the whole point.'

Tanner sat back and studied him. When she spoke again there was something close to a challenge in her tone. A dare. 'I don't want to get you into trouble.'

'Why don't I talk to the Honour Crimes Unit, at least?' Thorne looked to Helen and Hendricks for support, but both were looking elsewhere, seemingly content to let Thorne and Tanner argue this one out.

'Good luck with that,' Tanner said.

'I might be able to get them on board without rattling too many cages.'

'No chance.'

'Worth a try though.'

Tanner shook her head. 'I went to them with all this before what happened to Susan. Remember what I told you? Those "delicate sensibilities"?'

It was Hendricks that broke the silence. He nudged Thorne and said, 'Listen to you. Since when were you bothered about wasting anyone's time or money? Keeping the brass up to speed?' He smiled, happy as always to be the one with the smartarse remarks when things threatened to darken. 'It's like me sleeping with Kylie Minogue.' He cocked his head theatrically. 'Having said that, I probably *would* sleep with Kylie Minogue. I bet she's awesome at spooning.'

Helen smiled. 'Better than Liam?'

'Liam needs to cut his bloody toenails.'

'Do whatever you think is best.' Tanner had not taken her eyes off Thorne. 'But I'm going to talk to Amaya's brother.'

For the remaining few minutes they were at the table, the jokey exchange between Helen and Hendricks nudged Thorne's somewhat testy conversation with Tanner to one side. Helen got up to clear the plates away and Tanner moved quickly to help. They loaded the dishwasher together, then stood for a few minutes talking about Alfie, who had helpfully stayed asleep since Helen had put him to bed a couple of hours before.

From there, Tanner walked into the hall to get her coat and Hendricks announced that he too had better be heading home. Thorne seemed keen for his friend to stay a while longer, perhaps to talk about what Tanner had said, but Hendricks told him there were several corpses who would need his best endeavours first thing the following morning.

At the door, Tanner thanked Helen, and said, 'He was great in that school today. Your old man.'

'Yeah.' Helen glanced at Thorne, who was still sitting at the table, nursing a can of beer. 'Miserable old sod usually comes through when he has to.'

'The singing needs a bit of work though.'

Hendricks said, 'You should see him dance.'

When they had gone, Helen said, 'I get what she's doing.'

'I'm glad somebody does.'

'She doesn't really care about the official investigation into Susan's death because she's excluded from it.' She took a bottle of water from the fridge and poured herself a glass. 'I had the same thing with Paul, which is why I had to find out how he was killed myself. Tanner needs to feel like she's part of what's happening.'

'I understand that,' Thorne said. 'It's the "what's happening" bit I'm trying to sort out, that's all. That's what I was trying to tell her.'

'It's a way of putting off the grief, as well.' Helen drank, leaning back against the worktop. 'Throwing yourself into something. You can kid yourself you've dealt with it, you know? Until it comes back later on to bite you in the arse.'

'Yeah.' Thorne saw the look on Helen's face and understood that, once again, she knew exactly what she was talking about. He watched her rinse out the glass, then walk out into the hallway that led to the bedrooms. A last check on Alfie before bedtime. When she reappeared, she said, 'So, are you going to talk to the Honour Crimes lot?'

Thorne got up and walked into the kitchen. He drained his beer can and dropped it into the bin. 'I don't know.'

Helen sighed, fished the can out and threw it into the recycling box under the sink.

'Sorry,' Thorne said.

The truth was that only twenty minutes after suggesting they talk to the Honour Crimes Unit he was already having doubts of his own. He understood Tanner's lack of enthusiasm better than she thought he did, because there was at least one part of the investigation he himself was reluctant to hand over.

One victim.

He might well pay the HCU a visit, but not yet.

There was someone else he wanted to talk to first.

Outside, standing by Tanner's car, Hendricks said, 'You sounded like you were disappointed in there.'

'Did I?'

'Disappointed in him.'

Tanner keyed the remote and unlocked her car. 'I didn't mean to.'

'Not living up to your expectations?'

'Presuming I had any.'

Hendricks nodded, fingered his own car keys. 'I'm guessing that you checked up on him before you asked him to help you with all this. Decided he ticks all the right boxes. Cutting corners when he needs to, doing whatever it takes to get the right result, all that. Bolshie, with a nice fat file at the Directorate of Professional Standards. Right up your street.'

'If you're asking did I think he was the right man for the job, then absolutely. It wasn't quite as ... devious as you're suggesting, but I think the two of us are very well matched, yes.'

'Dream team.'

'If you like.' Tanner stared at him, the knowing grin that was spreading across his face. She said, 'Are you sure you're all right to drive?'

Hendricks took a few steps towards his car, then stopped and turned round. 'Yes, he *is* all those things you were counting on, or at least more often than not. Tom can be a right pain in the arse, tell you the truth. There's one other thing you should know about him, though.'

Tanner waited.

'He doesn't like being used.'

TWENTY-ONE

As she carried her basket to the checkout, Tanner was thinking about what she'd told Helen Weeks the night before. Living on cheese on toast. It hadn't been too far from the truth, and it was time to start making an effort. She hadn't been lying about the division of cooking duties between herself and Susan, but she wasn't hopeless, so she'd bought the ingredients she'd need to knock up a chilli and a spag bol. She'd bought some fruit and low-fat yoghurt. She'd thrown a few cheap ready-meals in there too, because there was no point trying to run before she could walk and often it was simply a question of getting something on a plate fast. Refuelling. To be honest, it didn't make much difference what she ate anyway, because she could barely taste anything. It was the same with most things; watching TV or reading a book.

Everything just washed over her.

Almost everything. There were always those stupid songs or TV shows that Susan had liked and once or twice Tanner had been ambushed; channel-surfing or listening to the car radio. A slap, a punch, before they were turned off as quickly as possible.

She accepted the pain, but she refused to wallow.

A sly glance from Haroon Shah told her that he knew she was there, that he recognised her from when she and Thorne had been in to talk to his parents ten days before. There was no obvious reaction. He went back to serving the customers ahead of Tanner in the queue, swiping and bagging, his demeanour every bit as truculent as it had been when Tanner had first walked in and spotted him at the till.

He was a good-looking boy though, Tanner thought, if you liked that sort of thing. Somewhere in his early twenties; well built, with a diamond in one ear and gelled hair that he clearly took more time over than she did over hers. She watched him snatch a twenty-pound note from an elderly man who'd bought cigarettes and a couple of scratch cards. He handed over change without a word and grunted when the customer thanked him.

His father might have owned the place, but Tanner doubted very much that Haroon would be winning employee of the month any time soon.

Another glance in her direction as the queue moved forward.

She might be misjudging him, of course. He might normally be a little ray of sunshine, with a winning smile and a cheery word or two for each of his customers. Perhaps Amaya Shah's brother was just having an off day.

A lot on his mind, Tanner guessed.

She checked the contents of her basket one more time as she stepped up to the till. Confident that she hadn't forgotten anything, she set it down then stepped back as Haroon Shah began removing the items one by one. He tore off a plastic bag and held it up.

'Bags are five pence,' he said.

'It's extortionate.' Tanner shook her head. 'Considering the ones in Waitrose are exactly the same price and are infinitely better. Much thicker plastic, you know? Those stupid striped ones tear the minute you walk out of the shop.'

He waited.

Tanner smiled. 'It's fine, though.'

Shah carried on bagging. He said, 'My dad's not here.'

'That's OK.'

'You local, then? Just popped in to do some shopping?' He held up a microwaveable lasagne, looked at it as though it were a box of rat poison, then tossed it into the bag.

'Thought I might as well pick up a few bits and pieces while I was here.'

'I told you, my dad's out.'

'Actually, it was you I wanted a word with,' Tanner said.

'About Amaya?'

'Won't take long.'

He shrugged and finished putting Tanner's shopping in the bag. He told her how much it came to and she handed the cash across, getting no more in the way of customer service than the man before her.

'Thank *you*,' she said, taking her bags.

Shah looked at her, ignoring the sarcasm, or unaware of it. 'So?'

'Not here,' Tanner said.

'Why not?'

'Really? You want to talk about what happened to your sister while you're bagging up baked beans?'

'Course not, but it's difficult, isn't it?' He pointed out the three people who were already queuing to be served.

Tanner turned and flashed a conciliatory smile to the woman directly behind her. 'Can't you get someone to take over for five minutes?'

He sighed, as though Tanner were asking the impossible, then shouted across to a boy of no more than fourteen who was stocking the shelves. When the boy came over, Shah told him to watch the till. Said he'd be keeping an eye on him.

The boy nodded, already smiling happily at the next customer in line.

133

By the time Shah had come around the till Tanner was already moving away, and he followed her to a quieter part of the shop. He stood against the wall and Tanner leaned back against a freezer piled high with ice creams and desserts.

'So, you caught him yet?'

'Caught who?' Tanner asked.

'Amaya's boyfriend. I mean, it was obviously him, wasn't it? I saw the thing on the news. The appeal for information or whatever.'

'There haven't been any further developments, I'm afraid.'

'He killed her though, right?'

'It looks that way. I probably shouldn't be telling you that, but—'

'Bastard.' Shah lowered his head then banged it back hard against the wall. 'Dirty little bastard.'

A woman with a basket hooked over the handles of a push-chair looked at them as she walked past. Tanner smiled at her, turned back to Shah who was shaking his head and sucking his teeth noisily.

'Well, I hope for his sake you get hold of him before we do.' Shah nodded, eyes narrowed. 'All I'm saying.'

Clearly keen that she didn't miss anything, the woman with the pushchair was taking cans from the shelves one by one and studying them. Tanner stared at her until she moved away.

'How's everyone holding up?'

'How d'you think?'

'I know. It can't be easy.'

'Might be easier if you let us have her back,' Shah said. 'We believe the dead should be buried quickly.'

'I know,' Tanner said. 'And while I respect that, I'm afraid it's not possible at the moment. When we do catch whoever killed her, there might need to be a second post-mortem.'

Shah shook his head. 'It's a desecration. All that stuff.'

'Look, I'm sorry if some of these things go against your

beliefs,' Tanner said. 'But there's things I believe in too, like doing my job properly.'

'It's OK, I get that.'

'Good.' She smiled at him. 'So part of me doing that means I need to ask you a couple of quick questions.'

'OK.' He was looking past her, towards the till, but Tanner didn't think it was because he was watching the boy at the checkout.

'We spoke to a friend of Amaya's, from college?'

'Who was that?'

'She told us that Amaya was absent a lot more than normal.'

'So?'

'Like she was unwell or something.'

He shrugged. 'Yeah, she probably was. Always coming down with something, since she was a kid.'

'Yes, that's what her friend thought it was. She also told us that you used to come to the college. Like you were spying on her or something.'

'Why would I do that?'

'I don't know, that's why I'm asking.'

'Yeah, I think I went up there a couple of times. I was supposed to pick her up, I think, or help her carry something. I can't remember.'

'Her friend thought you were just there to keep an eye on her.'

'Who told you all this?'

'It doesn't matter.'

'I bet it was the bitch who lied about where she was that night.'

'It was a friend of your sister's.'

'The night she went off with him. The kid that killed her.'

'She told us that Amaya was scared of you.'

'I'm right, aren't I?'

'Why would your sister be scared of you, Haroon?'

He shook his head, as though the question were ridiculous.

'Really scared.'

'I'm her big brother, aren't I?' He blinked. 'I *was* her big brother.' The head was lowered again for a second or two. 'We had arguments, course we did. Just normal, stupid stuff and yeah, I've got a temper. I shouted at her a few times when she didn't behave herself.'

'Behave herself?'

He blinked again. Once, twice. 'Stuff around the house she was supposed to do, you know? Not doing her fair share, helping out, whatever.'

'Just everyday stuff, you mean? Chores.'

'Right, like that.' He nodded. 'Sometimes she had college work and I might lose it a bit because it was her turn to wash up or something. I mean how do you think I feel about that now?'

'Guilty, I should imagine.'

'Right.' He looked over towards the till again. 'Scared, though? For real? That's what that . . . what she told you?'

Tanner looked at him for a few seconds; the diamond in his ear catching the glare from the strip light. The pained expression and the muscles bulging in his jaw.

She said, 'OK, we're about done.'

His face relaxed. 'Good.' He nodded towards the till. 'Cos you know, I've got a job to do as well.'

As Tanner bent to pick up her shopping, her eye caught something in the freezer behind her. She lifted the lid and took out a frozen cheesecake. 'God, this looks good . . . hugely bad for me, obviously.' She held it up to show him.

'It's one ninety-nine.'

Tanner glanced over at the checkout. The queue was bigger than ever.

'Just take it,' Shah said. 'No sweat.'

'Absolutely not,' Tanner said. 'If I want those gazillion calories badly enough, I'll just have to queue again.' She half turned back towards the freezer as though debating whether or not to put it back. 'What d'you think?'

'Up to you,' Shah said.

'Oh what the hell.' She clutched the package to her chest and smiled. 'Life's too bloody short.'

On the way to her car, Tanner called Dipak Chall.

'Look, I know you've done enough already and I don't want to put you on the spot.'

'What do you need?' Chall asked. He spoke quietly and Tanner could hear the hubbub of a busy incident room in the background. It was a noise she recognised, a buzz she missed.

'Anything else you might be able to dig up on Haroon Shah.'

'OK.' He didn't sound hopeful.

'Look, we know there's a chain, from the families to whoever hires the killers, and I reckon Haroon might just be the weak link.'

'I'll see what I can find,' Chall said. 'But there were no red flags first time round.'

'I know.' Chall had sent her the background information on both families immediately after Amaya and Kamal had gone missing. 'I just think it's worth a second look.'

'Is everything OK?'

Tanner looked down at the bag she was carrying. The sharp edge of the cheesecake box had already ripped through the plastic. A few steps further on, she stopped at a litter bin and dropped the bag into it.

'Yeah,' she said. 'All good.'

TWENTY-TWO

The late great Merle Haggard provided the accompaniment on the drive to a retail park in Wembley and Thorne sang along to 'Silver Wings' with rather more gusto than he had managed in that school hall the day before. In an electrical chain store the size of a football pitch, he spent a few minutes browsing the stereo equipment and staring at 54-inch TVs like a kid in a sweet shop. He asked for the manager, then got back in his car and drove to a pub a few streets away to find him.

Govinder Athwal sat alone at a corner table, looking up at a rather more modestly sized television above the bar. The remains of his lunch were still on a plate in front of him; an empty glass on the table and a bigger one, still half full, in his hand.

Thorne ordered a Coke, then walked across to join him and waited for the penny to drop.

It had been four years, so when it eventually came it wasn't the crispest of double takes, but Thorne enjoyed it nonetheless. 'I've probably put on a bit of weight,' he said.

'You look exactly the same,' Athwal said. 'I'm glad one of us does.' He held up his glass. 'Am I going to need another one of these?'

'Up to you,' Thorne said.

Athwal took a drink. 'Well, I don't suppose too much could shock me any more. Even if you've come to tell me you've found out who killed my daughter, I'm afraid you've left it a bit late.'

He held out his arms, inviting scrutiny. *Look at the state of me.*

Thorne could see what the man was getting at. Though still heavily accented, Athwal's English was as immaculate as Thorne remembered, but in most other respects the changes were obvious enough. The grubby edges of a grey turban, the lines on his face and the veins cracked-red in the yellowish whites of his eyes.

The drink in his hand.

It was clear that Athwal knew Thorne had seen it. 'As a Sikh, I was a man of faith,' he said. 'And then I wasn't.' He clicked his fingers, continued to speak as if he were talking to himself. 'I did not consume intoxicants, and then I did.' He smiled. 'All very well believing in the cycle of birth, life, death and rebirth until you see your flesh and blood laid out on a slab. Believing that God is inside every person until someone rapes and strangles your daughter and you learn that some people are empty, save for lust and wickedness. All very well believing that your three principal duties are to pray, to work and to give, and that by doing these things you are honouring God.' He studied his drink for a few seconds. 'All very well.' He brought the glass to his lips. 'Now, I just work.'

'I went to the shop,' Thorne said.

Athwal nodded, having clearly worked that much out for himself. 'I hope my staff were helpful.'

'Well, most of them look as though they haven't started shaving yet, but they told me where I could find you.'

'I like to take my lunch hour early.' Athwal smiled, looked at what was left in his glass. 'And the food is nice in here.'

Thorne smiled back, allowing the man his moment of self-delusion.

'I presume you didn't come because you are looking for a good price on a DVD player. Not that I wouldn't give you one, because I would.'

Thorne nodded and leaned towards him. 'I'm afraid I haven't come to tell you we've found out who killed Meena, but I wanted to let you know that we've reopened the case.'

Athwal looked at him. 'You have some new information?'

'We're chasing up some fresh leads, yes. It's looking hopeful. I just wanted to tell you personally, that's all.'

'That's good of you.'

'Didn't want you and your wife seeing something in the papers and wondering what was going on.'

Athwal nodded. 'Now, *there* was a woman who prayed, worked and gave until the very end.'

'Oh,' Thorne said. 'I'm sorry to hear that.'

'Nearly two years ago now.' He raised his glass and it wasn't clear if he were drinking in remembrance of his wife's death or indicating that it was another reason the glass was there in the first place.

Thorne lifted his own glass. Touched it to Athwal's.

'They talk about people dying of a broken heart, don't they? You believe that's possible?'

'People can . . . fade,' Thorne said. 'They can give up.'

'It burst,' Athwal said. 'That's the simple truth, just walking up the stairs one afternoon, but that would be splitting hairs. Burst . . . broken, doesn't really matter what they call it. My wife was dying from the moment we got that first phone call. When they found Meena.'

Four years on, there was no question that, if Meena Athwal's father was giving a performance, it was faultless. The crack in the voice and the tremor in the cheek. He'd had a lot of time to perfect the show of grief, Thorne thought. To really *inhabit* his loss. 'I know it doesn't get any easier,' he said. 'But like I say, we're making progress and hopefully finding out what really happened might make things less painful.'

Athwal licked his lips, rubbed hands across his face. 'What kind?'

'Sorry?'

'What kind of progress are you making?'

On the way to Wembley, Thorne had thought about this moment, or something close to it, and imagined how angry he would be; the fight to stop himself pulling Govinder Athwal out of his chair, driving his face into the table. Instead, he felt himself warming to the game he was being drawn into. Happy to let the man sitting opposite him believe he was getting away with it.

He said, 'Let's just say we're not sure it was a random attack.'

'What?'

'There's new evidence that suggests otherwise.'

'So . . . not a stranger?'

'It isn't quite that straightforward.'

'Are you suggesting Meena was killed by someone she knew?'

Thorne sensed nervousness and suddenly Athwal's performance did not seem as polished. This was not a role he had been expecting to play. 'No, but possibly by someone who knew her.'

'I don't understand.'

'I can't really say any more at this stage. Like I said, I just wanted to tell you that things are moving forward again. To let you know that personally.'

Athwal stared up at the TV for ten, fifteen seconds, as though trying to process the things Thorne had told him. Their implications.

Thorne did not believe he was acting any more.

Athwal pushed back his chair and asked if he could buy Thorne a drink, but Thorne told him he needed to get back to the office as quickly as possible, that there were still a few more of those fresh leads that needed following up.

'I meant what I said. If you ever need a new TV or whatever. A radio. It would be my pleasure to help, really. I haven't forgotten everything you did four years ago.'

Thorne said, 'I'll bear that in mind,' because he hadn't forgotten either.

Driving back to Colindale, Thorne turned the volume up when his favourite Merle Haggard track came on.

'Tonight The Bottle Let Me Down'.

Nosing into slow-moving traffic by Wembley Park station, he thought about Govinder Athwal, a glass in his hand and a dirty turban, dragging his past around like a ball and chain; a future no more than days to be counted down. A man who looked every bit as crushed, as haunted, as he deserved to be.

I've always had a bottle I could turn to . . .

Drinking to keep two women off his mind.

Watering down the guilt with Bell's and Sam Adams.

TWENTY-THREE

Back at Becke House, Thorne finally caught up with DCI Russell Brigstocke in the canteen. He bought a cheese and tomato roll and a bag of crisps and carried them across to join his boss.

Brigstocke grunted, his mood clearly not helped by the food in front of him. It was certainly a healthier option than the one Govinder Athwal had chosen, and clearly a weapon in the battle Brigstocke was waging against an expanding waistline, but nobody in their right mind could have called it appetising.

'Pulses,' he said. As though he'd far rather be looking down at a selection of things that had once had them. 'Fibre, vitamins, I get all that.' He glanced up at Thorne. 'Just the taste thing that's the issue.'

'I got your message,' Thorne said.

Brigstocke nodded and began to eat, chewing like it was actually painful. He swallowed and said, 'Amaya Shah.'

'Right.'

Brigstocke waited, pushed his pulses around.

'I've been looking into the possible connection with the

Meena Athwal murder we talked about. I spoke to her father this morning.'

'So, how did that go?'

'Well, I'm still convinced that she was killed by the same people that murdered Amaya.'

Brigstocke waved his fork as if a fly were annoying him. 'We'll get on to that in a minute. What else?'

'We also talked to Amaya's brother. Sarah Webster told us that Amaya was scared of him, hinted that he might have been violent in the past.'

'By "we", I'm presuming you're talking about officers on your team, as opposed to one who's still on compassionate leave and not actually part of this inquiry.'

'Right.'

'I'm presuming that, because if I found out this other officer *was* involved . . . you know, if you were stupid enough to make it blindingly bloody obvious, I'd probably have to do something about it.'

'You said.'

'Like have your bollocks on a plate.'

Thorne nodded down at Brigstocke's lunch. 'Tastier than that.' He watched his boss force another mouthful down. 'You really shouldn't eat that shit, Russell. It's clearly making you miserable.'

'No, you make me miserable,' Brigstocke said. 'This stuff makes me suicidal.'

Thorne laughed. Brigstocke didn't.

'What did the brother have to say?'

'I'm still waiting to hear from the officer who spoke to him.' Thorne ignored the warning look. 'But I should imagine he fronted it out, demanded to know when we were going to find Kamal because it's obviously Kamal that killed his sister.'

'Well, forensic science would appear to agree with him,' Brigstocke said.

'Kamal was gay.'

'According to this girl you talked to. Certainly not according to the DNA evidence.'

'Why would Amaya tell her friend that Kamal was gay if he wasn't?'

'If she was as scared as you say she was, maybe she didn't trust anyone. Maybe she said that to throw people off the scent, whatever.' Brigstocke didn't wait for Thorne to argue. 'Yes, it's possible that she was feeling threatened by her family, that the pair of them were planning to run off together. But that doesn't mean Kamal didn't rape and kill her.'

Thorne said nothing.

'Will you at least accept that's an explanation?'

'Yeah,' Thorne said, eventually. *And Shergar's giving rides to little kids on Southend beach.* 'It's an explanation.'

'Good. Thank you.'

'I just think it's the explanation we're meant to accept.'

'What, stupid coppers like me?'

'You know I didn't mean that,' Thorne said. 'Come on, Russell—'

'Oh, sod this.' Brigstocke pushed his plate away and got to his feet. 'I'm going to the Oak.'

Thorne knew that the DCI would never dream of drinking halfway through a shift and guessed that the lure of the local pub had more to do with the steak and kidney pie it was famous for.

Having only taken one bite, he rewrapped his lunch in the cling film it had come in and followed Brigstocke out.

Walking down the stairs, Brigstocke said, 'So, how's the search for Kamal going?'

'We're still doing everything we can,' Thorne lied. 'Obviously.'

'Bank cards, mobile phone?'

'Nothing. And there's not going to be.'

'Maybe we should think about a second appeal.'

'Really?'

145

The appeal for information following the DNA match with Kamal Azim had quickly yielded what, in any other circumstances, would have been positive results. Though they had yet to trace him through YouTube, the boy who had shot the mobile phone footage on the train had come forward, but only to confirm that Kamal and Amaya had been threatened by a well-built Irishman and rescued by an older Asian man who had led them off the train. It hadn't looked to the boy as if the abuser was following them.

There had been sightings of Kamal from all over the country and though he'd known it would be a waste of time, Thorne had dutifully followed up every one of them.

A woman who ran a café on the Holloway Road had come forward to say that two men matching the description of those in the Tube photograph had eaten breakfast there two days after the incident. Thorne had taken the information to Brigstocke but it had not cut a great deal of ice.

'There's a lot of well-built Irishmen around,' he'd said. 'A lot of middle-aged Asians. It's the boy we should be concentrating on.'

Nicola Tanner had been rather more excited.

'They're sticking around,' she had said. 'Probably waiting until Amaya's body was found because they wouldn't get paid until then.'

Thorne had said nothing, because he was worried about what else the killers might be sticking around for.

Now, descending the final flight of stairs, Brigstocke said, 'I think another appeal would be a good idea.'

Thorne trudged down a step or two behind him. 'We're doing exactly what they want,' he said. 'Buying the story they've set us up to buy.'

Brigstocke pushed through the doors into reception, stopped at the main exit. 'Listen, I've already given you a ton more leeway on this than I should have, OK?'

'I know, and I'm—'

'I've let you go down this other road, the honour killings stuff, this pair who are doing it for money. I've agreed to this second line of inquiry, but I can't afford to look like an idiot.'

Thorne stepped close to him, spoke low and urgent. 'They killed Kamal at the same time they killed Amaya. Did whatever they needed to create this DNA evidence. That was always the plan. Why are we wasting our time looking for someone who's already dead?'

'You sure about that?'

Thorne watched Brigstocke reach into his pocket then produce a folded sheet of paper with the same flourish he might once have used when he completed a magic trick. *Ta daaa!*

'Danny Mirza got in touch.' Brigstocke handed the paper across. 'He received this last night.'

Thorne unfolded the piece of paper and read the printout of an email sent just after eleven o'clock the previous evening:

hey Danny. just checking in, let you know i'm getting
everything sorted. all of a bit of a mess right now. don't
know what you've heard but will explain when i see you. it's
complicated, yeah? keep the faith, man. K

'Disposable email account,' Brigstocke said. 'The lab's on it, but I'm guessing an internet café or some remailer service. He obviously wants to stay hidden.'

'Or the killers don't want us to know it's them sending the email.' Thorne waved the paper at Brigstocke. 'Come on, this doesn't tell us Kamal's still alive.'

'It tells me that we aren't wasting our time,' Brigstocke said. 'And if I was to do anything else but make finding him our priority, it'd be *my* bollocks on a plate. So, Kamal Azim remains our prime suspect in the murder of Amaya Shah, OK?'

'Russell—'

'*Your* prime suspect.'

Before Thorne had a chance to fight his corner any further, Brigstocke was through the doors and away across the car park. Annoyance or just the thought of a decent lunch, he was moving faster than Thorne had seen him do in a long time.

When Tanner called, she said, 'I talked to the brother.'

Thorne was at his desk, after an hour of conversations with team members he did not want to have and pointless exchanges with technicians tracing an email sent by a young man he knew to be dead.

He was watching the clock.

He said, 'How did that go?'

Tanner described a conversation that was almost exactly as Thorne had told Brigstocke it would be, even if he had been somewhat evasive about which officer Haroon Shah had been talking to.

Well aware the whole time that Brigstocke knew exactly who it was.

'Shaken him up, I reckon,' Tanner said.

'You think?'

'Let's hope so.'

'I went to see Meena Athwal's father.'

'And?'

'Sounds like he's a better actor than Haroon Shah.'

'I was thinking,' Tanner said. 'Maybe we could put Haroon under surveillance. I'm pretty sure he's rattled and he might be just daft enough or scared enough to lead us straight to who-ever's organising all this.'

Tanner sounded fired up and Thorne knew he was about to piss all over the flames. 'I can't see it.'

'You're probably right, but we should be all over his mobile phone at least. Reckon you can twist your boss's arm?'

'Not a hope in hell,' Thorne said.

'What's happened?'

Thorne told her about the email from Kamal Azim, the clear instruction from Brigstocke to keep the investigation firmly on whatever track led them to him.

Tanner took the news better than he had expected.

'Not the end of the world,' she said. 'Actually, there's an argument for making it look like we've fallen for it. Like we're going in the wrong direction because we're daft. You never know, whoever's running this thing might get over-confident and then *they* might do something stupid.'

'You're staking a hell of a lot on people being stupid,' Thorne said.

'Because they are, most of the time. There's a lot of links in this chain and someone's going to mess up, because there's always someone stupid. But we're not.'

Thorne watched as Brigstocke wandered through the incident room on his way back from lunch. It didn't look like the steak and kidney pie had done much to improve his mood. Or perhaps they had sold out.

'We're back to where we started, that's all,' Tanner said. 'Dream team.'

'What?'

Tanner laughed. 'Just something Phil Hendricks said.'

Thorne turned to his computer screen as an email about an email pinged into his inbox. No, he wasn't stupid, not all the time, anyway. Which was why he knew there was every chance the dream could turn into a nightmare.

He said, 'Well, Phil Hendricks is a fucking idiot.'

TWENTY-FOUR

Haroon ended the call and tossed his mobile on to the bed. He dropped down next to it, then almost immediately stood up again, unable to settle.

One job sorted ... *boom* ... but a much bigger problem to think about.

From one wall of his bedroom to another in four paces. Four. How sad was that? What the hell was he still doing living at home, anyway? Mooching around above the shop in the same room he'd had since there were David Beckham posters on the wall? Assistant manager *sounded* good, was what he said to his mates and what he told girls whenever he had the chance, but at the end of the day, he was still a glorified till-monkey.

Taking as much shit as money from the winos and the chavs and the shoplifters.

Cider and cat food and bog-roll ...

Work hard, this place will be yours.

Like it was a done deal and there could not possibly be anything else he might want to do. Like maybe *he* fancied dossing about at college for a while; making some real money afterwards, opening a *string* of shops.

He felt guilty that he wasn't a bit more grateful. He felt disrespectful. He knew how hard his father had worked for all this, still worked.

And now, of course, Haroon was the only child.

Not that everything wouldn't have come to him anyway, being the only son. Not that his sister would have been a lot of help.

Glittery tops and eyeliner, when there was stock that needed shifting.

He picked up his phone and checked the time.

He needed to get back down to the shop and give his father a break. His old man's arthritis was getting worse by the day and he could only manage a couple of hours at a time. His mum did what she could, but she still got flustered dealing with the customers and that boy they had helping out was worse than useless.

Kid wasn't all there, to be honest. A favour for one of his father's cousins.

He had to make some decisions though before he went back to work. Take some steps, or figure out what they should be, at least. He didn't want to worry his mother and father with any of this; it was still tough enough as it was. Tough for all of them, because it wasn't like Amaya had never existed, was it? Like they hadn't loved her. More important, he wanted to show his parents and anyone else who'd been part of this business that he could deal with the problem himself.

He was going to be the one to step up. It was about responsibility and doing what was expected, simple as that. Besides, taking this on would make him feel better about those occasional doubts. Those disrespectful thoughts when he saw his mates out in flash cars until all hours and lying in bed until lunchtime.

Maybe he needed to write it all down, he thought. Get organised.

What did she really know, anyway? That stupid woman copper with her basket of crap and her questions about spying.

Fishing, that was all. We heard this, we heard that.

Who should he talk to first? Who had it started with?

He couldn't think straight.

He'd get it all down on paper, once the shop was closed, then start talking to people tomorrow. He'd make it go away, so that his father would never even have to know about it.

His mobile pinged. A mate he knew he could trust.

SORTED 4 L8R.

Haroon was in a much better mood as he walked downstairs. Past the calendar, the photographs of Rangpur and Chittagong where so many of his family still lived, the pictures of his sister.

At least he'd have something good to think about, help get him through his shift.

He showed respect and now he would earn it.

And those who did not know what it meant would have to learn.

A wake-up call, wasn't that what they called it?

Govinder Athwal would never use such a phrase, but he knew what it meant and it certainly summed up the way he felt about his conversation with Detective Inspector Tom Thorne in the pub. Sitting there telling a virtual stranger all that, the car crash that his life had become, in such detail. Since when had he sounded like one of those terrible TV shows he sometimes watched in the middle of the morning, when he'd found some excuse to take the day off work? Maybe what he really needed was a jeering audience. Some arsehole in a suit shoving a micro-phone in his face, telling him to pull himself together.

People die. What sort of excuse is that? What sort of man are you?

Perhaps now was the time to do something about it, he

thought. To change once again. Since his lunchtime conversation, he had thought about little except the man he had once been.

Two children once upon a time, and a wife.

A life.

He looked around the room and the shame was like acid in his stomach. He hadn't told Thorne about this place, though he might have done if Thorne had accepted his offer of a drink. The family home unnecessary, now that there was no family to live in it. A poky flat, a *flat* ... with noise from the street and damp creeping up the bathroom wall like a shadow; with just enough space for his son to stay when the boy needed his bank account topping up and bothered coming home from university.

Meena's little brother. All that was left of Govinder Athwal's family.

There had been lies told in that pub, of course. Or at least a few half-truths, but that was the man he had become. As much point fighting this new nature of his as there would be the grey in his beard or the loss of hearing in one ear.

A losing battle.

He did not drink simply because his faith had gone. He drank because he needed to and, right this minute, he needed to drink more than he had in a long time. Tom Thorne had probably worked that out, because he wasn't a stupid man, like so many of them. Even if he had failed to solve Meena's murder four years before.

Was he really as close to doing so now as he'd suggested? There was confidence, certainly. Another thing Govinder had lost.

What was this new evidence the police had found? This progress?

He walked across to the wardrobe and reached inside for his copy of the *Guru Granth Sahib*.

One more thing he had lied about.

He carefully removed the holy book from its silk wrapping and carried it across to the small, cushioned altar he had built beneath the window. He laid it beneath the canopy, then sat down to take off his shoes.

Ten minutes later, having washed, he sat clutching his chain of steel *mala* beads and began to pray.

TWENTY-FIVE

More often than not, Alfie was the reason Thorne and Helen stopped arguing. His simple demand for attention would tend to defuse tense situations, making them realise that what they were fighting about was unimportant, or, at the very least, could be put on hold.

It wasn't usually Alfie that started the row.

Close to bedtime, he had been sitting with Thorne on the sofa, happily hypnotised by a Peppa Pig DVD. Thorne was quietly succumbing to the charms of the winsome porker himself. Already a lot more relaxed than he'd been when he'd come home, he was looking forward to an evening of slobbing out with Helen; to some comfort food and TV, and, if at all possible, staying on that sofa until he was forcibly removed.

To not thinking about woodland, or darkened dead ends; the bodies waiting and the two men for whom these were workplaces.

It was a perfectly good plan, but it had all unravelled very quickly when Helen told Alfie it was time for bed and her three-year-old son had calmly glanced up and told her to 'fuck off'.

There had been some angry words exchanged before Helen had picked her son up and moved towards the bedroom. She had pointedly – and somewhat ludicrously – suggested that Alfie had not heard those words from her. Thorne had tried to make light of it, insisted she was over-reacting, but Helen was not to be appeased. The bemused child in her arms had waved on his way out of the room, looking from Thorne to his mother as though trying to work out what all the shouting was about.

It had not helped that Thorne's first instinct had been to laugh.

Now he awaited Helen's return, and with the imminent resumption of hostilities those thoughts and images he had felt able to escape for a while had begun to creep back into his mind.

She was a good girl.

I'd rather be ignored than controlled.

They killed Susan, but it was me they were after.

'Sorry, Tom, that was daft.'

Thorne looked up and was pleased to see that Helen was smiling. He nodded and said, 'Too right it was. I mean for a kick-off you swear like a bloody docker.'

'No, I mean being bothered about it at all.' She walked across and sat down on the arm of the sofa. 'Fucking stupid.'

'See what I mean?' He laughed again when Helen flicked two fingers at him. 'Anyway, the average child starts swearing at four. So Alfie's above average.'

'Or below. Depends how you look at it.'

'I don't trust people who never swear,' Thorne said. 'Always makes me think there's all sorts of dark stuff going on in their heads.'

Helen looked away, nodding.

'And there's plenty of kids with worse things in their heads than that. I mean, it's just a word.'

'Yeah.' Helen reached for the remote and turned Alfie's DVD off, though Thorne had barely registered the fact that it was still

156

playing. 'Sorry, though, I shouldn't have gone off at you about it.'

'I'll get over it.'

'Shitty job on at the moment.'

'OK.' Thorne waited. They were all shitty in Helen's line of work, so this one must have been particularly bad. He wasn't sure if she wanted to talk about it or not, if he really wanted to hear it, but the tone of his response had left the door open. Just an inch or two. 'Sounds like someone needs wine.'

Helen shook her head then stood up. 'Chocolate.'

Within thirty seconds she was back on the sofa next to Thorne and making short work of a large bag of Maltesers. Thorne watched; the closed eyes, the sighs and hums of contentment.

'Be honest. Is that better than sex?'

'It lasts longer,' she said.

'Only because it's a big bag.'

Helen polished off the rest of the chocolate. She dropped the empty bag on the floor and sat back. 'The best thing about having children is that you can buy stuff like this and kid yourself it's for them.'

'You serious? Alfie would never eat anything like that.'

'I *know*. What's wrong with him?' Helen shook her head, though she was of course delighted that, unlike most kids his age, her son had never shown any interest in sweets or chocolate bars. He'd spat out chunks of Dairy Milk on more than one occasion, preferring to snack on slices of cucumber and celery, and he was currently getting through a large jar of olives every few days. 'I mean, I know there's some doubt about who his dad was, but sometimes I watch him stuffing raw carrots into his mouth and I wonder who his bloody mother is.'

Thorne tried not to look shocked. Helen rarely talked about the uncertainty over the identity of Alfie's father, and he could not remember her ever joking about it. 'Maybe you just ate too many Walnut Whips when you were pregnant.'

157

Helen was staring ahead, her face creased in confusion. As though she were a little appalled at her own comment. She said, 'This bloody job's messing with my head.'

'I'd worry if it didn't,' Thorne said.

That door creaked further open.

She inched across, leaned into him. 'Two brothers, fourteen and twelve. Nothing that I haven't seen plenty of times before … strange behaviour at school and with other kids. Trouble sleeping, outbursts of violence, being inappropriately and overtly sexual. Like I said, the usual stuff.'

'The father?'

'Well it's always where they start. I'm waiting on the full report from Social Services, but yeah, probably.'

'So, what's …'

Thorne felt her stiffen slightly. 'I don't know. I think not being sure why this one's bothering me so much is getting to me every bit as much as the case itself.'

'It happens,' Thorne said. 'Certain cases. Sometimes you never work out why.'

'I saw the videos … the initial interviews with Social Services, and it's just something about those two kids. A look on their faces. In their eyes, you know?'

'Yeah.' Sometimes Thorne believed that having a decent idea about how killers felt, what drove them to do what they did, was what made him good at what he did. Better than some others, anyway. It was nothing mysterious, just how his brain was wired; the way some people were good at doing crosswords or had great hand-eye co-ordination.

But he hadn't had to kill anyone to acquire that … insight. There hadn't been a price.

'I'm probably being stupid,' Helen said. 'Maybe I just need a break.'

'Well, if you ask me, you need a break anyway.' Thorne rubbed her shoulder. 'Polesford was meant to *be* the break.'

Thorne had known since then that his partner understood what the victims she worked for were going through because she'd been where they were. Plenty of her colleagues had compassion, some had empathy, but Helen knew better than most what such children lived with every day. The things they felt and the things they carried around in their heads.

Terror, rage, bad memories.

'We should try and get away,' he said. 'Soon.'

Helen nodded.

There were plenty of things worse than words.

TWENTY-SIX

Sarah Webster could just as easily have told them that, after she'd finished college for the day, she was going into the West End for dinner with Leonardo DiCaprio. The Ivy or somewhere like that, then a limo back to his hotel afterwards. Her parents would have paid about as much attention. As *little* attention. As it was, she was happy enough heading for the pub with some of the people on her course, a kebab or some chips on the way to the bus stop at the end of the night. Not her proper mates, but they were nice enough, a good laugh, and it killed a few hours before she would eventually have to go home.

They'd be in bed by then, with any luck, and would still be by the time she had to leave for college the next morning. If she was unlucky, they'd be crashed out in the front room, off their faces with the TV still blaring. Then it would be Sarah's job to get them upstairs. Try and clean up a little. Empty cans into bin bags, a roll of kitchen towel for whatever they'd spilled, just so the place wouldn't stink quite so much when she was having her breakfast.

Toast and white cider.

On the bus home, she sat on the top deck same as always and plugged in her earbuds. Just her and a couple half asleep up the front, a group of Asian lads messing around on the back seat. She liked being high up and staring in through the windows of the houses they passed. If lights were still on, she might catch glimpses of people doing stuff. Watching TV together or saying goodnight then going upstairs like normal people, without falling over or being sick on the landing and laughing about it.

Telling her to chill out like *they* were the teenagers. Taking the piss. Leaving the bedroom door open and not caring that she could hear them doing it.

He wasn't actually her dad, just the bloke who'd moved in after her real dad had left, and it was him who'd kicked everything up a notch as far as the boozing went. The stupid, strong stuff. Her mum had always liked a drink same as anyone else, but it had never been about getting off her face. These days, it was hard to have a proper conversation.

Sarah couldn't remember the last time they'd really talked.

Behind her, the lads at the back were laughing and taking selfies. She turned the music down on her phone and thought she heard some comment about girls with short hair. She didn't turn round, but she thought they might be taking pictures of her, too.

She was wishing she hadn't bothered with that kebab.

The taste was rank in her mouth.

They'd talked about Amaya a bit in the pub. Most of them being nice, saying how awful it was and raising a glass to her. One of the boys Sarah didn't know that well had drunk too much and said he thought Amaya had secretly fancied him, that she hadn't really been as shy as she pretended. Sarah had told him to shut up. Told him that Amaya would never have been that desperate. The others had laughed, but she was thinking about that phone call from Amaya's father the morning after she'd gone missing. Screaming abuse so loud that Sarah could hear from across the room and her mother in tears, telling this stranger on the phone she didn't understand. The hangover, crippling.

She got off the bus and began to walk.

A few minutes to think about what might be waiting for her. To hope her luck would hold.

One of these days she'd get home to find the place on fire.

There was time for one or two more lighted windows, but there wasn't much to see. A couple of shapes, curtains being drawn. She was still enjoying the music and it wasn't until she turned a corner that she became aware that the boys from the bus were behind her.

Four of them, hoods up.

She took her earbuds out.

Fifty yards further on the street narrowed and she had her keys out, but by the time she knew they were following her, by the time she turned and saw them running, it was too late.

She started to run herself, moved the front door key in her hand, enough to take an eye out.

She had seen it on a cop show once.

She ran, but they were much too fast and she didn't have her trainers on.

Not going to happen, not here, they're not stupid.

There are houses, she thought; she could hear cars. There were still lights on.

She shouted and turned to face them and smelled grease on the hand that was pressed across her face.

TWENTY-SEVEN

They'd stayed in better hotels, but this was the second night, so they would probably be checking out later anyway. Never in the same place more than a couple of days, that was the rule. Never anywhere flashy, either. Same with hire cars, clothes, all of it. Nothing that was going to attract any attention.

Shame, because who didn't like a bit of luxury? Especially when you could afford it.

It was one of those cheapskate, help-yourself breakfast buffets, with slices of white bread that you put on to that belt contraption to toast. Horrible orange juice in a big carafe thing with a tap, mini boxes of Corn Flakes and Rice Krispies.

Muldoon was hungry, though.

He carried three slices of toast, some jam and a few bits of cheese over to his table, then went back to get coffee and biscuits. Whacked another slice of bread on the belt for good measure. Once everything was laid out, he got stuck in and tried to ignore the tinny jazz that whoever ran this poxy chain had chosen to give their guests a nice, relaxing start to their day.

If relaxed meant wanting to tear the manager's head off.

He leaned back, chewing, and looked across at Riaz eating his own breakfast at a table in the far corner.

Yoghurt and a bit of fruit, for God's sake. His own teabag, some herbal shit he always carried with him.

Head down over the newspaper he'd ordered the night before.

They had not fallen out, nothing like that, but it was always the same if they had an early start. If they were eating somewhere like this. His partner was not exactly chatty at the best of times, but first thing he preferred his own company, which Muldoon thought was fair enough. Nobody needed a gobshite like him firing questions across the table before they'd woken up properly, did they? Riaz was not a morning person, he'd told Muldoon, and he liked a bit of space at the start of the day.

It was nothing personal.

Miserable cunt . . .

Muldoon wasn't sure what sort of place they would be moving to. Riaz always made those arrangements, which was fine, because organisation had never really been Muldoon's strong point. Bits of paper to lose. Somewhere a bit nicer, with any luck. It would still be somewhere in town though, Muldoon knew that much. They still had plenty of work to do.

Riaz looked up and saw Muldoon looking. Muldoon nodded. Riaz nodded back and went back to his paper.

Muldoon started slathering butter on a second piece of toast.

Seemed like they were in demand right now, in London at least. Regular boom industry, it felt like. Always the same, Muldoon thought. Feast or bloody famine. Obviously they'd had to stick around until the thing with those two kids was finished, but now there was another job to do and, who knew, there was every chance something else might come along before they had to move on. Probably be Turkey or Pakistan, he reckoned – they'd done plenty over there the last few years – but it would be nice to stay in the UK for a while, at least. The food, the language, all that. Maybe something up north, or in the Midlands. Those were where the jobs usually came from.

Birmingham, Bradford. A few nice paydays up there in the past.

When he'd finished eating and found himself tapping his spoon on the table in time with the foul music, Muldoon got up and ambled across to his partner's table. A quick chat wouldn't hurt. Get the lie of the land.

Riaz sighed and looked up; folded his paper and waited.

'So, what's on today, boss?' Riaz wasn't his boss, it was just a word and Muldoon knew that it irritated the Asian for some reason. Which was why he said it.

'We watch the house again.'

'If you say so.'

'Get a sense of the routine, the timings. Do it properly.'

'Oh, I'm all for that,' Muldoon said.

'I'm very glad you agree.'

'Proper, but not . . . overdoing it. Like you said.'

'Bring a magazine or something, so you won't get bored.'

'So I won't start annoying you with my stupid chatter, you mean? Getting on your nerves?' Muldoon reached across and picked up the empty plastic pot. 'How was your yoghurt, by the way?'

'*I'll* bring a magazine,' Riaz said.

TWENTY-EIGHT

The crisp packet had been lying in the footwell of Tanner's car for several weeks. Normally it would have been removed immediately, of course, with a good deal of huffing and a telling-off for the individual who had left it there. Lovely as her partner had been, she was never much of a one for tidiness. *Up to you if your own car's a bloody pigsty, but don't throw your rubbish away in mine.* The packet – and a half-empty water bottle behind the seat – had been left the day her car had been borrowed, so Tanner was happy to let them sit there for a while.

Not *happy*, perhaps . . .

A reminder of Susan, obviously, and of her own guilt. A reminder why she was parked at the end of a side street, watching a convenience store in East Barnet.

Tanner had said something about the car, about not pranging it, the last time she'd seen her. A few words, only half tongue-in-cheek, before Susan had climbed in and driven off, grinning, to school on that final morning.

Never anything profound, was it? Never anything important.

That final conversation.

It hadn't been an argument, which was something to be grateful for, though there had been plenty of those in the weeks beforehand.

The drinking, the treatment she wasn't sticking with, the usual stuff.

So, it could have been a lot worse, but that didn't make Tanner feel any less wretched. Her precious bloody car, for pity's sake.

She drummed the steering wheel and told herself she was being stupid.

How many people got to say anything that actually mattered? Like, 'I'm sorry', or 'I should tell you that I love you more often', or 'I don't know how the hell you can stand to live with me'.

Those things they wished they had said.

She glanced down at the crisp packet then back up at the shopfront she had been watching since first thing this morning, and wondered what Amaya Shah's last words to Haroon had been. It was hard to imagine they had been . . . loving. Or perhaps they had, and Amaya's last words to her brother had been a lie.

The shop was doing pretty good business – on a busy road with plenty of footfall – so Tanner almost missed seeing Haroon Shah leave, strolling out into rare September sunshine in jeans and a baseball cap. Tanner checked her watch. It was just after twelve thirty, so he was probably heading to get some lunch from one of the many fast-food places within a few minutes' walk. Then she saw him reach into his jacket for what she guessed were car keys and jog across the road. She started her car as she watched him climb into a battered-looking Fiat Panda, and half a minute after Shah had pulled out and turned on to the main road, Tanner was sitting a few cars behind him.

She turned the radio off and sat up straight. She folded her collar across the seat belt.

She had attended a weekend vehicle pursuit course a few years

167

before and, as with the umpteen other courses she had completed in her time, she'd listened and learned, while a good many of her colleagues had been there simply to tick it off, treating the weekend like a mini-break and flirting or blowing their expenses in the bar.

Tanner had no trouble hanging back, while keeping Shah's Fiat in plain sight.

This was not an area of the city she knew very well. Besides living in west London, she normally worked out of a station in Belgravia, catching cases in Pimlico or Chelsea, or across the river in Battersea now and again. Murders with a more attractive postcode and a decent deli within walking distance of the crime scene. It was one of the reasons – a minor one, admittedly – why she'd approached Tom Thorne. He might currently be living south of the river – a situation that she sensed he was not altogether happy with – but this part of London was his patch and local knowledge would always come in handy. Contacts with those on local teams.

She followed the Fiat as Shah sped up a little past Arnos Grove tube station and on to the North Circular. A mile or so further on, he swung on to Green Lanes, and once he had turned right on to the next major road his destination became obvious enough.

Tanner could see the copper-coloured minaret above the trees, the crescent mounted on top.

Dipak Chall had yet to come back to her with any further information about Haroon, but in the notes that he had put together after the disappearance of Amaya and Kamal there had been no indication that the Shahs were regular visitors to a mosque. Not significant in itself, of course. She knew that even the most devout of Muslims could pray at home and that the shop kept both Haroon and his father busy. It would have made a visit for even one of the five daily prayers difficult, which left Tanner to draw one of only two conclusions.

Haroon Shah was squeezing in a quick *salah* on his lunch break. Or he wasn't going to the mosque to pray.

She drove slowly past the many worshippers arriving on foot and turned into the large car park in time to see Shah reversing into a space at the far end. Tanner quickly found a space of her own; one that was far enough away from the Fiat, but still gave her a good view of the main entrance.

She watched Haroon get out of his car, replace his baseball cap with a dark kufi and join the crowd heading inside. She saw him walk past two men on their hands and knees near the door, working hard with brushes and buckets, scrubbing at the brickwork.

The call to prayer echoed around the car park. Tanner could not tell if it was live or pre-recorded. She knew there would be a second one just before the prayers began, but had no idea how long the service would last.

Half an hour? More?

She turned the radio on again, pulled her phone out and opened the camera app. She took some pictures before settling down to wait.

The exterior of the building. A few number plates. The crisp packet nestled in her footwell.

TWENTY-NINE

'So, when am I going to see this glass of wine?'

Thorne looked up from his computer screen to see DI Yvonne Kitson standing in front of his desk. 'Sorry?'

'The drink I was promised for agreeing to hand over the Amaya Shah case.' Kitson turned and walked across to her own desk on the other side of the office they shared. 'A deal's a deal.'

'Oh, right.'

'So what about a quick one later on? You can settle up.'

Thorne grunted and looked back to the file on his desktop. An all-forces alert regarding the search for Kamal Azim – a new photograph, a more detailed description – to be circulated nationwide. He had been staring at it for the previous ten minutes, his fingers hovering over the keyboard, reluctant to do as he had been instructed first thing and send it out. To do exactly what was expected by those calling the shots on either side.

An impatient DCI. A pair of killers.

Hendricks had been right to point out that Thorne was not usually the sort to worry overmuch about waste; money, manpower or time. In the past, he had been guilty of wasting all three when it had suited him. Barking up a forest's worth of decidedly iffy trees, unwilling to accept that he had been wrong.

'It's fine to think you're the only one who's right,' Hendricks had said once, 'when it comes to liking cowboy music or a particular football team. I mean, obviously you're *not* right, but it's OK to think you are. When there's bodies involved though, lives at stake ... sometimes you just have to put your hand up and say "I'm an idiot."'

It was entirely possible of course that the same thing was happening now and that simple pig-headedness was why Thorne believed Kamal Azim was never going to be found. His own and Nicola Tanner's. Every few minutes he considered such a possibility and, every few minutes, he dismissed it. Tanner was by-the-book after all, Job-pissed; not a woman inclined to swim against the tide for the hell of it. Whatever her personal involvement might be, she had put the hours in on this already. It was her certainty that Thorne drew on to fuel his own, that kept him convinced they were right to ignore the evidence.

The DNA, the email.

He and Tanner were not the ones doing all the misguided barking.

He quickly configured the mail options that would distribute the file to every major incident room in the country. That would see Kamal Azim's name scrawled on whiteboards, mentioned at every shift briefing and scribbled in the notebooks of thousands of uniformed officers nationwide.

'Stupid,' he said.

Kitson glanced up. 'What?'

If they wanted to find Kamal Azim, they'd be better off calling in cadaver dogs.

Thorne pressed *send* and closed the file; found himself looking instead at the pictures of the Amaya Shah crime scene he had been studying before. A shallow grave left waiting to be found. The clods of black earth, a tangle of twigs laid out to one side for examination.

Naked flesh, muddied and mottled.

Leaves in her hair.

He closed that file too and sat back. He could feel a headache coming, the first nagging stabs at the base of his skull. He said, 'You can have a *bottle* of wine if you take it back. Two bottles.'

'What?'

'The Shah case.'

Kitson looked across at him. 'I thought it was sorted,' she said. 'You've got a prime suspect, haven't you? Enough to put him away when he turns up. I wish the case *I* had was that easy.' Getting no more than a non-committal hum, she stared at him for a few seconds. She narrowed her eyes and teased at a strand of brown hair in her recently styled bob. 'Why do I get the feeling there's something you're not telling me?'

Thorne stood up and walked across to close the door that Kitson had left half-open.

Then he told her. From Susan Best's death to the fake email.

Kitson sat back and puffed out her cheeks. 'Well, you've got a fair few balls to juggle, no question about that, but I can't see that you're actually in trouble just yet. No more than usual, anyway. I mean, you haven't actually lied to Russell, have you?'

'Depends how you define lying.'

'There you go then. Put a few extra hours in, a couple of cans of Red Bull every day, I don't really see the problem.'

'You'd be rubbish on the Samaritans helpline,' Thorne said.

'Seriously. Look, you either catch this pair, in which case everyone's happy. Or you don't and you just bumble along like a good boy with the official line of enquiry.'

'It's not our line,' Thorne said. 'It's theirs.'

Kitson nodded. 'Your hired killers.'

'The one they want us to follow.'

'Either way you come out of it smelling all right.'

'You reckon?'

'You've certainly smelled a lot worse. It's a win-win, mate.'

'Not how it looks to me.'

'Well, you're not exactly the glass half full type, are you?' Kitson turned her attention back to whatever was on the screen in front of her. Prodding half-heartedly at the keys, she said, 'Let me know how it pans out, OK? Obviously I won't say anything and I'm happy to pitch in if you start dropping balls.'

'Thanks.'

Thorne knew that he could trust her. She had helped him out a good many times before; allowed herself to get dragged down into shit far deeper than this. He also knew that Yvonne Kitson was just about as cynical as anyone who'd done the Job a few years and was not prone to outbursts of unbridled optimism. She probably had a point, but it wasn't doing much for the sinking feeling, the headache that was gathering strength.

He guessed that the men who had already tried unsuccessfully to kill Nicola Tanner were not used to failure. He tried not to dwell on that too much, because even an idiot knew what the opposite of win-win was.

Brigstocke walked in without waiting for his sharp knock to be answered.

'I sent it,' Thorne said.

'Good.' Brigstocke stared at him, sighed. 'What are you wearing?'

Kitson grinned. 'It's bit early for dirty talk, isn't it?'

Thorne glanced down at his brown leather jacket and denim shirt. A letter or two of the Willie Nelson T-shirt he was wearing underneath, just visible.

'I'm sure you can find someone to lend you a suit for half an hour.' Brigstocke tugged at his own crisp white cuff. 'Almost everyone in the building seems to be wearing one, or maybe you hadn't noticed.'

173

'What for?'

'We've managed to get a slot on *London Tonight*. Another appeal for information as to the whereabouts of Kamal Azim.' Thorne tried to interrupt, but Brigstocke was already opening the door. 'It won't go out until half six, but you'll be shooting it this afternoon.'

'You serious?' Thorne was aware of Kitson smirking from the other side of the room. 'Russell—'

'Borrow a tie as well.'

THIRTY

It took Tanner a few minutes to spot Haroon Shah among the large crowd gathered just outside the main entrance. She lifted her phone and pointed, zoomed in and focused. A good many worshippers had headed to their cars immediately or begun walking away towards the road, keen to get home or back to work as quickly as possible. There were still several dozen milling around near the doors though, chatting, shaking hands.

Men on one side, women on the other.

Tanner watched, waiting eagerly to see just who Haroon Shah might fall into conversation with.

He moved through the crowd, exchanging words with several men of his own age, including those she had seen scrubbing graffiti from the walls near the door to the mosque. There were smiles and outbursts of laughter, an embrace or two, and, though Tanner could not swear to it, something in the body language suggested that Shah's friends were pleased to see him. Surprised. Moving on, he joined a more senior group, the majority dressed somewhat less casually than he was. It was hard to tell if it was purely down to age difference, but Shah's demeanour during

175

these formal-looking exchanges certainly seemed rather more reverential: hands clasped behind his back, head slightly bowed.

The respect his faith demanded for elders, perhaps, no more than that.

Tanner shot video on her phone, moved the camera around a little, but knew she was unlikely to be capturing anything of any real use.

Not yet, at least.

Skulking in the front seat of her car, needing a piss sometime very soon, Tanner knew that spying like some tabloid hack might well prove to be completely pointless. Perhaps Haroon Shah was here simply to praise his God. And if he *had* come for rather less ... holy reasons, the conversations he would need to have were unlikely to be quite so public.

Presuming he hadn't simply picked up a phone and had them already.

When it came to arranging the murders she had begun looking at months before with the Honour Crimes Unit, Tanner had quickly become convinced that, whatever the particular faith, there was always a middle man. Perhaps more than one. As she had explained to Thorne, it would probably begin with no more than a few pointed comments; a complaint about a young woman's unacceptable behaviour, concern about the attitude of a dissenting wife. If this became something more serious and punitive action was demanded, then someone would have a word with someone else, until eventually, once the gravity of the complainant's intention had been confirmed, the man who brokered such deals would make the necessary arrangements.

Would contact the men who carried out the killings.

Tanner wanted to catch those men, of course, the men who had taken Susan from her, but she wanted the broker most of all.

She wanted to save lives as well as avenge them.

She had briefly taken her eye from the gathering in front of the mosque, lost for a while in thoughts of her partner. The sight of her getting dressed that final morning, the smile as she had climbed into Tanner's car, the hall carpet. Stains like rusted wings and a scattering of white spots.

When she looked back, Haroon Shah had moved away from the older men and was talking to someone near one of the tables a few yards from the doors. The man appeared to be somewhere in age between Shah and the group he had been with a few minutes before: fortyish, maybe, and heavily bearded; a smart black jacket over a blue robe and a gold skullcap.

The two men leaned close together, spoke with their heads lowered.

Conspiratorial.

Almost certainly innocent, of course, but all the same Tanner forgot how badly she needed the toilet and stopped worrying about how stupid she would feel if the meeting she was watching turned out to be of no real significance.

Nobody could ever accuse her of being lazy, and sloppy was simply unthinkable, but as things stood, she could live with stupid.

She began to take more pictures.

THIRTY-ONE

In the end, once it was established that Thorne would only be filmed from the waist up, he had only needed to borrow a jacket, shirt and tie. He had swapped with one of the civilian staff who was broadly the same shape and size, though the man had drawn the line at wearing Thorne's somewhat sweaty T-shirt and had clearly never heard of Willie Nelson.

Thorne and a humourless woman from the Media Liaison team had driven down to Colindale. The front of the police station would be more appropriate than Becke House, she told him, and would provide a 'more suitable backdrop'.

Thorne knew what she meant. Becke House might have been almost any anonymous office building. Still, it seemed a little over the top.

'They'll know I'm a police officer though,' he had said, in the back of the car. 'You know, because I'll be talking about a murder.' He'd smiled at her. 'And there'll be a caption.'

The woman had not smiled back. 'It's better,' she'd said.

Thorne watched as the cameraman set up his tripod and an assistant positioned a folding reflector to utilise such sunlight as there was. The Media Liaison officer stood to one side with her phone pressed to her ear, while, sitting on a low wall, the reporter from *London Tonight* looked through her notes. Thorne could only admire her professionalism, or perhaps she was just new and still keen. He knew she was there simply to feed him a question or two that would never actually be used, because he would be talking straight to camera.

Making his appeal directly.

'Just be a few minutes,' the cameraman said. 'If you could just move six inches to your right.'

Thorne stood where he was told and waited.

Mentally rewrote the script he'd been given.

He had done such things many times before, but this would be the first time he had asked the viewing public for help with a case knowing that it would be superfluous at best and, at worst, lead to a drain on resources that had already been needlessly stretched. Another flock or two of wild geese to be chased when there were murderers, sexual predators and terrorists demanding as much of their attention as was possible. Friends and families of missing persons who might actually be found.

'You sure you don't just want a bit of make-up?' The young reporter stepped across and smiled. 'I've got stuff in my handbag.'

'I'm fine,' Thorne said.

'You look a bit pasty.'

He was running through his last few lines when his phone rang and, after announcing that he'd try not to keep anyone waiting too long, Thorne walked away towards the car and took the call.

He told Tanner that he didn't have very long and explained why.

'I just got a call from Sarah Webster,' Tanner said.

'How's she doing?'

'Not brilliantly. She was raped last night.'

'Oh, Christ.'

'She just left the hospital.'

'How bad?'

'A few cuts and bruises. Has to be Haroon Shah.'

'Does it?' Thorne looked back to see that the Media Liaison officer was staring at him. She turned to the reporter and held her hands up by way of apology. The reporter did the same to the cameraman.

'His mates, anyway.' Tanner paused for a few seconds. 'There were a few of them.'

'Have we got descriptions?'

'It was dark, they had hoodies on, you know how it goes. I've told the team that's on it to look at Haroon Shah before they do anything else. He's not stupid, he'll have an alibi, but I'm sure he'll have set it up right after I talked to him.'

'You told him about Sarah Webster?'

'I told him a friend of Amaya's had told us she was scared and he kept asking me who it was. He called her a bitch . . . he knew it was her.'

The wind was picking up. Thorne fastened his jacket and turned away from a gust. He said, 'Don't feel bad about it.'

'What?'

'It wasn't your fault.'

'Of course it wasn't,' Tanner said. Quick and even, stating the obvious.

Neither of them said anything for a few seconds. The reporter and the cameraman were sitting on the wall drinking tea that had been produced from somewhere and the Media Liaison officer was texting and glancing at her watch. She saw Thorne watching and mouthed at him. *How long?*

Thorne shook his head. Maybe when he and Tanner had finished, he would call Phil Hendricks for a leisurely chat, see how much he could piss the woman off.

'Shah went to the mosque,' Tanner said. 'There was a conversation that looked interesting.'

'You're following him?'

'What else do you suggest?'

'Well, be careful.'

'Why?'

Because the people we're after have tried to kill you once already. Because one of our witnesses has just been raped.

'OK, so don't be,' Thorne said.

'If you're so concerned, maybe you could come and give me a hand,' Tanner said. 'When you've finished wasting your time on TV.'

'I'm doing what I'm told.'

'Well, I was given a bum steer.'

'What's that mean?'

'Didn't think you were such a good boy, that's all.'

The Media Liaison officer was talking to the reporter. She turned and shouted across to let Thorne know that the crew needed to be somewhere else in half an hour.

'Listen …' Thorne signalled to say that he would be two minutes, fought the temptation to turn the two fingers around. 'Doing what I have to on the official side of this gives us a chance to do the other stuff without attracting too much attention. It's misdirection.'

'If you say so.'

Saying it, Thorne had almost convinced himself, though he wondered just how long misdirection was likely to fool an amateur magician like Russell Brigstocke. 'What are you going to do now?'

'I'm going home,' Tanner said. 'Need to tidy a bit.'

'Really?' Thorne could not imagine any house that needed tidying up less than the one he'd visited a fortnight before.

'My brother and his wife are coming over. I could do without it, to be honest. I know they're only being nice, but I'd much rather be on my own.'

'OK.'

'You?'

'Well, as soon as I get a chance I'm going to see if I can get any change out of your old friends at the Honour Crimes Unit.'

'That really *is* a waste of time,' Tanner said.

Thorne walked back and stood on his mark, the station sign and the symbolic blue lamp nice and *suitable* behind him. The cameraman and the reporter put down their teas and wandered over to take up their positions.

'Ready, then?' The Media Liaison woman moved close to him, her lipstick still perfect and her hands deep in the pockets of an expensive-looking coat.

'Like a coiled spring,' Thorne said.

'They're looking at about thirty seconds.'

'Understood.'

'Have you got it written down?'

Thorne tapped the side of his head. 'All up here.'

'Really?'

He looked at her. 'It's a quick appeal, all right? It's not the fucking Gettysburg address.'

The woman looked as though he'd slapped her.

'Whenever you like,' the cameraman said.

THIRTY-TWO

Mid-afternoon was the quietest time in the shop. Business would pick up again once the kids came out of school, and then they'd all need to be around and paying attention, if half the stock in the place wasn't going to go walkabout. This time of day it was just dribs and drabs; bread and milk, a few cans of White Ace or Tennent's Extra for the tramps who hung around by the post office. The lull gave everyone in the family a chance to take a breather. Haroon's mother could make a start on dinner or sit with a crossword and his father might take the opportunity to catch up on some paperwork upstairs. While the kid who helped out sat with a comic somewhere or went off to play with himself, Haroon would usually look after the till for an hour or so; happy enough to ring up what few purchases there were with plenty of time to call his mates or catch up on Twitter.

Haroon's father had already gone up and, a few minutes later, Haroon watched as his mother put down her pricing gun and started towards the back of the shop to follow him. He moved to intercept her. He asked if she would be OK looking after the checkout for twenty minutes, told her his stomach was playing up. She told him he was eating too many takeaways, that he should be eating decent food at home, and she was still shaking her head and muttering as she wandered back towards the till.

Haroon hurried upstairs and found his father dozing in front of the television. He touched him lightly on the shoulder.

'There's a problem,' he said. 'With Amaya.'

Faruk Shah opened his eyes. He blinked, then sat up fast. 'What problem?'

'The policewoman was here.'

'When?'

'Yesterday, but it's fine.'

Haroon's father grabbed the remote and turned off the television. He pressed his palm to the sofa cushion next to him and said, 'Sit.'

Haroon did as he was told. He turned, about to speak, and his father slapped him hard across the face.

'Why didn't you tell me the police had come back?'

Haroon rubbed at his face, blinking back tears and began talking quickly. 'She came to see *me*. Asking me about Amaya, why I went to the college, why she was absent so much, all that.'

'What did you say?'

'Nothing ... just something about picking her up, how she was ill a lot. I made out like I was angry, like it was insulting or whatever.'

His father nodded. 'Why didn't you tell me afterwards?'

'I didn't want you to be worried.'

Faruk Shah raised his hand again, clenched it into a fist, then let it fall into his lap. 'Worried? What is going on in your head? I thought that boy downstairs was the halfwit, not my son.'

'Look, I told you it's fine,' Haroon said. 'It was just questions, that's all.'

'Questions are not fine. If it was fine, they would be looking for that boy Azim instead of coming here. If it was fine, they would be sending flowers and making us tea.' Haroon opened his mouth but his father quickly shushed him and sat forward. 'Shut up. I need to think.'

They sat in silence for a minute or more. Haroon felt sick and his face was stinging. The room was even warmer than usual.

He said, 'I've sorted it.'

His father turned to look at him.

'Yeah ... I mean it's probably *not* fine, like you said, so I just thought we needed to do something, right? I thought—'

Haroon stopped and pressed himself back into the sofa. He had seen his father angry plenty of times, had grown up listening to the shouting from the next room. He and his sister, holding on to one another. He had seen him really lose it in the weeks before the Amaya business, but he couldn't remember a look on his father's face like this one. He could not remember hearing anything like this in his father's voice.

'It's my name.' Faruk slapped his hand to his chest, his fist. '*Mine*. My name you have and my name that your sister had. You understand?'

Haroon nodded.

'*I'm* the one who sorts things.'

'I'm sorry.'

'What did you do?'

Haroon took a deep breath and told him.

He knew that his mother had seen the mark on his face, but she had said nothing when she had slipped from behind the counter and walked slowly away.

He knew she had covered up worse things herself. He had seen her once at the dressing table; the compact open and powder speckled on her hijab, a sponge dabbed against the bruise.

She had his father's name too, after all.

For all the shouting and the 'I'm the daddy' stuff, Haroon thought that deep down his father was proud of what he'd done,

185

the initiative he'd shown. Or he would be in time, anyway. His father would probably follow it up, put his own stamp on things, but the son had been the one to step up and put the word out.

It would not go unnoticed, he knew that.

People would talk about it.

He quickly forgot the pain in his cheek and was unusually good-humoured and chatty as he rang up the booze and chocolate bars and scratch cards. As the shop became busier again.

When he wasn't serving, Haroon checked the messages from his friend then immediately deleted them. He hadn't told his father about what he'd lined up for Amaya's gobby college friend the night before, but he didn't think there was any need. That was something extra, just for him.

What would that tight-arsed policewoman have called it? A loose end.

He called it a lesson.

THIRTY-THREE

Thorne took the stairs to the third floor of Belgravia police station and showed his ID. After being given no more than cursory directions, he followed a grey-carpeted corridor past a computer-aided dispatch suite and a busy-looking incident room to an unmarked office door.

He knocked, remembering what Tanner had said at their first meeting.

I did some work with the Honour Crimes Unit. Such as it is.

After an hour on the phone and online back at Becke House, Thorne now understood exactly what she had meant, and he was keen to see it for himself.

DS Soran Hassani was the officer Thorne had spoken to on the phone, and he seemed happy enough to see him when he opened the door and invited him in. The office was a lot larger than it appeared from the outside, with four desks arranged in the middle and a large expanse of grey carpet everywhere else. The same ratio applied to the pair of whiteboards and the blank walls around them.

There was plenty of free space.

Young female officers were working at two of the desks and both of them smiled as Hassani led Thorne to a chair. He was offered coffee, then immediately told how bad it was, so he politely declined.

'No sign on the door,' he said.

Hassani looked at him.

Thorne pointed back over his shoulder. 'This is the Honour Crimes Unit, right?' He smiled at the man behind the desk, who was rubbing a palm across his shaved scalp. Hassani was shorter than Thorne and certainly filled out his smart blue suit. He wasn't one of the officers Thorne had worked with briefly on the Meena Athwal case four years earlier, but, knowing what he now did, Thorne was not altogether surprised. 'I just wanted to check.'

'You're in the right place,' Hassani said.

'That's a relief. Because Honour Crimes isn't actually a *unit* at all really, is it?' Thorne looked around, but both the female officers kept their eyes fixed on the paperwork in front of them. 'I mean not officially. It's basically just a bog-standard community safety unit attached to the Homicide and Serious Crime command, right?'

'Yes, and that's because we're looking at murders.' Hassani sat back. 'I mean, that's all they are at the end of the day. Murders same as any other. Religion's got nothing to do with it.'

'Spot on,' Thorne said. 'Couldn't agree more.'

'Good.'

'But still.'

'Still what?'

'You find a body in Epping Forest with smashed kneecaps and a bullet in the back of the head, chances are you might bring in Gangs and Organised Crime, right? You find one next to a suitcase full of iffy cheques and blank credit cards, you're going to at least liaise with the Economic Crime Unit. It makes sense, doesn't it? There are specialist teams.'

'Not with you,' Hassani said.

'There's no Honour Crimes Unit listed anywhere on any Met police website or mentioned in any media release. It's as if it doesn't officially exist. There's a Royal Protection Unit and a Marine Unit and a big, hairy Dog Support Unit. There are specialist units to investigate money laundering and wildlife crime and let's not forget good old arts and antiques theft. There's a *Film* Unit, for Christ's sake.' Thorne summoned a smile and tried to keep his tone nice and light, as if the whole thing were no more than vaguely ridiculous. 'I mean, seriously.'

Hassani smiled back, and said, 'I take your point.'

'Three thousand honour crimes reported every year.' Thorne had made very sure he was well armed with the facts and figures. 'Nearly one hundred and fifty people killed in the last ten and obviously I'm only talking here about the ones we know about . . . and you don't even get a sign on your door.'

'Like I said. Murders.'

'So, nothing at all to do with the issue being politically sensitive. Not wanting to offend certain sections of the community, that kind of thing.'

'What is it you wanted, Tom?'

Thorne was thinking about Meena Athwal and Amaya Shah, and at that moment he wanted to kick a door in at New Scotland Yard. He very much wanted to pull some useless arsehole with lots of pips on his shoulder across a desk and ask him what the hell he thought he was doing.

Instead, he started to tell Hassani what he and his new partner were doing and he saw the man's expression change as soon as he mentioned Tanner's name.

He stopped, waited.

Hassani leaned back and shook his head. 'Horrible what happened to her other half.' He nodded across and the two female officers looked up and made sympathetic noises, though Thorne could not be certain if they'd actually known Tanner or not. 'I thought she was still on compassionate leave.'

'She is,' Thorne said. 'This is something we're working on together in our spare time. Like a hobby.'

'OK. Better than trainspotting, I suppose.'

Thorne quickly told him the rest. The link between several victims whose murders had been categorised as sex crimes or random attacks. A series of honour-based killings carried out by the same men. When he had finished, he said, 'So, what do you think?'

Hassani took a few moments. 'Yeah, Nicola was working on that theory when she was here,' he said. 'Bit of a project of hers.'

'And not one you took very seriously.'

The DS leaned towards him. 'There's been *one* case in this country where it's been proved that a family used what were essentially hitmen to kill their daughter. One. A young woman named Banaz Mahmod, back in 2006. They ended up putting seven men away for that. The two men who killed her along with various members of her family who'd helped dispose of the body.' He looked hard at Thorne. 'A Kurdish family. Like mine.' He sat back again. 'One case.'

'One that we know of. You know as well as I do that lots of this stuff doesn't get reported. Families close ranks; young women are taken abroad for one reason or another and never come back.'

'Of course, but I still think the idea that there's people who actually specialise in this is a bit far-fetched.'

'Would you think that if this was Pakistan?'

'Come again?'

Something else Thorne had come across when he was reading up on it. 'Over there, the family of the victim can choose to forgive the killer or killers and they get off scot-free. They get away with it. So you can pay someone to kill your wife or son or daughter, and if they're caught you just "forgive" them and they get to walk away, presumably with the money you paid them to do the job in the first place.'

190

'This isn't Pakistan.'

'No, because we're not going to let them get away with it.'

'But you're talking about Muslims, Sikhs, Hindus.'

'That's the point.' Thorne stabbed a finger on to Hassani's desktop. 'It doesn't matter to them. As long as they get their money and whoever's organising it all gets their cut, these people don't discriminate.'

'No.' Hassani rubbed at his scalp again. The stubble sounded against his palm. 'I'm sorry.'

'What for?'

'Sorry ... because I just don't see it. Of course the things you're talking about happen, it's why we're here, isn't it? But not like this.'

'What about Meena Athwal? What about Amaya Shah and Kamal Azim?'

'Well, I think I'm right in saying the Meena Athwal case isn't one that's still open. And it looks very much like Amaya Shah was murdered *by* Kamal Azim.'

'You're right,' Thorne said. 'It looks very much like it.'

They stared at each other for a few seconds.

'What exactly did you come here for?'

Thorne shrugged. He already had one eye on the door. 'Asking myself the same question. I thought you might be able to offer something in the way of support, but ... '

'But I obviously don't give a shit. Right?'

'I think you could do more,' Thorne said. 'I think you could do *something*.'

Hassani's expression hardened. 'I think what you and Tanner are up to is daft, I'm not pretending I don't, but if you think I don't care about the job we're trying to do here, you're even more stupid than I thought.'

'So, prove it.'

'I don't have to prove it.' He pointed over Thorne's head towards the whiteboards, the photos pinned up. 'Those are young

191

men and women who've been assaulted, kidnapped, raped. Murdered. I didn't just cut the pictures out of a magazine, all right?'

'I know that.'

'We're working closely with the groups that are campaigning against this stuff every single day, supporting the victims.' He nodded towards the whiteboards again and Thorne turned to see a number of flyers and posters, recognised the names of the organisations Tanner had mentioned to him. 'We're working with families in all these communities who are violently opposed to HBV. That's the majority by the way, the *vast* majority.'

Thorne nodded, as if he were impressed. He said, 'Well, seeing as you care so much, as this is all so important to you, I don't have to worry about you running to my boss and telling him what I'm up to, do I? Telling him about Tanner.'

Hassani held up his hands. 'Why would I do that?'

On his way out, Thorne stopped at the door and turned back to DS Soran Hassani and his two colleagues. 'Sorry for taking up so much of your time,' he said. He pointed back into the room. 'You know, you should seriously think about putting a pool table in here.'

THIRTY-FOUR

The appeal was due to air in a few minutes, but Helen had already decided that Alfie would have to go to bed before it was shown. Excited as he would obviously have been to see 'Tom' on the TV, Thorne would be saying words that Helen wasn't overly keen for her son to hear. Thorne was a little disappointed, but hadn't bothered to argue. Just words, yes, but Alfie had already demonstrated a knack for parroting them and it wouldn't go down awfully well if he started jabbering about rape and murder at nursery the next day.

Besides, Alfie was excited enough as it was, because Uncle Phil was here.

From the sofa, Thorne watched the two of them kneeling on the carpet, surrounded by toys, laughing their heads off. They had painstakingly assembled a complicated Thomas the Tank Engine playset, with ramps, tunnels and a bridge that would shake if they pressed a button. Predictably, Alfie had been pressing the button as often as possible, but now decided to mix things up by adding a new character to the action.

'You can't do that,' Hendricks said.

'Yes, I can.'

'You can't put Spiderman on Thomas's island.'

'Why not?'

Hendricks widened his eyes in mock outrage. 'Because it's stupid.'

'*You're* stupid.'

'You put Spiderman on there and he's going to get run over by Old Wheezy for a start.'

Alfie grinned and waved the action figure in Hendricks's face. 'You're stupid.'

Helen was putting potatoes into the oven to bake for later on. 'Don't call people stupid, it's not nice.'

'He's got a point,' Thorne said.

Hendricks held up a hand. 'Don't worry about me, I can handle this.' He raised himself up on his knees. 'I've dealt with all manner of little herberts a lot scarier than this one.' He narrowed his eyes, glared at the boy. 'Think you're a hard case?'

'Yeah.' Alfie narrowed his eyes too and stood up.

'Reckon you and Spiderman can take me, do you?'

Almost before he had finished, Alfie was laughing and rushing across the few feet of carpet between them. Hendricks roared and pulled the boy to him, began the squeeze-and-tickle manoeuvre that always reduced Alfie to hysterics. 'You're no match for me,' he shouted. 'You're weak and feeble.'

'You're bald,' Alfie shouted back, struggling.

'How dare you!'

'Bald! Spiky face.'

Helen was walking across. 'All right, that's enough ... you need to say goodnight to Tom and Uncle Phil.'

Hendricks let Alfie go, but the boy was content to stay nestled close to him for a few seconds. He reached up and gently touched a finger to the pointed stud protruding from Hendricks's bottom lip. He moved the finger away quickly, then put it back again. 'Spiky ...'

Thorne watched his friend's face as Helen picked Alfie up and carried him away to bed. His expression when the boy waved to him.

Hendricks was always joking about how great it was to come round and get Alfie worked up, let Thorne and Helen deal with the fallout. All the fun of having a kid, he said, but without the responsibility. Almost convincing, but Thorne knew how much Hendricks wanted a child of his own.

A few years before, he had confessed it. A drunken conversation during which he had told Thorne about his trip to some conference or other; a tour around cutting-edge mortuary facilities for children, each suite designed to resemble a child's bedroom. While those around him had been busy taking notes about temperature regulation and set-up costs, Hendricks had stood there, he had told Thorne, and seen a child on the bed.

The child I'd imagined on that bed wasn't anonymous, he wasn't a body I'd worked on. He was mine. *I'd bought him those pyjamas with rockets and stars on. I was the one who was going to have to bury him. I suddenly knew how much ... I could suddenly admit how much I wanted a child. Because I knew how terrible it would feel to lose one.*

Tears after that, while Thorne could only sit feeling awkward and helpless.

Now, it looked as though Hendricks was finally with someone who felt as he did. He and his partner Liam had discussed adoption, though the conversations between Thorne and Hendricks had thus far been no more than lighthearted; Thorne suggesting that Hendricks might need to modify his appearance a little, if he didn't want to frighten the horses.

'Unless you want to go to the interview inside a giant sack,' Thorne had said.

He knew that if it came to it, Hendricks would happily wear beige slacks and a sports jacket. He would have every tattoo removed by laser and take every piece of metal from his body in a heartbeat.

Hendricks trudged across and dropped down next to Thorne on the sofa.

'I'm knackered.'

'Still think you want one of your own?' Thorne asked.

Hendricks looked at him. 'Do you?'

They watched TV in silence for a few minutes: the mayor pressing flesh at a bus depot; another cyclist killed at a notorious black spot. Then the studio presenter cut to the reporter Thorne had met earlier in the day. She made a few introductory remarks and Thorne was on.

Hendricks laughed at the caption. 'Thomas?' He said it again, shouting the name like the maid in the Tom and Jerry cartoons.

'Hilarious,' Thorne said.

'Bloody hell, where did you get that jacket?'

'Shut your face.'

'*We are urgently appealing today for any information regarding the whereabouts of Kamal Azim. Kamal is twenty-one and from Whetstone. He was last seen just over a fortnight ago on September the fourth, getting off a Northern line train at Woodside Park . . .*'

They showed the CCTV still of Kamal and Amaya leaving the station, then cut to a photograph of Kamal. He was smiling, though he looked a little embarrassed, wearing one of the T-shirts from his father's printing business.

'*We're seeking this individual in connection with the rape and murder of Amaya Shah on September the fourth, so I must stress again how urgently we need to find him. If anyone has seen Kamal Azim or even thinks they've seen him, please contact the incident room at Colindale station and they will pass the information on.*'

A phone number appeared at the bottom of the screen as the reporter wrapped the piece up.

'How was it?' Thorne asked.

'You looked gorgeous, obviously.'

'How convincing was I?'

Hendricks thought about it. 'I reckon it was somewhere between Dick Van Dyke's cockney accent and Keanu Reeves in *Dracula*.'

Helen came back in as Thorne's phone began to ring. He knew who was calling before he saw Tanner's name on the screen.

'How did it go with the Honour Crimes lot?'

'I can see what you meant, put it that way. Did you see the appeal?'

'Yes.' Tanner said it as though she had been asked whether she'd watched *Saw* or *Debbie Does Dallas*. 'Very good.'

Thorne watched as Helen came across. She sat on the floor in front of the sofa, picked up the remote and began rewinding the programme back to the start of Thorne's segment.

'It had to be done,' Thorne said.

'I know. Misdirection.'

'Right.'

'So, now you've done it, how do you fancy coming with me to the AHCA meeting tonight?'

'There's one tonight?'

'There's one every week,' Tanner said. 'There was another attack outside a mosque a couple of days ago. They need to talk about a response ... and maybe one or two people have other things to talk about.'

'Maybe.'

'So, what do you think?'

Thorne hesitated, and Tanner's shrug was almost audible.

'Fine,' she said. 'It's probably better if I go on my own anyway. More discreet, less attention, whatever.'

'You think Haroon Shah will be there?'

'No idea who's going to be there, but there's only one way to find out.'

197

'Let me know how you get on,' Thorne said.

'If you're sure.'

'For God's sake, I'm working my arse off.' Thorne saw Helen and Hendricks react, shook his head. 'I'm working both sides of this thing, remember?' He took a breath or two. 'Of course I want to know.'

'OK,' Tanner said.

They watched the appeal again, for Helen's benefit. Thorne felt even more self-conscious seeing it second time round: his head held at a strange angle; the grey hair and the fact there was more on one side than the other; the straight scar across the bottom of his chin.

One of his chins.

'Very good,' Helen said. 'Not sure about the jacket, mind you. Or the tie.'

Hendricks snorted.

'Don't you start.'

'I think I was right not to let Alfie see it, though.'

Thorne kicked at Hendricks's leg. 'He doesn't think I was very convincing.'

Hendricks grinned and started channel-surfing.

'What did Tanner have to say?'

'That I'm not pulling my weight.'

'She said that?'

'No, but that's what she thinks.' He nodded towards the television. 'I mean, yeah, all that's a complete waste of time, but I'm not convinced *we've* got a whole lot either. Two blokes on a tube train and a couple of relatives we *might* have put the wind up a bit ...'

When Thorne stopped talking, they could hear Alfie crying from his bedroom. Helen swore and got to her feet. She said, 'I think I rushed his lordship's story.'

'I've changed my mind,' Hendricks said. 'More convincing than Keanu Reeves. Just.'

'Oh, cheers.'

'But he's far hotter, obviously.' Hendricks flicked through the channels. 'With less grey hair.'

Thorne let his head fall back and closed his eyes. He said, 'I turned down a room full of people shouting about hate crimes for this.'

THIRTY-FIVE

Riaz turned off the small TV that was mounted on the wall and tossed the remote on to the bed. He smiled, remembering the conversation with the Eastern European girl at the reception desk when they'd checked in. She had given them both forms, which they had filled in with false names and addresses, handed over the room keys, then reached under the counter for their TV remotes.

Riaz had laughed. 'People steal these?'

'Oh yes,' the girl had said. 'Sorry about that. You would not think it would you, but they do. People steal all sorts.'

'No problem.' He laughed again and studied the remote. There was grime around the buttons and the batteries were held in place with gaffer tape. 'You can never really be sure who you've got staying, can you?'

The girl had already lost interest, one eye on her phone. 'Anything else I can do for yourself?'

Muldoon leaned across. 'Are there dressing gowns in the rooms?'

He had carried on moaning all the way upstairs, demanding

to know why they always had to stay in fleapits. Riaz had quietly pointed out that the hotel was one notch above the places where the remote was attached to the headboard by a curly wire. It seemed clean and was handy for the job they were doing, besides which, as always, it would not be for long.

Riaz looked around. The majority of his clothes had stayed in the case, as usual, but his jacket was hung up in the narrow wardrobe and his toiletries had been neatly arranged in the bathroom. The room was clean enough, and that was important to him. He liked to bathe as often as possible, three times a day if circumstances allowed it. A bath whenever he had the chance, showers otherwise.

There were wet-wipes in the car, if it came to it.

He needed to be clean when he prayed, of course, but he also believed that it was important when the job itself was carried out. A simple matter of respect, that was all; for himself and, in those final moments, for the man or woman he was dispatching.

Muldoon, of course, had made some feeble joke when he had endeavoured to explain it to him. Something about a 'clean kill'. It was no real surprise that the Irishman had failed to understand, and these days Riaz tried to keep their conversations – beyond those that were strictly necessary – to a minimum.

Difficult, of course, when they spent so much time sitting together in cars, as they had done today. But even if Riaz had felt inclined to engage with his partner, finding any subject that might generate more than a word or two was next to impossible.

Muldoon enjoyed drinking and Riaz did not. Muldoon followed football and horses while Riaz had no interest in any sport aside from cricket. He was even less interested in the filth of tabloid newspapers or films about superheroes.

Once, letting his temper get the better of him, Riaz had

said, 'If this were a marriage, I would be looking for a divorce.'

Muldoon had laughed. 'Divorce? Not me, mate, I'm a good Catholic boy. I'd just be shagging around on you.'

Then, of course, there were the differences when it came to the matter of the killings themselves.

Riaz took his shoes off, set them down next to one another on the floor, then lay back on the bed.

It had been a productive day. Muldoon would not have thought so, but then he always grew edgy and impatient during the preparations. He was no better than a bull in a china shop and did not fully appreciate the importance of waiting and watching; of knowing as much as possible about your victim's routines and habits.

It would be especially important with this one.

He smiled; the blank television screen a reminder of just how important planning and preparation could be. Was this latest police appeal not a perfect example of what it could achieve? What they had done with the young couple had been distasteful, yes, but it had led the authorities where it needed to. The email he had sent from an internet café in Brighton had worked perfectly, too; cemented the assumptions.

The money had gone into an untraceable account the previous day, so now they could consider that job done. They could get on with this new one.

He wondered if Muldoon had seen the appeal.

Almost certainly not. He would be down in the bar already, or watching dirty movies in his room. Riaz doubted that his partner would care either way. He did not seem to care about a great deal, as long as there was money in his pocket and young women to brutalise.

A good team. The Irishman was always saying that, but Riaz was no longer so sure.

Perhaps it was time to start thinking about that divorce again.

*

They were talking about one of the local football teams, but Faruk Shah had stopped watching as soon as the policeman disappeared from the screen. He turned the television off and finished his tea. He needed to get back down to the shop anyway and it was good that he could work now without sweating and struggling for breath, that he would finish the day in a much better mood than he had started it.

What on earth had Haroon been thinking?

There was no problem, of course there wasn't. There never had been. Whatever that policewoman had come to see his stupid son about, everything was fine and would continue to be fine and the appeal on the television proved it.

They could forget Amaya and what she had made them do. They were still a family. They could go about their business.

Haroon had been panicking when, above all, he should have been remaining calm. He had talked to people who should not have been bothered with this nonsense and it had all been so unnecessary.

A boy who thought he was a man and had behaved like an old woman.

Faruk wanted to slap his son again.

Govinder Athwal had followed the story in the newspapers of course. People had been talking about it at work and in shops. A man he had overheard in the bar.

He had wondered then, as he always did when such things happened.

Now, he had seen Tom Thorne talking about the search for this boy and the murder of the young girl, and Govinder could not help thinking that this was what Thorne had been hinting at when he had come to see him the day before. The new information that he said might help him catch Meena's killer.

Alone in his room, Govinder had watched and begun to tremble; to speak things out loud that had, until now, been no more than whispers from the bottom of a glass or the noises in a bad dream.

He sat, frozen, until he could not bear to listen to himself any more.

He stood and rushed to collect his beads and his book, then hurried from the room to wash.

In a room several miles to the north of the hotel in which Riaz and Muldoon were staying, a man they knew but had never met had also just watched the television appeal.

He was thinking.

He had seen many such appeals in the past; by the police, by stricken families, and often he had watched as an interested observer, because he knew the precise whereabouts of the missing person. Because the service he had provided to those very same families was the reason they were missing in the first place.

The words were always more or less the same, but there had been something about this one that had bothered him. The police officer had seemed a little nervous and he found it hard to believe that it was simply down to the fact that he was appearing in front of the camera. Didn't they do this sort of TV appearance all the time? Weren't there training courses, that kind of thing?

No, not nervous exactly. Unconvincing.

It might have been that the officer was trying to put across the urgency of the situation, but it smacked a little of trying too hard. It looked as though he was giving a performance, and that in itself was worrying.

In theory, the fact that the police were making the appeal meant that they did not think the murder of Amaya Shah was anything it did not appear to be. Yet he had watched the police officer trotting out those familiar words and had felt uneasy.

He had met Detective Inspector Tom Thorne and he knew that the man was far from stupid.

He would need to be watchful.

THIRTY-SIX

Tanner had called her brother as soon as she'd got home; told him she wasn't feeling well and that there was no point in him coming round. He said that his wife had made some soup and that it was no problem to pop over with it.

'I think I'll just get an early night,' she had said.

From the Facebook group set up by the Anti Hate Crimes Alliance, Tanner had found out that the next meeting was taking place that evening at the Sikh temple on Harley Grove, in Bow. A few more minutes online and she discovered that there had been a gurdwara on the site since the late seventies, that it had once been a synagogue and that it had been extensively rebuilt after an arson attack in 2009.

It was a beautiful building. Grade II listed; she had found that out as well.

Approaching the entrance with several others, she could see that there were even more amateur bouncers outside than there had been at the meeting a week before. It made sense. There had been another attack after all, and if she could find out where the

205

meeting was being held, then so could those who might want to come along and cause trouble.

This time, Tanner just produced her warrant card, and a smile that was met with a series of blank stares.

She was already looking for a face that might be significant.

Inside, she followed the crowd past the main hall to a room at the back of the building. Having seen some of the notices, she guessed that this was where community groups would gather to play music, dance or take lessons in *gatka*, which, from the pictures, appeared to be some form of combat involving wooden sticks. Rows of chairs that might normally have been used for weddings had been arranged in rows on the crimson carpet and most were already taken. With five minutes before the meeting was due to start, most of those in attendance were engaged in conversation, standing between rows or grouped around the edges.

As before, the religious divides were obvious enough.

While discreetly checking the photos she had taken that morning on her phone, Tanner scanned as many faces as she could see. Though there were several she recognised from the previous meeting, she saw nobody to get excited about; nobody as yet whose presence might justify hers. When anyone turned to look directly at her, she let her gaze drift innocently up to one of the many colourful pictures that decorated the sky-blue walls. They were clearly sacred portraits, but Tanner was not sure who the men in the pictures were supposed to be. Were they gurus? Or saints?

Did Sikhs even *have* saints?

Some were of smiling older men with white beards and beatific smiles, while the younger men in the pictures looked like dashing heroes straight out of Bollywood. They had flashing eyes and coal-black beards. They wore heavily bejewelled turbans and their delicate hands carried curved daggers or provided perches for fierce-looking birds of prey.

Holy *and* hot, Tanner thought. If you liked that sort of thing.

Looking around, the crowd seemed bigger than at the last meeting, though the room was smaller, so it was difficult to be sure. There was no stage, only a trestle table at the front of the room, but there was certainly as much food as there had been at the school. In front of two tables in one corner, each laden with cling film-covered trays, three women in saris stood handing out paper cups of fruit juice poured from cartons.

Tanner's mouth was dry, so she walked up to take one. The woman clasped her hands together and bowed her head.

Tanner said, 'Thank you,' and bowed hers.

When one of the men she had seen at the door stepped to the front and announced that the meeting was about to start, those not already seated moved quickly to take empty chairs. Tanner did the same, which was when she saw the man to whom Haroon Shah had been talking privately at the mosque that morning.

Tanner double-checked her phone as she took a seat at the end of the back row. It gave her a good view of proceedings and more importantly of the man whose picture she had taken at the mosque.

The man in the gold skullcap.

The same three men as last time made their way to the front and took the seats behind the trestle table. Bannerjee, the Hindu businessman, Mansoor the imam and the Sikh community leader, Dhillon, who took the seat in the middle and spoke first. He was wearing a turban rather less ornate than those in some of the portraits and he spoke calmly and quietly. There were no microphones and one or two at the back began shouting for him to speak up, which was probably why he handed over to the imam so quickly.

The man in the gold skullcap applauded politely.

Mansoor was a little more demonstrative. He talked about the desecration of a mosque in south London a few days earlier; was resolute in his determination to oppose the cowardly attacks on all their communities, but urged restraint.

Bannerjee was the final speaker. He was immaculate in a well-cut, black collarless jacket and, as before, was by far the most charismatic of the three. 'I echo the imam's comments,' he said. 'If we resort to violence, then we lower ourselves to the level of the animals that are committing these crimes. There are other ways to fight.'

Tanner was keeping a watchful eye on the man a few rows in front of her, and it wasn't until the meeting was thrown open to the floor that she looked to her right and saw another face she recognised. Someone whose presence at the meeting was a little more worrying.

DS Soran Hassani.

There was a good deal of shouting from the audience, more than the previous week, but Tanner found it hard to concentrate on what was being argued about. She was doing her best to focus on the man Haroon Shah had spoken to, the man she believed he had been at the mosque to seek out, but her mind was racing.

Struggling to work out why Hassani was there.

As soon as the meeting broke up and people were on their feet, Tanner had to fight to keep an eye on the man with the gold skullcap. He was talking to those around him, but it looked to Tanner very much as if he was slowly making his way towards the trestle table at the front.

Towards Bannerjee and the others.

She thought about using the camera on her phone again, but decided that it might not be a good idea. As her quarry reached the table, she took a few steps towards the front herself, pushing through the crowd, at the same time trying to keep one eye on Hassani, who was chatting with a fellow Muslim in the queue for food.

It certainly looked as though the man in the gold skullcap was talking to Bannerjee, though Dhillon and several others were standing close by, perhaps in earshot, and Bannerjee had his usual support group around him: his son, Ravi, and some of his mates. The man moved away slightly and now he appeared to be saying something to the imam, Mansoor.

Tanner was craning her neck to see who was talking to who and was unaware of Bannerjee's approach until he was all but upon her.

'Don't you think this is getting a little ridiculous?'

'I told you I wasn't going anywhere,' Tanner said.

'When my son was advising me to complain about this, I warned him he was overreacting. I am starting to think he was right and that this is nothing short of harassment.'

On cue, Ravi Bannerjee appeared at his father's side.

'Why are you doing this?'

'Well, I'm not sure exactly what it is you think I'm doing,' Tanner said. 'But you certainly know why.'

'I know what you say you're doing.' The boy took a step closer. 'Hitmen and all that rubbish. But if you ask me, it's starting to look like something else.'

'What would that be?'

The boy grunted, shook his head. The beard he was trying to grow still looked unconvincing.

'You think I'm a racist, Ravi?' Tanner drank the last of her fruit juice. 'When I'm trying to catch men who are killing Hindus, Muslims and Sikhs? You seriously think that?' She stared at him. 'I can understand why people are getting worked up at these meetings, but the rest of the time you need to keep it in check, OK? It can upset people.'

Bannerjee senior laid a steadying hand on his son's shoulder. 'Yes, I think that's sound advice. It's never a good idea to throw such accusations around.'

'I didn't,' Ravi said.

Bannerjee looked at Tanner and shook his head. 'He's just a boy and he's only trying to stick up for me. Aren't you, Ravi?'

Ravi grunted again, looked at his feet.

'I might still have another word with your superiors, though.' Bannerjee wagged a finger at Tanner. 'You're making a nuisance of yourself.'

'Go ahead,' Tanner said. 'I'm on leave anyway, so I'm not sure anyone will really care.' She looked past him. 'Actually, the officer running the team in my absence is around somewhere, if you'd like a word now.'

Bannerjee seemed shocked and began looking around. There was no sign of Hassani.

'Probably saw whatever he needed to,' Tanner said. 'As did I, so I should probably be getting off.'

'What does that mean?' Bannerjee asked. 'What did you see?'

'I'll get out of your way.'

'Let's hope so,' Ravi said.

Bannerjee led his son away, but looked back more than once to watch Tanner heading for the door.

Hassani was leaning against his car on the other side of the road. He had his phone pressed to his ear, but put it away as Tanner crossed and walked towards him.

She said, 'Shouldn't one of us ask what the other one's doing here?'

Hassani smiled. 'Probably better if we don't.'

'In which case, I'm not sure we'll have much to talk about.'

'I'm sorry about your partner,' Hassani said. 'I never got a chance to tell you in person.'

'Thank you.'

'I hadn't realised it was a *she*.' He shifted awkwardly from one foot to the other. 'I mean, I didn't know you were ...'

'A rug-muncher?'

'A homosexual.'

Tanner tried not to laugh at the way he'd said it. 'That OK, is it?'

'Why wouldn't it be?'

Tanner turned back towards the temple, watched as those attending the meeting wandered out. 'Well, there's probably one or two in there who'd have a problem with it.'

'Not me.'

'Glad to hear it,' Tanner said. 'There's a fair number of us in the Job. Never really been sure why.'

'I've heard all the jokes.'

'Something about truncheons, was it?'

Hassani shook his head, disgusted, though it was not altogether clear why. He said, 'I saw your friend Tom Thorne today. He's a difficult customer.'

Tanner was pleased to hear it. 'Really?'

'It just seems stupid to be so . . . confrontational, when we are all on the same side.'

'Glad to hear that, too.'

'Having said that, I made my feelings about what the two of you are doing clear, I think. You already know what they are.'

'Oh yes. I also know that unless you've been promoted very recently I outrank you, but maybe you don't think that matters.'

Hassani nudged a shoe against the wheel of his car, ran his palm across his scalp. 'What matters is that others who are senior to both of us have already dismissed these theories of yours. No, not *dismissed*.'

'Chosen to ignore?'

They waited as a group of five or six men who had been at the meeting crossed the road on to the pavement a few feet away and walked towards a café. The heated debate looked as though it was continuing.

'Look, Nicola, you know how hard things are for us already. We're up against families closing ranks, whole communities if we're unlucky, and you and Thorne charging around is only going to make that worse. Talking about hired killers, all that nonsense . . . people are going to get angry. *More* angry.'

'I understand that,' Tanner said. 'And I'm sorry, but I don't much care.'

'That's a shame,' Hassani said.

It had begun to drizzle. Tanner took an umbrella from her bag as she walked away. She stopped and turned back to him.

She said, 'You shouldn't forget how angry *I* am.'

THIRTY-SEVEN

The girl hadn't enjoyed it very much – the look on her face when she'd left had made that pretty obvious – but Muldoon didn't care a great deal. She didn't have to like the things he'd done or made her do and he wasn't stupid enough to believe that any of them ever did. That wasn't part of their job, was it? The truth was, he rather liked the fact that she hadn't enjoyed it, got an even bigger kick out of the fact that she couldn't even be arsed to pretend.

She'd left with eighty quid in her purse, hadn't she? Forty more than the price advertised online. That could buy plenty of mouthwash and whatever that stuff was that got rid of bruises.

He walked into the bathroom, spread his legs at the sink and washed himself off. The girl had been keen to get away by the end, snatching up her clothes in a real hurry, and he wondered if she'd bother to clean herself up before the next punter. She might have called it a night, of course, and been heading straight home. All the same, it tickled him, thinking about some poor sod stumping up for sloppy seconds and licking Irish sweat off her.

Maybe she'd offer him a discount.

He walked back into the bedroom and flopped down on to the bed. He flicked through the shitty menu of TV channels and thought about Riaz a few rooms away. Mr Holier-Than-Thou, praying in his jim-jams like a good boy or already tucked up and dead to the world. Sleeping peacefully and dreaming sweet dreams, where animals didn't get eaten and girls did what they were told.

What had tonight's girl said to him? She'd been all smiles at the start, of course.

'You here on business, then?'

'Yeah.' He'd been sitting on the edge of the bed, watching her strip and stroking himself to attention. 'Supposed to have been a quick job, but it's dragged out a bit.'

'All good though, darling. More money, yeah?'

That was when he'd asked if *she'd* be interested in a bit of a bonus. Talked about a few of the things she might be willing to do for a couple of extra twenties.

He found some football highlights, but it was hard to concentrate. He was thinking about the girl and still thinking about Riaz. The things his partner had said about him enjoying the job too much.

It still rankled.

He thought about those teenagers, the ones they'd taken off the train.

They had both been crying, of course, the girl and her queer BFF, and in the end he'd had to *arrange* them. Heave the boy on top of her like he was a sack of spuds and use the edge of his knife once or twice to get the little poof's arse pumping. So then he'd had to watch, hadn't he? He'd had to make sure it was done properly, and it wasn't like Riaz wasn't getting an eyeful as well.

It was different, that was for sure. On other jobs he'd had to do the business himself, make it look like whatever girl it was had been killed by some random rapist, but this was a set-up they

214

hadn't tried before, what with there being two of them to get rid of.

So, had he enjoyed it? Had he ... whatever the word was ... revelled in it?

Listening to the boy blubbing and saying 'Sorry' over and over. And the girl underneath him with her eyes screwed shut, telling him it was OK and shushing and stroking his back. Wiping the blood away while he wept into her shoulder.

Had he?

It was seriously cold, he could remember that much. Like a freezer in that bloody warehouse, it wasn't like that lad could have got it up, even if he'd been that way inclined. His little cock all shrivelled up to nothing.

So, fine. He'd watched and listened to it all, and so what if it hadn't been the worst thing he could have been doing at that moment. So what if his own little cock had perked up a bit? At the end of the day, he'd been thinking about the money, hadn't he? Same as Riaz, however much his partner banged on about these things 'needing' to be done.

Goats and pigs and all that shite.

Always the money.

End of the day, very few people enjoyed what they did at all. Not people slaving in offices, or cleaning cars, and certainly not working girls. He was one of the lucky ones, so no way was he going to accept the suggestion that enjoying what he did meant there was anything wrong with the way he did it. He wasn't going to feel guilty about that, either. It was a perk, so why shouldn't he grab it with both hands? Bankers had bonuses, didn't they?

This next job might not be quite so much fun, though. All a bit round-the-houses for his liking. Nothing to see at the end of it, which was a shame because that was the part he enjoyed the most. The looks on faces those last few moments, the noises they made. So, there wouldn't be any of that with this one, but like the girl said, it was extra cash, so he wasn't going to complain.

He'd do what he was told and let Riaz get all creative about it.

Normally it was up to them, how they did things. Once in a while a job came with special instructions – 'make sure she doesn't suffer', or now and again, 'make sure she *does*' – but most of the time they were free to improvise and that was always the bit Muldoon liked best.

Mixing things up a bit.

He reached behind him and undid the buckle that had fastened his belt to the batten at the base of the headboard. The girl hadn't been mad keen about all that, either, had squeaked a bit when he'd tied it around her wrist. Fair enough, Muldoon had thought. Not everyone wanted to improvise.

Witch hazel. That was what it was called, the stuff for bruises.

The nurse had it in the cupboard at school and his grandmother was always dabbing it on him. He could still remember the bloody awful stink . . .

As West Ham and Sunderland ground out a tedious draw, he lay back and thought about the old woman who'd died almost ten years before, who he'd spent so much time with growing up. Three husbands she'd had, and there'd been a fair few adventures before any of them. She'd happily tell him all about the stuff she used to get up to, the men she'd been with; cackling and chain-smoking Players and giving him little nips of Bushmills.

They were great stories, no more than that.

There might have been a few whispers around the town back then, some graffiti on a toilet wall, but that was the only price his grandmother ever paid for having fun and she didn't much care one way or the other. Her good, God-fearing parents might not have liked it, but that was as far as it went.

They hadn't sent men to kill her, had they?

There was no shortage of good reasons for killing someone, he knew that better than most. Money, obviously, which was why he was doing it. Sex, revenge, the usual stuff.

216

Plenty of good reasons, but this ... nonsense wasn't one of them.

Still, he was making a living, wasn't he? Muldoon smiled, remembering the look on the face of the girl who'd just left, who was probably dropping her knickers for someone else already and thinking much the same thing.

Now he came to think about it, they had a fair old bit in common.

Difference was, his job paid a lot more and he was the one doing the hurting.

THIRTY-EIGHT

Neither of them, had they been inclined to talk honestly about it, would have claimed it was the best sex they had ever had, but both would have said they had enjoyed it. They were tired, that was all, and nobody had been in the mood for gymnastics or looking to break any records. While managing to avoid waking Alfie, who was asleep in the next room, both of them had got what they needed.

It had done the trick.

Thorne lay staring at a crack across the ceiling rose while, next to him, Helen re-read a page of the novel she had been struggling with for at least a month. Some paperback thriller Thorne had seen people reading on the Tube.

'Are you actually enjoying that?' he asked.

'Not really.' Helen turned the page, turned it back again. 'I can't get into it.'

'What you reading it for, then?'

'It's not going to beat me.'

Thorne laughed. 'I thought reading was supposed to be fun. Why don't you just wait for the film to come out?'

'It's probably really good,' Helen said. She held the book in front of her as though she'd never seen it before.

'Yeah, sounds riveting.'

'I can't concentrate when I'm this knackered, that's all. I read a few pages, then fall asleep and when I pick it up again I've forgotten what I've read.'

'Knock it on the head then,' Thorne said. 'Read a magazine or something.' Thorne had certainly given up on more books than he'd ever finished, but there were not a great many of either and it probably had more to do with attention span than high standards. Phil Hendricks, who devoured dark fantasy novels almost weekly, had told Thorne that perhaps he should try books with fewer long words in them. Or more pictures. 'There's some great books for kids around, you know. What about one of them pop-up ones?'

There was a cobweb dancing around the ceiling rose; a few strands, like an old lady's hair moving underwater.

'She's pissed off because apparently I'm not what she thought I was,' Thorne said. 'Tanner.' He turned towards Helen, but she carried on reading. '"Didn't think you were such a good boy", she said. Like I was letting her down. Because I wasn't charging around like an idiot or tearing up the rulebook or calling the DCI a twat.' He lifted his head, punched the pillow good and hard into a more comfortable shape. 'I don't know what she thinks I can do. What she's *expecting* me to do.'

Helen put her book down and took off her reading glasses. 'You think you should have gone with her tonight? To that meeting?'

Thorne said nothing. Shrugged. Then: 'It's like I told her, I'm working both ends of it. Doing that stupid appeal, wasting my breath with an Honour Crimes outfit that's as much use as tits on a fish and all I'm getting is grief. I've got Brigstocke on my back one minute and her having a pop at me the next and it isn't like I'm not on her side, is it?'

Helen smiled.

'What?'

'You sound like a whiny teenager.'

'Do I hell as like.'

'It's so *unfair.*'

'Oh, cheers.'

'Come on, nobody made you get into this, did they?'

'Phil said—'

'You'd have done it anyway,' Helen said, 'you know you would. You can't resist it.' She turned on her side to face him. 'If you ask me, what's really getting under your skin is the accusation that you're being a goody-two-shoes. I'm right, aren't I?'

Thorne said, 'You're such a smartarse,' but now he was smiling too.

'I mean, we all know that the truth is you're exactly what she wants you to be and you're just frustrated because you haven't had much of a chance to show her yet. Yeah, you've been playing fast and loose with Brigstocke a bit, being economical with the truth and whatever, but that's just an average day at the office for you, isn't it? Bending a few rules . . . you're not even trying, are you? Bending rules is for lightweights. You wouldn't be the you we all love if you didn't smash a few.' She left it a few seconds. 'I say *we*; obviously I'm just talking about me and Phil.'

Thorne moaned with the effort of moving closer to her. He rubbed his foot against hers. 'It's a bit bloody rich, that's all I'm saying. Because she's the one who isn't what it says she is on the tin. Little Miss Paperwork with her nice neat folders and her expenses forms. I'm betting she hasn't given Professional Standards too many sleepless nights.'

'Most of us don't,' Helen said, giving him a little kick.

'Now she's all "whatever it takes", you know? Tearing around and not giving a toss if what she's doing might be dangerous, for herself or anyone else. Not caring about whose toes she steps on. Not thinking.'

Helen thought, and said, 'Grief changes people.'

Thorne nodded, stubble rasping against the pillow. 'I suppose. Your priorities or whatever.'

'Everything.'

'Did it change you? After Paul?'

'Oh God, yes.' She thought for a few seconds, as though unsure how much to reveal. 'Obviously, it's like part of you dies, and that's horrible for a while, but it's weird, because what's left actually feels more alive. I suppose it's like you say and loads of things seem stupid and unimportant, but it's like you're in a hurry and you suddenly get greedier about stuff, you *want* it more. Basically, you're not the same person you were before. *I* certainly wasn't.' A smile began to form, then died quickly. 'Actually, I'm not sure you'd have liked me very much.'

'It feels wrong,' Thorne said. 'Having a dead person to thank. Obviously if Paul hadn't been killed, we wouldn't be here.'

Something tightened around Helen's eyes. She swallowed and said, 'I'm happy, *really*. You need to know that. But I want to be honest with you, and if I could go back and stop him being killed, I would. I'd do anything to have Paul alive again.' She laid a hand on Thorne's shoulder. 'This is great ... you and me and Alfie ... but I want you to understand that.'

'Course,' Thorne said.

Helen nodded. 'And Nicola's the same. You need to understand that, too. How she's acting ... it might not be who she really is, or who she was, but she can't stop herself. It's a part of her that's come to life.'

They lay together in silence for half a minute and then shifted apart, though it was impossible to say which of them moved first.

When they were still again, Thorne said, 'Why wouldn't I have liked you? Before?'

But Helen had already picked up her book again.

*

221

Haroon Shah liked being the one who locked up.

After emptying the tills, his mother and father had gone upstairs fifteen minutes earlier and he enjoyed this time last thing every night, when he would walk the length of the shop checking that all was in order. Turning out lights, his father's bunch of keys heavy in his hand.

He liked the responsibility, the feeling of being in charge. At the same time, as he moved up and down the aisles, he liked to imagine that he was the one taking the money upstairs, with a wife to make him tea and a son downstairs doing the locking up. Checking that everything he'd worked for was safe and secure. Not this place, obviously. Somewhere bigger, one of many, and a lot more money to bank at the end of the week.

Two sons, maybe three.

Each one as strong, as ready to step up and be a man, as he had been.

He turned the key to lower the metal shutters on the shopfront and it was only when the clang and clatter had finished that he heard his phone ringing.

The number was withheld.

The voice was not one that Haroon recognised. The man on the other end did not bother to introduce himself, did not even say hello. He just waited for Haroon to answer and said, 'Listen, that problem you have, the one you've been talking about. It's already being taken care of.'

THIRTY-NINE

The call had come in late the night before. A woman, convinced she knew the two men from the footage shot on the underground; the picture that had been in the papers a few days earlier. With the hunt for Kamal Azim now top priority, nobody had been awfully excited, but Thorne had quickly volunteered to follow it up.

A break that he and Tanner could certainly do with.

'Probably nothing,' he had said, already on his way out of the office, taking no notice of the knowing smirk from Yvonne Kitson. 'Can't be seen to be ignoring the public though, can we? We have been asking for their help, after all.'

Now, he and Tanner were driving towards Earl's Court. Though Tanner had been pleased about this new information – if indeed there proved to be any – she clearly had other things on her mind.

'What the hell was he doing there?' She had told Thorne about Hassani being at the meeting the previous evening as soon as he had called.

'A concerned citizen?'

'Come on.'

'Maybe someone at the meeting has a connection with a case

he's working.' He looked across and saw that Tanner was every bit as unconvinced by the suggestion as he was himself. 'I don't know. Maybe he was just curious.'

Tanner stared out of the window at the houses and office blocks that bordered the A4, the multicoloured blur of warehouses and megastores. 'He wasn't there by accident,' she said. 'He went because I did.' She looked at Thorne. 'So I'd love to know how he knew I'd be there.'

'Unless he was just as surprised to see you. He might be sitting in his office right now trying to figure out how *you* knew *he'd* be there.'

Tanner thought about that, then shook her head; dismissed it. 'He told me he'd seen you. Said you were difficult. A "difficult customer".'

'Pleased to hear it.'

'So was I.'

Thorne glanced across. 'A bit closer to what you were expecting, right?'

'What I need,' Tanner said.

They didn't say much else until Thorne had turned off the Cromwell Road and pulled up on a side street opposite the old exhibition centre.

Tanner nodded towards the CD player. There had been music in the background ever since Thorne had picked her up. 'What is that, anyway?'

'It's country,' Thorne said. 'Well, sort of. Sturgill Simpson.'

Tanner grunted. 'Susan liked country.'

'Did she?'

'I think that's what it was anyway. Taylor Swift?'

Thorne tried to hide his reaction as he turned the engine off. 'What do you like?'

Tanner undid her seatbelt. 'Nothing, really. It's all just background noise, isn't it?'

*

The Palm Court hotel was one of several similar establishments in the street. Guest houses with ideas above their station, they had probably done regular business before the exhibition centre, which was currently being demolished, had been sold off. These days, the Palm Court and places like it were probably grateful for customers of any sort, but were clearly not getting enough to maintain themselves. Losing what few AA stars they might have had hand over fist.

In unexpected September sunshine, Thorne and Tanner stood and stared at the cracked and flaking sign outside. A picture of a palm tree above the room rate and a smaller sign that showed VACANCIES. The word might just as well have been painted on permanently.

'Forty quid a night,' Thorne said. 'Can't argue with that sort of value.'

Tanner was already climbing the steps to the glass doors. 'It'll cost you more than that in antibiotics afterwards.'

Thorne wondered if Noreen Shepherd would have made quite so much effort had she not been expecting them. The manager of the hotel, who was somewhere in her early sixties, was dressed up to the nines in a print dress and pink silk jacket with boot-black hair that was stiffly lacquered and full make-up. It might well have been the kind of thing she wore every day, he decided. Perhaps she took such pride in her own appearance that there was none left for the place she ran. He remembered walking into a front room a few years before to find an elderly man sitting there in a collar and tie, his shoes like mirrors, seemingly oblivious to the movement of insects in his carpet and the moonscape of dog-shit in one corner.

Shepherd showed Thorne and Tanner into a small office behind the reception desk.

'There's been a spot of thieving, you see.' She sat down at a small desk and began slowly tapping at a computer keypad. 'That's why I was looking.'

'It happens,' Thorne said. 'I blame the price of towels.'

The woman looked at him. 'No, I don't mean stuff from the rooms. Well ... that happens as well, obviously. No, I'm talking about ...' she nodded back to where a young girl was sitting at the reception desk, flicking through a copy of *Heat*; her voice dropped to a whisper, 'the staff.'

'That happens too,' Tanner said.

'She's Romanian,' Shepherd said, as though that explained everything. 'Not that I'm saying it's her, mind you. There's a couple of other girls and I wouldn't want to be unfair to anyone.'

'Course not.' Thorne looked around. There was a calendar with pictures of Jack Russell terriers, though the one that stared up at him from a basket next to the filing cabinet was rather less appealing than September's dog of the month.

'That's Rascal,' Shepherd said. 'Don't make a fuss of her, because she can be a bit snappy. She's not got long left, bless her.'

Thorne and Tanner exchanged a look.

'So anyway, that's why I put a camera in at the reception desk and I always have a look through the film last thing every night. Just to make sure everything's above board, you know. Like I say, you don't want to accuse anyone, do you?'

She looked at Tanner who managed a smile, but Thorne could see how impatient she was getting. Or perhaps she was still thinking about Hassani. Thorne had said little about it to Tanner in the car, but it was certainly of concern. Was the Honour Crimes officer keeping an eye on what they were up to? Was he trying to muscle in? He had seemed unthreatening enough, ineffectual even, but perhaps he wanted to appear that way when in fact he was every bit as difficult a customer as Thorne was.

The manager was still typing, searching for the pictures Thorne and Tanner had come to see. 'That was what rang a bell last night, see? Sitting here, looking through the footage from yesterday, I see these two checking in and straight away I

226

remembered that picture in the papers. That thing on the underground train.'

'They checked out this morning?' Tanner asked.

'First thing,' Shepherd said. 'Paid in cash. I did call last night though. I thought it might be important, you know.'

'Yeah, thanks.' Thorne saw Tanner shake her head. If these two men turned out to be the ones they were looking for, they had missed them by a matter of hours. If only Thorne had been on shift when Shepherd's call had come in. If only whoever had taken the call had understood the significance and called him.

This was what happened when you were working a case off the books.

'Here you go.' Shepherd pushed her chair away from the desk, inviting Thorne and Tanner to move closer and look. She nodded towards the reception desk. 'That's where they were, checking in, yesterday morning. That's a different girl on the film, see?' She pointed. 'Estonian, I think, that one. I get confused about where they're from.'

Thorne and Tanner leaned in to watch.

'Is it them?'

Thorne nodded.

The Asian and the Irishman were standing close together at the reception desk. There was no sound on the hotel's cheap CCTV system, but the Asian seemed to be doing most of the talking. The girl handed him something and at one point he laughed at whatever she had said. The Irishman leaned in to speak just before they walked away from the desk and out of shot. The image was black and white and far from pin-sharp, but there could be no doubt that these were the same men who had abducted Amaya Shah and Kamal Azim; who had killed one and probably both of them.

Who had almost certainly murdered Meena Athwal and probably several others.

Who had stabbed Susan Best to death in her own home.

227

A matter of hours ...

'Oh, hell's bells,' Shepherd said, behind them.

They turned to look at her. She had clamped a hand across her mouth. The terrier in the basket began to bark and she told it to be quiet.

'What?'

'The rooms have already been cleaned.' The woman was shaking her head and now the hand was pressed to her chest. 'I mean, I didn't think and we always send the girl in to do the rooms first thing.' She stared at them, as though amazed that they weren't screaming at her. 'Well, that's buggered up the DNA, hasn't it? I'm no expert, but I watch enough bloody police shows on TV to know that much. Oh, what a bloody shame.'

'It's fine,' Thorne said.

He and Tanner had talked about this on the way over and both knew that, for all sorts of reasons, the state of the rooms the men had stayed in would make no difference. Clean or dirty, hotel rooms were always a forensic nightmare, containing traces from hundreds of former occupants which would take many weeks, if not months, to process, even if they had the money or the permission to do so.

They knew very well they would get neither.

'Hang on,' Shepherd said. 'They filled in registration forms, didn't they? Maybe you could get fingerprints or something.'

Thorne was about to tell her that this too was of no real use, but the manager had already begun rooting excitedly through the filing cabinet. He and Tanner could only watch, saying nothing, as she searched for several minutes, then drew the forms out triumphantly. She held each one gingerly by a corner, looking to Thorne for a nod of approval, before dropping it into an empty plastic bag.

'Best I can do,' she said. 'Not exactly *CSI*, I know.'

'We'll manage,' Thorne said.

He knew that even if they were given the go-ahead to test and came back with the cleanest set of prints the forensic team had ever come across, they would be wasting their time. Tanner had said as much, back when Hendricks had been carrying out the post-mortem on Amaya Shah. There would be nothing on record, nothing to match a fingerprint or a DNA sample with.

The only forensic evidence these men had ever left at a crime scene had been Kamal Azim's.

They were never going to catch them that way.

'Did they have a car?' Tanner asked. She had spotted a CCTV camera outside the entrance, where there was room for two or three vehicles.

'Well, if they did they didn't park it here.'

Tanner nodded. She had been pretty sure that the men they were looking for would not have been so careless as to provide them with a nice checkable number plate, but it had been worth asking.

Noreen Shepherd handed the plastic bag across. 'There you go,' she said. 'Never know your luck.'

Tanner closed the car door and fastened her seat belt and, watching her sit back, Thorne got the sense that he was as much a chauffeur as anything else. He actually preferred being in his own car, but on top of everything else, it rankled. He decided that, wherever they went next, it might be nice if Tanner offered to do the driving.

'All good,' she said.

'Really?'

'So, we missed them, but not by much.'

'We missed them, that's the point.'

'No, the point is that they're still here. That's good news for us.' Tanner turned in her seat to look at him. 'That last sighting, the woman from the café? As I said at the time, I'm fairly sure they were still working the Shah and Azim killings then. Hanging around just long enough to make sure Amaya's body was discovered, that it looked the way it was supposed to. If they're still here, it's because they've got another job to do, and I think we're getting close to whoever's putting these jobs their way.'

Thorne said nothing. He started the car.

'Men like that don't hang around any longer than they have to,' Tanner said. She sounded fired up again, keen to crack on. 'They're on their toes with the money. In the wind, first chance they get.'

As Thorne nosed the BMW into traffic, he saw how relaxed Tanner looked suddenly, how confident, and he remembered what he'd said about her to Helen the night before.

Not giving a toss . . . not caring...not thinking.

Thorne was not convinced the news was nearly as good as Tanner thought it was.

FORTY

Thorne had offered to drop Tanner at home before heading back to the office, but five minutes into the journey back to Hammersmith, she suddenly asked if he could let her out at a tube station instead. It appeared that she had suddenly decided she needed to be somewhere, but she showed no inclination to explain, and when Thorne pulled over in a bus lane opposite Baron's Court station she did not seem in any hurry to get out of the car.

Thorne flicked his hazards on.

Taking rather less care with them than Noreen Shepherd had done, Tanner was examining the registration forms filled in by the two men who had spent the previous night at the Palm Court hotel.

She said, 'No point running these.'

Thorne took the forms, looked at the names the men had given. Block capitals and scrawled signatures.

Michael O'Toole and Hassan Ali.

'Not massively imaginative,' Thorne said.

Tanner's thin smile was no more than automatic. She quickly

sat back and began to talk, describing her trip to the Palmers Green mosque in detail; her subsequent sighting of the man in the gold skullcap at the AHCA meeting the night before.

'It wasn't a coincidence,' she said. 'He'd gone there to see someone.'

'Right.'

'To pass on whatever Haroon Shah had told him.'

She might simply have been thinking aloud, running through the salient points of her investigations over the previous few days, but to Thorne it sounded rather more as if she were recapping for the benefit of a dimwitted sidekick.

Watson, again.

Thorne wondered if Watson ever told Sherlock Holmes that he should think about counselling. That he was starting to sound slightly crazed. He wondered if Watson had ever lost his rag and kicked the Great Detective out of a hansom cab.

'So, who's our friend in the gold skullcap then?'

'Not sure it matters,' Tanner said. 'He's probably just a go-between. One of the links in the chain. In *that* chain, obviously. Somebody else would be doing it if it was a Hindu or Sikh family. It's whoever he delivered the message to that we're after.'

'It would help if we knew, though.'

The look Tanner gave him suggested to Thorne that perhaps she really did think he was a little slow on the uptake. 'Obviously, and I'm going to find out.'

'I wonder if the mosque keeps records of worshippers?' It was Thorne's turn to think aloud. 'Not sure they'd be very forthcoming, mind you. Certainly not without a warrant.'

'Probably simpler if I just go and ask him,' Tanner said.

'You think that's a good idea?'

'I don't see why not. I mean, he's not going to give me a false name, is he? Wouldn't want to arouse suspicion.'

Thorne shook his head. 'You really like getting in these people's faces, don't you?'

'You went to see Meena Athwal's father.'

'I don't think I was that ... obvious, though.'

'You telling me you didn't enjoy it?'

'I'm just saying ... there's a difference between rattling someone's cage a bit and pretty much making it clear you're on to them.'

'I know that.'

'Sometimes, there are consequences.'

Tanner lowered the sun visor and checked her make-up in the vanity mirror. 'If you've got any better ideas I'm keen to hear them.'

Thorne glanced at the rear-view and saw a bus approaching the traffic lights behind them. They probably had no more than a couple of minutes, but he didn't want to move just yet.

The picture was already in his head and he wanted to tell her why.

'There was this case, years ago,' he said. 'A man called Frank Calvert.'

Tanner turned, recognising the name. 'You caught Calvert?'

'Yeah, I caught him,' Thorne said. 'I *found* him ...'

Half a dozen gay men slaughtered in eighteen months and a city-wide manhunt that was going nowhere. Francis Calvert had been one of hundreds of builders questioned; a line of inquiry based on the one solid lead the investigation had. Thorne had been a DC back then and had been sitting in on the interview.

A stroke of luck, good and bad.

'Something happened, as I was showing him out of the station,' Thorne said. 'I'm not sure I really *knew*, even though that's the story that was put around afterwards ... but I thought that something was off, and, for whatever reason, he saw it in my face. I shook his hand and he walked out of those doors convinced I'd sussed him.

'I went round to his house a couple of days later, to prove to myself I was being stupid as much as anything else. Just to try and work out what was bothering me so much, you know?' Thorne paused and opened the window a fraction to suck in some fresh air. It was still sunny, but that wasn't why his shirt was sticking to his back as he leaned forward. 'I knocked, but nobody answered, and I almost walked away. Then before I knew what I was doing I'd fetched a truncheon from the car and I was smashing the front door in.

'His wife was dead in the kitchen. Strangled. He was on the floor in the living room, his brains all over the mirror above the fireplace.' He reached forward and slowly wrapped his fingers around the steering wheel. 'The girls were upstairs.'

'I remember,' Tanner said. Whispered.

'Lauren, Samantha and Anne-Marie. She was the youngest . . . five years old. *Just* five. He thought it was finished, so he took them all with him.'

In the small back bedroom.

Laid out next to one another on the floor.

The smell of shampoo in their hair and of freshly washed nightdresses and six tiny, white feet in a row.

The picture in his head.

'Not your fault,' Tanner said quietly.

Thorne shook his head, not because it didn't matter and not because he disagreed. Shaking the picture away. 'He did it because he thought we were on to him, simple as that. That's all I'm saying. Somehow I . . . pushed him.'

A horn sounded behind them, but neither of them moved.

Tanner closed the sun visor and lifted her handbag on to her lap. 'You think we should be playing our cards closer to our chests?'

'Not sure we've got any cards,' Thorne said. 'But yes.'

The bus driver leaned on his horn again and braked hard a few feet behind them.

'You should probably move,' Tanner said.

The horn sounded again, several seconds of it. Thorne looked in the mirror and watched as the bus swerved sharply around him and drew alongside. The driver lowered his window and shouted.

'You can't stop there.'

Thorne reached for his wallet then lowered the passenger side window. He leaned across Tanner, showed his warrant card and shouted back.

'I can stop where I like. Now fuck off.'

Muttering curses, the driver pulled away, and Thorne was looking a little happier as he tucked his wallet back in his pocket again.

'You shouldn't have done that,' Tanner said. 'Misuse of warrant card. Arguably discreditable conduct.'

Thorne nodded. 'Well, that's both of us finally living up to our reputations, then.'

This time, Tanner's smile was a little more genuine. She said, 'Sorry for being a pain in the arse the last couple of days.'

'I can cope.'

She opened the door. 'I'd love to say it was down to grief. But there's no point in lying.'

FORTY-ONE

When Thorne got back to his office, Kitson was watching a video on her iPad, eating lunch from a Tupperware container. She looked up when he walked in, turned the video off.

'Worth it?'

Thorne tossed his jacket on the back of a chair, which he dropped gratefully into. 'Depends what you're talking about. Getting out of bed in the morning? Probably not.'

Kitson got up and closed the door. 'The hotel.'

'Well, it was definitely them,' Thorne said. 'The pair that abducted Kamal Azim and Amaya Shah.'

'The ones Tanner thinks killed her girlfriend?'

Thorne nodded. 'False names, everything paid for in cash . . . DNA and prints a non-starter, obviously.'

'Yeah.' Kitson walked back to her desk and sat down. 'Tricky to get forensic back-up on a case you're not supposed to be working.'

'What case?' Thorne held up his hands. 'No idea what you're talking about.'

'Ignore me.' Kitson shook her head. 'I'm probably just

delirious with hunger.' She plucked out another sandwich and took a bite. 'Still, a couple of hours away from the office is always nice.'

'Oh yeah, and I got to meet Noreen, the hotel manager . . . and Rascal, of course.'

Kitson looked at him.

'Dog.' Thorne let his head drop back, rolled it from side to side. 'Yappy little shit.'

'The manager or the dog?'

While Kitson continued to eat, Thorne opened a couple of drawers and closed them again. He sent a text to Phil Hendricks suggesting a drink later on. He logged on to his computer and saw a message from the tech support team confirming that the email supposedly sent by Kamal Azim had been traced to an internet café in Brighton. A second email confirmed that Sussex police were intensifying the search for their prime suspect.

'God help us.'

Kitson looked up. 'What?'

'Doesn't matter,' Thorne said. He groaned with the effort of getting up and walked across to sit on the edge of Kitson's desk. He helped himself to a cherry tomato from her lunch box. 'Did Brigstocke notice I was gone?'

'Don't think so.'

'Good.' He reached for the lunchbox again, but Kitson slapped his hand away. 'Not that he doesn't *know*. He's just playing the game and pretending not to.'

'Just don't rub his nose in it.'

'I'm not stupid.'

Kitson pretended to choke on her sandwich.

'Hilarious.'

'Just saying. Stay on the right side of him—' She reached to answer the phone that had begun to ring and grunted a couple of times before she'd managed to swallow what was left of her sandwich. She said, 'Right . . . I'll tell him,' and looked knowingly at Thorne as she hung up. 'There you go. Now there's something you can do on the case you're supposed to be working *and* the one that doesn't exist.'

'What?'

'Kamal Azim's father just walked into Colindale station. Doesn't think we're doing quite enough to find his son, apparently.' She carried on over Thorne's harsh bark of laughter and industrial-strength muttering. 'He's demanding to see someone, because he reckons he's got a way to help us.'

Thorne stopped swearing. 'Oh, does he?'

'Want me to go?'

'Finish your lunch.' Thorne was already moving back to his desk. 'I mean, how can we turn down an offer like that?' He grabbed his jacket and walked quickly towards the door, feeling a lot better suddenly than he had five minutes before, and remembering what Tanner had said to him in the car.

You telling me you didn't enjoy it?

It would normally be no more than a five-minute walk from Becke House to Colindale station, but on this occasion Thorne took his time.

It was a nice day, after all.

Hamid Azim did not look best pleased at having been kept waiting. He stood up as soon as Thorne walked through the main doors into the reception area, but Thorne did not acknowledge him, waiting until he was past the main desk and swiping his entry card before he turned and politely said, 'This way, sir.'

Azim picked up a large cardboard box he had presumably brought with him and, struggling to carry it, followed Thorne through into the station and along a corridor to one of the interview rooms.

'Bog-standard, I'm afraid,' Thorne said, as he closed the door. 'Everywhere else is busy.'

Azim did not appear overly concerned by the spartan surroundings. As soon as Thorne had sat down, he laid the box on the table in front of him and stepped back, seemingly happy to remain standing. He looked agitated. He took off his rimless spectacles and quickly cleaned them as he shifted from one foot to the other.

Thorne nudged the box aside. 'What can I do for you, Mr Azim?'

The man looked at him. He seemed even slighter than Thorne remembered, wearing a black windbreaker over brown slacks. His hair looked a little messy. 'Well, I suppose it would sound rather rude if I said you can find my son. So I will simply say that you could perhaps make a little more effort to find him.'

Thorne did not have to pretend to be taken aback. He said, 'I can promise you that we're doing all we can. We put out a fresh appeal on television yesterday.'

'I saw that. There was an . . . implication I did not like.'

'What was that?'

'A suggestion that he might be missing because he was somehow involved in what happened to that poor girl? "In connection with" you said.'

'That's right.'

'You think my son is a murderer?' Azim swallowed hard. 'You think he's a rapist?'

'We're looking at several different possibilities,' Thorne said.

Azim was blinking fast, staring at Thorne's face, then at his feet. 'So, did this appeal help with any of them? Your *possibilities*?'

'Not yet, I'm afraid. We haven't located your son, if that's what you mean.'

'There we are.'

'We got a good response, though, and we're working through every call that came in.'

'I understand, but there is always more that can be done.'

'I assure you that people are working very hard to find Kamal,' Thorne said. 'Going the extra mile in many cases.'

Azim nodded and screwed up his eyes for a few seconds. 'Have you any idea what my family is going through?'

Thorne said 'No,' because he really didn't. Now that their son was gone, how were they with one another, behind closed doors? If the man in front of him had been the only member of the family involved in Kamal's death, how did he behave towards his grief-stricken wife and their surviving daughters? Thorne wondered if there had been any communication between the Azims and the Shahs since the murders. They claimed not to have known one another, yet Tanner still believed that the families had planned the killings together.

Thorne was starting to believe it himself.

Had they met somewhere to talk about how it would be done? Over coffee or dinner, maybe? Somewhere they could get authentic Bangladeshi food and discuss the best way to dispose of their troublesome children?

'It's a living nightmare,' Azim said. 'So, we would be grateful if you could do everything in your power to bring that to an end.'

A week earlier Thorne had wondered how Faruk Shah had behaved identifying his daughter's body, but this was surely a performance that topped it.

Oscar-worthy.

'Like I said, Mr Azim—' Thorne's phone pinged to indicate a text message. He took it out and saw that the message was a response from Phil Hendricks. 'I'm sorry, I really need to deal with this,' he said. 'It's about the search for your son.'

'Is there news?'

'Not news, I'm afraid, but it's from another officer working on the investigation, so . . . '

coming 2 ur place later. double stabbing in edgware. beer after? ☺

Thorne typed a reply. He looked up and said, 'I won't keep you.'

Oak at 5?

He stared at the screen, waiting for Hendricks to reply. He glanced up at Azim once or twice to see if there was any change in the expression.

Nothing.

c u there!

Thorne apologised as he slipped his phone back into his pocket. 'Now, apparently you said something about a way you might help?'

'Yes.' Azim stepped smartly forward and opened the cardboard box. Thorne leaned over to look inside and saw a pile of neatly folded white T-shirts. Azim pulled one out and held it up.

'We did these,' he said. 'We printed them in the shop.'

The same picture of Kamal that had been used in the TV appeal. Above it the word MISSING and below the phone number of the incident room. Azim stepped back and unzipped his windbreaker to show that he was wearing one. 'We have done five hundred of them and we've handed them out to everyone in the area.'

'You think Kamal is still in the area?' Actually, Thorne thought there was every chance he might be. He didn't believe that the men responsible for his disappearance would have travelled far to dispose of the body.

'I have no idea where my son is. We thought it would be good if perhaps you could help distribute them. Then we might find out.'

'Us? You mean the police?'

'Yes, of course.'

'I'm afraid we simply don't have the manpower for that,' Thorne said. 'Every available officer is already working all the hours God sends.' He tried to look sincere, knowing full well that each one of those officers would be doing a lot more good hosting a bring-and-buy sale for local widows and orphans.

'Perhaps if I leave them then. You could just give them to everyone here. Everyone who comes in.'

'OK,' Thorne said, getting to his feet.

Azim dropped the T-shirt back into the box. 'We don't know what else to do,' he said.

On the way out, Azim stopped and said, 'What do you think has happened to my son?'

It was a convincing display of helplessness. Of despair. But to Thorne, the man's question sounded rather more like a taunt, or a simple attempt to gauge the degree to which he and his family were in the clear.

The distance between the truth and the story.

Thorne said, 'I know as much as you do, sir.'

FORTY-TWO

Sarah Webster answered the door wearing sweatpants and what looked like a man's cardigan over a faded T-shirt. She peered out, cradling a mug close to her face, the door open no more than a few inches.

She said, 'Oh.'

'I tried to call,' Tanner said. 'But it went straight to voicemail.'

'Phone's turned off.' The girl opened the door and stepped back, inviting Tanner inside. 'I should probably listen to the messages.'

Tanner followed Sarah into a living room and watched her sit down in a chrome and leather armchair. The girl pointed as she drew her knees up.

'Just move all the shit.'

Tanner gathered up the newspapers and bits of clothing that were spread across the sofa and moved them aside so that she could sit down.

'Keep thinking I should tidy up,' Sarah said. 'But then I just forget.'

'It's fine,' Tanner said.

There were several beer cans on the glass coffee table and Tanner guessed they were all as empty as the wine bottle on the floor near her feet. An ashtray full of butts sat in a pool of liquid in the corner of the table and a sodden magazine flopped over the edge.

'Where's your mum and dad?'

'He's not my dad.'

'Sorry,' Tanner said.

Sarah glanced at the ceiling. 'Still in bed.' The look on Tanner's face prompted a thin smile. 'Yeah, I know. He usually drags himself downstairs in time for *Tipping Point*. You know, that stupid quiz that's like the game at the fair. The one with coins?'

Tanner shook her head.

'He'll sit and watch *The Chase* after that, then switch over for *Pointless*. Even if they've had a heavy session, and he's not down in time, he's got them all on Sky, so he can sit there and watch quizzes right through to dinner time.' She sipped her drink. 'He's pretty clever, actually. Not that you'd think it.'

'What about your mum?'

'Don't know.' The girl shrugged. 'Shopping or something?'

There was a low hum coming from somewhere. A fridge, maybe, or the central heating. Voices bled through from a television next door, a smattering of applause for one of them.

Tanner leaned forward and stood a fallen beer can back up.

'You heard anything?' Sarah asked.

'I talked to the team leader this morning.'

'Only I've heard nothing, you know? They were really on it after it happened, doing all the tests or whatever.'

'The rape kit.'

'Yeah, the kit.' Sarah nodded. 'Then one of the female coppers rang yesterday, see how I was ... but I still don't really know what's happening.'

'It's difficult without DNA,' Tanner said. 'There was nothing under your fingernails.'

'One of them was holding my arms.'

'I know.'

Sarah rolled up the sleeve of the cardigan to reveal a cluster of purpled bruises. 'Kneeling on them.'

'And nothing internally, because . . .'

'They were wearing condoms. I *know*, I was there.'

'Sorry.'

Sarah shook her head, as if it didn't matter. 'A woman came to see me in the hospital straight afterwards. She told me I might feel angry.' Her shoulders tensed and the smile was momentary. 'Angry or frightened, she said. She gave me a booklet and said I might get headaches or feel sick, or get too scared to leave the house.'

Tanner waited.

The girl moved the tip of her finger slowly up and down the side of her ear; touched each stud once on the way up and again on the way down. 'She never said I might get all of them.'

'Sorry.'

Sarah stared into her mug. 'You don't have to keep apologising.'

'It was Amaya's brother,' Tanner said. The hum sounded louder for the second or two before she spoke again; said what she'd come to say. 'He did this.'

Sarah looked up.

'Not himself, and it probably wasn't any of his close mates, because they've all got alibis. They might just be giving one another alibis of course, but all the same . . . I know Haroon Shah organised it.'

Sarah looked stunned. 'Because I lied about where Amaya was?'

'No—'

'I was raped because I said she was at my house that night?'

'They did it because I told him you'd spoken to us.' Tanner shuffled forward. 'I didn't mention a name, I would never have done that, but I did tell him I'd talked to one of his sister's friends. He guessed it was you.'

Sarah's hand fluttered to the side of her head again, then the fingers crept across her scalp and she began to tug at the blonde spikes.

Tanner could see that the dark roots were coming through.

'It doesn't matter,' Sarah said, finally. 'Doesn't matter why in the end, does it?'

'You've got every right to be angry though. Angrier.'

'Will they get him for it? Him and the lads who did it?'

'I'm going to get him.' The other thing Tanner had come to say. 'And then I'll get all of them.'

They sat in silence for half a minute, the leather on the sofa sticky beneath Tanner's hands. She heard what sounded like someone turning over in bed upstairs. She said, 'My ex-partner used to drink.' A nod towards the coffee table. 'I had to deal with the empties, same as you. Try and find the full ones, where she'd hidden them.'

Sarah nodded. 'Ex because you got rid of her? The drinking.'

'She died,' Tanner said.

'Oh. Sorry.'

Tanner smiled. 'Don't you start.'

'Cancer, was it?' The girl shrugged. 'I mean, it usually is.'

'No, it wasn't cancer,' Tanner said. That was enough. It was the girl's tragedy and not her own that she had come to talk about.

Though arguably she had ultimately been responsible for both.

Sarah put her empty mug down on the coffee table and stared at it. 'I never even offered you a drink or anything.'

'It doesn't matter.'

'Yeah, it does. The kettle's just boiled anyway.'

Tanner was already getting to her feet and talking quickly.

'Don't worry, I'll do it.' She pointed. 'Kitchen through there, is it?'

'Yeah.' Sarah stood up and they looked at each other. 'I just need to nip to the toilet. Milk's in the fridge.' She laughed. 'Mind you, you'd be a rubbish detective if you couldn't work that out.'

Tanner could not hear Sarah come into the kitchen a few minutes later and it wasn't until a hand was laid softly on her shoulder that she even knew the girl was there.

'It's good to do that,' Sarah said. She tore off several sheets of kitchen towel from a plastic dispenser and handed it over. 'That's one of the things it said in that booklet they gave me. Letting your feelings out or whatever. Not bottling it all up.'

Tanner spluttered a 'Thank you'.

She pressed the towel to her face with one hand while she used the other to steady herself against the sink. Her legs were trembling.

This was not the first time she had cried since Susan's death. But it was the first time she'd made any noise.

FORTY-THREE

'You'll have to stand on a chair,' Riaz said.

'You're kidding. Isn't there a stepladder?'

'I've looked.'

'I'm not standing on a chair.'

'How else are you going to do it?'

'Why don't *you* stand on a bloody chair?'

'I don't have a problem with it, but I'm still not sure I would reach. You are what . . . six feet?'

'Six two.'

'Right.' Riaz smiled at Muldoon. 'Shall I look for one?'

'I'll do it,' Muldoon said. 'I want to make sure it's good and solid. I'm not breaking my neck for this load of old nonsense.'

Riaz watched his partner lumber off towards the kitchen, then reappear a few seconds later with a chair that certainly looked sturdy enough. 'That will do.'

'You're not the idiot who's going to be standing on it.' Muldoon put the chair down. He looked up at the ceiling and adjusted the chair's position.

Riaz stepped away to give him room.

'You want to talk me through this again?'

'Really?'

'I know what we're doing, I just don't get it. Why does it have to be so . . . ?'

'I told you why—'

' . . . elaborate?'

'This one is different, so it needs to be handled differently, that's all.' Riaz leaned back against a wall. 'And actually, I think you're wrong. I think the job we did with that couple was actually *more* elaborate. The various stages of it. Even though it was rather more hands-on.'

Muldoon thought about it, cocked his head as though conceding that Riaz might be right. He said, 'Still think it's bollocks, though,' and grunted as he climbed up on to the chair.

'Careful,' Riaz said. 'Don't want you doing any damage.'

Muldoon blew him a kiss.

'I meant to the chair,' Riaz said. 'Or to anything else. In and out like we were never here, that's the whole point.'

Muldoon reached, then stopped and looked down. 'How did you get into this?'

'*What?*'

'This game. Not like it's something you dream about doing as a kid, is it?'

'Is now really the best time for a chat?'

'While we're doing it. Don't see why not.'

Riaz looked down at his shoes. The silence made it clear that Muldoon was waiting for an answer. 'My sister.'

'Your sister what?'

'Look—'

'Oh . . . you mean she was your first one? No way.'

Riaz looked at him, unblinking.

'So, what did she do?' Muldoon sniffed. 'Naughty girl, was she?'

'It doesn't matter.' Riaz bent to pick a worm of dried mud

from the carpet. 'Word got around, I suppose, and a few months later I was asked to help another family.'

'Help?' Muldoon's laugh was a dry rasp. 'You make it sound like you gave them a hand putting up a shed or something.'

Riaz thought how easy it would be to kick the chair away, enjoyed the image of the Irishman flailing then crashing to the floor. 'What about you?'

Muldoon reached up again and went about the job. 'Well ... I'd been involved in a bit of stuff with the boys back home, you know? Not like this, just punishment, that kind of thing.' He glanced down and saw the look on Riaz's face. 'What?'

'What you're talking about is political and it surprises me, that's all. Doing things because of what you believe in.' He shook his head. 'I thought it was all about money for you.'

The dry rasp again. 'Oh, even working with that lot there was plenty of money to be made, don't make any mistake about that. Protection, drugs, you name it.' He cursed under his breath, said, 'This is proper fiddly.'

'Take your time.'

'So, anyway ... eventually I came over here to see if I could make a bit more. Made a lot more, as it turned out. I ended up helping this bloke out in Birmingham and that's where I ran into you.'

'Yes.' Riaz tried to sound as though he recalled the memory a little more fondly than he now did.

'Looking for a big stupid mick who didn't mind getting his hands dirty, so you were.'

'It was not a job I could do alone, that was all.'

'And now look where we are. Ten years on.'

Riaz checked his watch.

'Well, I'm standing on a chair like a bell-end and ... done it.'

Riaz flinched as Muldoon jumped down, losing his balance and stretching out a hand to steady himself on the banister. 'Right. Kitchen.'

Muldoon looked along the corridor. 'Oh, now you're taking the mickey. I could have done that while I was in there.'

'Why didn't you?'

Muldoon stared at him for a second or two, knuckles whitening as he grabbed the back of the chair again. 'I thought I'd wait for you to tell me.' He picked up the chair and carried it back towards the kitchen. 'I know how happy it makes you, thinking you're the one in charge.'

Riaz followed him, bending to collect a few more crumbs of dirt from the carpet. He said, 'Check the bottom of your shoes. You've walked mud in.'

FORTY-FOUR

There was a scrum of officers – uniform and plain-clothes – gathered around the bar in the Royal Oak. Most had just come off shift at Colindale or the Peel Centre, eager for the drink they had probably been thinking about since lunchtime. Something to take the edge off. Or, for those who had paid the price that the Job often demanded, something with which to steel themselves for the journey home to empty flats or houses to rattle around in.

A quick drink before going home for a few more.

Thorne reached between two men who appeared welded to the bar and took his change. 'The smiley face was a nice touch,' he said.

'I couldn't find a slab or a bone-saw,' Hendricks said. 'Whoever designs those emoticons is missing a trick.'

They carried pints of Guinness back to a table near the Gents. They sat and touched their glasses together.

'How you getting on with Tanner the Planner?'

'Well, that might be what she's like most of the time, but she's definitely winging it on this one.' Thorne brought him up to speed with events since they had last spoken: Tanner's visit to the AHCA; their trip to the Palm Court.

'She says she's going back to the mosque.'

'Maybe she's converting,' Hendricks said.

'And she's not nearly as bothered as she should be about the two hitmen still being around.'

'If I didn't know what a heartless bastard you were, I might think you were worried about her.'

Thorne shook his head. 'Worried about myself, mate. Any trouble and I'm going to end up copping for it.'

'Right,' Hendricks said. 'Course.'

Before Thorne could say any more, an officer he had worked with a few years before wandered over to chat. Something about a DCI they had both served under, a scandal of some sort. It was pretty clear that the man wanted to share his gossip and was itching to join them, but Thorne offered no invitation and very little in the way of conversation.

When the officer had ambled back to the bar, Hendricks said, 'So how did the appeal pan out?'

'Badly. By which I mean very well.'

'Ah . . . the helpful general public.'

'More than a dozen sightings, one of which was just outside Brighton, annoyingly. So, plenty more dicking about on the cards.'

Hendricks nodded and took a swig of Guinness. 'I'm just being devil's avocado here, mate . . . but there *is* more evidence that Kamal's alive than there is to suggest he's dead.' He saw the look on Thorne's face, held up his hands. 'Just saying.'

'Whose side are you on?'

'Not about sides, is it?'

'Yeah, I think it is, now,' Thorne said.

'You know me, I'm above all that. I wield the sword of truth and justice. Well, the scalpel of truth.' He took another drink, enjoying himself. 'And the rib-cutters of justice.'

Thorne looked up to see Russell Brigstocke approaching the table with a plate of food. 'Try wielding a bit on him, would you?'

Brigstocke pulled back a chair and laid down a plate of steak and kidney pie. He grabbed his cutlery then saw that Thorne was watching him. He pointed with his fork.

'Don't say a *word*.'

Thorne shook his head. He was remembering what Kitson had said only a few hours before; her advice to keep on the right side of their boss. 'Actually, I was just thinking you could probably afford the odd blow-out, sir. I reckon you've lost a few pounds.'

Brigstocke studied him.

Thorne tried and failed to look convincing. The 'sir' had probably been overdoing it.

'Piss off,' Brigstocke said.

Hendricks laughed. 'Didn't know you ate dinner in here?'

'Wife's doing fish and salad,' Brigstocke said. 'I hate bloody fish.'

He ate the rest of his meal without speaking, while Thorne and Hendricks talked about football. There was an Arsenal–Spurs fixture coming up in a few weeks and they agreed that it would be great to go, though both knew the chances were very slim. Job demands meant that they had not been to a game together in over a year.

'Last time you went, Tottenham were title contenders, weren't they?' Hendricks grinned. 'Wasn't Jimmy Greaves still playing then?'

Brigstocke finally pushed his plate away and sat back. The look on his face told Thorne that the DCI was not there purely for the food and certainly not for the pleasure of their company.

'Heard you had Kamal Azim's father in this morning.'

'Yeah. He wanted to show off his new range of designer T-shirts.'

'Sorry?'

Thorne explained. 'There's a boxful in my office if you fancy wearing one.'

Hendricks said, 'What are you, Russell, a small? Medium?' but neither Thorne nor Brigstocke was interested in joking about it any more.

'Look, it's . . . understandable.' Brigstocke leaned forward. 'He wants to know what's happened to his son.'

'He knows.'

Brigstocke shook his head, unwilling to go in the direction Thorne was pushing him. 'It's the same reason Amaya Shah's father is on the phone to me every day. Their kids are dead or missing, so I wouldn't expect them to act any other way.'

'Which is exactly why they're doing it,' Thorne said. 'Come on, Russell.'

'Come on, *what?*' Brigstocke was becoming tetchy. 'We're simply pursuing a line of inquiry suggested by solid evidence. That's what we do, Tom. It's what we're supposed to do.'

Thorne put his pint glass down a little harder than he intended. 'Right. And I suppose that after Kamal raped and murdered Amaya Shah then vanished for a bit, he popped back to rape Sarah Webster.'

Brigstocke straightened the cutlery on his plate. 'Well, as it happens the chief superintendent did mention that we shouldn't be ruling that out as a possibility.'

'You're kidding,' Thorne said. He looked to Hendricks for support. 'Why the hell would he rape Sarah Webster?'

'Why the hell would he murder his closest friend?'

'He didn't.'

'Look, he knew Sarah Webster,' Brigstocke said. 'We know that. There's simply a suggestion, and it's no more than that, that he might have attacked her because he was afraid of what she might tell the police.'

'So, why not kill her?' Thorne threw up his hands. 'Have you

255

any idea how ridiculous this all sounds? There is no motive for Kamal Azim to do any of this. It's just nice and convenient, you know ... to clear another offence while we're putting him in the frame for murder.'

'You can tell the chief superintendent that.'

'You want to talk about motive? Let's talk about Amaya Shah, murdered because she didn't want the life that had been planned out for her and decided to marry her best friend instead. Let's talk about Kamal, running away with her because he didn't want to marry the girl back home and didn't want Amaya to marry someone she'd probably never even met. Oh yeah, and because he was gay.'

'It's hard to accept that these are motives.'

'Because they're not,' Thorne said. 'Not to you or me or to anyone else with an ounce of sodding humanity. The people we're dealing with here have different ... standards. A different code. If you can kill your own flesh and blood because something they've done means you don't think you can hold your head up in a temple or in some poxy neighbourhood café ... Jesus, I think I understand serial killers better than I understand that. I'm never going to understand that.'

He let out a long breath.

He picked up his beer and sat back.

Brigstocke nodded slowly. He looked exhausted suddenly, as though he were finally admitting defeat. Accepting that he was fighting a losing battle with Thorne, and with the part of himself that knew, that had always known, Thorne was right.

The fight between the copper and the politician.

Brigstocke looked at Hendricks. 'You helping him out with this, are you? Egging him on.'

'Nothing to do with me,' Hendricks said. 'As a completely impartial observer, though, I think he's right. And I'm speaking as the man who found Kamal Azim's semen inside the body of Amaya Shah.'

Brigstocke nodded again. He sighed and said, 'Ever felt like drinking and drinking until you forget all the shit you have to deal with? Until you don't give a toss about anything any more?' He reached for his wallet. 'Ever thought about knocking it all on the head?'

Hendricks grinned. 'Existential crisis, Russell?'

'Shut it, Phil.' Brigstocke drew out a twenty-pound note and glanced towards the bar.

'Well, I don't know about drinking and drinking,' Thorne said. 'But I could certainly handle another pint.'

As Brigstocke walked away from the table, Hendricks said, 'There you go. One more on your side.'

Thorne nodded and watched the DCI pushing through the crowd to get to the bar. He said, 'I feel quite sorry for him.'

Hendricks shrugged and downed what was left of his drink. 'He's always got the magic to fall back on.'

FORTY-FIVE

One by one, the majority of Helen's colleagues had left, but she was not watching the clock or thinking about the overtime she was earning. She was thinking about Alfie. Though she had taken care to make the necessary arrangements for her sister to pick him up from the nursery, though she knew he would be safe and well cared for and that Jenny would bring him home later on ... sitting alone in front of that computer screen, she was thinking about her son.

How could she not?

The boy on the video was nine years older than Alfie, but he was still a child.

You could disassociate all you liked, you *had* to, and Helen had always thought she was better at that than most, but still there were times when it was impossible to hold that question at bay; to prevent it from worming its way in and doing its insidious worst.

What if ... ?

She had watched the video all the way through once already,

but this time she was making notes. Jotting down anything that occurred to her as she watched, that she thought might be important. It was normal procedure. Pausing and playing; rewinding several times and watching sections through repeatedly, to be sure she hadn't missed anything or confirm that her reaction to something she had seen or heard was sound.

Evasive or naturally shy?

Liking for fantasy films/TV shows etc.

Where did that anger come from?

This was one of several initial interviews already carried out by a social worker Helen had worked with for several years and trusted implicitly. The woman had done her job brilliantly, as patient and sensitive with her subject as always. If, after police and social services had put their heads together, they decided that further inquiry was warranted, Helen would probably end up interviewing the boy herself.

Close enough to see the bruises.

It was a standard young persons' interview suite. Comfortable chairs and colourful paintings on the walls. Helen knew that in the locked cupboards behind the boy there were toys and games that would be used with younger children. Male and female dolls that were rather more anatomically correct than those you could buy from Toys 'R' Us.

No need to open that cupboard, not for this one.

The boy and his brother were already too old and evidently too anatomically aware for any of that.

There was drawing equipment – felt-tips and large sheets of paper – on the red plastic table and Helen had already seen some of the pictures the boy had produced during an earlier session. As far as Helen was concerned, they in themselves had been enough to merit continued investigation. She knew what to look for by now. The boy had not exactly drawn a juvenile version of *The Scream*, but there was plenty of pain and violence.

Plenty of things there should not have been.

The social worker had agreed. It was pretty much textbook.

Staring at her screen, she watched the boy shift awkwardly on his chair then sit on his hands. He had already got up several times and walked around the room for a few minutes, muttering to himself. He had been talkative enough to begin with, as the social worker had eased him into the conversation; football, TV, where his trainers were from.

Getting him to talk about his family was proving a little more difficult.

Did he and his big brother see much of their grandfather? Yes? That must be fun. Did they spend a lot of time alone with their father? How well did they know any of his friends?

Still, as she watched the video again, Helen could not identify what it was about the case that was making her uneasy. That had bothered her enough to discuss it a few nights earlier with Tom. Perhaps it was merely down to the fact that since she had finally talked about what had happened to her as a child – to Tom, to her superiors, in a courtroom – something had shifted; had attuned her to subtleties hidden within cases like this one that she was, as yet, unable to identify.

Or perhaps she had simply lost that ability to disassociate and was letting empathy cloud her judgement.

Thinking about Alfie when she shouldn't.

Thinking this was not quite as textbook as the social worker believed it to be.

She glanced at the clock. Her sister would probably be giving Alfie his tea around now; the promise of staying up past his normal bedtime, which Helen knew was the real reason he was always mad keen to spend time at Auntie Jenny's house.

She couldn't really give her a hard time about it though. Not when Jenny was doing her a favour and certainly not if she wanted to hang on to the option of free babysitting.

Nearly six o'clock . . .

She knew that the sooner she left, the sooner she could call Jenny and have her bring Alfie home, but she didn't think another half an hour would make a lot of difference.

Watching a bit more TV wouldn't hurt him, and Helen wanted to take one more look at the interview with the older brother.

FORTY-SIX

Tanner saw no reason to lurk in the car park as she had done the first time she had been here, so instead she stood waiting outside the main entrance to Palmers Green mosque. A little after seven o'clock, and though it was not as warm as it had been that morning, it was, thankfully, still dry. Darkness was beginning to settle across the adjacent football pitch, but the exterior of the building was illuminated by uplighters: blue and white columns rising over the ornate brickwork towards the bronze dome, its crescent outlined against the charcoal sky.

The lights also clearly showed the tracks left by a paint-roller; an attempt to cover up the latest slew of abusive messages. Hate from a spray can. The outline of several words remained, just visible through the whitewash.

ISLAM ... SHIT ... PRIDE

She leaned against a wall and sent texts to both her brothers. She spent a few minutes checking her email. When the doors opened to indicate that the *Salat al-Maghrib* – the sunset prayer – had finished, she moved to watch the worshippers come out.

They emerged over the next five or ten minutes, in small groups for the most part, and Tanner engaged happily with several of them as they lit cigarettes or checked their phones. She said, '*As-salaam-alaikum,*' and exchanged a few words about the weather. Though there were one or two looks that bordered on the suspicious, everyone she spoke to was friendly and extremely polite.

Happy.

Keeping one eye on the door, Tanner wondered – not for the first time – what it was about organised religion that brought such contentment and joy to people, when it left her so completely cold. She watched another group emerge, saw the smiles on their faces. Was this true faith, or simply the demonstration of it? For some people, she suspected, attendance would be as much about duty as anything; about being seen to worship by others. She knew plenty of Jews and Christians who went regularly to church or synagogue because they thought they ought to, while cheerfully cheating on husbands and wives or scoffing bacon sandwiches when nobody was around to see it.

Were these killings as much about duty as they were about conviction? Was it really rage and shame that had choked the life from Amaya Shah, or was it about being seen to do the right thing?

Tanner told herself it didn't matter and turned her eyes back to the door.

It was not just the honour killings that had given her cause to consider such things recently, of course. When they finally saw fit to release Susan's body, there would be a funeral to organise and she was not looking forward to that for all sorts of reasons.

Susan had been every bit the heathen that Tanner was, but they had never sat down and talked about ... arrangements. Tanner had tried to initiate a discussion on several occasions, to make Susan's life easier as much as anything. After all, weighing up the risks inherent in their respective lines of work, it was

Tanner who had been by far the more likely to go first. Susan had always dismissed it, told Tanner she was being 'morbid', when the truth was that she had only tolerated Tanner's organisational leanings when it suited her. When there were forms to be filled in or accounts to be done.

Susan's lack of belief had led Tanner to start thinking about a humanist service. She wasn't sure she could bear to listen to some vicar neither of them had known blathering on, or friends and family wailing their way through hymns they didn't know the words to. A God in whom Susan hadn't believed sticking his beard in.

Susan's family, though. That was quite another question.

That sort of thing was important to them; the show of it. They weren't even churchgoers as far as Tanner was aware, but Susan's mother had already made it clear what would be expected. It was convention, as much as anything else; Tanner knew that. They had accepted the fact that Susan was gay – she hadn't given them a lot of choice – but that was as far as it went. It was rarely acknowledged and never discussed. They didn't kid themselves that she and Tanner were just 'good friends' or – that hideous euphemism – 'companions', but it might well have been what they told their friends if the subject ever came up.

'So, still no sign of your Susan getting married . . . ?'

Tanner and Susan had not seen much of them, not together. Christmas was always spent with Tanner's family, and Susan's mother sent them separate cards. They used to joke about going to stay with them and being made to sleep in separate rooms; sneaking across the corridor in the middle of the night like horny teenagers.

Now, though, there were the funeral arrangements to navigate and Tanner knew that the wishes of Susan's mum and dad would not be the same as hers. For them, the blathering vicar would do nicely. She should assert herself, she knew that, but as things stood she did not have the strength.

They could bury Susan at sea and she would raise no objection.

As soon as the man with the gold skullcap appeared, Tanner walked over and asked casually if she could have a quick word.

'Do I know you?' the man asked.

Tanner produced her warrant card, ignoring the stares from several onlookers, which were not quite as friendly as they had been a few minutes before. She said, 'I won't keep you.'

Up close, despite the fulsome beard, the man was younger than she had first taken him for. Early thirties maybe. He had soft brown eyes and flawless skin, and the smile he'd been wearing as he'd walked out of the mosque would not have been out of place on one of those absurdly handsome gurus whose portraits she had seen the night before.

Though it had gone now.

'Could you tell me your name?' Tanner asked.

'Do I have to?' Earnest, but polite enough.

'Well, I'm hoping that by answering a few quick questions you'll be able to help me with an ongoing investigation. So, if you don't, I'll probably just be asking myself why you wouldn't want to do that.'

'My name is Ilyas Nazir.'

'And what do you do, Ilyas?'

'I work in IT,' he said. 'Very boring, I'm afraid. I'm a computer nerd, basically.'

'We all need nerds,' Tanner said, laughing. 'I'm probably a bit of a nerd myself, actually. Not computers or anything, but I like details. I like to know stuff.'

Nazir was wearing a dark jacket over a collarless white shirt with fancy stitching, the same gold as his cap. He reached inside for a packet of cigarettes and Tanner watched him light up, saw the plume of smoke curl away and vanish in a column of blue light.

'Shouldn't really do this,' he said.

'You could switch to vaping, maybe.'

He smiled. 'Not because it's bad for you, but because the Prophet, peace be upon him, said "Do not harm yourselves or others".' He shrugged and nodded towards a group of men a few feet away, each member of which was also smoking. 'These things weren't around back then though, so it's a bit of a grey area.'

'Can you tell me where you were yesterday evening?'

He looked away, just for a second or two, and took a drag. He said, 'Of course. I was at a meeting in Bow. It's a multi-faith . . . action group, I suppose you'd call it. They meet to discuss how best to deal with the rise in attacks on Muslims and Sikhs . . . anyone who certain sorts of people might think has got a bomb in his pocket.' He nodded towards the area of fresh paintwork, the words bleeding through it. 'Morons, obviously, but morons who can still hurt you if they feel like it.'

'Yeah, I saw that.' Tanner looked up towards the small camera on the side of the building. 'What about the CCTV?'

'Makes no difference. They always wear masks or have their hoods up. We pass the tapes on to the police, but nobody has ever been prosecuted.'

'I'm sorry.'

'This morning there was a pig's head on the doorstep.' Nazir shook his head and took another drag.

Tanner watched him smoking for a few seconds. 'Can you remember who you spoke to at the meeting?'

Nazir took a moment to think and his eyes narrowed suddenly. 'You were there,' he said. 'You were sitting at the back. Why would you ask me where I was if you already knew?'

A man slightly younger than Nazir stepped across and laid a hand on his shoulder; asked if everything was all right. Nazir said that it was and the man walked away, though he did not go very far.

'So?'

'I talked to a lot of people,' Nazir said. 'Several of my friends are as concerned as I am about these attacks, so obviously I spoke to them. I talked to some of the organisers afterwards, too.'

Tanner tried not to react. The three men in control of the meetings: Bannerjee, Dhillon and Mansoor.

'What did you talk to them about?'

'I wanted to let them know I would be happy to help, get a bit more involved. They've got a website, but it's pretty basic, so I offered to give them a hand with it. I talked to a lot of people.'

'Do you know Haroon Shah?'

'Yes.'

'Did you talk to him here, yesterday morning?'

'I have a feeling that's another question you know the answer to already.'

'Can you tell me what you talked about?'

He waved an arm around slowly as though trying to recall the conversation, or to buy himself a few seconds. 'He hadn't been here for a while, so I said it was good to see him. I told him I was very sorry to hear about his sister. I presume you know about that?'

Tanner said that she did.

'I told him that extra prayers were being said.'

'What did Haroon say to you? Can you remember?'

'Yes, of course. He was very happy to be among friends, happy to be here. We talked about how tragedy can sometimes bring back those who have drifted from their faith a little, how it can help them find their way back to God. How good can come out of evil.'

'Every cloud, right?' Tanner looked at him. 'A silver lining.'

'Yes, if you want to put it like that.'

Before Tanner could ask any more questions, another man arrived from behind her and moved close to Nazir. He nodded politely at Tanner, said, 'Sorry to interrupt, but I need to drag

267

Ilyas away.' He looked at Nazir. 'We need to talk about those network problems before tomorrow's meeting. I still haven't seen the spreadsheet.'

'I'm sorry,' Nazir said. 'I have to go.'

Tanner guessed that he had managed to catch the other man's eye over her shoulder, to signal that he needed 'rescuing'. She and Susan had done the same thing more than once, on those rare occasions when one had been dragged along to a work do by the other and found herself pinned against a wall by someone desperate to discuss teacher shortages or morale among beat officers.

'No problem,' she said. 'You've been a big help.'

Nazir dropped his cigarette and stood on it. 'I'm glad to hear it.' There was a glimpse of that smile before his friend ushered him away. 'You know where you can find me.'

Tanner walked back to her car, thinking that a name was somewhere to begin, and about those who claimed to live by certain rules, as long as they could pick and choose.

Thou shalt not steal, but it's OK to cheat on your taxes. Love thy neighbour, as long as he believes in the same God you do, and he's not gay.

Thinking about Amaya, Kamal, Meena.

Susan . . .

Do not harm yourselves or others.

Wondering which part of that simple commandment was so hard to understand.

FORTY-SEVEN

'You're funny when you're pissed,' Helen said.

'What?'

'You want some tea?' She walked across and flicked the kettle on.

'I'm not pissed.'

Helen turned and grinned at him.

Thorne grinned back at her as he sat down at the kitchen table. He hadn't stopped grinning since he walked in. 'OK, pissed . . . ish.'

'How many did you have?'

Thorne shrugged. 'Not many. Four?' The grin became a grimace at the taste of the 'spiced Mexican melt' he'd eaten in the Royal Oak. The pub's signature burger, according to the menu. Hendricks, who had also eaten one, had pronounced the signature 'distinctly fucking illegible'.

'Did you drive?'

Thorne was peering at his phone, slowly stabbing at the keys.

'Tom?'

Thorne looked up, blinked.

'Did you drive?'

He shook his head. 'I left the car there. Got the Tube to Brixton then a bus up the hill.' He carried on, laboriously trying to type. 'Buses are quite nice, aren't they? Haven't been on a bus for ages.'

'What are you doing?'

'I'm trying to text Nicola Tanner ... just ... bloody autocorrect.' He put his phone down. 'Sod it, I'll do it tomorrow.'

'Why are you texting her?'

'Just to tell her that I've managed to get Russell onside.'

Helen mashed the teabag in Thorne's mug. 'How pissed was *he*?'

'No idea. Good though, don't you reckon? I mean we'll probably have to stick with the whole missing persons business for a while, you know ... like Kamal's still our prime suspect ... but at least I don't have to pretend we aren't doing all the other stuff. He knows we're on to something and that's the main thing.' He laughed. 'Phil chipped in, you know? Helped me persuade him ... like a pincer movement or whatever. "Spit-roasted him", that's what Phil said.'

'Yeah, that's what Phil would say.' Helen carried the tea across and put it down. 'And Russell's fine about you working with Tanner, is he?'

'Well, he didn't say he wasn't.' He picked up his tea, blew on it. 'Buses are so much nicer than they used to be, don't you think?'

He began humming a song that had been playing while he'd been in the pub, though he would not have been able to name it and would have been horrified to discover who it was by. Helen smiled.

'What?'

'You *are* funny when you've had a drink.'

'Thank you.'

'A bit louder and a bit ... happier.'

'I'm always happy.'

'Some people get a bit nasty when they've had a few, don't they? Phil can get chopsy, for a start.'

'Yeah, well, he's northern.'

'You actually get nicer when you're drunk.'

'So.' Thorne narrowed his eyes, mock-serious. 'You saying I'm nasty when I'm sober?'

'Well . . . '

'Fair enough.' He picked up his phone again and studied it. 'I'll settle for that.'

'Have you spoken to Tanner about these two men still being around? About the fact that she might want to be careful?'

'She's not stupid,' Thorne said.

'No, but sometimes when you're obsessed with one thing, you can miss something else that's blindingly obvious.'

'I'm sure she knows,' Thorne said. 'I definitely mentioned it.'

Helen stood up and walked across to the sink. 'Yeah . . . you're probably right. She strikes me as the type who doesn't like to admit there's anything to be scared of.'

Thorne nodded and hummed through the fuzzy remembrance of saying something about the two hired killers to Hendricks in the pub; Tanner in his car and a picture of six tiny white feet.

'You do know that's a Coldplay song, don't you?'

Thorne wasn't listening. He nodded again and sipped his tea. He said, 'I think Nicola Tanner can take care of herself.'

Tanner felt something move across her face and woke up choking. She sat up quickly and heard the thump as the cat that had been pawing at her chest jumped, yowling to the floor.

The bedroom was hot and full of smoke.

She threw herself out of bed and stumbled to the light switch, but the room stayed dark. Blacker than dark. Even if the lights had not already fused and she had still been wearing the contact lenses she had taken out before going to bed, she would have been unable to see what was six inches in front of her. The smoke was thick enough to feel as it rolled across her arms and legs and, gasping for air, it felt as though she was breathing in oily water.

She knew she had to think fast.

She needed to cover her face.

The front bedroom was her best chance.

Get down . . .

She knew it was important to stay as low as possible, that any clean air would always be nearer the floor. She dropped to the carpet and began to crawl towards the door. Holding her breath, struggling to focus, the smoke she had already inhaled burning in her chest.

The phone was down in the hall.

Her mobile was in her handbag in the kitchen.

The only way out was upstairs.

She pulled the door a few inches further open and squeezed out on to the landing. Her face was pressed into the carpet and she could hear the crackle from below through the boards. Looking down into the shifting wall of smoke, she could see the glow of the fire downstairs, the flames that had begun to climb.

She sucked in fumes as something shattered loudly downstairs, turned away from a surge of heat and the next moment she had no idea where she was. She groped forward, feeling nauseous and disorientated, struggling suddenly with the familiar geography of her own home.

Come on . . .

Bathroom to her left: she could soak a towel to cover her head. She peered into the blackness. Front bedroom to her right: no more than a few feet down from there to the sloped roof above the bay window. She needed to go left, then right . . . quickly.

She turned sharply and cried out as her head smacked hard into the newel post at the top of the stairs.

A few seconds, ten, until the pain gave way to panic.

She would not have enough time.

She moved quickly backwards into the blackness towards her bedroom; towards where she guessed her bedroom was. Hands sweeping the floor until she felt the burn of the metal carpet divider, before she dragged herself across the threshold, reached for the door and slammed it shut.

Keeping low was safest, she knew that, but it was taking too long. There wasn't time to play things by the book. She took a deep breath, retched as she took the poison into her lungs, then got to her feet and ran to the window.

It would not open.

She screamed with the effort, but the frame would not shift.

Susan had painted the damn thing shut.

Remembering the bottle of water on her bedside table, she launched herself towards the bed. She grabbed for the T-shirt she had taken off the night before and quickly soaked it before clamping the material across her mouth and nose.

Minutes, now; she had no more than that.

She turned back to the window. A twenty-foot drop on to the patio below, maybe fifteen if she could hang on to the window ledge. It wasn't like she had a lot of choice.

She fought to picture the room, to locate an object in the dark she could use to break the glass.

The lamp, unreachable, plugged in somewhere behind the bed.

The heart-shaped box she kept jewellery in. Soapstone, heavy ...

She moved for it, then stopped.

The cat. Where was the fucking *cat*?

She removed the T-shirt from her mouth and called the cat's name. Gagged as she shouted. She dropped to the floor and moved her arms back and forth, searching beneath the bed, once, twice ... until she could barely lift them.

Every ounce of strength in her was gone.

Easy enough to just close her eyes against the stinging of the smoke and the tears. To crawl beneath the bed or clamber on to it; curl up and let it happen. She knew she would lose consciousness before the flames arrived ...

A thought.

A basic instinct, the *most* basic. A jolt of adrenalin and a surge of energy, but it all began with a thought.

I will not die face down on an oatmeal carpet. Not both of us.

She reached for the edge of the bed and hauled herself to her feet. She lurched towards the door, which she knew would very soon begin to crack and blister. The doorknob was not yet hot enough to burn.

I'm not going anywhere without the cat. Without Susan's cat.

Tanner pressed the soaking T-shirt to her face, opened the door and stepped back out on to the landing.

FORTY-EIGHT

Thorne could smell it as soon as he turned on to Tanner's road, well before he saw the cones and the crime-scene tape, the line of vehicles parked outside the house. A couple of marked cars either side of the CSI van, several others that probably belonged to exhibits officers and fire service techs. He recognised Tanner's blue VW Golf parked fifty feet away. It had recently been cleaned and, unlike those parked nearer to the house, was not coated in soot.

She would have been pleased about that.

He showed his ID to a uniformed constable and walked across Tanner's front garden. Forensic equipment had been arranged on a trestle table on the small patch of grass and a number of fire-damaged items had already been laid out on a sheet of white plastic: shoes; a singed blanket; what looked like one of the prints he'd seen on the wall in Tanner's front room. He couldn't tell which one.

Stedman – the officer from the Fire Investigation Unit Thorne had spoken to on the phone – was waiting for him by what was left of Tanner's front door. It hung oddly, warped and splintered, though it was hard to tell how much of the damage was down to the fire and how much to the firefighters who had kicked it in just after three o'clock in the morning.

Stedman reached into a cardboard box and handed Thorne a blue forensic suit, gloves and a mask. He watched as Thorne took his jacket off and climbed into them.

'OK?'

'Fine,' Thorne said. 'Just the smell.'

Stedman swigged from a bottle of water. The suit made it all but impossible to tell how old he was, but the accent was most definitely Scottish. 'I would have thought you Homicide boys smelled much worse things than this.'

Thorne leaned against the fence to pull on a plastic bootee. 'My father died in a house fire.'

'Oh.'

'A while back.'

Stedman nodded, then stepped away and spent half a minute or so pointlessly rearranging the items on the trestle table until Thorne was ready.

'Let's have a look then,' Thorne said.

The reek was even stronger inside. The hall carpet had burned through to the underlay, its remains damp and spongy underfoot. The walls were jet black and the glass in the large mirror was cracked and coated in soot. Thorne glanced up past the charred spindles on the stairs then put his head round the living room door. He nodded to a CSI working near the bay window. The damage in there was less severe, though the walls were every bit as black and a layer of soot lay across the sofas and TV.

He turned back to Stedman. 'No doubt, then?'

Stedman shook his head and pointed to a square of blackened floorboards just inside the front door, from where what was left of the carpet had been removed. 'Obvious evidence of accelerants there. We'll need to analyse the ILR ... ignitable liquid residue ... but I'm guessing a rag soaked in petrol or paraffin and stuffed through the letterbox. Same thing at the back of the house.'

He walked away towards the kitchen and Thorne followed, noticing another CSI crouched on the landing at the top of the stairs. Scraping and bagging.

In the kitchen, Stedman pointed again. 'Put it through the cat flap, see?'

Once again, a square had been removed from what remained of the twisted linoleum. Once Thorne had finished coughing and lowered his mask to spit in the sink, he looked around. The cupboards had burned back to their frames and the black walls were still slick with foam and water. The door of the dishwasher was open and he could see that the innards had melted, fusing with the blackened crockery inside.

'She's OK, by the way,' Stedman said.

'Sorry?'

'The cat. It *is* a she, isn't it?'

Thorne nodded. He remembered Tanner telling him the cat's name, remembered enjoying the joke.

'She's with the neighbour ... same one that called the fire brigade. Poor wee thing's a bit blacker than she was, but she'll be fine.'

'What about smoke alarms?'

'Ah.' Stedman stepped across to the kitchen door and motioned for Thorne to follow. He pointed to the ceiling, the melted remains of the familiar plastic disc, its lid hanging open. 'No batteries, see? Same with the one in the hall.' He shook his head. 'Bloody stupid.'

Thorne was staring. 'No.'

'No, what?'

'The alarms would have had batteries in. I *know* her. She would have put fresh batteries in everything.'

'*Everything?*'

'What?'

The look on Thorne's face quickly wiped the smirk off Stedman's. The FIU man looked at his feet for a second or two. 'Do you want to see upstairs?'

'No,' Thorne said. He knew what he would see. 'I'm done.'

Walking back towards the front door, Stedman said, 'House should actually be all right, once it's cleaned up. Fire brigade got here before there was any structural damage.'

'Still not quickly enough,' Thorne said.

Stedman said, 'No,' and as soon as they were outside he took off his mask and picked up another bottle of water. He stood watching Thorne removing his bodysuit. 'Was it deliberate? The fire that killed your dad?'

Thorne grunted, though it might just have been the effort of climbing out of the suit.

'Did they catch them?'

Thorne froze, just for a second.

He thought about a man who had once been the head of a Turkish gangland family. A trail of blood behind him as he crawled across the floor of his own restaurant; screaming into the napkin that had been stuffed into his mouth, both knees shattered with a claw-hammer.

'Eventually,' he said.

The General Intensive Care Unit at Hammersmith Hospital was on the second floor of a block behind the main building. It was certainly good that it was a little out of the way, though Thorne had still needed twenty minutes on the phone – at least half of which was spent shouting – before he'd finally been able to persuade the consultant in charge of critical care that the patient needed a private room.

Having put a call in first thing to Tanner's DCI at Belgravia, it had been considerably easier getting authorisation to place an officer outside the door.

'Consider it done,' the man had said. 'I'll organise shifts, and I'll obviously try and get down there myself, as soon as I can find an hour or two.'

'I'm sure she'd appreciate it.'

'Give her all our best.'

'Course,' Thorne had said. 'Soon as she's conscious.'

Tanner's boss had been the one responsible for 'encouraging' her to take compassionate leave in the wake of Susan's murder. He might or might not have known that she had continued working off the books, but he'd certainly been well aware of the theory that she had been the target when Susan was killed. He must have understood the implications of the previous night's arson attack.

'Let me know if there's anything else I can do.'

Guilt cut through a lot of red tape.

Approaching the door, the plain-clothes officer on a chair outside put down his newspaper, stood up and demanded to see ID. Thorne nodded his approval as he reached for his warrant card. It was good to see somebody doing their job properly.

'There's a visitor in there already,' the officer said, sitting down again.

'Who?'

The officer looked embarrassed. 'Sorry, I've forgotten the name. He's definitely Job though. An Asian bloke.'

Thorne moved towards the door just as it opened and a doctor stepped out. She said, 'Oh,' and closed the door behind her, and there was a second or two of awkwardness as they both moved the same way, then apologised at the same time.

'How is she?' Thorne asked.

'Well, she's completely out of it at the moment. Will be for some time.'

'I meant how is she . . . generally?'

The woman looked down at her clipboard, lifted the glasses that were on a chain around her neck. 'Lucky, I suppose,' she said. 'Considering the height. But still … both ankles shattered, fractured arm, fractured pelvis, fractured wrist, severe concussion and major facial contusions. We can't be sure about the degree of the smoke inhalation injuries until we've run more tests, but we have to assume carbon monoxide poisoning.' She removed her glasses. 'Not good.'

Thorne nodded. 'You should print that list out and have it laminated for her. She'd appreciate that.'

The doctor smiled, though she clearly had no idea what Thorne was on about. 'We're still trying to schedule the surgery, but it's not life-threatening, so …'

'Right.'

She nodded back towards the door. 'I was trying to explain to your colleague in there. He wasn't very happy, but there's really not much I can do, I'm afraid. Obviously we'll continue managing the pain.'

Thorne nodded and moved past her to the door.

Thinking that Nicola Tanner was very good at doing that herself.

FORTY-NINE

Thorne said, 'You must be Dipak.'

Detective Sergeant Dipak Chall stood up from the chair next to Tanner's bed and stepped across to shake Thorne's hand. 'I know who you are,' he said. 'I was in court for a few days on the Finlay trial. Never got the chance to introduce myself.'

'You did a lot of good work on that,' Thorne said. 'I read the files before I got involved.'

Chall sat down again and reached across to pat the bed. 'All down to the boss.'

Thorne took the other chair, and for a few slightly awkward seconds he and the DS stared across the bed at one another. Chall was tall and skinny, early thirties, Thorne guessed. He was wearing a smart grey suit, all set to head to work after his visit, though it was obvious that he had not yet found time to shave. 'Anyway, nice to finally meet you,' Thorne said. 'I've heard great things.'

Chall grinned. 'From ... Nicola?' He said the name as if it were one he was not accustomed to using. 'Blimey.'

'She was grateful for all your help the last couple of weeks. She knew you didn't have to stick your neck out.'

'She'd have done the same thing for me.'

'Really?' Thorne looked at him. 'Unauthorised access to files from other teams' cases? Transcripts of emergency calls, CCTV footage ... passing all that information on to someone who was supposed to be on leave?' He smiled. 'I don't think she's broken that many rules in her life.'

'Well ...'

'Don't forget, I've been working with her the last few weeks.'

Chall laughed and nodded. 'Bloody nightmare, isn't she?'

Thorne looked at the table on Chall's side of the bed. There was fruit and a few paperback books, and he guessed that Chall had brought some of them. He didn't know if any of Tanner's family had been to visit yet. 'She thought you were probably doing it because you felt sorry for her ... after what happened to Susan.'

'Well, yeah ... maybe a bit.'

Chall turned to look at Tanner and for the first time, suddenly aware that he had been putting the moment off, Thorne did the same.

There were just about as many tubes and monitors attached as he had been expecting, as many machines humming and beeping. There were several intravenous drips, at least one of which, Thorne knew, was dosing her with diamorphine; the cannula taped to the skin of her left hand. Most of her face was obscured by dressings, and as Thorne had already been told that Tanner had escaped without any serious burn injuries, he guessed they were covering the contusions the doctor had mentioned.

She seemed to be breathing easily enough.

Looking down at her now, unconscious and broken, 'lucky' seemed a strange word to have used, but Thorne knew the doctor had been right. Lucky to have avoided the flames and to have survived the drop; twenty feet or more on to a concrete patio. A few seconds after she'd heaved a bedside table through the window, according to the neighbour who'd called the fire brigade and watched her jump.

Luckier than Susan had been, certainly.

'You been to the house?' Chall asked.

Thorne nodded. 'Petrol or paraffin, front and back,' he said. 'And they'd removed the batteries from the smoke alarms.'

'How the hell did they get in?'

'Maybe she leaves a spare key somewhere. They'll have been watching her. Doesn't really matter, does it?'

'I suppose not.' After a few seconds, Chall nodded towards the bedside table. 'Fruit. How bloody ridiculous is that? Be rotten by the time she can eat any of it. Didn't know what else to bring, though.'

'Not your books, then?'

He shook his head. 'I think those must have been from one of her brothers. He came first thing.'

Thorne nodded, imagining the officer outside demanding to see identification from members of Tanner's family. It was the right thing to do, he knew that, but still, it must have been alarming. He wondered if he should call and explain, though that would almost certainly make them even more worried than they already were.

When she was awake, he'd ask Tanner what she thought.

'So, where were you with everything?' Chall asked. 'The honour killings.'

Thorne told Chall about the visits to the AHCA meetings and Tanner's visits to the mosque in Palmers Green. He told him about the men who seemed to be in charge of the AHCA and a go-between named Ilyas Nazir. Tanner had mentioned the name in a message she had left late the night before. She had sounded excited, said that she thought the pieces were finally coming together.

Having been too drunk to send Tanner the message about Brigstocke, Thorne had already been in bed and dead to the world for an hour when she had called and left hers. Still feeling the effects of his night on the beer, he had eventually listened to it when he'd woken up, only fifteen minutes before hearing about the fire at Tanner's home.

The news had got rid of his hangover quickly enough.

Chall glanced at Thorne. 'Looks like you got too close.'

Thorne shook his head. 'No, I think they've been planning this a while. Ever since they messed it up the first time. They decided she needed getting rid of weeks ago.' He saw the look of confusion on Chall's face. 'They're the men who killed Susan. They thought she was Nicola.'

Chall nodded slowly, processing it. 'She never told me.'

'She said she tried to tell the team that was investigating Susan's murder, but between you and me I don't think she tried too hard. She said there wasn't much point, because nobody believed her theory about the hitmen in the first place. I think the real reason was that she wanted to catch them herself.'

'With your help, right?' Chall was still looking a little disappointed.

'What would you have done if she'd told you? I mean, it would have been perfectly understandable if you'd gone straight to the SIO on the Susan Best case.'

'I don't know,' Chall said. 'I think I'd certainly have told her to be careful.'

His mouth dry suddenly, Thorne spent a few seconds listening to the machines hiss and beep. He swallowed and said, 'Yeah, course.'

'You think she was close back then? When they killed Susan.'

'They knew she would be, eventually,' Thorne said. 'They knew she wasn't the type to give up.' He looked at Tanner. The wires and the bags, the bandages and the needles. 'Unfortunately, she's also the type who doesn't worry too much about herself, and some people who should have known better didn't do enough to talk some sense into her.'

'Easier said than done,' Chall said. 'She's stubborn.'

Thorne shook his head. 'I should have done more.'

Chall looked at his feet. His shoes were nicely polished. He said, 'They won't get away with it.' A shrug, a simple statement of fact. 'I know you'll do whatever it takes to make sure that doesn't happen. And you know ... if you need a hand.'

'Thanks,' Thorne said. 'But I'd be lying if I said I had the first idea what to do next.'

Chall nodded towards the door. 'Well, whatever happens, she's safe in here. Well done for getting that organised.'

'Yeah,' Thorne said. He looked at his own, somewhat less presentable shoes. He'd certainly made a very good job of closing the stable door after the horse had bolted. It meant nothing, though, less than nothing, because he knew damn well he hadn't done nearly enough to prevent its happening in the first place.

Tanner's DCI wasn't the only one feeling guilty.

Chall looked down at Tanner again. 'Stupid thing is, we've been working together for over a year and I can't really say that I know her. Not properly. I never met Susan and I'm not sure she even knows what my wife's name is. I've only been to her house once and that was just a couple of weeks ago. She's not the type for all that, you know? Going out with the lads, the banter, all the matey stuff. She just gets on with it. But she gave me credit whenever I'd earned it. She listens if I've got something to say and she's always straight. She never plays games, like a lot of them do. You know what I mean?'

Thorne said that he did.

'So, like I said ... whatever needs doing to help you catch the people that did this, I'm bang up for it. Seriously, whatever you need.'

Thorne thanked him again and nodded towards the fruit on the bedside table. He said, 'You could chuck me one of those bananas for a kick-off. I've not had any breakfast.'

PART THREE

FROM CHAOS

FIFTY

Friday, June 2nd

So, another night hiding in my room again, like I'm this house's dirty secret. Well, not hiding exactly, because they both know where I am. It's not like we live in a mansion or anything. Be nice though, obviously! Escaping to my room, that's probably closer to it. Trying to get away from more shouting and stupid arguments and it's starting to really wear me down. It's so unfair, and I know that sounds like whining, but it's the simple truth! No point lying in a diary, is there?

They go on at me like I'm such a disgrace and sometimes I catch them looking at me like I'm something on the bottom of their shoes.

And they've got NO idea! At work today, some idiot was ranting about muslims. 'Bloody muzzies' he called us. Only he used a worse word than 'bloody' and I lost it with him in the end and stuck up for us. I told him he was a moron and I defended our faith.

I COULD HAVE KEPT MY MOUTH SHUT, BUT I DIDN'T!

And then I have to come home to all this SHIT. To the rows and the rubbish that's got NOTHING to do with our religion. I mean, I know I haven't studied as much as I should, but I know the difference between what the faith teaches us and the things I have to put up with at home every day. Mind you, even if I WANTED to study the religion a bit more it would be tricky, wouldn't it? Say I wanted to be a proper muslim scholar (I DON'T by the way!), there's not exactly tons of places that would allow it. I don't even think there are any female imams yet, or only a couple anyway. And there's NOTHING in the Quran that forbids it and all these places that don't allow men and women to pray together are just basing it on something that the Prophet – peace be upon him – is supposed to have said. But nobody knows for sure, do they? None of it's about what God wants, it's just about men wanting to run everything and girls like me knowing their place.

Behaving PROPERLY.

What makes it all so much worse is that I know things would be easier if Mum was still around. Now she's gone, the pair of them can talk to me how they like and just treat me like I'm here to do stuff for them. Like I haven't got a full-time job already! When I'm not running around after them, I'm having to listen to them telling me what a disappointment I am to them, what a terrible sister and daughter.

Mum would have stuck up for me. She'd have tried to, anyway. She'd be here right now, listening to me ranting, rubbing my back and telling me how silly I am to be getting upset.

But I AM upset.

I'm SICK of putting my make-up on in the toilets at the office and taking it off again before I come home. I'm SICK of making excuses when the girls go for a drink after work. I'm SICK of creeping around like a spy and living in a corner.

Worst thing is, if I told them any of this, gave them a hint even, that's exactly what they'd think of me.

It's what they'd think I was.

SICK!

FIFTY-ONE

Muldoon sat down next to his partner on a bench in Soho Square Gardens. Riaz nodded a greeting and shifted across a little. Muldoon watched him fold the corner of a page in the book he had been reading and slip it, somewhat reluctantly, into the M&S bag at his feet.

Muldoon nodded down at the bag. 'Bought yourself some new pants?'

'I needed a few things.' Riaz did not look at Muldoon, but after a few seconds he caved in to the pressure to make conversation. 'What have you been doing?'

'Oh, all sorts.' Muldoon leaned back and stared around, watched the comings and goings, from Oxford Street to Soho and vice versa. It wasn't warm, but there was just enough sun to tempt people out; to eat their lunch on the grass, or, for those with rather more flexible hours, to drink their Special Brew and shout at passers-by. 'When *Cash In The Attic* and a quick wank are the high points of your morning, you realise that your life's going nowhere, you know what I mean?'

Muldoon had spent the morning in bed. Another dingy room

in yet another crappy hotel. He had seen little point in going anywhere, but, after a few hours, boredom had got the better of him and he'd called Riaz to see what he was up to. Riaz had got up bright and early, he had told him, and headed into the centre of town to do a spot of shopping.

Just a regular tourist.

'What the hell are we doing?' Muldoon asked now.

'I told you. We're waiting. We have to wait.'

'Yeah, and I told *you*, didn't I? That whole arson business was a waste of time.'

'You made your feelings very clear,' Riaz said.

'And I was right, wasn't I?'

Riaz said nothing.

'I said it was all too bloody complicated, didn't I? Too fancy. I mean, smoke alarms, for Christ's sake. What's wrong with a gun or a knife ... a hammer or whatever? We were inside, weren't we? We could have just waited for her, done it there and then.'

'That's not what was wanted,' Riaz said.

'You saying he specifically asked for a fire?'

Riaz nodded. 'He wanted her to burn. He wanted it to be slow.'

Muldoon shrugged, like that was fair enough. 'OK, so what now?'

'We have to wait. How many times do I need to tell you?'

'Yeah, I understand, but why do we have to hang around here? I mean it's not like we can get to her now, is it? They're not stupid; there'll be coppers all over the bloody place. Can't we go home and wait?'

Riaz shook his head. 'I think it's best if we stay where we are.'

'Come on, I could go home and sit on my arse there. I could be back here in an hour.'

'Until I hear otherwise, we're still working.'

Muldoon grunted his disgust and looked at Riaz, watched

him close his eyes; bored, or just enjoying the late September sunshine.

Muldoon lived on a modern estate just outside Guildford, which suited him very nicely. It was quiet, anonymous, within easy reach of several major motorways and only twenty-five miles from Gatwick airport. But he had no idea where Riaz called home, not really. It was always Riaz who organised the jobs, then made the call. Pack your bags, we're going to Istanbul, Karachi, Leicester or wherever. As to where he went when a job was finished, Muldoon had an idea there was a place somewhere in the north, and he had once let something slip about a flat in Islamabad. To be fair, there was no point either of them putting down roots anywhere, not when they both travelled so much, but it might have been nice if they'd talked about it once in a while. It wasn't like they'd be having one another over for cosy dinners or what have you, but it came to something when he didn't even know where his partner lived or who he lived with.

Muldoon was very happy living on his own, as long as there were some serviceable pubs around and a decent internet connection when he needed company, but he didn't know about Riaz. Anything was possible, of course, but it was hard to picture him with a wife and a couple of sprogs running around. I mean, how much of a family man could anyone be when they'd done their own sister in?

'When are we getting paid?'

'That's still being discussed,' Riaz said.

'Come on, we did what we were told. It's not our fault if she's still walking around.'

'I don't think she'll be walking anywhere for a while,' Riaz said.

Once each of them had completed his task at the front and back doors of Nicola Tanner's house, they had sat in Riaz's car to watch and wait. After twenty minutes or so they had seen the fire engine arrive and then, eventually, the stretcher being carried round from the back of the building.

'Tell him I'm not very happy,' Muldoon said. 'When you speak to him. Right? Tell him I want paying.'

'I'll pass it on.'

'Actually, why don't I tell him myself? About time I had a word, I reckon.'

'That's not how it works,' Riaz said.

'No?'

'You know it isn't. He talks to me and I talk to you.'

'Yeah, well maybe we should change the way it works.'

'I don't think so.'

That was what Riaz did, whenever Muldoon raised an objection to something or tried to suggest a different way of doing a job. He would close the subject down. Nice and friendly, nice and polite. 'I don't think so', or 'I'll bear it in mind', or 'Let's come back to that another time'.

Fuck's sake . . .

It drove Muldoon mental, but he knew there was no point forcing the issue. All he could do was seethe quietly, store up the frustration and maybe take some of it out on the next girl he bought for a couple of hours.

He stared at a young woman sitting a few feet away until she got up and moved. He narrowed his eyes at a passing teenager. He cursed under his breath, said, 'What are we supposed to *do*?'

Riaz waved lazily in the direction of Trafalgar Square. 'The National Gallery's that way. You could go and look at the pictures.'

'Oh right, yeah. Then maybe I could go to the zoo or catch a movie.'

'Why not?'

Muldoon swore again then fell into a sulky silence. After half a minute or so, he suddenly lunged for the plastic bag at Riaz's feet. Riaz moved quickly to stop him but Muldoon wrestled the bag from his grasp.

He pulled out the book Riaz had been reading. 'Right, what have we got here, then?' He grinned when he saw the cover, sniggered as he read the blurb on the back. '*Romance?* Ah, that's lovely.'

Riaz snatched his book back, cobra-quick. 'I'm amazed you could read it.'

Muldoon smiled and stretched out his legs and watched as a grown man on a scooter almost collided with a couple coming the other way. He pointed, laughing, said, 'See that daft bastard,' but when he looked, Riaz was already on his feet.

The Irishman watched him until he was out of sight, then got up and walked away in the opposite direction.

FIFTY-TWO

It was not as if Thorne had been expecting a branch of Tesco, but he was nevertheless surprised by the limited options on offer at the hospital shop, and it took him ten minutes of careful browsing before he eventually found something he thought Tanner might actually appreciate.

He had already brought in cards, of course – one from Helen and himself and a somewhat saucy offering from Phil Hendricks – but now he wanted to take something in that would prove he had at least thought about an appropriate gift. There were flowers for sale, of course, though nothing more exciting than the bunches you could pick up at the petrol station opposite, and he knew he wouldn't be allowed to leave those in Tanner's room anyway. There was a carousel of paperback thrillers and chick-lit. There were plenty of sweets, chocolates and teddy bears wearing 'Get Well Soon' badges, but little else besides.

Nothing that would be any less pointless a gesture than Chall's rotting fruit.

Paying for his purchase, Thorne wondered if perhaps there were only so many things that patients ever wanted – even those that weren't heavily sedated – beyond toiletries and the like, which their nearest and dearest could always bring from home. Thorne thought back a couple of years, to a week he had spent in hospital with a gunshot wound; tried to remember if there had been anything at that time he had been desperate for someone to bring in. With alcohol and pornography frowned upon even in the most progressive hospitals, he had spent the majority of his time awake with headphones on, listening to music. Hendricks had brought some Johnny Cash CDs in, cracking predictable jokes about country music and mercy killing. Helen had made him a couple of compilations.

There were a few CDs for sale in the shop, but Tanner had already made it clear that music was not exactly one of her passions, so that was never going to be an option.

What had she called it? Background noise.

Thorne smiled, remembering, and on his way to the till he had glanced at some of the musical delights on offer. Michael Bublé, Little Mix, Gary Barlow. He had to concede that, in certain instances, Tanner had a point.

Coming out of the lift on the second floor, he saw the doctor he had spoken to on his first visit and hurried over. She told him she was on her way to the ITU, so he walked with her.

'No change,' she said. 'But that's hardly surprising since she's still under heavy sedation.'

'Probably for the best,' Thorne said.

'Absolutely.'

'She's a pain in the arse when she's awake.'

The doctor blinked, stared at him.

'Sorry.' Thorne felt himself begin to redden. 'Stupid joke. I get a bit nervous around . . . you know.'

'Women?'

'Doctors,' Thorne said.

Now the doctor was smiling. 'Anyway, the good news is that I've finally managed to schedule a date for the surgery.'

'That's great,' Thorne said.

'Well, not entirely. It's three days away, but obviously we'll keep her nicely drugged up until then. The main thing is, she's in no danger.'

Thorne nodded, thinking about the reason why there was a police officer posted outside Tanner's door, which was when he heard the sound of a commotion around the next corner, precisely where that officer was supposed to be.

Before the doctor could react, Thorne was running, and he rounded the corner to see two people he recognised having a stand-up row with a uniformed PC. He slowed to a quick walk, keen to listen.

'It's ridiculous, completely ridiculous.' Arman Bannerjee was shouting and waving an enormous bunch of flowers around. 'I've taken time out of a busy day to come here, and now I'm being treated like a criminal.'

'Not at all, sir,' the officer said.

'Just because you say "sir" doesn't mean you're showing us any respect.' Bannerjee's son, Ravi, stood just behind his father, hands deep in the pockets of his hoodie. 'You get that, officer?'

'Respect's got nothing to do with it.'

'You reckon?'

The PC was on his feet and did not appear to be the least bit intimidated. He said, 'It's very simple. I've got a list and if your name isn't on it, you don't get to go in.' He brandished the all-important piece of paper, then carefully folded it and put it away in his pocket.

Now only a few feet away, Thorne was pleased to see the hint of a smile on the young officer's face. The list he had been talking about was a very short one. Thorne himself, Dipak Chall, family members ... and even if the visitor was on the list, the officer on duty had been instructed to demand ID.

'Can I help?' Thorne sauntered up, smiling as the Bannerjees turned to look at him. He nodded to the PC. 'I'll take it from here.'

The officer said, 'Sir,' and sat down again.

'Problem?'

'Yes there is.' The elder Banerjee took a breath as though to calm himself down. As though he had done all his shouting at the monkey and was now ready for a more reasonable discussion with the organ grinder. 'As I was trying to explain to your colleague, I have simply come to visit Miss Tanner and to deliver this.' With a crackle of cellophane, he once again held out what was certainly an impressive bouquet. 'But it seems as though we are not permitted to do so. We are not on a list.'

Thorne nodded and smiled again, nice and reasonable. 'The fact is that Detective Inspector Tanner is in hospital because someone tried to kill her.'

'Yes, I know that.' Bannerjee shook his head sadly. 'I was extremely shocked to hear it. We all were.'

'So, we are simply taking reasonable precautions to protect her while she recovers.'

'Yes, I understand, but you *know* us.'

'I certainly do.'

'I think that's the problem,' Ravi Bannerjee said.

Thorne looked at the son. 'I'm not with you.'

'You think someone tried to kill her because of this honour killing business, right?'

'I think it's a reasonable assumption, don't you?'

'Not really. I mean, someone could try and kill a copper for all sorts of reasons.' The boy was pushing twenty, perhaps older, but his demeanour was that of a typically sulky teenager. 'They make enemies, don't they?'

'Nobody's arguing with that.'

'For whatever reason, you've got it into your head that these supposed honour killings might have something to do with the organisation my dad's involved with.'

300

Arman Bannerjee turned to his son. 'Please, don't start with all that again. There's really no need for any . . . confrontation.'

Ravi had not taken his eyes off Thorne. 'So obviously he's not going to be on this precious list of yours, is he? This list of people who can be trusted.'

'Oh, I wouldn't get too worked up about it,' Thorne said. 'There's all sorts of people who aren't on that list. Right now, the Archbishop of Canterbury wouldn't be able to get into that room.'

'It's a shame, that's all.' Arman Bannerjee looked down at his bouquet. 'I come all this way in good faith to make a gesture, to show support, and the door is closed to me. A very great shame.'

'Nice flowers,' Thorne said.

Bannerjee nodded, sniffed at them. 'Yes and I should point out that they are not just from me. They are also a gift from imam Mansoor and Mr Dhillon, from all our communities. We clubbed together.'

'Three of you?' Thorne said. 'That's very generous.'

'The least we can do.'

'Why don't I take them and I'll make sure they're put in her room?'

Bannerjee nodded and handed the bouquet over.

Thorne took a sniff himself, then said, 'Oh, now I come to think about it, Detective Inspector Tanner isn't actually allowed flowers. Risk of infection. Sorry.'

Bannerjee stared at him, the muscles working in his jaw, as though struggling to keep his anger in check, or simply trying to decide if he should take his bouquet back again. In the end he just turned and walked away.

The boy walked slowly backwards after his father, then pointed. 'Like I said to PC Plod.' The finger moved to Thorne. 'Like I said to *you* last time, it's about respect.'

Thorne watched them go, then turned to the officer who had sat staring at the wall opposite throughout the exchange. 'You married?'

The PC shook his head.

'Girlfriend?'

'Yeah.'

'Here you go.' Thorne thrust the flowers at him. 'You might get your leg over tonight.'

Leaving the officer looking somewhat ridiculous, sitting and clutching the ostentatious bouquet, Thorne pushed open the door and walked into Tanner's room. Today there was light rain spattering the window, but little else appeared to have changed. The machines still hummed and hissed and Tanner was still connected to them.

She was every bit as insensible.

He carefully removed his gift from the plastic bag he'd been given in the shop and set it down on the table next to Tanner's bed.

Then he dropped into a chair and waited.

Just once, he thought he saw her eyelids flutter and a few moments later her mouth appeared to tighten as though something was happening in a dream of which she seriously disapproved.

A sloppily completed expenses form maybe, or a misfiled document. Thorne hoped it was something like that.

After a minute or two he heard voices outside and a few seconds later the door opened and Dipak Chall walked in.

He said, 'I heard there was some trouble.'

'Unwelcome visitors.' Chall looked at him, concerned, but Thorne shook his head. He watched the DS take his jacket off and fold it across the back of a chair. 'No big deal.'

Chall pulled a selection of magazines from the satchel he was carrying and set them down on the table next to the cards, the water jug and the gift Thorne had deposited. He carefully straightened the pile. He sat down and, once again, he and Thorne looked at each other across the bed, and the unconscious woman who was in it.

FIFTY-THREE

In the dream there was blood in Susan's hair, streaked through the curls like a cheap dye job, and she had no eyes. Such horrors aside though, it was recognisably her. The tatty old sweatshirt she would put on the moment she came in from school. The freckles and the crooked smile and the gap in her teeth that she could whistle through.

If she wanted to attract someone's attention.

If something surprised her.

If she thought Tanner was looking particularly gorgeous.

There were times when it felt to Tanner as though she were drifting in and out of consciousness, only for a moment or two perhaps, and whether it was actually happening or not she somehow understood exactly where she was. *How* she was. There was a memory, a dream within a dream, of the paramedic giving her something as she lay sprawled on the patio, and then being given something else once they arrived at the hospital. She'd known she was going under, had thanked God for it, and she still did, because she knew very well that, back in the land of the living, there was nothing waiting for her but pain.

In the dream, Susan spoke to her, the flames rising up around both of them and the smoke like oily hands pressed across their faces. Susan smiled and shook her head, the blood flying from her hair. She said, 'See, Nic ... this is what happens when you get a bee in your bonnet. You just need to step away sometimes, let it go. Like the song.'

That soppy Disney film they had watched a couple of Christmases before. A song Susan had sung to her many times since.

Tanner was crying and Susan told her not to, told her that none of this was her fault. Tanner knew very well that it was, but she understood that Susan would never blame her and that she would have seen the affection in her partner's eyes had there been anything to see but blackness and blisters.

The damage they had done to her.

In the dream, there were other voices, drifting like snippets from a badly tuned radio. Names mentioned that Tanner recognised, that sparked something in her; the people she believed had brought her to this. The people who had done these things to both of them. So, when Susan began to hum that stupid song, burning, bloody and eyeless, Tanner could only shake her head, because, even in a dream, she could never let go of anything.

FIFTY-FOUR

Three days later, on a bright but cold Tuesday afternoon, Thorne stepped out of Aldgate East tube station and set off along Whitechapel High Street. He called the hospital and, after several minutes of irritatingly upbeat hold music, he was finally put through to a nurse who was willing to give him the information he was after.

Albeit a little brusquely.

Tanner's surgery had gone well, he was told, and she was now on her way back from the recovery area. Thorne thanked the nurse, and as soon as he had ended the call he made another, to ensure that once again there would be an officer stationed permanently outside Tanner's room.

Thrusting his hands deep into the pockets of his leather jacket, Thorne turned left on to Brick Lane and picked up his pace. He smiled as he passed the first piece of street art – an enormous mural of a vaguely furtive hedgehog – or perhaps he was simply looking forward to passing on the good news about Tanner's operation to the man he was on his way to meet.

It had been a while since Thorne had been on this street, one of the most famous in east London, and his last visit had not ended well. A stag party he had been roped into had ended, predictably, in one of Brick Lane's famous curry houses, and a row with a group of braying City boys on the adjacent table. When the groom-to-be – who Thorne had never liked much to begin with – had picked up an empty Kingfisher bottle, Thorne had been forced to step in and produce his warrant card, quickly defusing an ugly situation and almost certainly saving the bolshie DS his job.

Walking past another colourful mural and getting his first sniff of one of those curry houses, Thorne decided that this street was a perfect example of everything that was great about living in a multi-ethnic city. Fifty yards further ahead was the Brick Lane mosque. Once a home for French Protestants, then later the 'great synagogue' for the East End's influx of European Jews, it was now a place of worship for the area's Bangladeshi Muslims, whose culture and cuisine gave the street its unique flavour. Its sights and sounds and smells.

God, those amazing smells.

The Royal Taj was at the north end of the lane, across from the old Truman brewery, and Arman Bannerjee was sitting at a table with a view of the door. Best in the place, Thorne guessed. The businessman looked up as Thorne came through the door and, walking across to the table, Thorne saw no reason to disguise his delight at the fact that he was eating with friends.

Dhillon and Mansoor were watching him, too.

'I'm sorry to interrupt your lunch.' Thorne spoke directly to Bannerjee.

'How did you know I was here?'

'I spoke to your secretary,' Thorne said. 'She was very helpful.' He nodded towards Dhillon and Mansoor. 'She didn't tell me that you'd have company.'

Bannerjee shrugged. His napkin was tucked into his collar to protect his expensive-looking jacket. 'We don't just have weekly meetings, you know. We have a lot of other things to discuss. There's a website to keep on top of, and newsletters ... and we're trying to co-ordinate a demonstration.'

'A peaceful demonstration,' Dhillon said. The Sikh, who was a little older than his companions, smiled and passed a hand across the front of his turban. 'Above all, it must be peaceful.'

'Of course,' Thorne said.

'That goes without saying,' Bannerjee said.

Mansoor, the imam, pointed to the empty chair at the table. 'Would you like to join us?'

Thorne hesitated, glancing at the waiter standing expectantly nearby. 'Are you sure?'

'Of course,' Mansoor said.

'Please.' Bannerjee looked down at his food, and was already eating again as Thorne said 'That's very kind' and slipped into the chair next to him.

Dhillon signalled to the waiter and, once an extra plate had been laid down, he nudged several of the serving bowls towards Thorne. 'We always order too much, anyway,' he said.

Mansoor grunted, then he too went back to his lunch.

The meal, unsurprisingly, was vegetarian, and though Thorne's favourite Indian dishes all contained lamb or chicken, he was hungry enough to make the sacrifice. He eagerly helped himself to aubergine, dhal and okra. He took two large spoonfuls of rice and tore off a healthy section of roti.

He turned to Bannerjee and said, 'I wanted to tell you that Detective Inspector Tanner had her surgery this morning and that it went well.'

The three of them looked up.

'I thought you'd like to know.'

'That's wonderful news,' Mansoor said.

Dhillon nodded enthusiastically. 'Yes, very good news. We were all so shocked at what happened to her. A very bad business.'

'Who would do such a thing?' Mansoor looked around the table. 'A fire.'

'Really?' Bannerjee stared at Thorne, chewing. 'You came here just to tell me that?'

'Well . . .'

'Of course it's excellent news, but could you not have just telephoned?' He smiled, a sliver of something caught between his teeth. 'You could have left a message with my secretary.'

'I suppose I could,' Thorne said.

Bannerjee's smile was suddenly a little thinner. 'It's odd, that's all. I mean, a few days ago we were not even on the list.'

There were knowing nods from Mansoor and Dhillon.

'Yes, well, I also wanted to apologise for what happened at the hospital,' Thorne said. 'I understand if you were offended, but you must appreciate that my primary concern must be for my colleague's safety.'

'It was unfortunate,' Dhillon said.

'You weren't there,' Bannerjee said, quickly. 'It was humiliating.'

Mansoor reached across to pull a dish towards him. 'So, are you?'

'Am I what?' Thorne asked.

'Are you apologising?'

Thorne tried to hold the stare but the imam had the beating of him. 'I'm sorry Mr Bannerjee was offended,' he said.

Mansoor scoffed and shook his head. 'A politician's answer.'

'We talk to politicians,' Dhillon said. 'On behalf of our organisation. We tell them they are not doing enough to prevent or punish these attacks on our communities. These hate crimes. Oh, they are always so very sorry that such things are happening, sorry that people are afraid and angry. They are never sorry that in many ways they are allowing it to happen. Never sorry that it's their fault.'

'I'm just a copper,' Thorne said.

Dhillon grunted, used a piece of bread to mop up his plate. Mansoor muttered something and brushed crumbs from the sleeve of his dark tunic.

A waiter cleared the table and asked if they wanted anything else. Mansoor and Dhillon asked for mint tea and Thorne ordered coffee.

'How is the investigation going?' Bannerjee said. 'If you don't mind my asking.'

'Which one?'

'Excuse me?'

'You mean the attempt on Detective Inspector Tanner's life or the series of honour killings?'

There was no noticeable reaction from Bannerjee. Dhillon and Mansoor drank their tea. But Thorne felt the atmosphere change at the mention of those two charged words. He smiled into the silence.

'Miss Tanner,' Bannerjee said, eventually.

'Of course, it doesn't really matter, because it's the same investigation. The two things are connected. The honour killings are the reason someone tried to burn her house down while she was still in it.'

'How can you possibly say that?' Dhillon said.

'Because it's the truth.'

Mansoor was quick to back his friend up, eyeing Thorne across his teacup. 'Nobody is questioning that there was an attempt on Miss Tanner's life. There is very clear evidence of it. Honour-based violence is a deplorable activity which all our communities must engage with, but the idea that there is a *series* of ...' He shook his head as though he could not bring himself to say the word. 'That people are carrying out these ... acts for money. Nobody has ever produced a single piece of evidence.' He brought his hand down on the table, rattling the cups. 'Not a single piece.'

'You said it yourself.' Dhillon held out his arms. 'You are just a police officer, so surely evidence is your stock in trade.'

'Usually,' Thorne said. 'When I can get it.'

'Take that poor young Muslim couple who went missing three weeks ago. This is a very good example.'

'An example of something, certainly.'

Mansoor nodded sadly. 'Amaya Shah and Kamal Azim.'

Dhillon leaned across the table. 'There is a good deal of evidence to suggest that this was, in fact, anything *but* an honour killing. So how can you sit there and—?'

Bannerjee raised a hand and said, 'Yes, well.' His words brought an abrupt end to an exchange that was threatening to become heated. It was the same tone Thorne had seen him use to rein in his son at the hospital a few days before. The Hindu businessman seemed to be the unofficial leader of the triumvirate. Or perhaps he was simply paying for lunch.

He looked at Thorne. 'If I might repeat my question, how is your investigation going?'

Thorne leaned back. 'As a matter of fact, I was going to ask for your help.'

'Us?'

Suddenly, he had the attention of all three.

'Well, yes . . . of course,' Mansoor said. 'Anything we can do,'

'Absolutely,' Dhillon said.

'That's good to hear.' Thorne picked up one of the chocolates that the waiter had left and began to pick at the gold foil. 'When's your next meeting?'

FIFTY-FIVE

Ilyas Nazir was as observant as he was devout.

He had first noticed the man a week or so before at Tuesday morning prayers, and seen him at every session since. An unassuming individual, seemingly alone, and always laying his prayer mat down towards the back of the room. A new face would usually catch Nazir's eye, but something compelled him to seek that particular face out again each time he entered the mosque, and now he found himself drifting through the crowd, looking for it. New worshippers were always welcome, of course, but this man had an almost visible fervour about him; a need that Nazir had picked up on almost straight away.

He looked troubled.

Nazir prided himself on an intimate knowledge of this congregation. He had been worshipping here for many years and knew exactly who was who. He saw allegiances forged and watched enmities develop. He understood the make-up of every clique and faction and was very well aware which people were here to be seen and who came to genuinely surrender themselves to the True and Only Creator. More important, everyone knew who *he* was. He enjoyed the fact that he was known as someone to whom others turned for advice or expertise. Someone they looked up to. He was not the imam, of course, and only the imam himself could offer genuine guidance, but he was most certainly respected and, other than those precious moments of *salah*, five times daily, when, like everyone else, he was necessarily prostrate before God, Ilyas Nazir walked around the mosque with his head held high.

Exchanging pleasantries with fellow worshippers and asking after their families. Humbly accepting the occasional gift or acknowledging good wishes.

Smiling beneath his gold skullcap.

Immediately following the noon prayer, the congregation was moving towards the exit, and once again Nazir spotted the newcomer. Was it not a tradition to welcome strangers? A pillar of the faith? He quickly extricated himself from his conversation and finally caught up with the man just outside the main doors. Groups had gathered as usual to gossip and smoke, pulling on overcoats against the cold.

He put an anorak on over his white jubba, then reached to lay a hand on the man's shoulder.

'*As-salaam-alaikum.*' He held out a hand, which the stranger took, if a little cautiously.

'*As-salaam-alaikum.*'

'I'm Ilyas.' He smiled. 'Ilyas Nazir.' He looked for something in the man's face to suggest that the name was familiar to him, and was disappointed to see nothing. He waited.

'Oh, I'm sorry . . . Jad Hakim.'

'Good to meet you, Jad. You've not been coming here very long.'

Hakim stared at his shoes. Shy, or nervous. 'No. Just a week or so.'

'Well . . . welcome. You could not have chosen a better place to worship. You will make many friends here, I can promise you that.'

'Thank you,' Hakim said. He did not sound overly thrilled at the idea.

Nazir waved at someone passing behind Hakim, promised to call someone else who stopped briefly to say goodbye. He shook his head and smiled, as though exhausted by the demands on his time. 'So, have you been attending a different mosque? Wood Green, perhaps, or Haringey?'

'No.'

'They are very good, too.'

'We only moved to the area a few months ago,' Hakim said. 'From Slough.'

Nazir's eyes widened. 'Moving *to* London?' He laughed. 'That's a brave step, considering the house prices.'

Hakim smiled for the first time, but it didn't last long. 'I know ... but we had to move and I've got a cousin in London. It was his idea, actually. We've had some family problems. So ...'

'I'm sorry to hear that.'

'It's fine,' Hakim said, though Nazir could tell that it really wasn't. 'Family, right?'

'Of course. Things don't always go the way we would like them, but sometimes Allah tests us with such things.' He took a packet of cigarettes from the pocket of his anorak, shook one out.

Hakim stared at him.

'I know,' Nazir said, lighting up. 'But in terms of the commandments, these things are a grey area.' He smiled as he inhaled, remembering the conversation he'd had with the policewoman, Tanner. 'By "family" you mean ... ?'

'My sister,' Hakim said.

'Ah.'

'Where we were living before, she fell in with a crowd, you know? Girls who were not living the right way. There were boys.'

'What's your sister's name?'

'Raheema.'

'Merciful and kind.'

'Yes,' Hakim said.

'How old is she?'

'Nineteen. She is refusing to marry, to talk about it even, spitting in my father's face.' Hakim looked close to tears. 'We thought that by moving away things might change, that she might straighten up and see how much shame she was bringing on us all.'

'But they haven't.'

Hakim shook his head. 'We were stupid, really. In London there are so many more opportunities for her to stray, to be ... wild.'

Nazir took a long drag. 'You must talk to the imam.'

'I have,' Hakim said. 'Days ago.'

'What did he tell you?'

'To pray for guidance. To pray hard.'

'Well, I'm sure that it will come,' Nazir said. 'The Most Gracious will show you the way.'

'I hope so.'

'He always does.'

Hakim nodded, straightened his plain white skullcap, but once again he looked as though he might burst into tears. 'I have thought bad things,' he said. 'About doing bad things.' His voice dropped to a whisper. 'The *worst* thing.'

'I understand,' Nazir said.

'But I don't think I'm brave enough.'

'Then perhaps it is the wrong thing.' Nazir tossed what was left of his cigarette away and stepped close to the newcomer. 'Now you feel as though your back is against the wall, so you think about an extreme course of action. But in time, this may change and you will be able to forget you ever had such an idea. As I said, when the Almighty chooses to show you the way, you will know.'

Hakim turned and stared out across the playing field. He shivered and hunched his shoulders against the cold. 'Thank you,' he said.

Nazir shrugged, as though he had simply been giving him street directions. 'Any time you want to talk.'

Hakim nodded, then reached into his jacket and produced an envelope. He held it gingerly towards Nazir.

'What's this?'

'It's my sister's diary. Well . . . I couldn't take the whole thing because she would know. So I borrowed it when she was at work and went to the local newsagent's and copied a few pages.' He kept his voice low, as though he were a spy handing over state secrets.

Nazir glanced around then reached for the envelope.

'If you read them, you'll see.'

When yet another person stopped by to talk to Nazir, Hakim stepped aside and began to walk away, but even as Nazir was tucking the envelope into his pocket and greeting his new companion like a long-lost friend, he kept one eye on his newest. Laughing at a joke he had already heard several times, he watched Jad Hakim trudging across the car park; stooped, as though burdened with a terrible despair and desperate for its weight to be lifted.

FIFTY-SIX

Saturday, July 8th

    I used to try to keep these pages secret, I mean that's what you're supposed to do with a diary, right? But I always knew you would look for it, that you would keep searching until you found it, so what's the point in hiding it any more? I can't be bothered wasting my time.

    So ... HELLO JAD!!!

    I KNOW you're looking at this, so as a special one-off treat, today's ramblings are JUST for you.

    Hope it's a cracking good read.

    Same thing with the make-up. I used to stash it in plastic bags behind the radiator then fish them out with a coat hanger. Is that how you found it? I know you did, because lipsticks and things were always going missing and I know you threw them away. Unless you wanted to use them yourself. Course not, because I know what you think about boys who wear make-up!! Thing is, I always know when you've been

316

in my room because I can smell your stupid aftershave. You think it makes you smell like a man, sexy or whatever, but it makes you smell like old socks and cheesy feet. So when I come in, I know you've been poking about, searching for something to disapprove of. I can literally sniff you out, bro! Now I make a point of buying things like that, clothes or whatever. Because if you and dad would hate it, I know it must be pretty cool.

I mean it's not like any of this stuff is DRUGS, is it? I'm not taking anything. I don't drink much and I only smoke at parties or whatever, and I know that you do plenty of both and so does dad, puffing away on those stupid shisha pipes at the café like nobody's business.

Oh yeah, I forgot, it's all different if you're a man, isn't it?

STUPID ME!

Thing is, if I sound angry, it's because I am. I'm nearly twenty for crying out loud. I work, I pay taxes and I STILL do my fair share in the house. MORE than my fair share. If me wearing a particular top or hanging out with particular people makes you uncomfortable or OFFENDS you, that's your problem, not mine, because I won't be told what to put on my face or who to see or what music to listen to. I don't care what your pathetic friends are telling you or what you might see online or anything. You and dad are the ones that need to change, not me.

I like my life, OK? You need to DEAL with that. If I ever seem unhappy, it's only because you and dad and all your ridiculous rules have made me that way.

There. Did you enjoy that?

R xoxo

FIFTY-SEVEN

The boy had not smiled, not once.

He sat hard against one end of a sofa, a few feet away from the social worker, there because she had already established a meaningful relationship with the boy, as well as taking on the necessary role of appropriate adult. Helen sat in a brown corduroy armchair opposite them both. This was not the same room in which the social worker had conducted her initial interviews – there were no cupboards filled with therapeutic toys or drawing equipment – but they were in the same building. When Helen interviewed the boy's father, as she would do in a few days' time, it would be in a somewhat less comfortable room at the station in Streatham, where her team was based, but for this final round of conversations with the twelve-year-old and his elder brother it was important that the surroundings were familiar.

'I like it in here,' the boy had said when they'd come in.

'That's good,' Helen had said.

'It's very tidy.' The boy had nodded approvingly, ignoring a large, multicoloured beanbag and settling down instead on the sofa. 'Our house is always such a mess.'

Helen had laughed. 'You ought to see mine.'

'Are you messy?'

'I've got a little boy.' Helen had taken her jacket off, laid it on the floor next to her handbag. 'He's *very* messy.'

The boy was wearing his school uniform. Helen wasn't sure if it was because he was going to school once they'd finished or if it was simply what his mother had chosen for him to wear. It might have been the boy's choice, of course, but Helen doubted it. His mother was waiting in an adjacent room and his father was at work. They were both – so Helen had been informed – as alarmed as they were confused by the initial inquiries by social services, and were now hugely distressed at the involvement of a Met police child abuse investigation team.

They were loving parents, they said. They had nothing to hide.

Helen would have been surprised, and not a little suspicious, to have heard anything different.

'Do you like school, Kyle?' she asked.

The boy scratched his head, tousling his dirty-blond hair. 'It's all right.'

'Have you got lots of friends?'

'Depends what you mean.'

'Well, the boys you hang around with at playtime.'

The boy shook his head, serious. 'We don't call it playtime. That's what you call it at baby school. We call it break.'

'Sorry. At break, then.'

The boy shrugged. 'There's a few different ones. Depends if anyone's been annoying me. I normally hang around with my brother.'

'Isn't he usually with the older kids, though?'

The boy sniffed and began picking at something on the arm of the sofa.

Helen looked down at the iPad on her lap. She scrolled through her notes. 'Looks like you're pretty good at sport. Football and swimming . . . bit of a star at sports day.'

Another shrug.

'But you haven't been doing as much sport lately, have you? Your teachers say that you've been pulling out of a lot of lessons and practices because you're not feeling well, or you've hurt yourself.'

'I couldn't play football a couple of times because I'd hurt my leg.'

'How did you hurt your leg?'

'I can't remember.'

'OK . . .'

'Oh yeah . . . I think I fell over when I was running for a bus. I remember because that was when I broke my phone.'

'Was that how you got the bruise? Here?' Helen patted her thigh.

The boy nodded. Helen had seen photos of the bruise; purple and saucer-sized, a little bigger than those on both his arms.

'Your teachers also say that you haven't been doing as well in class as you used to.'

'Which teachers?'

'Well, it doesn't matter which ones, but several of them. You were doing really well, they reckon.' Helen scrolled and nodded, as though impressed at what she was seeing. 'Top of your class in several subjects, always handing your homework in on time . . . but in the last few months your work's not been any-where near as good. And you're not joining in as much.'

'It's boring,' the boy said.

'Really? Why wasn't it boring before?'

'Sometimes I just don't feel like it, that's all.' He watched Helen working at her iPad. 'What's on there?'

'Just my notes,' Helen said. 'So I don't forget anything.'

'I'd love one of them.'

'They're very useful.'

'You know you can watch videos on them? Do you watch videos on it?'

Helen shook her head. 'You like to watch videos?'

The boy said yes, that of course he did, and sat forward slightly. This was a subject he was obviously far happier discussing than school.

'What do you like to watch?'

'*Game Of Thrones.*' The answer was instant, definitive. 'Best TV show ever.'

Helen nodded. She had never seen the programme, but knew that it was pretty violent. She also knew that it contained a fair amount of sex, but she wasn't naïve enough to presume that this was in any way significant. Unless they were very closely monitored, most twelve-year-olds had access to sexual content far more explicit than anything they might see on television, with parents who were guilty of no more than simple carelessness.

'There's a lot of violence, isn't there? In *Game Of Thrones*?'

'Yeah. There's loads of battles, so people get killed.'

'Is that the sort of stuff you were thinking of when you did some of your drawings? There was a lot of blood and knives and things.'

The boy blinked and looked away. 'Yeah. Like on TV.'

'Why do you like that kind of thing so much?'

'Because it's funny,' the boy said.

Helen exchanged a look with the social worker. 'Funny?'

'Yeah. It makes us laugh.'

'You and ... ?'

'Me and my brother, and my dad. Not my mum though, because she hates all that. Says it makes her feel sick.'

Helen sat back and let a few moments pass. The boy was still picking at the arm of the sofa. A stain, or a loose thread, or nothing at all.

'What about when it's just you and your dad? What kind of things do you do together?'

The boy puffed out his cheeks as though slightly bored. This was an area he had been drawn into before. 'Watch videos ... watch TV ... he helps with my homework sometimes, but not if it's maths, because he's rubbish at that.'

Helen looked at the social worker again. It was much the same response *she* had got, that Helen had seen in the videos she'd watched.

Casual and apparently stress-free.

No obvious red flags.

'I've got a sister,' Helen said. 'She's a bit younger than me ... same sort of difference between us as you and your brother.'

'What's her name?'

'Jenny,' Helen said. 'I remember when we were your age, we used to play all sorts of special games that we didn't want grown-ups to know about. Things that were just ours, you know? Most of all, we liked to have *secrets*. We had a code that nobody else could understand, so we could talk about things without anyone knowing. We'd sit in a corner and whisper things to each other ... *our* things. Do you do anything like that?'

'What do you mean?'

'Do you have special secrets?'

'*What?*'

'You and your brother.'

The boy began scratching hard at the arm of the sofa and then stood up suddenly. He said, 'Can I have a drink?'

'We're nearly finished,' Helen said.

'I'm thirsty, though.'

'Just a few minutes.'

The boy let out a long sigh and began to walk around the room, just as Helen had seen him do in the video. He looked closely at random points on the walls and at the window frames. He picked up a decorative vase from a low table and examined it, his eyes everywhere but on the two women in the room with him.

'I've only got a few more questions,' Helen said. 'Then I'll get you a drink. A Coke or something?'

The boy trudged back towards them, then dropped with a grunt on to the beanbag. He shuffled a few feet to the right then looked from the social worker to Helen, and back.

He suddenly seemed absurdly relaxed and confident.

The social worker said, 'Is everything OK, Kyle?'

The boy nodded, and for the first time there was the trace of a smile. He said, 'I can see right up your skirt.'

The social worker reddened and quickly crossed her legs. She took a few seconds to compose herself, then said, 'I'm sorry if I embarrassed you.'

'I think you embarrassed yourself.' The boy's smile became a smirk. 'Sitting there with your legs open.'

Helen said the boy's name, but he wasn't listening. She watched as he began waving his hand in front of his face as if trying to get rid of a terrible stench.

'Can you smell *fish*?' He began to laugh, then stopped, screwed up his face in mock-disgust and laughed again. He rolled back on the beanbag, helpless with laughter and repeating what sounded very much like a joke someone else had told him.

'I can smell fish!'

FIFTY-EIGHT

'I think she's been feeling a bit ignored,' Hendricks said.

Tanner nodded vigorously and said, 'Too bloody right I have. Miserable bastards.'

'I told you, I've been in to see you several times already,' Thorne said. 'But you weren't exactly great company back then. This is the first time you've actually been . . . chatty.' He looked across at Hendricks who was sitting on the other side of the bed and rolled his eyes.

'Too bloody chatty if you ask me,' Hendricks said. 'Having said that, I'm still waiting to hear about the burly firemen.' He shook his head. 'Fifteen minutes I've been sitting here and she's said nothing about their nice shiny helmets, nothing about the size of their hoses.' He sighed. 'All be lost on her, obviously.'

'I know,' Tanner's voice was a little deeper than usual, slow and slurry.

Thorne looked at her. 'You know what?'

'I know you were here.' She smiled. 'I mean, I knew you were here when you were here.'

'I don't think so.'

There was more nodding from Tanner, who had been raised up a little in her bed. Two days on from her surgery, there were still dressings on her face and tubes attached to the back of one hand. In the other, she clutched the clicker for an infusion pump, which she was using to administer morphine to herself intravenously. She had been pushing the green button every few minutes since Thorne and Hendricks had arrived. 'Oh yes,' she said. 'You and Dipak Chall. Sitting in here and rattling on about Bannerjee and the rest of them. Mumbling about meetings and flowers and whatever. Blah blah blah.'

'You heard what we were saying?'

Tanner moaned and Thorne heard the beep as she pushed the green button again. He was not overly concerned, because he knew that the pump was fitted with an interval breaker, designed to prevent the patient from giving herself more of the drug than was needed. He looked at Hendricks and shook his head. It was apparent to both of them that she'd had more than enough already.

'Anyway, I was busy,' she said. 'Susan and I had things to talk about.'

'How did that go?' Hendricks asked.

Tanner turned to look at him. 'Please don't talk to me as if I'm an imbecile, Philip. I didn't land on my head when I jumped out of that window. I'm well aware that Susan's dead and that I only saw her because of the drugs, but that doesn't mean it didn't feel very real at the time.'

'Sorry,' Hendricks said. He looked towards the window and dipped his head, like a chided schoolboy.

'Oh, Christ.' Tanner tried to sit up, moaning in pain with the effort.

Thorne reached for her hand. 'What?'

'The cat. What happened to Susan's cat?'

'The cat's fine,' Thorne said. 'I told you when we came in.'

'She's with your neighbour,' Hendricks said.

Tanner let out a long breath, stabbed at the green button again. 'You need to make sure that woman's all right to take care of her for a while, that she knows what kind of food to give her. I'll sort it all out when I get home. Well, obviously I won't be *home* for a while ... God knows when that'll be, but when I get out of here, I mean. She needs to know what kind of food to give her.'

'Cat food?' Hendricks said.

'She's very fussy, you know?'

Thorne nodded. Tanner had said all this once already. 'You don't need to worry about any of this stuff,' he said. 'Just concentrate on getting back on your feet. The good news is that there's no major damage to your lungs, so now you just have to give everything time to heal properly, get started on your physio—'

'She saved me, you know? The cat.'

'Right.' Thorne caught the look on Hendricks's face, sensed a sarcastic remark coming and softly shushed him.

'She woke me up.' Tanner slowly lifted the hand to which the drips were attached. She brought it to her chest and gently kneaded with her fingers. Then she screwed her eyes shut and shook her head, confused. She turned to Thorne. 'Why didn't the smoke alarms go off?'

Thorne looked away for a few moments. Some of the fruit Chall had brought was still there in a bowl on the bedside table, alongside a good many cards and the gift that Thorne had delivered several days earlier. He didn't know if she'd seen it yet. 'They took the batteries out,' he said.

'Who?'

'They were in the house. Before.'

Tanner nodded and pushed the control for the morphine pump. 'The Asian and the Irishman.'

'I presume so,' Thorne said.

'Well, that's one thing Susan can't blame me for,' Tanner said.

'Her stupid idea to leave a spare key under that plant pot. I never got round to moving it.'

'It doesn't matter.'

'Too many other things to do.' Tanner was shaking her head, grimacing as the words tumbled out. 'I had to replace the carpet for a start and sort the bills out. I had to decide what to do with all her clothes and I was trying to deal with her mum and dad and then those two went missing off the Tube and you know what they did to her eyes?' She turned to look at Thorne. 'Tom? Do you know what was left of them?'

Thorne reached for her hand again; a fist tightly wrapped around the morphine pump.

'Holes. That was all, holes.' She snatched her hand away from Thorne's. She said nothing for half a minute. Her eyelids fluttered and finally closed softly, and she said, 'Fuckers.'

Hendricks folded his arms, as though disgusted. 'Well, I'm not sure if those drugs are helping with the pain, but they certainly aren't doing a lot for your vocabulary.'

They watched her for another minute or so. It looked as though she was asleep, but just as they were about to stand up and leave, she said, 'And you can fuck off as well, Philip.'

Waiting for the lift, Hendricks said, 'She's off her tits.'

'I reckon it suits her.' Thorne pushed the button again. 'She should do it more often.'

Hendricks nodded. 'Maybe I should take her down Old Compton Street one night, when she's up and about again.'

'Good luck with that.'

'We'll do a few poppers, go mental.'

'You think she'll remember? When she comes off the drugs. What she's like now, I mean ... the things she's coming out with.'

'Depends,' Hendricks said. 'I'm a bit hazy after a couple of pints on a night out with you.' He looked at Thorne. 'Why?'

Thorne shook his head. 'Just not sure she'd like it, that's all. You know how ... buttoned up she normally is.'

The lift arrived and they stood aside to let its occupants out.

'So, how's it all going? Your pair of honour killers.'

'It's going backwards,' Thorne said. 'We rattled a few bars, but it didn't really get us anywhere.'

They walked into the lift and Hendricks pushed the button.

'So?'

'So, I thought I might go to the next meeting, see if I can rattle them a bit harder.'

'By doing what?'

As the lift door closed, Thorne started to tell him.

A minute or so later, stepping out on to the ground floor, Hendricks said, 'You two make a good pair.'

Thorne waited.

'You're *both* off your tits.'

FIFTY-NINE

Prostrate, he muttered in Arabic. 'Glorified is my Lord, the most great.' He said it three times, but on another day it might have been five, or seven; always an odd number.

The clearly prescribed movements and recitations of the prayer ritual were, by now, second nature to Ilyas Nazir, but, as always, he carried out each one with strong purpose and feeling, with devotion in his heart. Now, after almost ten minutes of prayer – of bowing low to await God's orders, of speaking verses from the Quran aloud and of silent supplication – he lifted his face from the floor and sat on his knees to ask for the Lord's forgiveness. Half a minute later, he moved again until he was sitting with his feet folded beneath him. This was the position demanded for the *salam*, the salutation; the concluding moments of the final *rakat* or round of late afternoon prayers.

Nazir turned his head to the right and spoke the prescribed greeting to the angel who recorded his good deeds. He turned to his left and spoke the same words in acknowledgement of the angel who recorded his wrongdoings.

'*As-salaam alaikum wa rahmatullahi wa barakatuhu.*'

May the peace and mercy of Allah be upon you.

He stood and turned, and, straightening his gold skullcap, he saw that Jad Hakim was watching him. Hakim was near the back, as usual, standing very still with his prayer mat carefully rolled beneath his arm. Nazir met the man's eyes and nodded twice, enjoying, as he always did, the soft and honeyed babble of those around him who had not yet finished praying.

All praise is to you.

Show us the straight path.

Forgive me . . .

He nodded once to let Hakim know he had seen him, and once towards the exit.

Outside, Nazir ignored the overtures of several people who seemed keen to discuss business of one sort or another with him, and walked away across the car park. He guessed that Hakim would follow, and just as he had predicted, the newcomer had caught him up by the time he reached his shiny black Audi.

Nazir unlocked it and they climbed in.

'Nice car,' Hakim said. He ran his fingers across the walnut dashboard, the leather of his seat. 'Very nice.'

'It does the job.' Actually, Nazir's business as a self-employed IT consultant had been going very well for several years and he could easily have afforded a model with even more bells and whistles than this one. He did not, however, believe in being overly ostentatious. He was an ordinary man who was good at his job, who believed that spiritual rewards were of rather more value than material ones. He was also a man with extremely generous pension provisions.

He said, 'How are you, Jad?'

The drift of the man's chin towards his chest and the set of his shoulders answered Nazir's question. Told him that Hakim's situation had not improved since they had first spoken three days before.

'No better, then?'

330

'Worse,' Hakim said.

Nazir nodded, serious. 'I read the diary.'

'So you know. Last night, she . . . '

'What?'

Hakim raised his hands and pressed them hard against the sides of his head, as though they might stop it shaking.

'You can talk freely, Jad.' Nazir reached across and touched his passenger's shoulder. 'I have a daughter about the same age as your sister, so I know how difficult it can be, and whatever you want to say to me, I promise that I won't be judging you. OK?'

Hakim nodded.

'I mean, I don't have the wisdom of the imam, but—'

'I've already tried talking to the imam.' Hakim raised his hands, then let them drop into his lap. 'Several times I've spoken to him about all this and I do what he tells me to do. I pray for guidance, any kind of guidance, and all I'm left with are these . . . thoughts.' He turned to look at Nazir. 'Thoughts that no loving brother should have rattling around in his head. And I do love my sister, you need to know that.'

'Of course you do,' Nazir said. 'That goes without saying.' They both stared ahead for a while, watched as other cars left. It had begun to rain and the windscreen was steaming up a little. Nazir started the car and turned on the heater to clear it. 'So, what did Raheema do last night?'

Hakim let out another long sigh that rattled in his chest. 'It was just the way she was talking to my father, the things she called him. Called both of us. We were trying to reason with her, you know? Letting her know what she was doing to the family.' He turned to look at Nazir. 'My mother died a couple of years ago, so it's just the three of us now. I don't know, maybe that's why she changed. Up until then she'd been fine, working hard at school and showing respect. A bit wild now and again like any teenager, but basically being a good daughter, and then she just started to go off the rails. It's not like my dad's been strict with her, not really, but she's always known what's been . . . expected of her, same as I have. It's not always easy, but you just get on with it, right?'

Nazir nodded.

'She was talking to us like we were filth. Like we were destroying her life, when she's the one who's destroying ours. My friends have started to say things about her, and my dad can't cope with any of it any more. It's not been easy for him the last few years. Since my mum, you know?'

'Hard enough raising a family when there are *two* parents.'

'Her language was just . . .' Hakim shook his head again. 'Spitting these words at us like she was drunk.'

'You think she was?'

'I couldn't smell anything, but I know she drinks. And there's this boy. This *man* . . . older than her. We'd thought she was seeing someone . . . we'd heard things, and there was what she wrote in her diary. So we tried to talk to her about it, to reason with her. That's when the argument really started.'

'You know this man?'

'No.'

'Married?'

'I don't think so.'

'A Muslim?'

Hakim shook his head.

'You think she has been intimate with him?'

'I know she has.' Hakim's voice was raised now. 'She told us all about it. Bragging about it, wanting us to know everything.'

'Unbelievable,' Nazir said. He tapped his fingers against the leather steering wheel. 'I've heard stories like yours many times before, but it's still so . . . shocking. I can't imagine what it must be like putting up with it.'

It was raining harder now. Nazir flicked on the wipers.

'We don't want to put up with it,' Hakim said. His fist was

bouncing against his leg and his chin was quivering. 'Not any more.'

Nazir nodded. 'You don't have to.'

'I know.'

'Have you spoken to your father about this? About a course of action?'

'Yes.'

'That's good.'

'But—'

'You should not be ashamed of these thoughts you are having. It's very clear to me which member of your family should be ashamed. It would be clear to anyone.'

Hakim nodded and let the tears come. 'I know it should be me that sorts all this out. My dad isn't strong enough. I know it's down to me to make things right, but I'm not sure I can do it. I'm so bloody scared.'

'Of course you are.'

'Too weak.'

'No.'

'If anything went wrong, if there was . . . prison or whatever, what would my dad do? I don't think he could manage on his own.'

'It's OK,' Nazir said. 'I know people who can help you.'

For half a minute or more there was only the sound of the wipers, and the sobbing of the man hunched in the passenger seat. Eventually he sat back and pushed the heels of his hands into his eyes. He said, 'Thank you.'

Nazir leaned across once more to lay a hand on Jad Hakim's shoulder. 'I'm sorry.' He squeezed. 'I'm so sorry you and your father are having to go through this.'

SIXTY

Thursday, August 17th

It's like having a split personality, like one of those psychos you see in scary films, except I don't want to kill anyone. Well, sometimes I'm tempted. Ha! At work, I'm the Raheema who everyone seems to like and even if my boss – who's a prick – has a go at me now and again, nobody's giving me a hard time because I'm good at the job and I get on with everyone. I can say what I think and LOOK HOW I LIKE and nobody's throwing up their hands in horror and telling me how much I'm letting them down. Nobody's ashamed of me.

Then, there's RAHEEMA AT HOME ...

It's OK when I'm in my room I suppose, but I can't hide away up there all the time. I don't want to hide away. And my brother's such a computer nerd that he can always find out where I've been online and who I've been talking to. It's just a break from them, really. Otherwise, I'm downstairs with them and then they want the girl who does all the cooking and cleaning up and never complains. The girl who sits quietly and presents herself correctly. Who dresses appropriately and lowers her head when her father has something to say. I'm ACTING when I'm that girl and the truth is I'm a rubbish actress and I'm getting more sick of it every day.

My brother knows all this because I've told him, but he seems to think it's just a phase, like I'm twelve or something and I haven't grown up yet and seen the error of my ways. He thinks I'll change and learn respect and he says it's all just because I'm hanging around with the wrong people. Like I'm being brainwashed or something.

They're the ones doing the brainwashing, him and my dad.

What makes me angriest is that I know Jad doesn't believe a lot of this stuff any more than I do. But he doesn't have to, does he, because all these rules suit him just fine. It's perfect for him, and all because of what he's got between his legs. He gets to do what he likes while I'm bringing dishonour into the house because I'm not ashamed to use what's BETWEEN MY EARS!

I don't mean brains either, because he knows I'm the smart one, I mean who's the one that got a job straight away after we'd moved, and him and dad never say no to the money I bring in from working my backside off. I'm talking about having the imagination to CHOOSE.

What I wear.

Where I go.

Who I sleep with if I feel like it.

Talking of sleep, I need to go to bed. I'm wiped out,

because tonight I cooked dinner and washed up as soon as I got in from work. Period's arrived as well, which doesn't help, but at least it gets me out of praying!

So enough for now.

I'm sure if there was some way for them to decide what I could and couldn't dream about, they'd do it.

SIXTY-ONE

Thorne carried the box over and laid it down by one of the trestle tables. A middle-aged woman in an elegant green sari was
busy arranging bhajis in concentric circles on a large metal plate.
She smiled at him.

'Is it OK if I leave this here for a while?'

The woman looked around, as though searching for someone
from whom to seek permission and unable to find anybody.

'I'm sure it'll be all right,' Thorne said. 'It's not for long.' He
slid the box underneath the table, then straightened up and
nodded towards the food. 'Looks good.'

The woman leaned across and made subtle adjustments to her
layout. She seemed a little uncomfortable at having her food
scrutinised.

'Can I have one?'

'No.' The woman clearly needed nobody's say-so to make this
decision. 'No food until afterwards.'

'Shame.' Thorne shoved his hands into his pockets and
turned to watch as people began taking their seats, picking up
the leaflets that had been left on every chair, in case they had not

all been given one on the way in. The meeting was a lot busier than the one he had been to with Tanner. There was a crowd outside, too, though not one comprised of people who would be welcome in the hall. These were the very people the meeting was about, and though Thorne had been unable to stop on his way in – lugging that stupid cardboard box from the car – those who did had plenty to say before the police on duty moved them towards the entrance, wary of the conversations becoming too heated.

'So, what do you think?' Thorne asked.

'Excuse me?'

He stepped closer to the woman, saw her step back a little. 'What do you think should be done about these hate crimes? The attacks.'

The woman wrung her hands. 'I don't know.'

'You've listened to the speakers, right?'

'Yes, of course.'

'What do you think about them?'

'They are very good speakers. They all have nice voices, I think.'

'What about what they're saying, though?'

The woman instinctively turned towards the stage, in front of which Bannerjee, Dhillon and Mansoor were deep in conversation. When she turned back, she looked nervous. Or perhaps, Thorne thought, she was just shy. He felt a twinge of guilt at putting her on the spot.

'These attacks are terrible,' she said. 'Something definitely needs to be done.' She looked at him, unblinking. 'But that's not why you're here, is it?'

'Why do you think I'm here?'

Another glance towards the stage. 'Honour killing.' The words were almost whispered. 'Someone heard you talking to the imam and the others. You and the woman. We were all talking about it after the meeting.'

'Do you mind if I ask what you were all saying?'

'What do you *think* we were saying?' She looked at him as though it were a very stupid question. 'Sometimes our children do things we wish they hadn't. Sometimes they do very bad things, but they're our *children*. They were given to us by God and only God can take them away.' She nodded and opened her hands. 'Only God.'

'There are people who don't agree with you,' Thorne said.

The woman shook her head quickly, pointed a finger. 'Nowhere does it say that this kind of thing can ever be allowed. Not in the *Guru Granth*, not in Hindu scripture and certainly not in the Quran. Nowhere, you understand?'

Thorne nodded.

'Same as in the Bible. Thou shalt not kill. I really don't think it could be any simpler.'

'Neither do I,' Thorne said. 'Personally, I'm not that bothered by what the Bible says. Too much stuff about coveting and taking names in vain. But the law is something else.'

Now the woman nodded. 'Of course, and you must catch the people who disobey it.'

'Simple, like you say.'

'I know some people are afraid to speak up and say what they really think. I know it makes your job difficult. But trust me, we want the people who do these terrible things to be caught and punished.'

'I'm doing my best,' Thorne said.

'These men who beat their wives and daughters because they feel dishonoured, who think they have the right to murder them, they are not men of God.' She half turned away towards her arrangement of platters and trays, then looked back at Thorne, eyes wide and fierce. 'They are not men at all. They are animals.'

Thorne watched as she glanced once again towards the stage and thanked her for her time. Seeing that he was about to leave, the woman nodded towards the table, and said, 'I'll save one for you.'

Thorne thanked her again and walked away. Looking across, he caught Bannerjee's eye. The businessman waved and Thorne waved back. Dhillon and Mansoor were looking at him, too, as was Bannerjee's son; scowling from the platform as he arranged the microphones, while a couple of his friends laid out water jugs and glasses, and emptied sweets into decorative bowls.

Thorne summoned a decent scowl of his own and the boy looked away. He picked up one of the leaflets, then sat down at the end of a row. He checked the messages on his phone, then played *Temple Run* for a few minutes while he was waiting for the meeting to start.

Dhillon, the Sikh community leader, was the first to address the audience. He spoke with sadness about the recent arson attack on a temple in Hendon and the abuse, both verbal and physical, levelled at several shopkeepers near his home. Bannerjee followed him, as charismatic a speaker as always, though when he spoke about the need for a measured response he struggled to make himself heard above the noise of those trying to shout him down and appeared to cut his speech short. The imam, Mansoor, waited for silence, but found it no easier to make his points than his predecessor had done. By the time he sat down again after only a few minutes, and Bannerjee got back to his feet, the meeting was threatening to get out of hand.

It was understandable, Thorne thought. He had been expecting nothing less. Considering the recent rise in the number of attacks and the crowd of 'well-wishers' waiting outside.

Bannerjee held out his hands and urged the audience to settle down.

'Please,' he said. 'I have something very important to say.'

The noise slowly began to abate and Thorne watched those

340

who were on their feet return reluctantly to their chairs. He looked across to check that his box was still there beneath the trestle table, then sat back to let Bannerjee say his piece.

'We have a police officer with us this evening.'

Bannerjee had to raise his hands high again and called repeatedly for quiet above an outburst of boos and catcalls. Many of those not shouting out or pointing angrily towards the stage were looking around, searching faces in the hope of identifying the officer in question, while those sitting close to Thorne glared openly at him, having clearly decided that he was the most likely suspect.

Thorne raised his hands in mock surrender.

Got me.

'Detective Inspector Thorne is here tonight to ask for our help,' Bannerjee said. 'I know that much of your anger this evening is understandably directed at the police, but this is something altogether different. This is something very urgent, so I'm asking you ... ' he nodded towards Mansoor and Dhillon, 'we are *all* asking you to hear him out.' Clearly well aware of exactly where Thorne was sitting, he looked across and beckoned him forward. 'Please ... '

Thorne stood and walked towards the stage, stopping on the way to retrieve the cardboard box and smile at the woman in the green sari, who now looked even more nervous than before.

When he had reached the platform, Bannerjee and the others hurriedly moved their bowls and glasses aside so that Thorne could drop the box down on the table. He took the microphone that Bannerjee was offering him and turned to face the audience.

There were still one or two voices raised in dissent, so he gave it a few seconds.

'Almost four weeks ago, two young people went missing.' Thorne waited until he had their full attention. 'Amaya Shah and her friend Kamal Azim, who were both just eighteen years old, were Bangladeshi Muslims.' He turned and looked at Mansoor, who nodded gravely. 'I'm sure I don't have to tell you how concerned their families were and how distraught Amaya's family was when her body was discovered nine days after she disappeared.' He saw heads being shaken or lowered in sorrow and was aware that the same thing was happening on the stage behind him.

He unfastened the zip on his leather jacket.

'While it was understandably terrible for Amaya's family, the agony for Kamal's loved ones continued, because he remained missing. But rather than sit there waiting for news they decided to *do* something, and as Kamal's father runs a printing business they had T-shirts made with their son's face on, in the hope that they might help spread the word.' He reached behind him to touch the cardboard box. 'In the hope that someone, somewhere, might recognise him and come forward with information.'

He slowly opened his jacket and eased it off.

There was a beat before those lowered heads began to crane forward and the pointing started.

Thorne carried on as though oblivious.

'I've brought them with me tonight, so please feel free to take one – to take several – and, who knows, perhaps seeing one of these will jog someone's memory ...' He stopped, as though confused by the shouting and the angry gestures, and looked down at the T-shirt he was wearing as though he had only just remembered that, above Kamal Azim's face, the word *MISSING* had been crossed out and the word *MURDERED* scrawled above it in black marker pen.

'Oh ... *this*,' he said.

He turned around so that Bannerjee, Dhillon and Mansoor could get a good look. When Bannerjee opened the box and began furiously pulling the T-shirts out to examine them, Thorne put his hand over the microphone and said, 'I wouldn't bother. They're all exactly the same.'

342

'What do you think you're doing?' Dhillon asked.

Mansoor slammed his hand down on the tabletop. 'This is not what we agreed to. You lied to us.'

Thorne shrugged, then turned back to the audience and spoke over the steadily increasing clamour.

'Yes, Kamal Azim is missing,' Thorne said. 'But I very much doubt that he will ever be found, and certainly not alive. He was murdered by the same people that killed Amaya. The same people that fabricated forensic evidence to make it look as though he was responsible. The fact is their murders were arranged and paid for by people close to them, by people they loved and trusted, and I'm sure there are several people in this room who understand exactly what I mean by that.'

He stared out for a few seconds, letting the noise wash over him.

'So, please help yourself to a T-shirt ... they're *very* good quality. Why not get one for a friend? Oh, and if anyone *does* have any information and feels brave enough to come forward, the phone number remains the same—'

Thorne stopped, aware suddenly that Bannerjee was standing next to him, red-faced and breathing heavily. He snatched the microphone from Thorne's hand. Said, 'That's enough.'

'Really? I thought I was going down pretty well.'

'You should leave.'

Thorne picked up his leather jacket and folded it carefully across his arm. He leaned down suddenly to take hold of Bannerjee's hand, pulled the microphone back to his mouth and said, 'Thanks for your time.' Then he marched down the stairs and out towards the door.

He smiled at the woman in the green sari as he passed her.

Doing his best to ignore the industrial language being spat in his direction, including several comments about his mother that were less than flattering, Thorne remained well aware of one man in particular; a man he had spotted within moments of arriving at the meeting, and whose dark eyes never left him as he walked towards the back of the hall.

His face oddly expressionless beneath the gold skullcap.

Those gathered in an ugly scrum outside were making almost as much noise as those in the hall. There were only about a dozen of them, but they'd come prepared with plenty of flags and banners; with well-rehearsed chants and less than artfully reworded football songs.

No surrender, no surrender, no surrender to the Taliban.

I'm England till the day I die.

Who the fuck, who the fuck, who the fuck is Allah?

Arms aloft in celebration of themselves, fists pumping in time to each bellowed chorus of tuneless bile.

A line of uniformed officers in high-vis jackets stood between the protesters and the entrance, barring any further progress and keeping them well away from a group of AHCA activists who looked more than ready to get stuck in. Thorne put his jacket back on. His palms were already slick with adrenalin as he reached for his warrant card and showed it to one of the officers. When the PC moved aside, Thorne stepped forward, until he was face to face with the individual who appeared to be co-ordinating the demonstration.

The singing petered out and finally stopped.

'So, who are you lot, then?' Thorne asked.

'Sorry?'

'EDL? Britain First? I suppose you *could* be the East London Gay Men's Chorus.'

'I'm a patriot,' the man said.

'Oh, really?' Though several of those brandishing flags on either side of him looked predictably thuggish – bullet-headed; football shirts stretched across beer guts and barrel chests – their leader was skinny and rat-faced. He wore a cream-coloured polo shirt buttoned to the neck; a flag of St George was badly tattooed above the collar. 'Proud Englishman, are you?'

'That's right.'

'Want to clear the scum off the streets?'

'Yeah.'

'Me too,' Thorne said. 'Only thing is, I think we might differ about exactly who the scum are.' He pointed to the man's tattoo. 'You do *know* St George wasn't English, don't you?'

'What?'

'Half Turkish, half Palestinian.'

'Come again?'

'Matter of fact, he's patron saint to plenty of Muslims in the Middle East.'

The man blinked. 'You're talking bollocks, mate.'

Thorne leaned in close and lowered his voice. 'I tell you what, *mate*, why don't you ask your Neanderthal friends to toddle off home to their inflatable girlfriends, I'll put my warrant card away, then you and me can go somewhere nice and quiet and settle this like men. Like *Englishmen*. What do you reckon?'

The man shifted from foot to foot. He sniffed and swallowed.

'I thought not,' Thorne said.

SIXTY-TWO

'Is this Jad Hakim?'

'Yes, who's this?'

'I'm sorry for calling so late,' the man said. 'We haven't met, but I was told you have a problem that you'd like dealing with. A family problem?'

There was a long pause, filled only with the sound of breathing through the crackle on the line. The man who had made the call guessed that Hakim was now moving through his house, quietly closing doors behind him. Trying to find somewhere nice and private, where he could talk.

'Yes, hello,' Hakim said. 'I'm here ... sorry about that.'

'It's fine.'

There was the hiss of a deep breath being taken.

'Take your time, Mr Hakim. Sit down. Maybe you should get a glass of water or something.'

'I'm OK.'

'Good. Well, let's not waste any more time. I need to ask you a very important question before this conversation goes any further. Do you understand?'

'Yes.'

'Do you still feel the same way you did when you spoke to Mr Nazir yesterday?'

'I think so.'

'I'm sorry, but that's not good enough. If you aren't one hundred per cent sure that you want to move ahead with this, I'll just hang up now.'

'No, I—'

'I'm not calling with *advice*, you understand? I'm calling to discuss how we can get something done.'

'Of course, yes. I'm sorry ... I'm sure.'

'One hundred per cent?'

'Yes, I'm sure. It's just a bit ... ' A gulp, another deep breath.

'I understand.' He knew exactly what Hakim was going through, because this was the way it usually went, the way it *should* go. The apprehension and the dread, the squirm of terror deep down in their guts. He could not recall a single client simply answering his call and saying, 'Right, let's do it.' This was not insurance they were buying, after all. They were not debating whether to move house or splash out on a new car. This was not something that could be returned or undone.

They would have to live with it.

'I have some questions,' Hakim said.

'I'd be worried if you didn't.'

'Well ... how much it will cost.'

'Really? That's your first question?'

'I need to know.'

The man sighed. 'Obviously I will be talking to you about money at some point, and let me say straight away that the people I use for these things are professionals and you need to be prepared for that. But it bothers me that you think you can put a price on such things.'

'I was just wondering.'

'What's the value of honour, Mr Hakim? Seriously, tell me. A hundred pounds? A thousand? How much is it worth, being able to hold your head up? For your father to walk down the street and look his friends and neighbours in the eye, and come home to a house that isn't tainted with shame? Such things are priceless, surely. I mean, you must know that. It's why you can't sleep or concentrate on anything, why you and your father are so miserable all the time. Isn't it why you reached out for help in the first place?'

There was another pause, then a soft, 'Yes.'

'OK then.'

'And what you said about ... professionals. That's good to know.'

'Is there anything else?'

'I want to ... be there. When it happens. Is that all right?'

'Well ...' He was accustomed to certain requests. Particular methods or perhaps a location that meant something to the family. It wasn't normally a problem. If such things were significant, he would always try to accommodate a client's requirements.

'I want her to know why. I want to see it ... and I want it to be quick. That's important.'

'I'll talk to the people responsible, but I'm sure we can sort it out.'

'Thank you.'

'So, tell me about Raheema.'

'What do you want to know?'

'Let's start with her movements and routines. Places she goes or any regular appointments she might have.' He reached for a notepad and pen. 'We need to make arrangements.'

Riaz had taken business calls in deserts, in medieval towns and in the foothills of snow-capped mountain ranges. This was the first time he had done so while watching his partner try to knock a golf ball through the mouth of a skull, on the deck of a miniature pirate ship.

They had driven down to Brighton four hours earlier, at the tail end of the rush hour. Riaz had been keen to eat at a wonderful vegetarian restaurant he had discovered when he was in the city sending the fake email from Kamal Azim, and this time Muldoon had insisted on going with him. Riaz was not thrilled, but he was not surprised either. They had been in something approaching a state of limbo since the arson attack at Tanner's house, and despite his best efforts, and much to his annoyance, he had been unable to shake his partner off for more than an hour or two.

'I want to be there when the call comes,' the Irishman had said. 'I want to know when we're getting our money.'

When the call *had* come – from a man he had spoken to many times, but never met – Riaz had been drinking herbal tea at a table near the booking office, overlooking a floodlit course festooned with Jolly Rogers and plastic parrots. Such a game was unquestionably a pastime for imbeciles, but even so he had been enjoying the sight of Muldoon growing increasingly frustrated at being held up by the family in front of him; red-faced and ready to bludgeon them all with his putter.

It had almost been a shame to look away.

'Should be fairly straightforward,' the broker had said towards the end. 'The brother wants to be there, by the way.'

'I can't say I'm altogether comfortable with that.'

'I've told him there will be a premium to pay and that will of course be passed on to you.'

The money meant less to Riaz than it did to his partner, and he had more than enough anyway, but he did not see much point in arguing. He said, 'What about payment for the Tanner job? The Irishman's nagging me about it.'

'You'll get that when this one's done. Both payments together. Then I think it might be a good idea to disappear for a while.'

'Happy to,' Riaz said. 'Just to get away from *him*.'

'Obviously I'll be in touch if other jobs come in, but in the meantime it would be best to keep your heads down. Let things settle. Tanner might be out of the way for a while, but now others are making a nuisance of themselves.'

'So, when are we talking?' He looked down at the name he had scribbled on a paper napkin. *Raheema Hakim.*

'Within the week. It shouldn't be too complicated. I'll be in touch with the details, but I know you'll want to do some work in advance, so I've got some useful information already . . .'

When the call had ended, Riaz looked up to see Muldoon striding across the course towards him, tossing his club away and kicking aside several other players' balls as he came.

Riaz sipped his tea and waited.

'So?' Muldoon had clearly seen Riaz on the phone.

'Another job.'

'We finishing the copper?'

'No. I think that's been set aside for a while.'

'Makes sense.' Muldoon sat down. 'I mean, what are we supposed to do, march in there dressed as doctors?' He looked at Riaz. 'You might get away with it, mind you. You know, plenty of your lot in hospitals and all that.' He laughed, failing to notice Riaz wince at the sound of it. 'But I don't think anybody's going to buy *me* as a quack.'

'This is something else.'

'Right, but what about—?'

'We're getting the money for both jobs when it's done.'

'Fair play, boss.' Muldoon leaned back, seemingly satisfied. 'So, what's the story?'

'Just the usual,' Riaz said.

Muldoon nodded. 'Usual's good. Can't be doing with any more of that complicated crap, fucking smoke alarms. Something nice and easy.'

Riaz let out a long breath and stared past him; out across Madeira Drive, towards the grey sky and the black sea beneath, crawling to kiss the shingle, then slinking away again. 'As a matter of fact I think we already have the ideal scenario.'

SIXTY-THREE

Coming along the corridor, Thorne saw the door open and watched a man he recognised step out of Tanner's room, exchange a word or two with the officer outside the door. There was still a list of those allowed access, but Tanner had insisted that it be enlarged a little, aware that some of her colleagues were keen to visit. Now, a warrant card was enough to get you inside.

DS Soran Hassani, acting SIO of what was nominally the Honour Crimes Unit, glanced up before he began walking. He had clearly spotted Thorne, but kept his eyes on the polished grey linoleum as he closed the gap between them.

'You got time for a quick chat?'

'As long as it *is* quick,' Thorne said. 'I've got a lot on.'

'Yeah, I know.' Hassani smiled. 'Busy man.'

They took the stairs to the small cafeteria three flights up. Hassani bought himself a latte and a tea for Thorne, folded the receipt into his wallet and carried their drinks across to a table near the window.

'She's doing well,' he said.

Thorne nodded through the flutter of irritation in his chest,

351

annoyed suddenly at Hassani's show of concern for Tanner. *We're* the ones who care about her, he thought. Me and Helen and Phil. It was momentarily disconcerting, how ... territorial he felt. 'Yeah, she's on the mend.'

The small talk dispensed with, they turned to look out of the window at the same time, as though it had been rehearsed. The few seconds of calm before the commencement of hostilities. A line of yellow ambulances idled below them. Cars nosed along Artillery Lane looking for a parking bay and, visible in the gaps between buildings, the walls of HMP Wormwood Scrubs rose just a hundred metres away; dirty brown blocks and ornate Victorian turrets.

'So, come on then.' Hassani sat back and folded his arms. 'What the hell was that stunt about last night?'

'Stunt?'

'At the meeting. Pissing about with T-shirts.'

Thorne cradled his mug. 'I was asking the community for their help.'

'Really?'

'It's modern policing. Inclusive, you know?'

'Do you think I'm stupid?'

'Is that a trick question?'

Hassani grunted and said, 'I can see why Nicola wanted to work with you.'

'I presumed it was something to do with my sunny disposition.'

'Because you're good at making trouble.' Hassani sipped his coffee. 'It's not something that comes naturally to her.'

Thorne looked at his watch. 'Quick chat, you said.'

Hassani leaned forward. 'Trouble isn't something we need right now. It's really not helping.'

'Not helping you.'

'Look ... we've got several sources at these meetings, OK? People embedded in this organisation who are providing us with information, some of the groups I talked to you about the other day. That's why we were monitoring the AHCA. Except for this honour-killers-for-hire business, it's the same reason Nicola was so interested. It's how I found out she was going in the first place, what the pair of you were up to. It's how I heard about that stupid bloody circus last night.'

'Information about what?'

'I would have thought that was obvious, but as you've already made it very clear that you think our unit's a joke—'

'Unit? One room with a couple of whiteboards in it?'

'Whether you believe it or not, and I really couldn't give a toss either way, we're investigating several serious honour-based crimes right now and everything you're doing is seriously threatening to screw them all up.'

'So, what? Your cases take precedence over mine?'

'You know how this stuff goes. It's hard enough to stop the community pulling the shutters down as it is. With crap like you pulled last night ... ranting about murders being arranged, veiled accusations ... important people in that community are starting to talk about a witch hunt, and they've got a point. You aren't doing yourself any favours and you certainly aren't helping me.'

'Have you finished?'

'More or less.'

'OK, then. I'm sorry.'

Hassani nodded, pleased. 'Good. That's ... good. Surely it's better for everyone if there's some co-operation.'

'Oh, I think you've got the wrong end of the stick,' Thorne said. 'I meant I'm sorry if my accusations were "veiled". I thought I'd made them perfectly clear.' He shook his head. 'Must be losing my touch.'

Hassani stared at him for a second or two then pushed his chair back hard. 'Fine. I'll have to take this somewhere else then.'

'Fill your boots, mate. There's probably a Witch Hunt Unit

just down the corridor from yours, in Tumbleweed Towers.' Thorne took a drink and winced. 'Christ, I really hope your coffee's better than my tea.'

'I'm spoiled for visitors today,' Tanner said.

Thorne nodded, fingers drumming against the arm of his chair. 'That prick's enough to spoil anything. What did he have to say for himself, anyway?'

'Probably much the same things he said to you.' She reached behind herself to adjust her pillow. 'He made a few sympathetic noises to begin with: how much I was missed, how he hoped I'd be back on my feet before too long. He told me he'd been praying for me, actually.'

'Really?'

'I know.'

'That must have been an enormous comfort.'

'Obviously . . . but as soon as I told him how grateful I was, he started going on about how we were messing up his investigation. Well, *you*, actually.' She slapped her hands down on to the bed. 'I mean I can't be causing too much aggravation stuck in here, can I?'

'Which means he's the one that should be grateful.'

Tanner laughed. She was sitting up in bed now. There was still a saline drip, but the morphine pump had gone, and though both lower legs were plastered up to the knee, the dressings that had covered most of her face had been removed, leaving only scabs and a few butterfly stitches.

She was starting to look – and to sound – more like herself again.

She said, 'Well, at least it explains what Hassani was doing at that meeting. How he knew I'd be there.'

'Yeah, maybe.'

'You think he's up to something else?'

Thorne shrugged. 'I don't like him. It's probably just that.'

'Yeah, well, he's never been top of my Christmas card list either,' Tanner said. 'He does have a habit of forgetting that I'm still technically his senior officer.'

Thorne was the detective sergeant's senior too, of course; technically and in every other respect. It was not the kind of thing he normally paid a lot of attention to, but ten minutes earlier, running out of patience in that cafeteria, he had come close to pulling Hassani up on it. Telling him that in order to earn respect you had to show some; trotting out the same tiresome lecture he'd been on the receiving end of himself, more times than he could remember. In the end, he'd decided that Hassani was one of those who assumed respect was something he deserved.

Or maybe he just thought he'd get some if he prayed hard enough.

Thorne looked across and saw that Tanner was grinning.

'What?'

'He told me what you did with those T-shirts.'

'Very creative, I thought.'

'It's good to keep putting the wind up them,' Tanner said.

Thorne's smile faded. 'Not sure it's actually achieving anything.'

'It might put a hold on any more killings being arranged. Just them knowing we're around. Then, once I'm out of here we can ramp things up even further.'

'Oh yeah,' Thorne said. 'You can chase after them in your wheelchair.'

Tanner laughed, but it petered out fast.

'When do you think you'll be coming out?'

'Tomorrow, they reckon, maybe the day after.' She picked at the blanket. 'Can't say I'm thrilled about the wheelchair thing, crutches, all that. Once the plaster's off I'll be doing physio for God knows how long.'

Thorne knew that Tanner was not someone who enjoyed sitting around doing nothing for as much as five minutes. It was clear how little she relished the prospect of weeks, or even months, out of action. 'Where are you going to go?'

'I'll stay with my brother while the house is getting sorted.' A nod, another tentative smile. 'His wife works from home, so she can help. Drive me around or whatever.'

'It'll go quickly,' Thorne said.

'Yeah.'

For the next fifteen minutes or so they talked about anything but the Shah and Azim case, the woman whose murder had brought them to this. They talked about TV, hospital food, the latest political scandal. Tanner did most of the talking, while Thorne was happy enough to chip in where necessary, doing his best to disguise the fact that he had other things on his mind.

When he was getting up to leave, Tanner said, 'I never thanked you for your present.'

Thorne looked to the bedside table, saw that the bag had been opened. 'Oh, I hope you like it.'

'It's perfect,' she said. 'How did you know I liked jigsaws?'

'Just a guess.'

'Loved them ever since I was a kid.' She shook her head, mocking herself. 'Probably my stupid fixation with making order out of chaos.'

Thorne leaned down to kiss Tanner goodbye, which seemed to surprise both of them equally. He said he wasn't sure if he'd be back in to see her again before she was discharged because his shift patterns were a bit up in the air. He left the room thinking that, sometimes, a little chaos might be exactly what was needed.

SIXTY-FOUR

'What kind of name is *fluxx*, for God's sake?' Muldoon shook his head and muttered the name again as he picked up a fat chip from his plate and dragged it through a smear of ketchup. 'What's it supposed to mean, anyway, and what's with the stupid spelling? In my day, clubs had proper names, like the Delta or the Plaza. Talk of the Town ...'

Next to him, Riaz sat staring through the window, towards the pair of central-casting bouncers on the other side of the road, arms folded like shaven-headed bookends beneath the neon sign. The name of the club in lower case. They wore black jackets and earpieces, as if they were high-status protection officers and didn't spend their working hours tossing drunks into the street or selling coke and MDMA to make a few extra quid.

In front of him on the scarred plastic tabletop sat a cup of lemon tea and a photograph of the girl. A printout of a photograph.

'Probably talking to the wrong person, aren't I?' Muldoon said. 'I doubt you were ever much of a clubber.'

Riaz looked at him. 'Actually, I am a pretty good dancer.'

'What?'

'Not like that.' He nodded across at the club. 'Proper dancing.'

'You're messing with me, right?'

Riaz glanced down at the photograph, then back across at the entrance to the club. 'I don't really care if you believe me or not.'

'Oh, I'd like to see that.' Muldoon laughed and picked up what was left of his burger. 'That's one for my bucket list, that is.' He counted off his fantasies on thick fingers. 'I want to swim with a great white shark, slip Angelina Jolie a length and I want to watch you doing your *Strictly Ballroom* bit.'

They were sitting in an all-night café on Shoreditch High Street, opposite the club inside which, according to information provided by her brother, the girl would be drinking, dancing, whatever else. They could not be sure what time she'd be coming out, but people were already beginning to leave, so Riaz guessed they would not have much longer to wait.

'Trendy as fuck, this place,' Muldoon said.

Riaz looked at him.

'Shoreditch. Where all the hipsters are. I read an article in some magazine while I was waiting to get my wisdom teeth done.' He peered out into the street. 'Not seen any so far, like.' He sounded rather disappointed that he had yet to spot anyone matching the description in the magazine he'd read. 'They have them skinny jeans, and a checked shirt with the top button done up and a stupid big beard, like they're farmers.' Grinning, he looked over at Riaz. 'Or—'

Riaz raised a hand to silence him, then pointed across to the club. A group of eight or nine had just emerged and were milling around on the pavement; lighting cigarettes, talking and laughing. Men and women, black, white and Asian. He said, 'There,' then stabbed at the photograph. 'Raheema.'

Muldoon leaned close to the window. 'Where?' Outside the club, hugs were being exchanged before several people moved off together. The remainder began to drift slowly away in the opposite direction and that was when Muldoon spotted her. 'Oh, right, I've got her.' He nodded, impressed. 'She looks pretty fit.'

Riaz said nothing.

The girl whose photograph lay on the counter in front of them was wearing jeans and a red leather jacket. She was tall and slim. Her hair was down and she pushed it away from her face as she leaned close to one of the men in the group.

Muldoon said, 'What now, then?'

Riaz had already folded the picture in half and was slipping it into his jacket. 'Nothing. We're finished.'

'So, we've seen her, and that's it? Job done?'

'I like to see them in the flesh beforehand,' Riaz said. 'A photograph is never enough. They might look different when the time comes and it's easy to make mistakes.'

Muldoon shook his head. 'Come on, it's not like we won't know who she is. The brother's going to be with her, isn't he?'

'So, what does *he* look like? We don't even have a photograph of the brother. This is the only way to be certain.' Riaz got to his feet, watched as Muldoon grabbed a last handful of chips. 'What, you think we should do it *now*?'

'Why not?'

'You seriously want to go after her?'

'Just saying we could.'

'Right. Of course. With crowds of people walking around and cameras everywhere. I don't know why I didn't think of it myself.'

Now Muldoon stood up too. 'There's always cameras. There'll be cameras when we do it.'

'So, what are these cameras going to see? Nothing suspicious. Nothing out of the ordinary. Certainly not a young woman being attacked on a busy street with dozens of witnesses.' Riaz allowed himself a patronising half-smile as he waited for his partner to see the sense in his argument.

359

It didn't take too long.

Muldoon was smiling himself as they walked towards the door and was laughing by the time they stepped through it on to the street.

'What?'

The Irishman tried to look serious, struggling to keep a straight face as they stood buttoning their coats. He said, 'Not sure there's any Muslim hipsters, like. But it'd be easy enough.' He raised his hand and waggled fingers beneath his chin, miming an extravagant beard. 'I mean, you're halfway there already, right?'

Riaz turned and walked away towards the street where he'd left the car.

Muldoon took a step after him, then saw that he was being stared at from the opposite side of the road. He grinned and waggled his fingers in the bouncer's direction, then casually gave him the finger.

SIXTY-FIVE

Tuesday, September 12th

Met P for coffee after work!!!

He held my hand under the table, and we talked about going clubbing again, but we spent most of the time with me moaning about how bad everything is at home and it's not like he hasn't heard it all before. Not exactly a romantic chat, but great to see him. Good news is, he's every bit as good with computers as J is and says there's a way he can show me so we can talk online and J won't ever find out.

Doing happy dance. Well, inside my head, anyway.

I try not to let them see when I get upset, but last night my dad was in a particularly vicious mood for some reason and said that it was worrying about me that had driven my mum to an early grave. I'm not an idiot, I know it was cancer and not me, but just the fact that he would SAY it had me crying like a baby. Like I haven't done in front of him for a long time. J agreed with him, of course, nodding like a dog, saying that she would be spinning in her grave if she knew how I'd turned out. He was grinning as I ran out of the room and I know the two of them sat and talked about what a problem I was afterwards. All the trouble I'm causing.

I told P what had happened when I saw him and he was sweet. He says I shouldn't put up with it, that there are all sorts of groups I can join to get help. He says he'll do whatever he can and kept reassuring me that I haven't done anything wrong.

I know he's right, OBVIOUSLY, but I'm not quite as brave as I like to make out when I'm scribbling in here every night. In the end though, it probably won't be a question of being brave or choosing the right moment. I can feel a time coming when something will just snap and then I know it'll all just come pouring out. I'll tell them EVERYTHING I'm thinking and feeling and exactly what I think of them and their rules.

What they can do with them.

Time to stand well back when that happens though. I might need to get stuck into that bottle I've got hidden in the airing cupboard first.

Because the SHIT . . . will hit the FAN!!

SIXTY-SIX

Thorne called Helen's mobile from his car just after eight, and wasn't surprised to find that she was still at the office. The case she was working involving the two young brothers was proving rather more complicated than she had first thought, and with Thorne trying to catch up on several cases of his own, neglected as a result of his ongoing off-the-books activities, the two of them had seen little of each other over the last few days.

A snatched conversation at breakfast.

A grunt of acknowledgement as one or other of them crept into bed.

The necessary abandonment of routine meant that domestic arrangements were now being made on the hoof, if they were made at all. Shopping, cleaning, childcare. The only constant was the unwelcome tension that such a 'ships in the night' existence inevitably bred.

'Alfie's at Jenny's,' she said. 'No idea when I'll be able to get round and collect him.' Her implied question was obvious enough.

'I don't think I can do it either.'

'Right.'

'Sorry.'

'It's not a problem,' Helen said, though it clearly was. 'He'll be happy enough to stay over. Staying up late and watching telly.'

'How much longer are you going to be?'

'Another couple of hours, so it's not really worth it. By the time I get over there and wake him up, get all his stuff together ...'

'Easier to leave him where he is.'

'Right. So, what about you?'

'What?'

'When do you reckon you'll be done?'

'Later than that,' Thorne said. 'I'm not sure when.'

'OK.'

'I was hoping I might be able to get away, then twenty minutes ago they pulled some bloke out of the reservoir in Lea Valley. Been in there a couple of days, looks like.'

'Nice.'

'Last thing I could do with.'

'Well, I'm sure he wasn't too thrilled about it either.'

Thorne stared out of the car window. People who'd already worked later than most were beetling through the drizzle towards the trains and buses that would take them home. Others had been home and were now heading out to eat somewhere or to meet friends; to the pub or the pictures.

Ordinary things. Harmless things.

'So, how's it going, anyway?' he asked. 'Those two boys.'

'Well, either a lot of people have got this spectacularly wrong, me included, or we just haven't found the source of the abuse yet.'

'Your money still on the father?'

'Yeah, but I've got nothing to back it up.' She sounded tired, suddenly. Frazzled. 'The boys haven't said anything that implicates their dad and the parents are rock solid. So we're widening things out a bit, looking at friends and neighbours. I don't know what else to do. They don't go to after-school clubs or scouts, nothing like that. They don't go to church.'

'You'll get there,' Thorne said.

'Or I won't.'

'Right, or you won't.'

'Then all I'm left with is a hideous mess. All *they're* left with is a hideous mess.'

Thorne said nothing, thinking suddenly about his own father. Towards the end, the old man had developed the habit of taking apart vintage radios and TVs, carefully dismantling them piece by piece, until their innards lay spread out across his kitchen table. Afterwards he would become agitated, unable to put the things back together again, but the delicate process of separating each valve, tube and circuit board had unquestionably been therapeutic; calming him and dampening down, for a few hours at least, each misfiring synapse.

Slowing the decline.

'Tom . . . ?'

Thorne knew that it was never about the mess, but the reason you made it.

SIXTY-SEVEN

In the end, they had plumped for the 01:05 train from King's Cross; the Northern City line, overground towards Hatfield and Welwyn. The train an hour earlier was not direct, and anything before that would probably have been too crowded.

No point making things hard for themselves.

Muldoon had no idea where Hakim had taken his sister that evening and didn't care a great deal. Riaz was the one for the details. All that mattered was that, afterwards, the two of them caught this train home together and from that point on there shouldn't be any problem, with the brother on board in more ways than one.

Muldoon was pleased with the pun he had thought of, checking his watch as the train began to move, and happy to see that they were on time.

Twenty minutes until Hakim and his sister were due to be getting off.

Thirteen until they would be.

He dropped into the seat opposite them just as the train pulled out of Finsbury Park, five minutes in.

He was wearing stained jeans and a paint-spattered sweatshirt beneath his old green jacket. A pair of muddy Timberlands. Just your average meat-headed paddy working man, which was exactly what he might have been in another life, had he not discovered talents that had taken him in a very different direction.

There was a moment's eye contact with the brother. He looked suitably nervous. The sister was staring at her phone, as yet unaware of him.

Sulky little cow.

There were two other people in the carriage, a man and a woman, but Muldoon didn't anticipate a problem. Even if either of them fancied chipping in, they would almost certainly bite their tongues and leave it to Riaz once he'd joined the party. Happy to stare at the floor and let someone else risk a beating; to pretend it wasn't happening.

He waited another few minutes – just a bit of drunken muttering, enough to make the girl look at him – before kicking things off properly. Leaning across, as the train rattled through the dark between Harringay and Hornsey.

'Look at you pair.' His voice thickened, a growl in it. 'Been anywhere nice?'

The girl wasn't looking at her phone any more.

'Pakis on the piss, was it? What does Allah have to say about that? Eh? Fucking Isis chopping up our soldiers and you two sit there like you own the place.'

Funny, but the girl was the bolshie one, same as last time. Her brother with his eyes screwed up, like he was trying not to wet himself, while she stared straight back and told Muldoon to shut his mouth.

Standard stuff after that, into Hornsey station and out again. Shouting over the stroppy little mare, waiting for Riaz to step in: a cod-Paki accent; the joke about the Muslim who was bisexual because he owned a camel *and* a goat; a nice phlegmy spit for good measure.

Then it was the boss's turn.

Riaz was on top form, Muldoon had to give him that much. Even more convincing than he'd been a few weeks before, when they'd taken that couple off the Tube. Angry enough, but still reasonable. Someone the poor, put-upon brother and sister could trust.

Telling Muldoon, or the character he was playing, exactly what he thought of him.

A bully, a coward, a *disgrace* . . .

With just a minute or two to go, Muldoon looked away, giving Riaz a chance to whisper his instructions, and when he looked back, he knew they were on.

A smile on the girl's face, something like defiance.

The second the doors opened at Alexandra Palace, the three of them were up and away. Muldoon stayed in his seat, shouting after them, glaring at the onlookers. He knew exactly how long he had before the doors would close again and, for those few seconds until he stepped off after them, he sat marvelling at Jad Hakim; at the stone-cold front of the bastard.

The fact that, despite being the one who'd set the whole thing up, who'd signed his sister's death warrant and paid good money for it, he had still been holding her hand as they ran.

SIXTY-EIGHT

It was no more than half a minute from the station exit to where he'd left the Astra, but with Hakim and his sister walking quickly just a few feet behind him, Riaz took careful note of everything.

Eyes everywhere as he shouted for them to hurry.

A couple of empty cars in the spaces next to his own. Another on the opposite side of the road, the dense line of trees beyond, at the edge of Nightingale Gardens. Up ahead, he saw two boys, fifty yards or so away, strolling down towards the station.

He wasn't concerned.

After all, as he'd said to Muldoon in the café, what was there for anyone to see? For any camera to pick up? Three people in a rush to get to their car, that was all. A fourth joining them a few seconds later. He knew they'd been caught on camera plenty of times before, but it had never been a problem. They changed cars as often as they could and they always made sure to change their appearance regularly. They'd be gone soon enough anyway.

He turned when the girl shouted, 'He's coming,' and was happy to see Muldoon on his way, lumbering along the pavement. The man was an animal, but Riaz could not fault his timing.

'Quickly,' he said.

He keyed the remote in his hand, and it was just as the indicators flashed that the door of one of the parked cars ahead of his opened, one of the cars he'd thought was empty, and a man stepped out.

Riaz saw the open wallet in the man's hand, the face bleached beneath a streetlight, but still recognisable.

The police officer he'd seen on TV.

Thorne.

'Stay where you are.'

Riaz slowed a little, but kept moving, and now just a few feet from his car, he turned quickly to Hakim and his sister, in time to see them stop and step back towards the shopfronts.

They too were brandishing warrant cards.

'It's all over,' Hakim said.

For a few seconds, all Riaz could hear above the sound of his own ragged breathing was the noise of Muldoon's boots, thundering towards them, then the cry of warning from Thorne, which only made Riaz smile, because he knew immediately it had come just a moment too late.

'Is it?' Riaz asked.

Hakim, or whoever the hell he really was, turned at the same moment as the girl shouted her own warning, but Muldoon was fast for a big man and on him before he could react; grunting with the effort of pushing him back against the shop window and punching the knife up into his ribs.

Even before the officer had fallen to the floor, Riaz had a knife of his own in his hand. Again, Thorne told him to stay where he was, but Riaz ignored the instruction. He ran towards the girl as Thorne began running towards him.

Then he heard another shout.

Two words which proved rather more effective at getting his attention.

SIXTY-NINE

'Armed police!'

Thorne stopped and watched Dipak Chall drop a few seconds after Muldoon's knife had clattered to the pavement. He turned to see the armed officers on the other side of the road. They had moved from their hiding place in the trees and now had their weapons levelled above the roof of a parked car.

They shouted again.

Thorne shouted back immediately. 'Hold your fire.' He turned quickly towards to the two boys who had been walking towards them and now stood frozen; shouted at them to get down.

He spun around and saw Chall raising an arm, waving to let Thorne and the officers with the guns know that he was all right. Thorne was relieved to see that the stab vest Chall was wearing beneath his shirt – identical to the ones he and DC Charita Desai had on – had done its job. A broken rib perhaps, a few bruises, but that was all.

Then he heard Desai scream.

He had shifted focus for no more than a few seconds, but it was enough time for everything to change.

Muldoon had his hands in the air. In view of the situation, he was not quite brave enough to risk picking his weapon up again, but the grin on his face suggested that he was anything but afraid.

He nodded. 'Nice one, boss.'

Riaz was standing by the boot of the Astra. He said, 'I think everyone needs to calm down a little.' One hand was wrapped across Desai's face while the other pressed a knife to her neck. 'Don't you?'

He began to inch around the car, one small step at a time, keeping the female officer's body between his own and the guns that were trained on him.

Muldoon said, 'Right, so I'll just walk slowly to the car now.' He was still grinning, nodding across the road. 'You boys be OK with that?' He took a step. 'Yeah, I guess you will.' Arms still raised, he held up both thumbs. 'That's grand.'

'This is a really stupid idea,' Thorne said.

Still moving slowly, his back pressed against the side of his car, Riaz kept his eyes fixed on the vehicle opposite. On the men taking aim from behind it. 'You think so?'

'You really want to add kidnap to the list of charges?' Thorne took a small step towards him. 'On top of everything else?'

'I don't think it will make a lot of difference.'

'Course it bloody won't.' Muldoon was reaching for the handle of the passenger side door. 'So we'll probably just kill her anyway.'

'In retrospect,' Riaz said. '*Yours* was the stupid idea.' He pulled Desai's head back. The knife was drawing blood. 'I'm sure your colleague here would agree.'

Thorne froze and held out his arms. As Muldoon slowly opened the car door, Thorne glanced across the road. He saw one of the officers look up and shake his head.

They had no shot.

'It's OK, Charita.'

The woman moaned against Riaz's hand.

Thorne saw her eyes straining to meet his own. He knew that, like any other officer, she was trained for situations such as this. He knew she would not panic, but that didn't mean she wasn't terrified.

Muldoon climbed into the car and immediately reached across to open the door on the driver's side.

'Give it up now,' Thorne said. 'Give it up and co-operate and things will be easier.'

'What, twenty years instead of twenty-five? That kind of thing?' Riaz took a final step then began to shuffle back towards the open car doorway. 'I've never gambled, but even I know that this way the odds are on my side.'

'Jesus,' Muldoon shouted. 'Enough jabber. Get in.'

Riaz took a deep breath, then fell backwards like a dead man on to the driver's seat, pulling Charita Desai down, screaming, on top of him. There was a moment of focus, of recalibration from the officers on the other side of the road, but it was clear there was still no possibility of shooting without risk to their colleague, and by the time they had looked up from their weapons, Muldoon had hauled the policewoman's body across to his side and Riaz had closed the door.

Thorne turned and ran to his car.

By the time he had started the engine, Riaz was pulling out and accelerating away, and the armed officers had finally begun to shoot.

SEVENTY

Muldoon heaved the female cop across the seat and into the back of the car, then reached over to punch her hard in the face. He wrapped a hand around her neck before turning to talk to his partner.

'Well, you're full of surprises.'

Riaz kept his eyes on the road. He raced along the edge of Nightingale Gardens, then, with only the most perfunctory check for oncoming traffic, turned hard left on to Bounds Green Road heading north.

'Didn't think you had it in you.' Muldoon shook his head. 'All I'm saying.'

'You do whatever is necessary.'

'Yeah, obviously. I mean, don't get me wrong, I've seen what you're capable of when it's just you and some teenage girl. Like cutting a pig's throat or whatever you said. You know, when it's work.' He opened the passenger side window, just an inch or two, and leaned towards the rush of air. 'Armed police though ... that's a different thing altogether.'

'If we're caught then there won't *be* any more work. So you do what you have to, to make sure that doesn't happen.'

The girl in the back seat moaned, so Muldoon leaned over and squeezed a little harder. He looked up and saw the headlights of the car that was following, growing in size through the rear window. He said, 'Behind us.'

'I know.'

'So, what's the plan?'

'I don't have a plan.'

'Well, don't look at me.'

'I wasn't,' Riaz said.

Muldoon grunted. 'I think the first thing we do when we get a chance is to go and pay your friend a visit.'

'*My* friend?'

'Well, you're the one who talks to him, sets things up.' The Irishman took another breath of air. 'I mean this is down to him, has to be. He's the one who arranges everything, so the way I look at it, this holy fucking balls-up is all his fault. He's got to carry the can. Am I right?'

Riaz pushed the car up to sixty-five past the tube station, the treeline a dark blur to their left. 'We can have this discussion later on, but for now we need to get rid of this car.'

'What about the girl?'

'Not important.'

Muldoon looked over his shoulder. The headlights were still there. 'Can't you lose him?'

Riaz shook his head and pulled hard on the wheel, fighting the car's drift towards the middle of the road, as he had been since they'd first driven away from Alexandra Palace.

'They shot one of the tyres out.'

Vehicle pursuit had never been Thorne's strong point.

He was grateful that there was very little traffic on the road, that it wasn't raining, that the armed officers had managed to hit at least one of the tyres on the car he was chasing. The Astra would struggle to go any faster than it was, and even without the benefit of blues and twos on his BMW he wasn't having too much trouble keeping it in sight.

Enough time to think, which, in reality, meant a few seconds of blind panic for every ten he spent shouting at himself. Slamming his hands against the steering wheel and telling himself what an arrogant idiot he'd been.

Planning was clearly not his strong point either.

They had guessed that the men they were after would be armed, which was why Brigstocke had stepped up and authorised a couple of officers from SO19. They had not banked on things playing out the way they had, though, and Thorne knew that they should have done.

That *he* should have done.

Why the hell had he ever thought they would simply give themselves up quietly?

Perhaps if Chall had been quicker ... if Desai had seen the danger earlier ...

He slammed a hand against the wheel again, a fist against the window.

There was nothing to be gained by blaming anyone but himself. He should probably just have let them shoot the Irishman when they had the chance, but he'd known that Chall was in no real danger and they had all agreed that the use of lethal force was to be a last resort.

He wanted these men alive.

He watched the Astra cross the North Circular, touching seventy past New Southgate station, where 'Jad Hakim' and his sister had been supposed to get off. It turned right on to Friern Barnet Road and barrelled across a major roundabout without stopping.

Thorne could only see the silhouettes of two occupants and guessed that Charita Desai was down on the back seat, being thrown about as the driver struggled to keep control of the car.

Unless they had killed her already.

Some people who should have known better didn't do enough to talk some sense into her.

She's stubborn.

I should have done more . . .

Remembering his conversation with Chall about Nicola Tanner, Thorne knew deep down that this whole half-arsed operation had been, at some level, about dealing with his guilt. Now, the plan he had hatched with Chall at Tanner's bedside had put another officer in harm's way.

Charita Desai was only twenty-eight, with two kids under six.

What had he been thinking as he'd left Tanner's hospital room the day before?

Some shit about chaos . . . ?

Ahead of him, a car emerged from a side street without looking and straightened up dangerously close to him. Fucking boy racer. Thorne flashed his headlights and the driver slowed, braking once, twice; trying to wind him up. Thorne leaned on his horn and watched the driver calmly stick his arm out of the window to give him the finger.

'Good,' Riaz said, accelerating as much as he dared, his eyes on the rear-view. 'That may help us.'

Muldoon wasn't really listening. With one arm still reaching behind him to pin down the female copper in the back seat, he continued to rant about the man he clearly believed to be responsible for their current predicament.

'I mean he's supposed to check everything out, isn't he? Before he brings us in. He's supposed to make sure it's all kosher.' He flashed a grim smile. 'No offence, like. It's his job to, what do you call it, facilitate everything and see that the risks are kept to a minimum. Right?' He glanced across at Riaz, but wasn't really expecting an answer. 'Yeah, well, he dropped the ball big time with this one, far as I can see. Coppers, for Christ's sake. I mean come on, how messed up is that?' He leaned towards the open window again, sucked in some more fresh air. 'Seems to me he's getting careless because he's getting greedy. Cutting corners when he smells money, and now we're the ones in the deep end for it. Couldn't say no to another payday, could he?'

'You're wrong,' Riaz said.

'I don't think so.'

'He doesn't do this for the money.'

'Oh, sweet Jesus.' Muldoon let his head fall back. 'You're telling me he's another one like you, is he? Does it because he thinks it's right? Another fucking . . . zealot?'

Riaz stiffened in his seat; breathed out slowly.

'Sounds like he's another one needs to hear my joke.'

'I don't think so.'

'Maybe you can tell him, when we see him.' Muldoon slammed his hand against the dash. 'Second thoughts, I'll tell the fucker myself, while I've got my hands around his neck.'

Riaz quickly checked the rear-view. There was still a car between his own and the policeman's. He scanned the road ahead.

'What's the most difficult thing for a religious fundamentalist who's killing his daughter?' Muldoon grinned.

Riaz knew there was no way to prevent Muldoon repeating a punchline he had heard several times before. His hands tightened a little more around the wheel.

'Hiding the hard-on.'

Muldoon had begun laughing before he'd even said it, but stopped abruptly when Riaz hit the brakes and dragged the car off the main road, on to an unlit driveway.

'Hell we going?'

'Dump the car.'

'Then what?'

'We need to split up.' Riaz threw another glance at the rear-view, then craned forward towards the sprawl of rusted skips and darkened buildings ahead. 'He can't go after both of us.'

Muldoon pointed to Desai, groaning on the back seat. 'What about her?'

'Leave her,' Riaz said. 'You're the one I'm worried about.'

'Ah, boss ... that's sweet.'

'Some people don't know when it's time to shut up.'

The boy racer ahead of him accelerated away in time for Thorne to see the Astra's tail-lights swinging off the road. By the time he reached the entrance to the industrial estate there was no sign of them, so with little choice he accelerated down the rough, unmarked driveway in an effort to catch up. He pushed the BMW hard past a builder's merchants as big as a football pitch, a timber supplier, a car-repair yard; the track lit only by emergency lights on top of each warehouse and industrial unit.

He stopped at a T-junction.

He knew that heading left would eventually bring him back out on to the main drag, but guessed that they had not turned off the road in an effort to shake him off.

He spun the wheel right and drove further into the estate.

He flicked on his main beams as he bounced over a series of grids and speed bumps, slowing just a little to peer into each car and van parked in front of a sheet-metal workshop, a tool-hire company, a joinery warehouse. He had no option but to take the car left and he accelerated again as he followed the road around to the rear of the estate, navigating the fists of darkened loading docks and weaving through a fleet of branded lorries. As he rounded the final corner, Thorne saw the Astra's tail-lights; watched them brighten, because the car was slowing.

Because they had run out of road.

He pulled up fifty feet behind the car, which had come to a stop with its engine still running. He got out when he saw the driver's door open and watched the Asian clamber out and bolt into the darkness.

Arms punching, shoes slapping the concrete.

There was a moment when Thorne felt the adrenalin kick in, when he was ready to give chase, but it was only a moment, because his first thought was for Charita Desai; had to be.

He had only taken a few steps towards the car when the rear door opened and the DC emerged.

He shouted her name and she raised an arm. Shouted back, 'I'm good.'

Before he could get any closer, Desai was running after the driver. He watched as she sprinted into the shadows, towards the black outline of trees beyond. He shouted after her, 'He's still got a knife,' but there was no acknowledgement that she had heard him.

Out on the main road, he heard a siren scream, then slowly fade.

Thorne walked towards the Astra, spitting out the acrid taste of metal and breathing against the tattoo beating in his chest. Slowly, because who knew what other weapons might have been stashed under the seats or in the glovebox.

Because the Irishman was still inside the car.

SEVENTY-ONE

The milky beams of the Astra's headlights were reflected by the water puddled in ruts, picking out the weeds and smears of oil against the dusty concrete. An indicator was flashing. Moving carefully through the livid red wash of the tail-lights and circling in a wide arc around the passenger side of the car, Thorne began to get a clearer picture of exactly where they were.

It was a small triangle of semi-enclosed waste ground. Ranks of graffiti-covered metal shutters stretched behind him and to the left a chain-link fence ran along the edge of a building site. On his right was the thick line of trees into which Desai had chased the driver. There were lights in several windows of the houses beyond and Thorne knew that if the driver had made it through one of the gardens and across the street on the other side, he would be away into the grounds of Southgate cemetery.

He hoped that Desai had given up the chase.

With front and rear doors open, the car's interior light was on too. Stepping closer, Thorne could clearly see the stitching on the cover of the steering wheel and the green glow of the dashboard. A satnav unit, and a string of beads hanging from the rear-view mirror.

So, why couldn't he see the passenger?

He had been watching the driver heading for the trees, Desai running after him. Was it possible that, in the darkness and confusion, he had missed seeing the car's other occupant jump out and slip away in the other direction?

He didn't think so.

Thorne opened the door and stared down at the figure slumped low in the passenger seat, his legs buckled in the footwell.

The blood explained everything.

The Irishman's hands were thick with it, clasped across his belly. The sweatshirt was sodden where it was pumping through his fingers. It ran down the edge of the seat and had begun to pool in the sill of the door, to drip.

Thorne said, 'Well.'

The Irishman gasped and smiled, blood between his teeth. 'Fucker knifed me.'

'Why would he do that?'

'Can't take a joke.'

Blood was running down the man's chin. Thorne watched him try to heave himself up in his seat and cough a red cloud on to the windscreen. He listened to him grunt and swear for a few seconds.

'You . . . got a phone?'

Thorne reached into his jacket pocket and took out his mobile. He held it up. 'Yes, I have.'

'Christ's sake, call an ambulance, will you?'

Thorne looked at his phone.

'You don't call someone, I'll bleed to death.'

'You'll be fine,' Thorne said.

'Do you not think I know what I'm talking about? Look at me . . . I'm bleeding to death here.'

'OK.' Thorne looked at the blood, the puddle that had now formed outside the car, and thought that the man was probably right. There was not a great deal of time. Chall or one of the SO19 boys would have called for support as soon as Thorne began the pursuit, but being as far as they were from the main road, there was no saying how long it would be until back-up arrived.

Unless Thorne phoned in to let them know where they were, of course.

'Call the ambulance.' The Irishman grimaced with the effort of shouting. 'For the love of God . . .'

Thorne looked at his phone again. He had a full signal and plenty of battery, but he was thinking about the real reason the Irishman's partner had decided he could not risk leaving him alive.

'You need to talk to me first.'

'*What?*'

Thorne crouched down and leaned towards the dying man, scrolling through the apps on his phone until he found the voice recorder. 'I want to know about Meena Athwal, OK? About Amaya Shah and Kamal Azim. I want to know exactly what you did and where Kamal Azim is buried. Then, you need to tell me which members of their families paid to have them killed, and last of all, the name of the person who organised it. I want to know who the broker is.'

The man turned his head to look at Thorne, then shook it and sputtered out a string of blood and curses.

'You'd rather die, would you? Bleed out like a stuck pig, protecting the people that got you into this?'

The man squeezed his eyes closed.

Thorne held the phone close to the man's mouth. 'Just tell me, and I'll call the ambulance, get you sorted out.'

'You swear?'

Thorne tapped the record button and nodded.

It took about a minute and a half, the words spewed and spat between hacking fits and moans; the breaths wet and rattly. By the time the man had finished, had given Thorne the information he wanted and spluttered out a familiar name, his jeans were black with blood and his eyes had begun to roll back in his head.

Satisfied, Thorne clicked the voice recorder off, then stood up and calmly slid the phone back into his pocket.

'The fuck d'you think you're doing?' The Irishman reached out a hand slick with gore and flapped at Thorne's leg.

Thorne stepped away.

He said, 'The honourable thing.'

SEVENTY-TWO

The detached Edwardian house in Enfield was testimony to how well Arman Bannerjee's business was doing. Thorne had discovered that the company specialised in purchasing job lots of used office furniture, doing it up, and selling it on through their own showrooms and others. Desks bought for a tenner each were stripped, waxed and sold on for ten times that. Gunmetal grey filing cabinets were dipped into acid, then polished until they were every bit as shiny as the Lexus on Bannerjee's driveway, and could fetch three hundred pounds a pop in Islington and Notting Hill.

A shame how things had panned out, Thorne thought, as he rang the bell.

He quite fancied jazzing up his office.

There were a number of symbols painted on a wooden board above the front door: several letters in a language Thorne did not recognise; a lotus leaf; something that looked like a Christmas tree but probably wasn't; and the one he'd seen on that website Tanner had shown him, that he'd thought was a swastika. A symbol of the god Vishnu, Thorne had since discovered, as well as of the Hindu sun god, Surya.

A charm to bring good fortune, though this one was clearly not doing its job.

Bannerjee's wife wore a simple blue sari and her hair was tied back to better display the jewelled bindi on her forehead. She said, 'Yes?' though the polite smile that went with it slid from her face when Thorne produced his warrant card.

'Sorry to disturb you so late,' Thorne said.

The woman did not appear to need telling who Thorne had come to see. She was all but bowing as she backed away from the front door, then gently ushered Thorne along a thickly carpeted corridor towards another. She stepped in front of him to put her head around it, and Thorne could not quite make out the whispered exchange before she waved a hand to invite him into the room and closed the door behind him.

Bannerjee was watching what appeared to be a nature documentary on a huge wall-mounted Samsung. Thorne just caught sight of a large insect scuttling towards a smaller one before Bannerjee switched the TV off and sank back with a sigh into a deep, cream settee. He was wearing jeans with a perfectly ironed crease and a collarless white shirt. When he held out his arms, helpless, as though the weight of the world were on his shoulders, Thorne saw the fancy buttons and the details picked out in red on each cuff.

'You are certainly a piece of work.' Bannerjee's smile was almost as polite as his wife's, but there was no trace of courtesy in his voice. 'Not content with disturbing my lunch, or interrupting an important meeting with offensive theatrics, you now come into my home.'

'I'm sorry,' Thorne said, though he was anything but.

'I think I'm right in saying that unless you have a warrant, I can ask you to leave.'

'You can ask.'

Thorne walked across to an armchair, the same cream leather as the sofa, and sat down. Looking past Bannerjee, he could see a small shrine set up on a gleaming sideboard against one wall. There were pictures of Hindu gods in wooden frames, though Thorne only recognised the one with an elephant's head. There were plastic flowers arranged carefully around a bowl of fruit. In the centre sat a large metal tray holding candles in each corner; a bowl, a spoon and what looked like a small handbell.

'So?' Bannerjee sat forward. 'Have you just come to gawp at my sitting room?'

'It's very nice.' Thorne smiled. 'But I'm here because of a significant development in the case I'm working on. Those offensive theatrics you mentioned?'

'Your pair of so-called honour killers.'

'Bang on.' Thorne could taste adrenalin for the second time in twenty-four hours, but for a very different reason. 'The fact is, we caught them.'

Bannerjee blinked. 'Really?'

'Well, we caught *one* of them, but in the end we only needed one. He told us everything we wanted to know.'

Thorne heard the sound of footsteps, quick and heavy on the stairs. He waited, until a second later the door burst open and Bannerjee's son Ravi stood glaring at him from the doorway.

'Seriously?' Ravi looked to his father. 'Why are you even talking to him?'

'Same old story,' Thorne said. 'I'm harassing your father. What can I tell you?'

'Yeah?' The young man's weight shifted from one expensive training shoe to the other, his hand still on the doorknob. 'Well I can tell *you* that we've had just about enough of this. You can't keep treating my father like this, like a criminal, and getting away with it.'

'Oh for God's sake, Ravi.' Bannerjee was irritated suddenly, the skin tight around his mouth. 'Shut up and go away or come in and shut the bloody door, one or the other.'

Ravi nodded, acquiescent, and closed the door quietly. He

crept into the room, keeping tight to the wall until he moved across to sit at the other end of the sofa from his father.

'Go on,' Bannerjee said.

Thorne nodded, grateful. 'I was just saying that we'd apprehended one of the men who carried out the series of killings we've been investigating. Amaya Shah and Kamal Azim, Meena Athwal, and several others here and overseas. This man, who we've now identified as Martin Muldoon, gave us all the information we needed to make several more arrests. All the names—'

Ravi sat up, about to speak, but his father quickly raised a hand to silence him.

Thorne stared down at the patterns on the carpet. A series of red and yellow swirls against an emerald green background. 'So ... I'm here because I now know that you are the person responsible for arranging all these killings. For making the deals with the families and paying the men who carried them out. I'm here because you're the broker.'

'This is ridiculous.' Ravi Bannerjee sat forward again and pointed. 'How dare you march in here and accuse my father of this? Where's your evidence?'

Thorne looked up. 'I wasn't talking to your father, Ravi. I was talking to you.'

The colour drained from the elder Bannerjee's face. He turned to watch his son fall back against the thick cushion; a hiss between the teeth, a shrug, as though he'd just been accused of stealing pocket money and knew that it could not possibly be proved.

'*What?*'

The boy waved his father's question away, took his own turn at studying those colourful swirls at his feet.

'Sadly, Mr Muldoon is no longer with us.' Thorne shook his head. 'Killed by his partner, would you believe? But he was *very* keen to get things off his chest before he died.' He set down his mobile phone on the glass-topped table between them. He opened the voice recording and pressed PLAY. 'A confession, I suppose you'd call it . . .'

When it was finished, Thorne picked up his phone and slipped it back into his pocket. 'Sorry the quality's not great, but he wasn't at his best. Clear enough, though.'

Arman Bannerjee was breathing heavily, his hands clenched into fists and banging against his knees. He stood up suddenly and walked to the far end of the room. Thorne heard a noise low in the man's throat and wondered if he was crying, but saw no tears when Bannerjee turned and walked back again, stopping finally to brace himself against the sideboard, clearly in need of physical as well as spiritual support.

His head shaking slowly, lowered above the fruit and plastic flowers.

'What do you know?'

'Sorry?' Thorne turned to look at the young man whose anger he knew had been a disguise. A useful smokescreen. He and Tanner had put the showy, self-righteous claims of offence on behalf of his father down to youthful posturing, but now he understood – as far as he could understand *any* of it – that they hid something far darker and more determined.

'What do you know about anything? Men like you . . . without faith, without a belief system that goes beyond the whims of judges and the pantomimes of overpaid lawyers. You really think there is nothing higher than the law of the land? If that's the case, I feel sorry for you. I feel sorry for anyone who can't see beyond that, because part of them will always be empty and ignorant.'

Thorne listened, happy enough to let things play out. Ravi Bannerjee leaned towards him and, for the first time, Thorne heard a voice that was not being manufactured for effect.

Soft and certain; appalling.

'You don't seem to understand just how many people can't

depend on people like you, the laws you claim to uphold. They aren't *our* laws. A community needs to protect itself, and it does that through a shared belief in what's really right and wrong. In what matters.

'The people I've been working to protect have traditional lives and traditional values. The most important thing is that the family is one unit.' He held up a finger. 'One unit ... one entity, and when someone in that family breaks a rule, the family itself has broken a rule. Is that really so hard to understand? If the part of the family that's rotten is not dealt with, that rot will spread and then the community can't protect you. It *won't* protect you. Everyone in that family is guilty, can't you see that? As far as the community is concerned they are all liars, thieves, whatever ... until they take steps against the person who is responsible for it.

'The men and women who come to me love their children. Course they do, every bit as much as anyone else. But they have other children who need to be protected and they can never really be safe unless the ones who break the rules are made to pay. It's important to remember that these people have raised their children, taken care of them. They brought them into the world, so it's their right to take measures when they have no other choice.

'Respect is important, and you hold on to it by weeding out those who are misled. Those who choose to ignore the rules about how to behave, how to dress, who they are supposed have children with. Nothing is more important than dealing with dishonour in the right way.

'Cutting out the rot ... '

Thorne watched Ravi Bannerjee sink slowly back and stretch out his arms, seemingly pleased with himself. He glanced across and saw that the boy's father had turned to stare, slack-jawed, at his son.

It was easy enough, easy and pleasant, to imagine the boy's

face opening up beneath his fists; a blow for each of the victims and for those left mourning them, until there wasn't much of a face left.

Easy enough.

He said, 'What's *important* is that I know what murder is. The fact that there are officers in the street outside and a few more waiting at the end of your lovely garden.' Thorne smiled and got to his feet. 'And that there are handcuffs in my pocket.'

PART FOUR

SOMETHING BRIGHT

SEVENTY-THREE

'So, good news on Ilyas Nazir,' Tanner said. 'The CPS thinks there's enough to make a case for conspiracy.'

Thorne almost dropped the phone. 'How come you're hearing this before I am?'

'Would you believe, Soran Hassani?'

'You're kidding.'

'Oh, he's my best mate all of a sudden. Sucking up, in case I decide to go back to Honour Crimes when I'm fit again. And there's a spot on the team for you too, if you want one.'

'Come again?'

'He wanted me to tell you what a great job you did.'

'Yeah, well tell him I'm sorry for being such a ... trouble-maker.'

'I think a troublemaker's exactly what he's looking for.'

'You think you will?' Thorne asked. 'Go back there?'

'Not in a million years. But it's fun to let him think that I might.'

Thorne could hear the glee in Tanner's voice, even though she was talking quietly, so as not to be overheard. She had been staying with her brother for almost a week since leaving hospital, and the help from her sister-in-law that was gratefully received for the first day or two had now started to become a major source of irritation. 'She follows me from room to room,' Tanner had told him. 'It's getting on my tits, to be honest. I think I'd rather be at home on my own. I'm like lightning on these crutches and I can always shuffle up the stairs on my arse.'

'Thank you for that lovely image,' Thorne had said.

Nazir, the go-between, had been the toughest nut to crack in terms of formulating charges that might stick, and there were still the other go-betweens to track down; those with connections to the Sikh and Hindu communities. The rest was looking straightforward enough, though the sheer number of suspects involved at different levels of the inquiry had meant a division of the caseloads between units. Hassani had taken charge of putting together the case against Ravi Bannerjee and would do the same with the man known to Muldoon only as Riaz, if and when he was taken into custody. Thorne had laid claim to those involved in the Shah and Azim murders and, of course, to the Meena Athwal case, which had been his to begin with.

Three days before, breaking it all down for Nicola Tanner had not only meant shocking her with the identity of the broker, but admitting to more than a few mistakes.

'We were wrong about Kamal's family being in on it,' he told her. 'It was all Haroon Shah and his father. They wanted Kamal killed as well as Amaya, because he was the one she was planning to run off with. They paid for both.'

Tanner said, 'In that case, we probably owe Kamal Azim's parents a visit.'

Thorne nodded slowly and felt the solid knot of shame in his chest tighten a little. As far as Kamal's family went, he had got it badly wrong. It wasn't the first time, of course, and he knew it wouldn't be the last, but that didn't help him sleep any more easily. Yes, he had believed that Hamid Azim had paid to have his son killed, had treated him the way he did *because* he believed it, but it was no excuse, and now Thorne was the only one feeling guilty.

'I'll go and see them when we find Kamal's body.' Fighting for his life, Muldoon had not been able to give Thorne any more than the vaguest location of Kamal's burial site. A team was searching several acres of wasteland between the M1 and the Great North Way. When Kamal's body was found, Thorne would visit Hamid Azim and his wife himself to deliver the death message.

'I mean, we should apologise for what you did to that poor man's T-shirts for a start.'

Thorne had laughed along with her and tried not to look too shocked, thinking that bereavement and a near-death experience seemed to have given free rein to a pitch-black sense of humour he had not known was there.

In truth, he had further penance of his own to pay.

'And I was wrong about Meena Athwal,' he said. 'It was the mother who arranged the killing, not the father. She's dead now, so . . .'

'Have you been to see him yet?'

'No.'

They'd been sitting in her brother's front room. Tanner's legs were still heavily plastered and resting on what Phil Hendricks always called a 'massive pouf' and she had leaned across to whisper that 'Nurse Nosy' – who had already provided them with tea and Jaffa Cakes – was almost certainly earwigging just outside the door.

'Well, I'm sure you'll get round to it,' Tanner had said. 'It's been a hectic few days, right?'

Now, talking to Tanner on the phone and listening to Helen murmuring to Alfie in the bedroom, Thorne was still trying his best not to dwell on the conversation he had yet to have with Govinder Athwal. The one about the dead wife to whom he had been so devoted being responsible for the murder of his daughter.

Another mistake, another in a catalogue. Thorne could always tell himself that the final result justified the stupid assumptions and excused his treatment of a man already destroyed by grief. If he was pushed, he could probably make a convincing case for behaviour which, in retrospect, had been profoundly unfair.

But it wouldn't make him feel any better.

He leaned back against the kitchen worktop. 'Oh, there is another bit of good news. Faruk Shah's a stubborn sod, saying bugger all, but Haroon's being pretty talkative. So, on top of all the other stuff, I think I can get him to cough to Sarah Webster's rape. Give us those lads' names.'

Thorne heard relief in Tanner's noisy exhalation.

'Can I tell her?' she asked. 'When you get the names?'

'Absolutely.'

'Something to look forward to.' She moaned and swore again under her breath; shifting position, Thorne guessed. 'OK, so is that it?'

'Yeah,' Thorne said. 'That's about all, I think.'

All except the one thing he had chosen not to tell her; that he would probably never tell her or anybody else.

The truth about Martin Muldoon's final moments.

He had told Tanner the same thing he'd told Brigstocke, Hassani and the rest of them. That he'd told Charita Desai when she'd finally come running out of the woods a minute or so after Muldoon had died, and the paramedics who'd arrived shortly after that.

Muldoon had expressly told him not to call for medical assistance. He had known it was too late by then and was far keener to have his confession recorded while he still had the chance. By the time that confession had been taken and Thorne had tried to call an ambulance, the battery on his phone had died.

Unlucky, but at least Muldoon had died having told the truth.

Even if the Nicola Tanner Thorne had worked with for the previous month or so had not been quite the stickler for procedure that her reputation would suggest, that was the only version of events Thorne had been prepared to share with her.

There had been a look between them, once he'd told her. Nothing overt, but a look that was held a few seconds longer than it might otherwise have been.

Thorne was thankful that had been as far as it went.

A few minutes after Thorne had hung up, Helen emerged from the now silent bedroom. She smiled, her fingers crossed, and went straight to the fridge in search of wine.

'We should celebrate,' she said.

'I thought we did.' That morning, they had each downed half a glass of Prosecco, topped up with orange juice. Breakfast, once Thorne had finally come home; Alfie smearing porridge across the table and Muldoon's blood still tacky on the tips of Thorne's shoes.

'Not properly.' Helen was pouring the wine. 'And anyway, I'm talking about *my* case.'

'The brothers?'

She handed Thorne his glass and raised her own. 'Finally cracked it.'

'Oh ... I'd been meaning to ask how it was going. Sorry.'

'It's fine. You've had a pretty full-on week.'

'Still.'

It was more or less what Tanner had said a few minutes earlier on the phone.

No excuse.

'So, come on then.' They carried their drinks across to the sofa and sat down. 'Was it the dad?'

'Nope.' Helen shook her head, pleased with herself, as though Thorne had just fallen for a trick question.

'Mum?'

'You're never going to get it.'

'Was it . . . someone off a popular seventies TV show?'

'It was the older brother.'

'What?'

Helen nodded. 'The fourteen-year-old is our abuser. Turns out he's been abusing his younger brother for years, making him do all sorts. A couple of local cats had their heads cut off, a few mysterious fires, and we've just started to dig up some very nasty stuff with girls on the same estate. The twelve-year-old was so petrified of him, he'd go along with whatever his brother wanted.'

Thorne puffed out his cheeks. 'So, why does a fourteen-year-old kid start behaving like that? I mean, something must have happened to *him*.'

Helen shook her head. 'No evidence to suggest that so far, and trust me I'm looking. Maybe that's just how he is.' She looked at Thorne. 'I swear to God, he is a seriously messed up boy.'

'So how did you work it out?'

'I didn't. I mean, I *said* I cracked it . . . but in the end he just decided to tell us. Came out with it yesterday afternoon, like it was something that had slipped his mind. Like he just got . . . bored.' She let out a long breath, downed what was left of her wine, then stood up to fetch some more. She turned at the fridge. 'What was the name of the school that Tanner's girlfriend worked at? The one where you went for that memorial thing?'

Thorne told her.

'Thought so.' Helen poured herself another glass. 'Same one those boys go to. Well *went* to, anyway.'

Thorne said, 'Oh, right,' while his hand was slowly moving up to brush at a familiar tickle at the nape of his neck. Spidery legs creeping across the soft hairs...

Remembering a picture.

Thinking about a clumsy scatter of painted freckles, and white spots on an oatmeal carpet. Thinking about the one thing Martin Muldoon had not confessed to.

'What's the boy's name?'

SEVENTY-FOUR

However Ryan Smedley had appeared when he'd let Helen know exactly what he'd been up to at home, he now seemed anything but bored. He looked excited. Sitting up good and straight in the plastic chair; wide-eyed, drumming his hands against the edge of the table, as if he was itching to get started.

Thorne guessed that the boy enjoyed being the centre of attention.

He now had plenty of it.

The interview room was certainly as crowded as Thorne could remember, but it was usually the way with underage suspects. There were necessary procedures to follow. There were crucial requirements in regard to legality and pastoral care. Nobody could afford to take chances when the person you believed to be a murderer hadn't started shaving yet.

Under normal circumstances, Thorne might have had a DC in tow, but today he had asked Yvonne Kitson to sit in with him. He didn't doubt that a certain morbid curiosity had played a part in her instant agreement, but it didn't hurt to have a DI as experienced as she was alongside him. Across from them, the social worker Helen had been working with on the abuse case was sipping from a bottle of water, in attendance as appropriate adult, while the solicitor hired by the family took a notebook and pens from his briefcase, doing his best to look as though he'd handled dozens of cases as notable as this before.

Like it was just another day at the office.

Between them, Ryan Smedley tapped at the table, buzzed up and keen as mustard. He was wearing jeans and a red Gap sweatshirt. A few strands of gelled blond hair were sticking up at the back of his head. He might have been waiting to be interviewed for a Saturday job in some café or local supermarket and, watching him, Thorne was reminded of another young man who had turned out to be anything but what he'd seemed.

What do you know about anything?

Once the red light on the box built into the wall was glowing, Thorne ran quickly through the usual routine, the announcements and disclaimers. For the benefit of the various recordings, he spoke the names of everyone in the room and their reasons for being there, but before he had a chance to kick things off properly, Smedley was already speaking up.

'So it's on tape or whatever and it's also being filmed?'

'Correct,' Kitson said.

Smedley craned his head around and looked up at the camera mounted in the corner of the room. 'Like on DVD?'

'Yes, and the audio recording's digital. It'll be stored on a central data system and automatically burned on to a CD.'

'Cool. And I can have copies, right?'

Kitson nodded towards the social worker. 'As soon as we're done, Miss Anderton will sign a form on your behalf to say she's accepting a copy of the CD, which will then be given to your solicitor. The video will be disclosed a bit later on.'

Thorne looked at the boy. 'OK, Ryan?'

'Yeah, cool beans.'

Thorne smiled and nodded. He said, 'You did a picture, of Susan Best . . . of Miss Best. A painting.'

'Yeah, at school. You know I did. You saw it.'

Next to him, the solicitor was becoming agitated. Smedley was clearly not following his instructions, which had presumably been to say nothing at this stage. 'I want to put on record my objections to this interview, on the grounds that, as far as I'm aware, you have no evidence whatsoever linking my client to this offence. There is no physical evidence, certainly.'

Thorne could not really argue. Forensic evidence gathered at the crime scene over two months before had done no more than point to the presence of two intruders: patterns on the soles of two sets of shoes taken from the hall carpet. Prints had been lifted, but nothing that had matched with anything in the database. A new team would obviously fingerprint Smedley and his brother, would take all their shoes away for examination, but Thorne doubted that any of it would ultimately prove useful. Any forensic evidence they could now look for, in a specific effort to link Ryan Smedley and his brother to Susan Best's murder, had been destroyed in the fire at Tanner's home.

Thorne wasn't overly concerned.

If things went the way he hoped they might, even eyewitness testimony would be no more than icing on the cake.

Kitson pointed to the red light. 'Your objection has been noted.'

'Tell me about the painting,' Thorne said.

'What about it?'

'Why did you do it?'

'Because I'm good at painting.' He frowned. 'Did you not think it was good?'

'It was very good,' Thorne said. 'Very lifelike.'

The boy looked pleased.

'Did you like Miss Best?'

'Not particularly.'

'So you did the painting because you're good at it, that's what you're saying? You did it because you could.'

'Yeah, why not?'

'Is that why you do lots of things, Ryan?'

The lawyer looked ready to speak up again, but the boy was too quick for him. 'Why else does anyone do anything? I bet you think you're good at what you do. I mean, you'd be an idiot if you did your job thinking you were rubbish.'

'I think I'm good at my job,' Thorne said.

Smedley nodded, as if his point had been proved, then sat back and folded his arms. 'I knew you were a copper, by the way. When I saw you at the school.'

'How did you know that?'

'Well, you look like one for a start, and you obviously weren't there because you were that other copper's boyfriend. I knew she was the one who lived with Miss Best.'

Thorne remembered what Smedley had said to Tanner. He remembered the headmaster's words too.

He's very bright.

'How did you know that Miss Best had a girlfriend?'

'Because I saw her, didn't I? Outside school.'

'You saw her, or you watched her?'

'Watched her, obviously. Me and Kyle.'

'Kyle is your younger brother?'

'You know he is.'

'For the benefit of the tape,' Thorne said.

'Oh right, cool beans.' Smedley grinned. 'Yeah, he's my annoying little brother.' He held up a hand. 'Sorry.'

'That's OK.' Thorne glanced at Kitson. As he had suspected, it looked as though there would be little need to go too far around the houses.

The boy had come to tell them, simple as that. Not because he thought it might save his life, as Muldoon had done, but because he wanted them to know.

404

'Why were you watching Susan Best, Ryan?'

'So we could get her. What else would we be doing it for?'

Even having sensed that the admission was coming, the calmly spoken words and the half-smile that went with them caught Thorne a little off guard. He took a breath and Kitson stepped in.

'What do you mean by "get her"?'

'*Get* her . . . like we *got* her. *End* her, right?' He rolled his eyes, then leaned towards Thorne, jabbing a thumb in Kitson's direction. 'Jesus, *this* one's a bit slow on the uptake, isn't she? I bet she only got the job because she's a woman, right?'

'Tell me what happened,' Thorne said, 'when you went to Susan Best's house.'

'You know what happened. It didn't go well for Miss Best, did it?'

'I want to hear it from you.'

'The last time, you mean? We'd been there a few times just to check it out or whatever.'

'The last time.'

The boy said, 'Cool beans,' and smiled, enjoying the game. 'We waited behind the trees opposite, playing on our phones or whatever until she got back. Me and Kyle.'

'Why did you take Kyle?'

'Well, I thought it might need both of us, in case she struggled. Because she wasn't small, you know. She was big, like a lot of them.'

'A lot of what?'

The boy looked at Kitson. 'Lesbians.'

Kitson looked right back at him. 'Kyle didn't want to go though, did he?'

Smedley shrugged. 'He does whatever I tell him. I swear, if I want him to do something, he does it. He stubbed a fag out on his cock once, because I told him to.' He chuckled. 'Honestly, he's such a plum.'

405

'What happened in the house?' Thorne asked.

'Well . . . once we'd got in there it was pretty easy really.' The boy's face hardened suddenly and he rounded on his solicitor. 'Oh, and by the way, what the *fuck* are you talking about "physical evidence" for?'

'Excuse me?'

'There wasn't any "physical evidence". Seriously, do I look like an idiot? Do you not think we wore *gloves*? I mean . . . *duh!*' He shook his head. 'I don't know how much my parents are paying you, but it's clearly far too much.'

The solicitor blanched as though he'd just been given a dressing-down by the Attorney General. He stared down at a notebook which was still blank, pens that remained untouched.

Smedley turned back to Thorne, the temper tantrum over as quickly as it had begun. 'I mean, the gloves made it a bit harder to use the water pistols, but it wasn't a problem.'

'Water pistols?'

'For the bleach. Deadly accurate they are, if you know what you're doing.' He turned to mime firing at the social worker, who flinched and leaned away. 'Wicked little jets, you know? I practised shooting at birds and the cat next door.'

'Who had the knife?'

Smedley stared as though he wasn't expecting such a daft question. 'Me, *obviously*. Kyle would have probably ended up cutting his own fingers off or something.'

'You stabbed Susan Best.'

'Yeah, course. That was the fun bit, wasn't it?'

Thorne could feel Kitson relax a little next to him. Job done. He watched the solicitor finally start to write something in his notebook, though he could not see what.

A letter of resignation? A suicide note?

'Why, Ryan?'

Smedley leaned back, tipping the chair on to its back legs, staring up at the polystyrene tiles on the ceiling. 'Why not?'

'Come on ... and don't say it was just because you could. There must have been a reason. I mean, why her and not one of the other teachers? Why not a stranger at a bus stop?'

The boy eased the chair slowly back down and reached to pull up his hood. 'She was on my case, wasn't she? Always telling me how *clever* I was, how much *potential* I had.' He cocked his head, put on a high, whiny voice. "You've got such a good brain, Ryan, but you're letting yourself down by not using it and not working hard enough". She told me I was lazy, basically. I'm *not* lazy.'

'Really?' Thorne leaned across the table. 'That was why you blinded a woman with bleach and stabbed her to death?'

Smedley sniffed, rolled his head back and around. 'I did this geography essay, right? Agents of coastal erosion. You know, sea and weather and all that, and I did this whole bit about people ... about *people* being agents of erosion, which was pretty clever, I reckon. Guess what mark I got for it?'

He waited. Thorne shook his head.

'C. I got a fucking *C* ... because Miss Best said she could hardly read it. Said it looked like it had been scrawled by a pig or a five-year-old or something. She told me I had appalling penmanship ... I mean, who uses words like *penmanship*?' He smiled. 'Someone who needs teaching a lesson, that's who.' He nodded and looked around the table. 'You see? I mean, fair enough, yeah?'

Thorne began gathering his papers together. The statements from investigating officers, the crime-scene photographs he had not needed to produce.

'Oh yeah,' Smedley said, 'and you can tell that copper, the one I gave the painting to, that we didn't do any ... other stuff or whatever. You know, that it was quick and poor old Miss Best couldn't see shit by then anyway.' He looked around, seeking approval for his generosity and compassion. 'So tell her if you see her, because there's no point *her* feeling bad. I mean it's not her fault her girlfriend was a bitch, is it? Will you tell her?' He waited, but did not seem bothered when he got no response.

He said, 'Cool beans.'

Thorne began to terminate the interview for the tape, even though Ryan Smedley was still muttering, something else about pigs and potential. The solicitor was already on his feet. Anderton, the social worker, was staring at the floor, but Thorne could see the tremor in her fingers.

Thorne pushed his chair back, thinking about the call he would need to make to Nicola Tanner. To let her know that she and everyone else had been wrong to assume Susan's murder had been a case of mistaken identity, and that a child named Ryan Smedley had targeted her very carefully.

That she had died because a fourteen-year-old psychopath had terrible handwriting.

SEVENTY-FIVE

The landlord had taken on an extra member of staff for the afternoon, but the extra wage was more than made up for by the increased takings across the bar. It was always the case when everyone in the pub was wearing black.

Tanner turned from the buffet table and saw Phil Hendricks marching towards her. She popped the sausage roll into her mouth just a second before he wrapped her in his arms, a few seconds before she put her arms tentatively around him.

Patted his back.

When they separated, Hendricks turned towards the man who stood waiting just behind him. 'This is Liam.'

Tanner stepped forward to shake hands.

'Lovely service.'

'Not really,' Tanner said.

Hendricks laughed at his partner's effort to mask the shock. 'I told you what she was like,' he said.

'All a bit . . . Goddy, if you ask me.'

'Why didn't you do the humanist thing?' Liam asked.

'This is what Susan's mum and dad wanted.' Tanner half

turned towards the food. 'Didn't even get much of a say in the buffet. I'd have been happy with Nando's, to be honest, and so would Susan.'

Hendricks nodded down towards Tanner's two walking sticks. 'So, how's it going, Hopalong?'

'Pretty well,' Tanner said. 'Another few weeks' physio and I should be off these things. It won't be much fun going through metal detectors at the airport, but my arms are a damn sight stronger than they were, and I've got calves to die for.'

'Yeah?' Hendricks crouched down to check for himself and moaned approvingly as he squeezed.

'Really?' Liam said. 'At a funeral?'

'Oh, shut it.' Hendricks straightened up. 'I've always said, if I'm ever tempted across to the dark side, it'll have to be a lesbian.'

'Piercings might be an issue,' Tanner said.

'Oh, I don't know, I'm sure we can get you a few.' He smiled when Tanner laughed, and leaned forward to rub her shoulder. 'Just think, a couple of months ago you were still calling me Philip.'

She said, 'A couple of months ago, a lot of things were different.'

Hendricks saw that someone else was waiting to speak to Tanner, so he ushered Liam towards the bar. As he passed the man, he dropped a hand on to his shoulder. 'Don't bother with the "lovely service" stuff. We've covered that.'

'Ignore him,' Tanner said.

The man stepped forward, smiling awkwardly. 'How you doing, ma'am?'

Tanner reached and took Chall's hand in both of hers. 'No need for that, Dipak.'

Chall nodded, the smile widening. 'Yeah, sorry. Bit daft.'

'I never really thanked you properly.' Tanner had not let go of his hand.

'Now you're the one being daft.'

'Stupid really, what you did. What you let yourself get talked into doing. But thanks for doing it.'

'He didn't need to talk us into anything,' Chall said.

Tanner let go of Chall's hand, smoothed down the black dress she had last worn for her mother's funeral. 'How's Desai?'

'Oh, Charita's fine,' Chall said. 'She's great.'

'Well, thank her again next time you see her.'

Chall said that he would.

'I sent her a note and I'll thank her in person when I can get around a bit more easily.'

'There's no need, honestly.'

Tanner picked up a glass of wine, watched Chall sip at his orange juice. 'I heard that she was the one who wrote the fake diaries.'

'Yeah.' Chall's expression darkened momentarily. 'She never said as much, but I think she knew what she was talking about, if you know what I mean.'

'You both deserve medals,' Tanner said.

'Yeah, well.'

It had been more than a turn of phrase. Both Chall and Desai had been put forward for the Queen's Police Medal for their actions in the sting operation against Martin Muldoon and his partner. No decision had yet been made as to whether the medals would be awarded.

'Seems to me like DI Thorne should be up for one as well,' Chall said. 'Going after them on his own.'

'Don't think he's the type for medals.' Tanner knew it was Thorne who had put Chall's and Desai's names forward. She was smiling because, when the suggestion that he might be in the running for a medal himself had been made, she was there to witness his reaction.

'They know where they can stick it,' he had said. 'I've got a gold life-saving medal, so why would I want another one?

411

Chasing two arseholes in an old Astra with three good tyres is bugger all compared to diving for a rubber brick in your pyjamas.'

Sitting with Helen at a table in the corner, Thorne watched Tanner talking to Dipak Chall, saw her glance in his direction more than once. She was looking well, he thought. Handling it all better than he had expected.

He couldn't think of anyone who surprised him so consistently.

'Phil looks good in a black suit,' Helen said. 'Don't you reckon?'

Thorne looked across to the bar, where Hendricks and Liam were deep in conversation with Soran Hassani. 'Looks like that bloke out of *Hellraiser* got a job as a bouncer.'

'Your suit's still holding up.'

Thorne studied a sleeve. The suit was starting to get shiny in places and it was no less tight than when he'd last had it on. The suit he'd been wearing the first time he'd met Nicola Tanner.

Helen said, 'I'm still a bit pissed off with you.'

'Only a bit?'

'For God's sake. Working late because of some non-existent body in a reservoir.'

Thorne's beer glass wasn't quite big enough to hide behind. 'I thought you'd tell me it was a stupid idea.'

'It *was* a stupid idea, but since when have I been able to stop you doing anything? Yeah, I'd've been worried.'

'Well, I didn't want you worrying,' Thorne said. 'I mean, don't get me wrong, I like it that you worry, because I think it means ... I don't know ... maybe it's more than just normal worrying, because of how well I get on with Alfie and everything.' He let out a long breath and took another drink, struggling to find the right words. 'You know, with Alfie's dad not being around any more.'

'I don't know what you're wittering on about.'

'OK ... so say you're on some girls' trip to the Maldives or whatever.'

Helen laughed. 'Like that's going to happen.'

'OK then, Glasgow ... doesn't matter where. Say the plane goes down, or there's a car accident. Or what if something happens to you at work? I mean, let's not kid ourselves, that's a bit more likely, right? It happens.'

She leaned forward, serious suddenly. 'Where's this going?'

'I just wanted to know, if anything happens to you ... if you'd thought about who you'd want to take care of Alfie. That's all. I mean your sister's probably the obvious choice ... and it's not like your dad's ancient, is it?' He lifted his glass again. 'I just thought I should ask.'

Helen leaned back hard. 'Shit.' She shook her head and looked over at the bar again. 'I've already asked Phil.'

'*What?*'

Helen stared at him, but could only manage a few seconds before cracking and beginning to laugh. 'You are *so* easy to wind up sometimes.'

Thorne's head dropped and he let out the breath it felt as though he'd been holding for minutes. 'You are properly evil.'

'Of course I want you to look after him.'

'Yeah?'

'I mean we can put it in black and white if you think we need to.'

'I think it's best to get things sorted,' Thorne said. 'Make arrangements.'

'Fair enough.' Helen nodded, then pulled a face. 'I mean ... my *sister*? Really?'

Thorne sat back and finished his drink. He stretched out a foot to touch Helen's leg and wondered just how much grinning you could get away with at a funeral.

*

413

Tanner came over and sat down while Helen was at the bar. She said, 'I know what you were up to, Tom.'

'What was I up to, Nicola?'

'Misdirection.'

'You think?'

'I know. All that messing around at the AHCA meetings, getting in their faces, while you and Dipak were busy setting everything up.'

'Dipak did the donkey work,' Thorne said. 'He might even be a better actor than he is a copper, and he's a good copper.'

It was not quite the look Tanner had given him when he'd told her about Muldoon, but it was not a long way off. 'You were misdirecting me as well, though.'

'Only a bit.'

'Did you think I'd try and talk you out of it?'

'I thought that you needed to do nothing but lie there and heal. I knew you'd try to get involved and I didn't want you to be.'

'What the hell could I have done in that state?'

Thorne laughed, softly. 'You'd have given it a bloody good go. You'd have found some reason to argue with me, tell me what a ridiculous plan it was.'

'No,' she said. 'I wouldn't.'

They sat in silence for a minute or so, drinking and watching the mourners mingle. They saw Susan's parents chatting to the priest who was making his third visit to the buffet table. The neighbour, who was still taking care of Tanner's cat, propped up the bar alongside the headmaster and several other teachers from Susan's school.

Tanner stood up and said, 'I think I'm going to go.'

Thorne said, 'Oh,' and stood up too. 'Can you do that? Be the first to leave? I mean obviously you can do whatever you want, but . . . '

Tanner looked around. 'This is for everyone else,' she said, leaning close to touch Thorne's hand. 'I've already said goodbye to Susan.' She blinked. 'Anyway, there's still plenty to do at the house before I can move back in.'

'Right.' Thorne knew that Tanner's brothers had done sterling work in making her house fit to live in again. They had carried out a full structural survey and done whatever repairs had been recommended. They had redecorated from top to bottom and replaced damaged furniture. With luck Tanner would be at home again within a few days.

'Carpet fitters are coming first thing tomorrow,' she said. 'Second time in as many months.' They walked slowly away from the table towards the door at the far end of the pub. 'I should have some kind of loyalty card at Carpet Express.'

'Same colour as the last one?' Thorne asked.

Tanner glanced across at him, eyes wide, half smiling. 'No, something different this time,' she said. 'Something bright.'

AUTHOR'S NOTE

Because so many crimes are unreported due to the fear of reprisals, it is almost impossible to get accurate statistics for honour-based violence in the UK. According to *'Honour' Killings In The UK* by Emily Dyer, a report published by the Henry Jackson Society in 2015, twenty-nine murders were reported in the media over the previous five years. In 2010, the police reported a minimum of 2,800 cases of honour-based violence, including abduction, mutilation, acid attacks, beatings and murder. The Association of Chief Police Officers estimates that the number of victims of HBV may be up to thirty-five times higher than that reported and warns that the annual figure is closer to 20,000 offences. The Crown Prosecution Service claims that approximately twelve honour killings are carried out in the UK each year, but accepts that the actual figure is likely to be much higher. Karma Nirvana, a UK charity that supports victims and survivors of forced marriage and honour-based abuse, has a helpline that currently receives over 850 calls per month, the majority of which are from victims themselves. Between 2010 and 2013, the number of calls received by the helpline increased by forty-seven per cent.

The results of a ComRes poll carried out by the BBC in 2013 state that over two thirds (sixty-nine per cent) of young British Asians across all the major faiths believe that families should live according to the concept of honour, or *izzat*. Three per cent believe that the ultimate sanction of honour killings is justified, including the same number of Muslims and Hindus, but rising to four per cent of Sikhs and Christians.

Banaz Mahmod, whose story is referenced in this novel, entered an arranged and abusive marriage at the age of sixteen. Her crime was to abandon this marriage in 2005 and choose her own partner. Her father, her uncle and other members of the family met shortly afterwards at the family home to discuss killing Banaz and her boyfriend. After two separate visits to the police station in Mitcham, during which Banaz named the people she believed were planning to kill her, the first attempt was made on her life. This attempt was reported to the police and Banaz agreed to co-operate in bringing charges against her family. The following day, on January 24, 2006, following a two-hour ordeal in which she was savagely beaten and raped, Banaz was murdered by two men hired by her father and uncle. Three months later, her body was discovered in a suitcase, buried in a garden in Birmingham. Her killers fled to Iraq, but were eventually extradited and jailed, along with Banaz's father, her uncle and three others involved in the disposal of her body.

Rahmat Sulemani, the young man Banaz had chosen to spend her life with, and who himself had been targeted, said, 'My life depended on her. She was my present, my future, my hope. She was the best thing that ever happened to me. My life went away when Banaz died. There is no life. The only thing which was keeping me going was the moment to see justice being done for Banaz.'

In May 2016, while I was writing this book, a decade after the woman he loved was murdered, Rahmat Sulemani hanged himself. Though he was alive when police officers found him, he died in hospital five days later.

There is no life . . .

Mark Billingham
London, September 2016

ACKNOWLEDGEMENTS

I am grateful to the authors and editors of several books and academic publications that were enormously helpful in the writing of this novel: *'Honour' Killings In The UK* by Emily Dyer, published by the Henry Jackson Society (2015); *Honour Killing, Stories Of Men Who Killed* by Ayse Onal (2008); *'Honour' Killing & Violence, Theory, Policy & Practice* (2014), edited by Aisha K. Gill, Carolyn Strange and Karl Roberts; *Honour* by Elif Shafak (2015).

All were compelling and disturbing in equal measure, and *Love Like Blood* could not have been written without them.

I owe an enormous debt to the early readers – Nithya Rae, Manpreet Grewal and Afeera Ahmed – whose feedback was invaluable.

Thanks so much for taking the time.

Those who take the time with *every* book have once again confirmed how fortunate I am to have such amazing publishers. Ed Wood is a frighteningly smart, sensitive and eagle-eyed editor, and it's an unalloyed pleasure to work with him and the rest of the incredible team at Little, Brown and Sphere: David

Shelley, Tamsin Kitson, Catherine Burke, Robert Manser, Sean Garrehy, Laura Sherlock, Emma Williams, Sarah Shrubb and Thalia Proctor. At Grove Atlantic in the US, I am equally lucky to be working with Morgan Entrekin, Allison Malecha, Deb Seager, and Justina Batchelor, while in Germany, Tim Jung at Atrium has comprehensively saved my bacon. Or schnitzel ...

Thanks to my wonderful agent Sarah Lutyens and to Francesca Davies and Juliet Mahony at Lutyens & Rubinstein. Thanks, as always, to the wise and wonderful Wendy Lee and to Martyn Waites (and Killing Joke) for the title.

And, of course, to Claire.